Promise of Victory

Book 3

by

Clifford M. Scovell

First Printing

ISBN-13: 978-0-9908536-1-9
ISBN-10: 0-9908536-1-6

Printed in the United States of America

Cover artwork by Katie Boyer Clark

Other books by Clifford M. Scovell

Prison Earth - Not Guilty as Charged
Prison Earth - A Loss of Face
Prison Earth - The Resurrection and the Lie

Promise of Darkness
Promise of Salvation

Chapter 1

Gallic Belgia, Roman Empire, late September, 52 BCE

The heavy wooden sword slammed mine, sending shockwaves down my arm, straining my wrist, and taxing muscles as I shoved the weapon away and jumped back. My opponent followed in lockstep, inflicting a bruising shoulder strike that forced me to stagger left. His blade came at my face, but I punched it away with my shield and quickstepped to the right.

I had the advantage of years of hard-won experience over my much-younger opponent, but those same years had shortened my endurance. In addition, my opponent was not some lumbering Gallic farmer, fresh from plowing his field. I was fighting a highly skilled Roman Legionnaire who was trained to give no quarter. This fight had to end quickly or slowing reflexes would let him past my defenses, and I would be on the ground.

Using my sword to deflect another powerful stroke, I stabbed my shield at his head. He ducked, but the grazing impact still knocked him off balance. Taking the offensive, I slammed his parry hard, forcing him back, off balance. Windmilling my right arm gave my sword so much momentum that even though his shield came up to deflect it, the impact sent him to his knees.

Agile as a cat, he hit hard with his shield and jumped up, but before he could get his feet set, I double-punched him: shield hammering body, sword against shield. It took only three of these double strikes before his right arm folded, knees buckled, and shuffling feet sent dust flying. Since he was off balance, it took only one more left-right pair to knock him down. He somersaulted backwards and moved from under my attack. I followed close, and before he could fully regain balance, I hit him again and again until he fell on his back, his open thighs exposed to my finishing stroke.

"Stop!" shouted a deep, commanding voice behind me. "What in the Jupiter's name are you two doing?"

I stumbled, my sword still high, dust billowing around my feet as I fought to stop my well-earned momentum.

Lowering my weapon, I turned to see a helmetless *centurio*, the commander of our *centuria,* his armor glittering in the sunlight as he pointed his own wooden sword at us, but his attention was on thirty recruits lined up on his left.

"Who can tell me what these stinking Grecian sluts are doing wrong," he cried. "Anyone?"

The recruits shifted uncomfortably, shaking their heads and giving each other nervous glances. I had obviously made an impression on them, but not their instructor.

Lowering his sword, the *centurio* shook his own head. "Is that how we should fight," he shouted, "hacking it out *honorably*, like two senators fighting over a scrap of moldy bread?"

I watched my opponent jump to his feet as the *centurio* marched toward us, his weapon pointing at me. "It might seem manly to spend half the morning engaged with a single opponent, but in battle you have neither the time nor energy."

Stopping in front of us, he motioned my opponent aside, and for me to stand in front of him. I knew what was coming, but had a role to play in this demonstration. No matter what the outcome, it was why I was here.

"Since we don't always have the enemy outnumbered, we have to be more efficient. Attack fast and hard, dispatching them quickly, disabling if you can't kill, taking down two or more in the time you'd usually slug it out with only one."

"But Sir," a recruit called, and like many ignorant souls before him, immediately regretted the outburst.

The *centurio* jerked around, weapon at the ready, the top of his shield level with his left shoulder, his voice steady as he asked, "How can we kill the enemy at twice the rate they kill us?"

The row of helmeted heads nodded, but the one who spoke bobbed his like the idiot he was.

They all jumped when the *centurio*'s sword slammed his shield and before the sound of the impact faded, his blade was coming at my face. I ducked and blocked with my shield, but the reflexive move exposed my left side. Before I could cover it, he used the momentum of the stabbing movement to yank his own shield back and deliver a hard body blow. I staggered back, but he stayed with me. I had barely taken a step before he jerked the shield up to catch my chin and then stabbed the dull tip of his sword into my belly to knock the wind from my lungs.

I missed a step, lost my balance, and hammered the ground. In shock from the impact, I gasped in too little air and held up my shield as he pointed his sword at me.

"Did you see what I did there?" he demanded. "Hammer..." he thrust his shield forward, "...and thrust." He stabbed the air in front of him with his sword. "Hammer and thrust! Hammer and thrust! If your jab to the gut doesn't disembowel him, put those metal cleats on your sandals to good use and stomp his nuts. While you're moving to the next in line, the legionnaire behind you will finish him off."

Still struggling for breath, I looked up, surprised and at the same time upset to see his hand stretched down toward me. It was bad enough that I, an experienced Roman soldier, had been dispatched so easily, but to be helped up after such a disgrace was a complete and unequivocal humiliation. However, there is one rule a legionnaire learns early in his career: *never* defy, challenge, or question your superiors.

I grabbed the hand and was yanked from the ground while glaring at the recruits around me, but they were too mesmerized by the *centurio* to notice.

"Strike hard and fast! Hammer and thrust! Hammer and thrust!" he shouted after he turned toward the line of recruits. "The discipline of your fellow legionnaires is an advantage your enemy does not have. Fighting as a team will keep your tiny feral brains occupied, and when the enemy sees their comrades falling faster than harvested wheat, they'll soon run for the hills."

The group laughed nervously, obviously unconvinced it would be that easy.

I was still trying to catch my breath, and doing my best not to show it when the *centurio* turned to my original opponent.

"Take half of these children over there..." He swept his sword to my right, pointing needlessly at thick posts protruding from the ground in the exercise area. "...and have them practice their sword work." He scowled at the glaring sun. "Work them 'til mid-day, break for a short meal, and then get in a couple leagues marching through the hills."

He turned to me while waving his sword at the remaining recruits. "Those vestal virgins are yours. Do *not* baby them."

Instead of walking away, the *centurio* hesitated, his attention still on me.

"You are *evocatus*," he stated with a hint of curiosity. When I nodded, he sheathed his sword and looked around the parade grounds. "Very few re-up after serving their term. What made you come back?"

My breathing now nearly normal, I shrugged and tried to make it look casual, but the flashing mental image of two beautiful faces stirred up intense emotions, and it was impossible for me to know how I appeared. Painfully digging the fingernails of my free hand into my palm to regain focus, I turned to him.

"Some are content to be settled onto a farm and idle away their days, but it was not for me."

What a liar, I thought angrily. *Mother would be so proud.*

The last thought was not sarcasm. My whore of a mother was Italian, but not a Roman citizen. My father's heritage was unknown, and my two siblings would have slit my throat for a copper *as*, if I'd ever had even that small amount of money. Despite her flaws, mother taught me to survive in the dangerous back alleys and gutters of Rome, but what she knew did not save her. Truth be known, my rotting corpse might also have ended up in the Tiber had a junior magistrate not given me the choice between death and military service. Choosing the latter gave a young Italian with no real future an opportunity to do something worthwhile. Mother would be impressed that I survived my first enlistment and retired a Roman citizen with farmland in Southern Gaul. I would be there now had it not been for...

"A soldier's life is right for me," the *centurio* repeated the old soldier's chant, seemingly unaware of my internal commotion. "To fight and die for liberty." He shook his head. "But we no longer fight for liberty, do we?"

I bristled at the apparently innocent question, which only a few years ago might have provoked a heated discussion on the moral justification of surrendering the Republic to the rule of the "unofficial" Triumvirate run by Gaius Julius Caesar, Marcus Licinius Crassus, and Gnaeus Pompeius Magnus. Though the Triumvirate had ceased to exist last year when Crassus was killed in the humiliating Battle of Carrhae, the Republic was still just a ghost of the past. Pompey had taken control of the Senate, and our general, Julius Caesar -- a man whose leadership in battle was so impressive we called him *Imperator* -- fearing legal action if he stayed in Rome, accepted the governorship of Gaul. Everyone knew Pompey wanted Caesar disgraced, if not dead, but once here, our *imperator* used the pretense of Gallic unrest as an excuse to add two legions to the four he already had, giving him enough fighting power to keep Pompey and the Senate at bay.

You might think such a situation would be difficult for soldiers who were supposed to protect the Republic, but few complained because it changed our lives very little. The Republic may someday be restored, but I and my comrades of the *Legio XI Claudia* are professional soldiers, and our loyalty is to our general. As long as we get regular meals and pay, why would we care? Whichever way it went, any soldier wanting to keep his job -- and his life -- left that sort of worrying to others.

Snapping to attention, I slammed a fist against my chest in salute. "I fight for the Republic and the might of Rome."

*Centuriōnē*s never smile, but his scowl seemed less intense than usual, and that was as close to a smile as I would ever see.

"What rank did you hold before you left?"

"I served as *decanus* of the third *contubernium* of the first *centuria* with the *Legio III Gallica*, Sir."

He hesitated, as though contemplating what I was sure he already knew.

"I recently lost my *optio*," he said matter-of-factly, "and I need someone with actual fighting experience to keep these sheep in line. You will move up a notch in rank and be my second in command."

Still at attention, I saluted again. "Yes, Sir!"

The harsh scowl returning, he nodded. "Good. As of now, you are *Optio* Marcus Aremus. Find the *quaestor* and get yourself properly outfitted. You will report for duty in the morning."

The proper outfitting he was referring to was primarily a crested helmet and a staff nearly a head taller than myself. Unlike the *centurio*'s crest of horsehair and feathers, which ran from side-to-side on the top of his helmet, mine would run from front to back. The staff would not only be a sign of my rank, but was useful in keeping the men in line. Whether marching or fighting, the *centurio* is always at the head of his *centuria*, while his *optio* stays in the rear to make sure everyone stays in line. The discipline of Roman legions is maintained because leadership demands it, and my stiff rod made my troopers painfully aware that it was.

The *centurio* pointed at my new charges standing at attention in the bright sun, their heavy armor surely as hot as mine, undershirts soaked with sweat.

"Get to work."

Without waiting for a response, he marched away, bellowing orders at a cluster of soldiers resting against the stockade wall

Tempus fugit, memento mori, mother's voice echoed in my head. Time flies, remember death. An appropriate motto for a soldier…and maybe a family living at the edge of civilization.

That last thought brought a flash of anger. The anger you feel when everything of real value is brutally taken away. An anger so raw, so intense, so deeply imbedded in my soul, only death could erase it.

The moment was disrupted by a sudden bout of dizziness that made me stagger, my knees buckling as though I had been shoved from behind. Disoriented, I briefly felt like I had just arrived at a place I had never been. After two quick steps, my legs were under me again and I gave the dusty arena a quick scan to find everything as it should be. Turning to the recruits, I was relieved to see that none of them -- standing at attention; their bodies erect, though wobbling; eyes forward -- had seen me stumble. I was myself again in an instant, the memory chased away by the moment, with nothing remaining but the anger: my reason for re-enlisting. Where else can a person express all that pent-up rage but on the battlefield?

Primal anger is powerful, and I felt like I could bite the head off a spear, but this was not the place for such a display. Pushing the feeling deep into my belly, I turned to my new charges, and felt a new emotion: jealousy. Their squat, muscular bodies were much like mine, only younger. Thanks to that magistrate, my youth had not been squandered, but decades of military service had taken their toll. Like it or not, it was now my job to make sure these anemic sons of whores also had the chance to grow old enough to have aching joints, thin hair, and fading endurance.

"Listen up, you mindless shits! Play time is over." I pointed at the wooden posts where they had been practicing their hacking and stabbing for much of the morning. "Time to sweat more baby fat off your worthless bellies."

Chapter 2

Salem, Oregon, United States, Late September of 2012

"Aunt Jasmina!"

Alarmed by the sound of fists pounding her front door, Jasmina Maxell rushed to the entrance and yanked the door open to see her red-headed niece, Remmy Reed: a much younger and more agitated version of herself.

"What is all the…"

Jasmina's protest was cut off when Remmy charged in, forcing her to take a quick step to one side.

"It's Gerry," the girl announced excitedly, her green eyes wide as she stopped in the middle of the entryway and turned to face her. "He's in a coma."

"What happened?"

Swallowing hard, Remmy jerked her attention from one part of the room to another, her feet still shuffling under her, hands rubbing together as she struggled to find words to express herself.

"We were talking about an assignment in history class," she finally answered while brushing her auburn hair back. "We're supposed to do a paper about the life of Roman soldiers."

"And?"

"Gerry was in mid-sentence and then started acting weird."

Her head shaking slowly, eyes unfocussed, Remmy held up a hand as though reaching for someone. "He was mumbling in a strange language, but the only word I could make out was *evocatus*."

"*Evocatus*? What does that mean?"

Fresh tears streaming over flushed cheeks, she pressed the front of her green mini-skirt down against black tights, focused on her aunt, and sobbed, "The professor said it was Latin for someone who reenlists in the army."

"Latin? Gerry's made another past-life connection? He's a young Roman?"

"He's a Roman soldier and I don't think he is young," her niece corrected. "We learned in class that for most Roman soldiers the commitment was usually twenty-five years."

"That's kind of extreme, isn't it?"

Remmy shook her head. "Whatever, but that means this guy is probably in his forties."

"How does this matter?" Jasmina asked.

"It matters because Roman soldiers were kind of like professional football players with swords. Very few last into their forties because their bodies can't take the constant abuse. Since warfare at that time was pretty much a slugfest, a frontline soldier past his prime wouldn't live very long."

"Gerry's consciousness is linked to a guy with a death wish?"

"Exactly," Remmy insisted, "and Gerry nearly died because the last guy he was connected to almost died. If it's going to happen again, I need to be there to help him."

Stunned by her statement, Jasmina hesitated for a long moment before shaking her head.

"Oh no. You're not ready for that yet," she stated as she hurried into the next room to grab her coat and car keys. "Where is he now?"

"But you said I have the *touch*, and I've already done some past-life readings on other people. Why can't I do this?"

Stopping at the back door, Jasmina faced her niece. "Listen, just because you and I share the ability to see past lives, doesn't mean you have my experience in doing it. In Gerry's case, he is connecting in a way even I haven't figured out yet."

Remmy stared at her aunt, her eyes wet with tears. "But I touched him before the ambulance got there. I saw what he was seeing, so I think I know where he's gone, and how I can get back there."

Jasmina put a hand on Remmy's shoulder and stared into her eyes.

"Remmy. Trust me when I say this is very dangerous. You don't have enough information to know where you'll end up. You might never find the person he is connected to."

"But I have to try."

Shaking her head, Jasmina put on her coat and motioned for her niece to follow. "Once we've figured out what's going on, you and I can do this together, but you are not to go back there on your own." When Remmy did not follow, Jasmina turned back and added, "We've got to hurry. Where is he?"

Her arms across her chest, as though she were cold, Remmy responded, "They took him to the hospital, *o que imos facer?*"

Grabbing the doorknob, Jasmina pulled it open and started to move through. "I have to make physical contact with him, and..." She stopped abruptly, and turned to face her niece. "What did you say?"

Looking disoriented, Remmy responded, "*Que?*" then her eyes rolled up and she fell to the floor.

"Remmy!" Jasmina screamed as she dropped to her knees and rolled her niece over. "Tim! Get in here *now*!"

She barely heard her husband's heavy footsteps as he rushed into the room.

"Come on, Girl. Wake up."

"What happened?" Tim asked as he knelt beside her.

"I don't know. She was right behind me and started talking gibberish. Before I could respond, she just collapsed."

Leaning over the girl, Tim pressed two fingers against her jugular. "Her pulse is steady, and her breathing seems normal too."

"Oh my God! She's in a trance."

"A trance? Why?"

Jasmina shook her head. "Wherever Gerry is, she's gone to join him."

"Another connection to the past?"

She nodded. "And if I'm correct, I'm going to need your knowledge of history to figure out how to help them."

"Any idea where they've gone this time?"

Her head shaking, she let out a long breath. "Maybe Rome, but the bigger question is when." She put a hand on Remmy's forehead. "Whenever it is, I just hope it won't be as dangerous as their last past-life connection."

Chapter 3

Running! Searching! Frantic!

Where are they? Where could they hide?

My lungs ache as I force my heavy legs to move faster, but it still takes forever to get from the barn to the burning remains of our cottage. Nearly out of my head with panic, I round the corner and stop to gape at...

Gulping air, I fought briefly with my twisted blanket before sitting up, and realizing I was in an entirely different space. The flames were gone, along with the blackened walls, and corpses by the dozen. Still breathing hard, I recognized the sparsely-furnished tent filled with nine other still-sleeping troopers.

My home is gone. This is what replaces it.

I hugged my knees tightly until the pain in my chest eased. Sweat dribbled down my nose to splatter on my arms, but I barely noticed it.

If they can't come back then I must go to them.

I sucked in another breath, and shook my head to clear it. With sleep no longer an option, I rose, quietly rolled up my blanket, and stowed it away, the notion being so automatic, I didn't even think about it until I was straightening to see if I had missed anything.

Since the first day of boot camp, every soldier knows to keep his gear stowed and be ready to move out on a moment's notice. After all these years, it was as much a part of my being as breathing. In fact, I could go a fortnight without speaking, days without eating, even hold my urine from sunrise to sunset, but cannot get out of bed without immediately stowing my bedroll.

"You're up early," the *centurio* observed as I stepped from the tent and approached the small fire he crouched in front of.

He was a short, stocky man with thick arms, broad chest, and tiny eyes embedded in a wide ruddy-cheeked face. The harsh light made the old scar on his forehead stand out and gave an alien look to the puckered skin where his forearm had been burned. What was odd was that he was dressed in full armor, the fire's flickering light glittering off the polished rings and golden plaques on his breastplate and playing across the colorful transverse crest on top of his helmet.

Squatting beside him, I held out my hands to the warm flames.

"I have the feeling that something is about to happen."

My superior nodded. "Good instincts."

Knowing what his response meant, I felt a flash of excitement.

"We're moving out?"

He nodded again. "Our *imperator* is preparing for the final battle with the savage who calls himself Vercingetorix. Reports from our spies say the Nervii will be siding with the enemy. There are several Nervii villages five leagues to the north of us, and our job is to keep them from joining their brethren in that effort. We are to leave at first light."

My excitement spiked as the new opportunity became obvious. As *optio* I would be expected to show bravery in the face of the enemy. That meant I might get the opportunity to fight with my men in battle, spearheading the charge, and dying bravely.

"How many are we to face?"

He shrugged, as though the question were unnecessary. "Three or four hundred in the first village, but I am told better than half are non-combatants."

Non-combatants meant women and children, and though it had never bothered me before, I felt a strange sense of discomfort, my excitement cooling when I realized they would be part of the booty we would collect, either as slaves, or as something to play with before we killed them.

Why should it bother me? Everyone knew these Gauls were simple savages, little better than feral dogs. They probably ate their own children, treated their women like common whores, and peed on the dirt floors of the hovels they called homes. Why would it be any worse for us to do the same?

"Their women are stout and strong," the *centurio* continued. "The slave traders will pay handsomely for them."

"What about the children?"

The question was, of course, irrelevant, and his only reaction was a raised eyebrow.

"If they are healthy, we'll get a good sum for them too."

"Yes," I responded, feeling foolish, but knowing better than to say more.

The *centurio* was silent for a moment, and though I wasn't looking directly at him, I knew his eyes were on me.

"Do you regret your reenlistment?"

Finally looking at him, I felt my face flush with embarrassment, not only because he had to ask that question, but also because of my delay in responding.

"No, *Centurio*," I finally barked, maybe too aggressively to sound sincere. "I am proud to serve."

He continued to stare at me for a long moment before rising, and after I quickly matched his move, he said,

"We will be two *centuriae* strong, but the *centurio* in charge of the other *centuria* was killed recently, and since his replacement has not arrived, I will be leading them both. As my *optio,* you will stand in for him when I am otherwise occupied."

"Yes, Sir!"

"Get the men up and ready. We have a long march ahead."

"Yes, Sir!"

While hurrying toward the barracks, I still felt a confusing sense of hesitation, as though I wanted to go back and argue with him about our orders. Of course, to challenge a superior's command meant immediate execution, and I was not that kind of fool.

Passing through the entrance to the barracks, I swore under my breath, "I will not hesitate again."

The statement sparked a fire in me.

"Get up you lazy dogs," I bellowed as I grabbed my armor and the new crested helmet of my rank. "We are moving out."

As the men rose from their cots, my excitement increased.

We're going into battle!

On the battlefield, the difference between life and death is often the width of a knife's blade, but to simply die is not enough. I knew I had to fight and die honorably, and anything less might prevent me from entering Pluto's palace where my family almost certainly waits for me. The opportunity was mine, and I had no intention of letting it pass.

Wait for me, my loves. I will join you soon.

Chapter 4

"Remmy," Jasmina shouted as she patted her niece's cheek.

Staring over her shoulder, Tim asked, "Isn't there a way to snap her out of it?"

Her head shaking, Jasmina kept her eyes on her niece. "If she is in a trance, she put herself there, and only she can bring herself out of it." She waved a free hand toward the front hall. "Call an ambulance."

"Are you sure? If it's only a trance, what can they do?"

"The doctors can do nothing, but she needs to be wherever Gerry is so I can work on them together."

"Right," Tim said while rising. "I'll get my phone."

Nodding, Jasmina returned her attention to Remmy. "I'll try to talk to her before they get here."

"Yeah, but..." he started to say before snapping his fingers. "Oh yeah. What was I thinking?"

After he left, she picked up Remmy's hands and closed her eyes.

"Come on, Dear One. Speak to me."

Though her niece remained limp and unresponsive, Jasmina's mind filled with startlingly realistic image of a village. She could smell, hear, and even feel what was going on around her. The effect took her breath away, and it was a long moment before she could orient herself.

A slight breeze brushed her cheek as she walked down a wide, well-defined street, bordered with houses made of wood and stone. The roofs, though thatched, were well maintained, and the people she saw were clean and attractively dressed. She felt the sun on her face and the weight of the basket hanging from her arm. When the woman looked down, she saw a finely woven, embroidered skirt that barely exposed sandals she might well think were fashionable even in modern times.

Her host stopped and Jasmina felt her confusion, as though she had forgotten where she was going. After a moment, the woman shook her head while thinking, *Silly forgetful girl,* and continued on.

She was just about to round a corner when something shook her shoulder.

"The ambulance is on its..."

She jerked back, her hands pulled free of Remmy's, and the sudden transition elicited a groan from her as she looked around the familiar room.

"What's the matter?" Tim asked when she gave him a questioning look. "Couldn't you make contact?"

"Oh yeah," she sighed. "And it's like nothing I've ever experienced."

"What do you mean?"

She shook her head. "When I touch Remmy, I'm pulled into an entirely different person."

"You can sense Remmy?"

She shook her head insistently. "I'm not connected with Remmy at all. I'm actually in the body of a young woman. In addition to her thoughts, I can see what she sees, hear what she hears, and even smell the odors around her."

"Where is she?"

"In a Celtic village, and I think it's somewhere in Belgium."

"How do you know this?"

Jasmina shrugged. "Not sure. It's just a feeling I get."

"And what time period are we talking about?"

She shook her head. "It seemed to me like it was a very long time ago, but I'm not sure. The young woman is wearing a beautiful dress, and the place she's walking through could be a village, or even a city. I haven't seen enough to know." After taking in a deep breath, she let it out slowly and took Remmy's hands again. "I need to know more."

She closed her eyes and was immediately immersed in the young woman's world.

"Enid."

The girl looked up to see someone waving at her, and Jasmina felt strangely happy at the sight of the stocky, handsome man hurrying toward her.

"Philippe," she responded. "How is your papa this fine morning?"

She not only felt her face warm, but other places as well when the young man smiled. "He is doing much better since you started ministering to him. He sends his thanks for the help."

"And you too are well?"

He stopped in front of her, bowing his head as a sign of respect.

"I am all the better for seeing you today."

"You are too kind..."

When his expression turned serious, Jasmina felt a sudden tightening in her stomach.

"You have heard something?"

He nodded. "The Romans have besieged the *Arverni* and their allies in the fort at Alesia. Vercingetorix has called for all the tribes to send men to attack the Romans and free him. We leave at first light."

"Can we get there in time?"

He shrugged. "We can only try, but the council thinks we…"

"Alert! Alert! Romans! Two leagues from here and headed this way."

Philippe turned toward the speaker, and shouted, "How many are there?"

"Two of their centuries," the man responded. "Maybe one-hundred-and-fifty men."

Looking back at Enid, he smiled. "We outnumber them. That is good." Turning back to the other man, he shouted, "Go to the next village and warn them." He moved toward the center of the square. "Women and children: gather your supplies and hurry to the caves. Everyone else spread the word then gather your weapons and meet up at the east gate."

Facing Enid again, he opened his mouth, but before words came out, the scene vanished.

"The EMTs are here, Dear," Tim announced as he once again shook her shoulder. "We need to let them in to work their magic."

"No!" Jasmina protested.

She was preparing to say more when she saw the EMT standing behind him. Taking Tim's hand, she rose and moved aside as the newcomer rushed in, checking Remmy's vitals as Jasmina struggled to stop herself from telling him what was happening. Before she could decide what to do, Tim gently grabbed her shoulders and pushed her towards the front of the house.

"It was so real!" she gasped as they moved into the hall and out of earshot. "It was like I was physically in that village."

"But maybe that's not what you should be saying to the medic right now."

"What?"

"This guy's job is to help Remmy. I don't think telling him about your vision will help matters."

"But she's in danger!"

He shook his head. "Whoever she's connected to *was* in danger, and probably a very long time ago. Let's focus on the present, and work out the past later. OK?"

She took in a sharp breath, and was prepared to continue her argument, but his pleading expression changed her mind.

"You're right," she responded testily, and quickly regretted it. "Yes, I'm OK, but let's see how it's going."

As they reentered the room, the paramedic stood.

"Do you know what brought this on?"

Jasmina shook her head. "She had just told me her boyfriend was in the hospital, and we were headed to the car when she collapsed."

"Why was he admitted?"

Jasmina hesitated as the realization dawned on her.

"Oh my God. He fainted, just like she did."

"Any reason these two cases should be connected?"

Jasmina threw a desperate look at her husband, who returned a scowl as he shook his head.

"If you must know, I think they are connecting to their past lives."

To her surprise, the EMT did not look skeptical.

"Do people normally faint when this happens?"

Realizing he wasn't dismissing her, she jerked a no.

"Actually, I've done hundreds of past-life regressions, but this one is entirely different. It feels like she is actually back there, really experiencing this past life."

The paramedic's eyes widened slightly as he smiled. "You're Jasmina Maxell."

"Yes."

"I've been to one of your seminars. You helped my grandmother with her rheumatoid arthritis. I'm a big fan."

"Then you know why I need to stay with my niece. Her life could be in danger."

He nodded. "She's unconscious so I've got to take her to the hospital, but you can ride along."

"Can I come too?" Tim asked.

As a second paramedic entered the room, Jasmina smiled and patted her husband's arm. "Bring the car, Sweetie. I'll need a ride home."

When she turned back to the first EMT, he waved at his partner and said, "Let's load her up!"

Nodding, she looked at her husband. "This is going to be the most exotic ambulance ride anyone ever took."

Chapter 5

We marched through a wide valley, making no effort to hide our presence. After all, we were not just soldiers. We were Roman Legionnaires. There is nothing like us in the world and our very presence often makes these Gauls run into the hills like the savages they are.

That of course, did not mean we walked blindly through enemy territory. Our scouts ran ahead, watching for enemy scouts, and attack parties. The Gauls thought they were clever guerilla warriors, but in fact were easy to spot and their uncoordinated assaults just a mass of screaming maniacs easily slaughtered by disciplined troopers.

It was not long before one of our scouts signaled contact, but upon seeing them, the Gauls ran away. The *centurio* kept us marching and we finally turned a bend in the river to see a larger village than we had seen in many months of campaigning in this sorry land. However, we were on the opposite side of the river, and since I was at the head of the troops, I marched up to our scouts.

"Where is the best place to cross?" I asked while scanning the enemy warriors -- a title I use very generously -- gathered across the river.

"Probably a league back up stream, *Optio*," he responded. "The water here is too deep to risk crossing while they are so close."

"Why was this not reported before we arrived?"

The scout pointed at smoldering wooden posts on opposite sides of the river.

"The savages burned that down only a short time ago."

"*Optio*?" the *centurio* asked as he approached.

"*Centurio*," I responded. "The enemy has destroyed their only passage over the river. The nearest crossing is a league back up stream."

My superior walked to the edge of the riverbank, his attention on the gathering forces on the far side. I moved up beside him to stare at a large force, easily twice our own complement, but woefully undisciplined. They were gathered more or less in divisions, with many of them hooting and shouting in their strangled tongue. Small groups broke away from the main ones to ineffectively fire arrows at us. To a disciplined Roman Legionnaire it was an embarrassing display, and instead of striking fear in my heart, it only garnered contempt and pity.

I looked back at the remains of the bridge. The water at that point was less than one-hundred paces across, and not terribly deep, but undoubtedly deep enough to force our troopers to march with water up to their necks. To gather a strong enough force to take on the enemy, we would have to cross with a dozen or more abreast. Unfortunately, that would leave us vulnerable to enemy attack, and our soldiers would be slaughtered as they tried to climb the other side. In addition, a legionnaire already carries enough weight. The added burden of water-soaked clothes would be a disadvantage we could ill afford.

With a slow shake of his head, the *centurio* turned to us. "We will cross here," he announced matter-of-factly.

The much younger scout looked quite shocked, but was not so foolish as to challenge the order.

"Bring up the engineers," the *centurio* demanded as he turned back and scowled at the enemy. "Let them squirm while we build our own bridge."

Though my mind flooded with questions, now was definitely not the time, so I jerked around and marched back to the men lined up in perfect rows behind us.

"Engineers! Front and center."

Five of our troop marched out in double time, their faces expressionless as I led them to the river's edge.

"Engineers," the *centurio* announced after they stopped abruptly and saluted. "Build a bridge wide enough for four soldiers to march abreast, and complete it by end of day tomorrow."

"A floating bridge would be the fastest to build, Sir."

"Make it happen."

"Yes, Sir," they barked as one.

"Dismissed!"

As they marched away, I turned to the *centurio*. "I will bring up archers to keep the enemy at bay."

"Good plan, *Optio*," he said without looking at me. "Use as many men as we can spare to cut the logs they will need. I only wish to give them a day to sweat before we destroy them."

"May I offer one other suggestion, *Centurio*?"

"Speak."

"Our scouts also report that the enemy has withdrawn their own sentries in preparation for the battle. May I suggest sending a force of twenty men back up river to cross and attack them from the side while our troops cross the bridge?"

The *centurio* turned toward the gathering enemy force, his eyes scanning from left to right.

The valley was quite wide at this point, and the fortified village was surrounded by a cleared space of nearly a thousand paces on the sides we could see.

"Too broad a plain for a surprise attack," he observed.

"Even so, Sir. If their leaders are even slightly competent, they will surely attack before our full force is across the bridge. Our sudden presence on their flank will confuse them, and divide their forces. At the very least, it should slow them down. If they did nothing, we could join our troops prior to the engagement."

"And if they discover your plan and wipe you out?"

"Then their attention will be on us, and not our men crossing the bridge."

I looked at his scowling face, his eyes searching for a sign of doubt I was not prepared to let him see. He hesitated only a couple of heart beats.

"The recruits you have been training have shown themselves well on the archery range."

"The best in the *centuria*, Sir," I announced proudly.

He looked across the river again. "Here is what you will do."

Chapter 6

"We'll be arriving in a minute," the EMT announced.

"Any change?" Jasmina asked as she looked down at her niece, whose face was so calm, anyone else might think she was merely sleeping.

"No. She's stable. Have you learned anything else?"

Jasmina frowned. "Yes, but it's not good."

"Ma'am?"

"She's in a village in what is now Belgium and Roman soldiers are approaching. This was before Europe was unified into individual nations, and each region had its own governing Celtic clan. Unfortunately, this meant the clans couldn't work together well enough to drive the Romans out."

"The Romans are coming to take over the town?"

"The Gauls plan to resist, and when provoked, the Romans were known for their brutality."

"Why don't they just run away?"

"Where would they go? Through Remmy's connection, I've learned that not only did they not get along with the Romans, but there were regional rivalries that kept them always at each other's throats. If one clan wandered into territory controlled by another, they were just as likely to be slaughtered as when they stood their ground against the Romans."

"So they're going to fight?"

"Yes, but not before sending the women and children into the hills to hide."

"So, at least your niece will be safe."

Jasmina shook her head. "She knows what is at stake. If the Romans defeat their men, the women and children will be defenseless against them."

"Bummer!"

"Worse than that," she said while squeezing Remmy's hand. "She and fifty of the younger women have decided to stay and fight with their men."

"Women fighting?" he asked with surprise. "They did that in those days?"

Jasmina nodded slowly. "Unfortunately, it rarely did them any good."

"You mean, the Romans were just that much better at fighting?"

"It's worse than that. The Romans took a dim view of women combatants. If captured, women warriors were not treated well."

"They killed them?"

Her head shook slowly. "Death would have been preferable to being raped and mutilated. Those who did survive the brutality were forced into humiliating slavery, often as prostitutes."

"Shit! Seriously?"

"Yes, and my niece is in the body of a woman who may just have to experience that trauma if I don't get her out of there."

"Maybe the doctor can give her a stimulant and wake her up."

"And how can I make him do that when she isn't in any obvious danger?"

"That's a tough one, Missus Maxell."

"Could you give her the shot?"

His head shaking, the EMT pointed at blinking lights in a panel next to his head. "Sorry, but this stuff records everything that's going on, and I have to report any drugs I give her. If I didn't, the doctors might double the dose and it could get very nasty. You know what I mean?"

Jasmina nodded. "That would make matters even worse."

They felt the ambulance slowing, and the EMT shifted his position. "We're almost there, Ma'am. I'll talk with the doctor, but I doubt he's going to go along with this."

"Maybe if you left off the part about her ancient connection to the girl in Belgium he might."

"It's worth a try."

The ambulance doors opened and the paramedics hurried out to move the gurney into the emergency room. Jasmina followed closely as they transferred Remmy to a bed and a nurse did a quick examination before hooking her up to the equipment at the head of her bed.

"She ever have this issue before?"

"Not as far as I know."

"You're her aunt, right? Have you contacted her parents?"

"They're in Paris right now. Things happened so fast, I haven't had a chance to try."

"It'd be good if you did as soon as you can. We'll need to know if she has any allergic reaction to drugs we might want to give her."

"Yes. I will."

"She taking any kind of prescription medication right now?"

"No."

"Any other kinds of drugs?" When Jasmina hesitated, the nurse held up a hand, palm out. "We're not the cops here, Ma'am. I just need to make sure we don't prescribe something that might make things worse."

"No. Remmy would never use illegal drugs, but she is on the usual vitamin and mineral supplements."

The nurse finished her task, and turned to Jasmina.

"The doctor will be in to see her soon, but it would be really good if you got in touch with her parents and made sure she isn't allergic to anything, or if she has any special needs we should know about. They'll also need to give us their insurance information, if they have it with them." She waved at the entryway. "You can't use your cell phone here, but it's OK to call from the lobby. Come back when you're done."

Nodding, Jasmina hurried into the waiting area and dialed a cell phone number she knew by heart. Her heart sank when it went to voicemail.

"Marv! Wanda! Please call me on my cell as soon as you get this. Remmy's in the emergency room. I think she's going to be OK, but the doctor's not been here yet, so I don't have much more to tell you."

After rattling off her phone number, she rang off, took a deep breath, and let it out slowly.

Closing her eyes, she struggled to keep down the panic cramping her stomach. When the anxiety did not subside, she opened her eyes, looked back into the patient area and sighed,

"Now let's see what my niece is up to."

Chapter 7

Roman legionnaires excel at many things, but sneaking is not one of them. In most cases, it is not a major issue, but when twenty soldiers are on the march, with heavy armor slowing their movement, spear, sword, bow and arrows flopping around and twenty pairs of feet stomping dry leaves in the forest, we are anything but quiet.

After marching a league upstream, we found a narrow section of the river and I ordered the men to build a raft. While they were working, I sized up the challenge. Though narrow at this point, the river was also fast and dropped over a small rapids several hundred paces above where we were crossing. In addition, the men had to wade in calf-deep water for half the distance to get to a spot where the raft would not hang on the gravel bottom.

Naturally, the first trip was the most difficult. I ordered the best swimmer among them to strip down and pull one end of a rope across. Knowing that being unarmed and nearly naked in enemy territory made him quite vulnerable, I kept four men ready with bows. The tension made my gut ache because if the enemy attacked us at this point, the mission would most likely fail, and I would have to explain the unexplainable to the *centurio*.

I only allowed myself to relax when the soldier tied his end of the rope to a stout tree. From that point on, it was simple enough to pull the raft to and fro until all were across.

After stowing the raft and regrouping, we gathered in the forest, and waited for daylight before heading toward the village. It was not difficult terrain, but the going was still slowed by downed trees, clumps of brush, and an occasional gully that had to be skirted or crossed, as the situation allowed.

In keeping with standard protocol, I had two men scouting ahead, looking carefully for enemy sentries, but though we found several campfires in the wood, their embers were too cold for recent occupancy. Obviously, the Gauls were not eager to engage us.

I smiled as we came upon the third such campfire, its coals as cold as the others. Such was the reputation of the Roman army that even when our enemy outnumbered us by three to one, they still abandoned everything resembling good military tactics when we approached. Many simply fled, preferring to live under the yoke of their life-long enemies rather than face Roman steel. It did them little good. Caesar wanted all of Gaul under his control. No matter where they ran, our armies would find them and make them bow in service to him.

Sunlight streaked through the leaves above as we approached the forest's edge. A hundred paces out, we came across a Gallic soldier with a Roman arrow in his chest. Fifty paces further on, a second enemy lay on his belly with an arrow in the middle of his back. The next thing we saw was our scouts coming back to us.

"Only two enemy sentries spotted, Sir. None escaped," the lead scout reported. "The rest seem to have pulled back to their village and are unaware of our presence."

Moving to the forest's edge, I looked down at the village, its walls being only a rectangular ridge of dirt topped with wooden walls made from bare logs. It was similar to the defenses we erect nightly while on the march, but much cruder. Even so, to breach it, our soldiers would have to run up the steep slope and climb the walls against an onslaught of enemy arrows and spears.

Shaking my head, I looked back at where our engineers were completing the bridge. The *centurio* would undoubtedly be constructing catapults, which would make short work of these crude fortifications, and if there was to be a siege, it would not last long.

After pulling back into the forest and establishing our perimeter, I sent pairs of men in both directions along the edge of the forest to search for more enemy sentries. Each pair found another enemy outpost, their men huddled over a small campfire, and dispatched them quietly.

Moving back to the edge of the forest, I looked again at the engineers working diligently on the bridge, which was now nearly across the river. It was a simple affair, consisting of squares of logs lashed together and floated out to be attached in a single row across the river. At some point before they started floating the sections, someone had swum a line across, allowing them to secure each section and keep the whole thing from being pulled down stream by the current.

When my troop left camp to find a river crossing, Gallic archers had been trading arrows with us. As I looked now, it appeared the Gauls had abandoned their plan to harass us, and retreated behind the walls of their village. With no further resistance, it appeared the last section would easily be slipped into place a half-day ahead of schedule.

"*Optio*," one of my scouts announced as he approached. "They are evacuating women and children into the forest. Shall we capture them?"

I shook my head. "Watch them from a distance, and see where they go. We can pick them up once we have dispatched their men."

Then a thought occurred to me. "Are you sure there are only women among them?"

"Sir?"

"Some of their men might be disguising themselves as women and moving into the forest to outflank us."

"I have two men watching them, Sir."

I nodded. "Good. Get back and let them know what I suspect. If it is true, we will have a surprise of our own for them."

"Yes, Sir!"

Seeing the soldier salute, spin around, and hurry off, I felt a sense of pride. After all, it is Roman discipline that makes our armies nearly invincible, and our nation the most powerful in the world. Despite the odds, I had every confidence we would make short work of these savage Gauls.

Turning to my second in command, I said, "Get ready to move out. The enemy may be planning a sneak attack."

"Yes, Sir!" he responded and was gone.

I looked again at the village below. Our position was slightly higher, and allowed me to see some of the buildings inside, though not high enough to see people. Even so, I was sure they were hurrying around like scared rabbits. I chuckled at the thought that it would do them little good.

Their best option was to surrender now, before the fight. Our orders were simple, and consistent with any Roman campaign. If the enemy surrendered without a fight, we were to accept their tribute and hostages, and leave their property untouched. However, if they resisted, we were to kill everyone we did not take as slaves, and burn their village to the ground, leaving nothing but smoldering ash and rotting corpses to show other clans what resistance to Roman rule brought upon them.

The policy had been effective in southern Gaul, but the northern clans had declared they would rather die than give in, and die they have. It also produced so many captives to be shipped back to *Italia*, it took a legion just to handle them, and drove the price of slaves down to nearly half the usual rate. Since part of any Roman soldier's pay came from booty, including the proceeds from selling slaves, this brought about a definite slowing in the growth of our retirement income.

As I turned to watch my men break camp, I suddenly felt doubt, as though enslaving and plundering these people was somehow wrong. The feeling appalled me, and I quickly shook it off. This was how warfare had been handled since the gods first appeared. Who was I to question generations of tradition?

"Sir," my junior called as he snapped to attention in front of me. "The men are ready to move out, and await your orders."

I nodded. "The enemy may be sneaking troops over the wall," I announced, pleased to see the look of disgust on his face. "We will move further into the forest and set up a trap for them. If it turns out they are not, we will still be close enough to support our main force, should they need us."

"Yes, Sir!"

After instructing my advance scouts, I led my men back from the forest's edge until I was sure the enemy could not see us and then led them to the back of the village. We had gone barely half a league when a scout appeared from among the trees.

"*Optio*. There is a clearing half a league from here. It will make an excellent ambush."

We had only started to follow the scout when a second one arrived from our earlier scouting party.

"You were correct, Sir," he announced. "The enemy smuggled fifty men out of the village. They were still getting organized when I left them about a league from here, but from the way their leader was acting, I believe they are coming our way."

Without hesitating, I waved the men forward. "Let us show them what this trickery will earn them."

I set a brisk pace, unconcerned with the weight of the gear each man carried. After all, I carried the same amount. If I could march at double-time for half a league, so could they.

When we arrived at the clearing, I kept the men in the protection of the trees while I looked around. The opening before us was nearly five-hundred paces long by two-hundred wide. One of my scouts approached through the trees.

"*Optio*," he called when in hearing range. "The enemy is following an obvious trail through the wood, and will be coming out there."

He was pointing at a small opening in the trees less than a hundred paces from where we stood.

"The trail drops into a small draw lined with brush."

I looked to see a line of dark-green bushes that snaked across the clearing for at least two-hundred paces before disappearing into the wood. Moving over to look at the narrow bottom of the draw, it was obvious this was a well-established path along a meandering creek, but the Gauls could march at no more than two abreast, meaning their men would be hopelessly spread out. Even better, the valley was wide enough to allow all fifty men time to get into the depression before their leader reached the other side.

I stepped back to see the draw was nearly three-quarters-of-a-man's height at the beginning, but the low brush along its edge would make it hard for them to see my men hiding on each side until our arrows sent them to Hades.

"Send eight men with bows to the far side of the draw. Another eight, including me, will man this side, and four men at this end to stop them from proceeding into the forest beyond. No one is to shoot until our men stop their progress. They will be trapped like pigs in a pen and we will slaughter them to the last man."

Watching the men hurry to obey my orders made me feel confident, but for a Roman soldier, that is not necessarily a good thing.

"Give no quarter," I ordered needlessly as the men moved into position. Every one of them knew that even one escapee would put us all in needless jeopardy.

We did not have long to wait, and I was surprised to hear the enemy's feet noisily pounding the ground as they marched from the forest, being so confident of their safety they did not even bother to send out scouts. I stared in disbelief while their leader casually chatted with a subordinate as he led his men to their deaths.

Dropping into the draw, they rearranged themselves two abreast, and when the lead soldiers reached the designated point on the opposite side, all four legionnaires rose in front of them and released their arrows, sending three to the ground. To my utter disgust, my men fired again before any of the Gauls barked out an alarm. By this time the rest of my men were releasing their arrows. Most of the remaining shouts I heard were cries of pain.

When nearly all of them were down, I called for my men to stop. Only three of the original fifty remained, and they were retreating over the corpses of their comrades. Using hand signals, I ordered two men to slide down into the draw to stop them. One of the Gauls pulled his still-unused bow free and knocked an arrow. Three of our arrows sent him to the ground. Seeing the man drop, his comrades cried out, their own weapons falling to the ground as they yanked hands over their heads.

"Bind them and bring them to me," I ordered before pointing at the four men on the opposite end of the draw. "Dispatch any still living and cut off the heads."

Without hesitating, the men ran to the first of the fallen, but I was already turning my attention to the living captives as I waved over the only member of my troop who could speak their barbaric language.

When the captives were in front of me, my soldiers pushed them down onto their knees, and forced their heads down so they could see nothing but my feet.

"Tell them if they cooperate I will be merciful," I ordered.

The translator relayed my demand, and the spitting response of the left man required no interpretation. I pointed at the right one.

"Lift his head."

My soldier grabbed the prisoner's ridiculously long, greasy hair and yanked his head back. His tense muscles pulled his mouth into an elongated O, but it was not tense muscles that kept his eyes wide.

"Tell him again."

Though he said nothing in response, his shaking body told me what I needed to know.

"Cut the other's throat."

When my soldier pulled out his sword and dispatched his companion, a wet patch appeared in the right captive's crotch. The limp body fell forward onto the ground, its blood quickly pooling in the thin grass. His eyes wide, the remaining captive screamed something in his unintelligible tongue, and my translator only had to give a slight nod to tell me what I needed to know.

"Get the usual information from him."

Without responding, the translator moved closer and spoke softly to the man, asking him about troop sizes, leader's names, fortifications, and the like. The captive claimed more ignorance than he surely had, but I felt time was of the essence and a thorough interrogation would take too long.

"How would these Gauls tell the people in the village that they were in position?" I asked.

The man's response was so fast I had no doubt he was telling the truth, but just as a test, I asked one more question.

"Put a sword to his throat, and ask him where the women and children have gone."

The bloody sword that had been used to kill his companion pressed to his throat, the blade being pulled back slightly to make a shallow, painful cut in his skin. He hesitated for a long moment then closed his weepy eyes and answered.

"He confirmed what we already know about the caves half-a-league to the south," the translator said with disgust. "This one would do anything to save his skin."

"A life not worth saving," I said, giving a quick nod just before the sword was pulled back sharply and the gurgling captive slumped to the ground to suffocate in his own blood.

"The Gauls will come out as soon as they get the signal that this lot are in position," the translator announced as he turned to face me. "They have two-hundred-and-fifty men and fifty women."

"Women?" I asked incredulously. "They outnumber us and they still hide behind the skirts of their women?"

"That is what he said, Sir."

Nodding, I moved to the edge of the draw and watched my men working their way through the prone bodies.

"Send a man to let the *centurio* know what has happened, and what we know. This is going to be like cutting warm bread with a sharp knife."

"The signal they are expecting is one of their soldiers waving a red flag if they are ready, and a white flag if there is a problem." The translator held up the two flags while shaking his head.

"No special code to make sure we had not captured their flags?"

"Apparently not, Sir. It looks like the only problem we are going to have is finding a soldier willing to put on one of their disgusting, flea-ridden garments in order to give the signal."

I pointed at the blood stained white flag. "Thankfully, we have no use for that."

Chapter 8

Jasmina stood next to Remmy's bed and hesitated with her hands just above her niece's. Looking around the room one more time, she took a deep breath and slowly let it out as she flexed her fingers and gently took Remmy's hands in hers.

The move immediately put her in a small room, across a table from the young man she quickly recognized as Philippe.

"You shouldn't be doing this. Fighting is man's work."

Jasmina could feel Enid shaking her head. "Do not be a fool, Philippe. These are Romans. It will take every soldier we have to defeat them. I would rather die fighting with you than hide in the wood and wait for them to enslave us."

"But we have them outnumbered. They cannot prevail."

"And yet we hide behind our village walls like scared rabbits. We should attack them as they cross the river, or at least harass them as they build their ridiculous bridge. Our leaders are fools."

"Maybe," he responded angrily. "But they are our leaders, and without them we will not survive."

"Did they learn nothing from the defeats of the southern tribes? You cannot win against Legionnaires in the open field. If we attack now, we could eliminate a quarter of their force before they cross the river. Then we would have a chance against them in the open field."

"Their bows have a greater range than ours," Philippe argued. "We might lose even more men trying to kill them that way. By letting them get closer to our defenses, we eliminate that advantage."

Enid sighed. "It does not matter. We will not survive at all if we are divided. I will fight along with my tribe, as will you, and hope our leader's plan is enough to drive them away."

"Trust me," Philippe pleaded. "Our leaders know what they are doing. We have kept our lands secure for as long as our people have existed. We will defeat these Romans as we have all who came before."

"I wish I could be so sure."

He shook his head. "We have no choice but to defend ourselves, but you should go with the other women and children. They will need someone to protect them until we are done with these Romans."

She also shook her head. "If we do not defeat them here, a small troop of women warriors will be of little use."

Jumping to his feet, Philippe slammed a fist into his palm. "If you are to be my wife, you must learn to obey my orders."

Standing as well, Enid glared at him. "I am not yet your wife, Philippe. And until I am, I will do as my father permits."

Philippe started to speak, but bit down on the words as though they were bitter herbs.

"I must go to my unit," he announced. "You will do as you must."

Without another word, he rushed through the door, not bothering to close it behind him. Enid watched after him for a long moment before she picked up her gleaming sword – a gift from her father – and held it in front of her while praying,

"Bring us victory, oh Great Spirits. We seek your blessing in this bloody business."

Moving to the door, she peered out at the apparent chaos of people rushing to and fro, some carrying armor and sword, while farmers hefted wooden pitchforks and hunting knives and dodged around crying babies as their mothers hugged their fathers for what might be the last time.

Strapping the sword to her narrow waist, she looked down at her thick leather dress, a fine brass breastplate covering her chest, and shining copper sheaths on her forearms. While training to fight, the outfit made her feel confident, almost invincible. Now that she faced a determined enemy, she felt nearly naked.

"Naked or no, I will make them pay dearly for my death," she muttered while unsheathing her sword and shaking it at the ceiling. "Spirits! Be my shield against the unjust, and give me strength as I strike these Romans dead."

As she took a step forward, she felt a hand shaking her shoulder. Lifting her hands, Jasmina turned to stare into the questioning eyes of a nurse.

"Are you OK Ma'am?"

"Yes. Sorry," she responded. "I just...uh...fell asleep for a moment."

The nurse waved a hand at the curtain surrounding the bed. "The doctor will be here soon. I want to check vitals again before he arrives."

Though she wanted more than anything to grab Remmy's hand again, Jasmina forced herself to step back and watch the nurse check the readouts on the display next to her niece's bed.

Nodding when she was done, the nurse sighed. "If I didn't know better, I'd say she was just sleeping." She pointed at Remmy's closed eyes. "It looks like she's in deep REM sleep, and having a whopper of a dream."

"Is that normal?"

The nurse shrugged. "If there's no brain damage, sure."

"So is there some way to…"

"Hello," the doctor announced as he pushed through the curtain. "I'm Doctor Spain. What seems to be the trouble here?"

"My niece collapsed and she won't wake up."

Nodding, he gave the nurse a questioning look.

"Her vitals are all normal," she answered. "There's nothing to suggest the reason for her condition."

"The notes say she was under stress when it happened," he observed while looking at the metal folder in his hands. "Her boyfriend had also fainted for no reason and was in a coma as well?"

"Yes, and before you ask, these two are good kids. They don't use any kind of drugs or alcohol, and both are excellent students."

He looked at the notes again. "And where is this young man?"

"His name is Gerry Patterson, and I believe he was brought here, though I'm not sure. Remmy and I were just preparing to go see him when she fainted. She never got the chance to tell me exactly where he is."

Nodding, the doctor made some quick notes before he looked at the nurse.

"Let's do a tox screen anyway, and a CBC. Fluids?"

"She's halfway through her first bag."

"OK. Keep that going."

"But doctor," Jasmina pleaded. "Can't you give her some kind of stimulant to wake her up?"

His head shook as he passed his notes to the nurse. "I don't want to give her anything without knowing what's in her system. As long as she doesn't appear to be in any immediate danger, we'll just have to wait until the tests come back before taking the next step."

"And that's it?"

Shrugging, he pushed an opening in the curtain. "For now, yes."

Before she could protest, the doctor was gone.

His sudden departure shocked Jasmina, but when she turned back to her niece, what she saw took her breath away.

Remmy's eyes were open, and her normally green eyes were sky blue.

Chapter 9

I watched as the last section slipped into place on the bridge. Though none of the enemy soldiers had yet appeared, we had been given another mission. While the *centurio's* men were binding the last section and preparing to move a small contingent across, we were to run around the perimeter of the village and engage any other troops they might have sent.

We would have to travel several leagues if we stayed in the woods and kept far enough back to remain out of sight of the enemy. The distance did not concern me. My men were in excellent shape, and we had suffered no casualties, so we should make it before the battle was engaged.

I sent two scouts ahead, spacing them out so I could see the second one, and he in turn could see the lead man. I kept a steady but brisk pace, my eyes on the wood, alert for any kind of trap we might be walking into. A quarter of a league further on we crossed a well-worn path which undoubtedly would be the one the women and children had taken. The path would be easy to find again and I was sure we would find more men to kill, women and children to enslave, and booty to collect. If this pattern continued, we would all be rich men long before the full moon returned.

Another quarter-league further on, we picked up signs that another troop had passed ahead of us. The damage to twigs and grass was quite recent, even within half-a-day's time or less. From this position we could not see the progress our main force was making in crossing the river, but I was fairly certain they were nearly ready to attack. Though I wanted to charge ahead and catch up with whoever was ahead of us, I could not afford to take that kind of risk.

I stopped the troop and ordered them to stand down, leaving two men on guard. Calling back my scouts, I told them to rush ahead, knowing the enemy could be anywhere, and report back to me as soon as they saw them. When the enemy was located, I planned to lure them further into the wood and dispatch them quietly so as not to alert those inside the village.

The men had barely settled in before both scouts were back.

"*Optio*," the lead scout called. "There are maybe fifty soldiers no more than one-hundred-and-fifty paces beyond that clump of brush.

Clifford M. Scovell

"I also went to the forest's edge," the second scout announced, "to see that our main force has crossed the river and is preparing to engage the enemy."

"Has the enemy moved out to intercept them?"

"Not yet, Sir," answered the second, "but from the way the troop ahead of us is organizing, they are close to doing so."

Something about this struck me as strange.

"Why would they deploy thirty men on one side, and fifty on the other?" I asked no one in particular.

"My apologies, *Optio*," the lead scout blurted. "I did not mention that these soldiers are all women."

"*All* women?"

"Yes, Sir."

"You are not serious."

"Yes, *Optio*. I am very serious."

I looked in the direction of the enemy, wondering if the gods had intentionally given me easy assignments so that I would survive this engagement.

"How are they armed?"

"Short swords and longbows."

"Organized?"

"It appears they plan to come out of the forest five abreast, and from the quantity of arrows they are carrying, their role seems to be to harass and weaken our right flank."

I shook my head. The gods can be so cruel, and yet so generous. I had to wonder which this was.

"Women or not, we'll match our bows against theirs," I announced. "At the ready men. I do not want a single one of them to make it to the battle. Is that understood?"

"Yes, Sir," they barked enthusiastically.

After sending a scout to the edge of the forest, I moved to a position where I could see our main force through a narrow gap in the trees. After watching for a short time, I became frustrated with the limited view and moved back to where I could see my scout hunkered down beside a tree, his head moving back and forth as he followed the action.

It was not long before he signaled that the main enemy force was moving out of their fortified position.

"They must not have reinforcements coming," I muttered more to myself than anyone close to me. "Otherwise, they would have holed up until they got here."

I held up my sword as notice for the others to get ready. The tension of a surprise attack was always unnerving, because timing was everything. If the enemy learned of your plans before they were fully executed, things often got sticky.

When the scout eventually waved us forward, I indicated that the men should crouch down as we moved through the wood, keeping ourselves as inconspicuous as possible until the last possible moment. As we approached open ground, I looked over to see the last of the women marching into the clear, their pace steady, formation surprisingly tight.

I motioned for the men to straighten and increase their pace. Their gate no longer impeded by having to run bent over, they moved quickly into position, but it hardly seemed to matter. The enemy's attention was completely on the upcoming battle below, and none of them saw us. I glanced at what was going on below, only to make sure the enemy was not sending reinforcements, thankful that the screaming and shouting of the Gallic soldiers was covering any noise we might make.

After determining that no one knew we were even there, I stopped and watched my men hurry past me to form a double row parallel to the enemy. The front row kneeled in a tight line, holding their shields close together and in front of their bodies while lowering their heads below the top of the shields. The second row stood behind them, using the ready-made wall of shields as a barrier to enemy arrows.

The top of my own shield held just below my chin, I held up my sword while watching them knock their arrows and aim. At this distance, few would miss.

"Release!" I commanded and yanked the sword down.

As the arrows flew, I sheathed my sword, grabbed my bow, and joined in. The men fired quickly, and a dozen women were slumping to the ground before the others even realized what was going on. They were still struggling to react to the assault when more arrows landed hard on their flank.

A tall thin woman rushed around the front of the group, bow in hand, arrow knocked and ready. She screamed something unintelligible, and the other women turned quickly. I was impressed to see that even though many in their number had fallen, they kept their heads, brought their bows around, and fired back.

Despite the tremendous self-control they showed, their first volley was mostly high, and the miss cost them another ten of their comrades. My men were now in automatic mode, dipping slightly as they pulled an arrow from their quivers, snapping their bow strings back, straightening, and releasing.

Another quarter of the enemy were on the ground before they managed to improve their aim, but the lead woman continued to scream at them as she fired her arrows so efficiently I almost stopped to watch her skilled execution. But I was a professional, and though such sights were rare, I was not about to let a mere woman best me.

Re-aiming my arrow, I let loose. Though I automatically pulled a new missile from my quiver, my eyes stayed on leader until the arrow found a home in her left shoulder. The impact twisted her thin body around and her bow flew from her hand. She howled from the pain, and sank to her knees. Seeing she was no longer a danger, I turned my attention to the other ducks trapped in my "pond."

With their leader down, the remaining survivors turned to retreat. I released an arrow that hit the thigh of the straggler. Of those remaining, most dropped their weapons and sprinted for the wood. Two more went down before they reached it, and as the remaining disappeared from sight, I motioned to five of my men.

"Get them," I commanded. "Alive if you can."

After the men took off at a sprint, I looked at my handiwork for a moment. Most of the women combatants lay still, one or more arrows protruding from their bodies. Others squirmed and cried, but it was obvious they were no longer a threat to us.

I turned to assess the damage to my men. Despite the shields, two lay dead, and three others were too wounded to continue the fight. At the moment, there was little I could do for them until the battle was over.

As my men and I approached the women, I saw the enemy leader struggle to her feet, sword in hand. Weakened by her injury, she staggered as I came within striking distance, my own sword easily blocking hers. Rather than kill her, I slammed a fist into the side of her head, knocking her to the ground. Though obviously stunned by the impact, she struggled to rise. Another fist to the face put her down for good.

Is she still alive? You MUST help her! a voice screamed in my head.

The thought was absurd. Those women were enemy combatants, not sparring partners. If I did anything, it would be to dispatch anyone still breathing. Then again, I had to wonder why I had knocked her out instead of finishing her off.

Shaking my head, I turned back to face my men.

"We will deal with survivors after we help the *centurio* cut these savages to ribbons."

After ordering the men back into formation, I looked again at the unmoving woman then toward the wood to see the five I sent in pursuit running toward us.

"*Optio*," the leader called when he reached me. "They dropped their weapons and vanished into the wood. We destroyed the weapons and hurried back."

I nodded. "Join the formation."

The roar from the battle increased and I turned to see the front lines of the two armies below smashing into each other. Though I knew I should do a sweep of the fallen women and dispatch any still breathing, my orders were to engage the enemy and since the women were no longer a functional threat, I lead the men across open field until we were three-hundred paces from the enemy left flank. I was not surprised that they ignored us. We were a tiny force compared to the nearly two *centuriae* they were facing.

"Line up and drop shields," I commanded.

The men spread out and once again formed a single line parallel to the enemy. During the heat of battle when hundreds of men are caught up in a life-and-death slugfest, a small contingent like ours might go unnoticed. I had no intention of letting that continue.

"Bows up and release!"

The buzzing of flying arrows was barely audible above the din of the fighting, but it felt good. It was also like kicking a sleeping badger.

When their comrades along the left edge of their flank started falling, the enemy finally began to realize that we were more of a threat than they assumed. Dozens went down before a contingent turned toward us. By this time, we were out of arrows, and the enemy's rear guard archers were starting to target us.

"Drop bows and reform platoon," I shouted, and was pleased to see my men grab their shields, pull out their swords and form a tight box.

We were only fifteen men and stood little chance against such a large contingent, but our orders were to attack from the side, and attack from the side we would do.

"Tighten formation," I shouted needlessly.

Five abreast, and three deep, we were a tight cluster with each soldier's shield protecting his companion's, sword arm. The enemy might overwhelm us, but it would be like attacking a porcupine. True to form, the screaming savages attacked, each running alone, his sword held high, shield waving at his side. I kept the men marching forward until I saw their leader motioning for some of their men to move around behind us.

"Square up!" I shouted.

We stopped and formed a hollow square with four on three sides and three in the back. The charging savages completely lost any remaining formation, some slowing at seeing our shift while others continued to charge full out, their bodies slamming against our shields as we threw our shoulders in to counter the impact and then stabbed up into their bellies.

Men screamed, blood gushed, and guts flew. Dying men were pushed back to fall in front of their comrades whose hesitation was their undoing. Some lost their balance, or stepped on their dying comrades and fell. Those who did not fall on their faces, stumbled into us to be cut down. Others tried to attack our side and rear and got the same treatment, their bodies stacking against our shields, forcing those who followed to climb over them to get at us. The confusion in their attack left them vulnerable.

In no time at all, we were surrounded by corpses, and the confused faces of our frustrated enemy, obviously wondering why they had not crushed us before now. We had only two men killed in the fracas, but the confusion we created allowed our main force to push back the Gallic left flank. To make it worse for the enemy, when those just behind the front line saw what was happening, they quickly pulled back, as though to regroup. However, others in their rear thought they were retreating and also fell back, further weakening their left flank. As it continued to collapse, more enemy fell, and those behind them began to panic.

Seeing their line disintegrate, those attacking us turned and ran back to the main body. Taking the opportunity, I regrouped the men outside the circle of bodies and marched them double-time toward the rear of the collapsing left flank. Against a professional army, we would have been quickly annihilated, but in this case, our little force created even more confusion. It seemed as though these inexperienced farmer/soldiers did not know whether to keep attacking the main force, or turn their attention to us. Now being attacked from two sides, many in the front line dropped their weapons and tried to surrender while those behind struggled to get past them to attack.

We were again attacked by a small contingent from the enemy rear. True to their training, my men marched steadily ahead, their lines straight, shields locked together, swords opening bellies, chopping off arms. To my surprise, the enemy suddenly pulled away from us, giving me time to look back to see our main force's unyielding attack was finally collapsing their line.

Promise of Victory

I stopped to give the men a rest and turned to watch the enemy center falter as our main force's right flank turned on it, pinching those in the middle between two lines of legionnaires. Though we were no longer needed, I was here to fight, and standing on the sidelines was not in my plan. I hurried my little force forward to attack the center from behind and before we even reached them, men started dropping their weapons and running. With their center now in chaos, the enemy's right flank disintegrated into bedlam. At this point, fighting became hand-to-hand, my men maintaining a loose formation as they spread out to cut and hack anyone within range of their swords.

When the enemy lines completely dissolved, the Gauls retreated toward their village. Our legion reformed and pursued, and as they approached the walls of the city, the gates started to close. A good number of their men were still outside and when the latches slammed into place. Bedlam ensued. As we continued to approach, small contingents of their men tried to form up and take us on, but they did not have the numbers to slow us much.

Our forces pressed the remaining Gauls. Some pounded on the gates, foolishly pleading to be let inside. Others ran as fast as their terrified legs could carry them. However, since there was nothing but one-thousand paces of open field between the gates and the wood, our archers finished them off before they could reach cover.

I stopped my troop as the main force pressed into those still clinging to the gates, and told my men to move to a position outside the range of the enemy's arrows, and stand down.

Seeing that the battle was all but over, I approached the *centurio*.

"Sir," I called while saluting. "Permission to see to my injured men and clean up the women contingent we destroyed."

"He hardly looked around. "Permission granted, *Optio*."

Hurrying back to my men, I organized them in loose formation and marched back through the battle scene to check on the three who fell during our attack on their left flank, leaving two men to help them back to camp while the rest of us returned to the edge of the forest where we found the corpses of those we left behind, all five with their throats cut, bodies mutilated, genitalia removed, three of them while they were still alive. I was gratified to see that those still living took out two more of the women soldiers before they were killed.

"This is intolerable," I growled while turning my attention to forest. "This outrage will not go unpunished."

Marching my men to where the women's bodies lay, I spotted four places on the ground where someone had lain, but there was now only a bloody patch of grass. I was surprised to feel both pleasure and disappointment that their leader was among the missing.

"They will be moving slowly," I observed. "We can still catch them."

The ten of us headed into the wood, and I could feel my breath quickening in anticipation of the kill. Though I was eager to catch them, I was not going to needlessly sacrifice more men by rushing into a trap. I sent two scouts out, and though we were moving quickly, and making a considerable amount of noise, I kept my ears open for sounds of a possible attack from the side. That old habit served me well when I heard a sharp squeal of pain off to my right. Stopping the troop, I signaled to them to spread out, as we could not form a tight formation in this dense wood.

We moved as quietly as we could for about a hundred paces, my hearing now so sharp I could hear the movements of each of my men, and easily picked out a muffled groan, followed by the sound of someone shushing her. I quickly determined they were in a small triangle created by the remains of three fallen trees. A wide disturbance in the leaves, and blood on the ground made it clear several of those inside had been nearly dragged there.

Using hand signals, I sent two to swing around behind them, two to approach from each side, and the one remaining to join me in the frontal assault. As we moved in, I heard the rapid breathing of the man next to me. His face was full of anticipation, but there was something more, which I felt as well. After all, these were not just enemy soldiers who had murdered our people. They were *women* enemy soldiers, and the possibility of payback was energizing me in a sexually exciting way.

When I could finally see over the logs, three uninjured women rose to meet us, their swords at the ready. One other, an arrow still protruding from her left shoulder, also rose with sword in hand. This was the woman I shot at the beginning of the engagement.

The injury to her shoulder brought on an instant sense of respect, but I was not ready for the feeling that suddenly overtook me. Though lust and anger urged me on, a voice in my head was shouting, *Save her! You can't let them kill her.*

Stunned by the strange sensation that statement brought on, I hesitated briefly before shouting, "Attack!"

I could hear my men cry out as they leapt over the logs as the voice again screamed, *No! They can't hurt them.*

"Yes they can," I shouted at the invisible daemon.

The enemy leader screamed something unintelligible and her women fell back and prepared for our attack. My respect increased when the outnumbered women and their injured leader did not back down.

While my men overwhelmed the three uninjured women, I made straight for their leader, countering her stroke with my own, surprised with how powerful it was despite the painful arrow hampering her effort. Our eyes met -- combatant to combatant -- for a fraction of an instant, hers showing no sign of giving quarter. The challenge excited me even more as she blocked my thrust and staggered back with her sword up and ready for whatever I would do.

Motioning my men away from her, I faked a stroke to her right before bringing my blade up to smack the protruding arrow. Though she cried from the pain, her stance wavered only slightly. My situation was turning critical, however, as the voice in my head was relentlessly pleading with me to do her no more harm.

When I stabbed at the protruding arrow, she jumped back, and for the first time showed weakness when her face scrunched up from the pain she must have been feeling. Another stab with my sword forced her back another step, her expression still determined, stance still steady.

Confusion filled my head as I began to wonder if this woman was the one who would kill me. Weak as she might be, her weapon was still a threat, and if I continued to hesitate, she might nick something vital, bringing a humiliating end to this soldier's life.

It was then I noticed a slight tremor in her right arm as she held her weapon at the ready. I made a feint toward the arrow again, and when she brought her sword up to block me, I changed direction, slammed her blade, and knocked it from her hand.

Only then did I hear the cheering of my men, and the excited calls for me to take her down and do what the voice in my head said could not happen. She hesitated only briefly, her attention moving to her companions, her expression shifting to a determined resignation. The woman started screaming as she pulled a knife from her belt. Realizing as well what she planned to do, I did a quick spin toward her, bringing up the hilt of my sword. As the knife rose to her throat, the hilt struck her forehead before the knife could end her life.

My men howled their approval and her people screamed as she crumpled to the ground.

Suddenly, and inexplicitly, I no longer had the stomach for what I knew was going to happen. Stowing my sword, I grabbed the leader's hand and pulled her over my shoulder.

Turning to my men, I shouted, "Victory is ours! This one is mine."

One of the women was screaming something in their unintelligible tongue as I leapt over the log and marched back toward our camp. My newly-won captive was hardly a burden, yet I felt a heavy weight of disgust as the screaming and shouting from behind reached my ears.

These are the spoils of war, I chastised myself, my stomach churning so much I thought I might hurl. *As it has been and always will be.*

The thought did nothing to dampen my growing disgust…and confusion.

Save her! shouted in my head as I exited the wood and headed toward the *centurio*'s location. Complying with that request would not be as easy as one might think.

For a Roman soldier, much of the compensation for risking life and limb for the mother country is counted in booty collected from these kinds of raids. Unfortunately, this woman was part of that collection, and I did not have final say in what would happen to her. All spoils gained from our raid would be collected into one place and then be divided by the *centurio*. A percentage went to the men of our *centuria*, another bit would be distributed amongst the rest of our company, but the lion's share would be forwarded to Rome for Caesar's share of the take.

I looked toward camp, seeing men already moving in that direction as the *centurio* prepared for a siege. The thought of trying to hide her was absurd. I was a lowly legionnaire. Though I now had my own tent, she could not stay with me when we were on the march. In addition, this woman was a captured enemy soldier. Trying to hide her was an act of treason against Rome, punishable by death.

But you have to save her!

The voice in my head was becoming annoying and I struggled to ignore it, with little success.

Determined that I would not die an enemy of the state, I marched up to the *centurio*, and saluted.

"*Centurio*," I announced as I shifted my load. "I have the leader of their female troop."

When he looked at me, I tightened my grip on her legs, pulling the short leather skirt down to cover her genitals. The move surprised me, but not more than the voice.

Ask him if you can keep her.

I almost laughed out loud. A soldier did not ask his superior for favors.

Standing at attention, I felt uncomfortable that he did not immediately respond.

"You did well today, *Optio*," he said with a hint of admiration in his voice. "Our losses would have been much higher if you had not eliminated those extra troops."

"We still have to take the village, Sir."

He nodded slowly. "Do you have a suggestion for how we should do it?"

I wanted to drop the woman onto the ground like a bag of turnips, but something inside me would not allow it. However, it was not dignified for me to discuss battle tactics with an unconscious woman over my shoulder.

Realizing that this would soon become an uncomfortable situation, I flipped the woman off my shoulder, caught her across the shoulders with my free arm, and lowered her quickly to the ground. Stepping away from her, I tried to pretend that her condition did not matter.

"It is quite likely they sent runners to the next village for help, so we need to act quickly. I assume you have scouts watching for anyone coming to their aid."

When he nodded, I scanned the area, seeing the newly built catapults rolling across the floating bridge; the enemy uselessly shooting arrows that fell short of our position; and our soldiers were cleaning up the battlefield, carrying off our dead and wounded, and quickly dispatching any of theirs still breathing.

"I suggest sending burning projectiles into the village to set it on fire. Once the place is fully engulfed in flames, we can use the same catapults to punch holes in their walls, leaving these citizen soldiers to decide between saving their burning homes or defending against our attack."

He nodded. "Such an attack might route them out before the sun reaches the horizon, but what if they decide to escape their stronghold before we break in? We do not have enough men to encircle the village."

I nodded. "While moving around their fortifications, I saw two locations through which they might escape." I pointed to the right side of the town wall. "On the north side, toward the back, the wall bows in for a short stretch to avoid a rock outcropping. They could lower people over the wall and then crawl to the wood. Even if we had guards on the northern edge of the forest, they might not see them after dark."

"And the other location?"

"On the south side there is a shallow swale that runs from the fortified wall to the forest. They might dig under the wall, slip into the swale and leave without being seen."

"How would you defend against these?"

"I suggest we place obvious posts at the front and back of the village, but move men into the wood on either side to watch for enemy trying to escape. Ten men with bows on each side should do it, as many of the enemy will likely be only lightly armed."

"Why would you suspect that?"

"They need to escape quickly and quietly. It is nearly impossible to be quiet while weighted down with armor, and weapons."

"And which side do you think it most likely they will use?"

"The south side, *Centurio*. It is closest to where their women and children are hiding and this route would not force them to sneak past our rear guard."

"You know where the women and children are?"

"I have a very good idea, Sir. While moving around to intercept the female soldiers, I spotted a ridge about half-a-league behind the village. I believe we will find them hiding in the caves dotting this ridge."

"And would you collect them now, or wait?"

"Though their men have suffered a great setback, I would still consider them too great a threat to be diverting legionnaires from our primary task. In addition, I do not think the women and children will move from the caves until they know the fate of their men."

The *centurio*'s scowl vanished. Not a smile, by normal standards, but for a person of his position, he was almost beaming.

"You are quite the tactician."

Straightening my back, I hammered a fist against my chest in salute.

"Just doing my duty, *Centurio*."

He stared at me for a moment before shaking his head. "And how do you suppose I can reward a 'common' soldier for outstanding work?"

"I ask for nothing, Sir."

He looked at his captive. "Do you think that woman will survive?"

"I do not know, Sir," I responded, even though I was hoping she would. "If you will allow me, I will take her to the physician and see if she is worth saving."

He nodded, but with an upheld hand. "She is not to take precedence over our men, but if she survives, she is yours."

Why would I want such a strong-minded woman? I thought while snapping another salute, and shouting, "Yes, Sir."

He waved a hand dismissively. "Move your new possession off the battlefield and get back here. We have work to do."

Without further comment, he walked away, shouting commands.

I was initially stunned.

Get her to a doctor now! the voice in my head demanded.

Looking down at the unconscious woman, I shook my head. "The slavers might pay handsomely for such a fine specimen."

Grabbing her hand, I threw her over my shoulder again and marched double-time to the bridge and across. She regained consciousness as I was stepping back onto solid ground. Her legs started flailing, but when she tried to beat on my back the pain in her shoulder made her cry out.

I did not understand a single word she was saying, but was certain it was not flattery. Unconcerned, I kept up my pace, knowing the pain would keep her from doing more than scream as I jogged to my tent.

"Two leather straps," I demanded while hurrying inside.

A Greek slave near the door jumped up from the small wooden stool he had been languishing on and hurried to do my bidding. While waiting for the straps, I dumped her onto the ground, and she landed on her butt with a pained grunt.

"You stay," I commanded while pointing at her.

Certain that she understood as little of my language as I did hers, I was not surprised when she jumped back up and pulled a small dagger from her belt. My first reflex was to laugh, but this was the leader of her troop. She must have shown some fighting skill to earn that position.

Without hesitating, she lunged at me, but her attempt was weakened by her injury. I easily grabbed her wrist with my left hand, and slapped at the arrow with my right. Though she cried out, the knife stayed in her hand and she continued to struggle against my grip. The returning slave distracted her enough to allow me to give her a sharp head butt.

The knife and the woman hit the ground at the same time.

Chapter 10

Jasmina peered over the desk of the nurse's station, and stared down at the slender black woman digging through her purse.

"Can I help you?" the nurse asked without looking up.

Feeling hesitant, Jasmina paused for a moment before nodding.

"My name is Jasmina Maxell, and I'm looking for…"

"*The* Jasmina Maxell?" the nurse asked, her voice expressing disbelief as she rose and quickly turned toward Jasmina. "You wrote *If Goats Can Fly*?

"Why, yes. That is my spiritual book. Have you read it?"

The woman let out a high-pitched laugh. "Only about a dozen times. Sweet Jesus, woman. That book is my new Bible."

"It has been well received, but what I…"

The nurse grabbed her purse and started digging through it.

"I've got to call my mother. She really wants to meet you."

"Perhaps we can arrange that for another time. Right now I need to find a young man by the name of Gerry Patterson."

The nurse looked cautious. "Are you gonna cure him of something?"

Jasmina shook her head. "I just need to see him. I understand he is in a coma."

"You got that right. He hasn't moved a finger since they brought him in. The doctor is completely baffled."

"I think I know what is wrong with him, but I need to speak with his parents."

"Oh yeah. They came up with him from the ER." She pointed down the hall. "You'll find them in 308. It's the third room on the left."

"Thank you."

Her footsteps echoing in the hallway, Jasmina felt her heart race as she approached the room, but as she neared it, she heard a second pair of shoes squeaking on the linoleum and turned to find the nurse right behind her.

"I just gotta see how you do this," she said excitedly. "You talk about it in your book, but there's nothing like seeing it in person."

"Well, this should be a private matter," Jasmina said.

The nurse waved her comment away. "Oh Hell. I'm his nurse. I change his bedpan, and if he stays long enough, I'll be giving him a sponge bath. It don't get much more private than that."

"Well, I'm not sure if…"

"Oh. It's you."

Jasmina turned to see Miriam Patterson glaring at her.

"Missus Patterson. I want you to know I'm sorry to hear about Gerry."

Miriam stiffened, but her expression did not change. After a tense moment, she jerked a nod.

"Thank you for the sentiment, but if you're here to do some kind of voodoo magic on my son then I'm…"

"No," Jasmina interrupted. "My niece, Remmy has also gone into the same kind of coma, and I think I can help them both."

Miriam's eyes went wide. "Remmy too? But how?"

Jasmina shook her head. "She came to tell me about Gerry, and we were preparing to come to the hospital when she collapsed. The doctors are doing tests now, but we both know what is going on here."

Miriam's expression turned guarded again. "I know no such thing."

"What have the doctors told you?" Jasmina asked, but then quickly held up a hand. "No. Don't tell me. They are saying it is as though he is sleeping, and nothing they try will wake him up."

Though she said nothing, the expression on Miriam's face told Jasmina she was correct.

Miriam shook her head "They won't try anything. They say nothing is wrong with him."

Jasmina nodded. "The same with Remmy."

"What can we do?"

"I need to communicate with Gerry. If I understand the situation correctly, my niece has connected to a young woman in Belgium, during the time the Romans were conquering the tribes there. I think I know who Gerry is linked to, and there is a battle about to start that will put Remmy and Gerry in grave danger."

"What do you mean?"

"The Roman army is preparing to attack the village Remmy lives in, and she and her fiancé are going to join in the fight against them. I am guessing that Gerry is her fiancé, and if they get involved in this battle, they will be either enslaved or killed, and from what I know of Remmy's frame of mind, it's most likely they'll die rather than submit."

"So," Miriam said defensively. "This girl and her boyfriend will die and our children will come back to us."

"No. I don't believe that is the way it works."

"What do you mean?"

Jasmina clasped her hands together as she gave Gerry's mother a stern look. "Remmy, and I assume Gerry, are not linked to their past selves, as they were the last two times. They are becoming those people."

"Becoming? How?"

"I don't know. When Gerry was connected to his other past lives, I could sense the connection, but only Gerry could see what his past person was seeing. When I connect with Remmy this time, I am directly connected to the young woman she is becoming. I can see, hear, and even smell what she is experiencing. I've never been able to do that before."

"How does that make her become that person?" she asked tentatively.

"You know Remmy's eyes are normally the color of mine, right?"

"Well...yes."

"After the doctor examined her, I was surprised to discover Remmy's eyes were open, and they are now sky blue. Her hair is also getting lighter. Remmy is becoming this girl. If we don't do something very soon, we may lose them both, even if they survive this battle."

Miriam's hands flew to her mouth. "Oh Lord in Heaven, That explains it."

"Explains what?"

Miriam was quiet for a moment before she lowered her hands. "Do you know what color this other girl's fiancé eyes are?"

"Brown, I think."

"I was watching as the doctor was examining him, and Gerry's eyes are turning brown as well. Are you saying my son is becoming this person?"

After a moment's hesitation, Jasmina gave a definite nod. "Miriam. We have to work together to help them."

"But how?"

"I have to see Gerry now. I have to make a connection with him to see what he's seeing."

"Will that save my son?"

Jasmina hesitated, her eyes on Miriam for a moment before she shrugged. "I don't know, but we have to try."

Tears dribbled down Miriam's cheeks as she looked from Jasmina to the room where her son lay quietly. She stared at him for a long moment, her expression changing from desperate to determined and back several times before a long-held breath hissed through her teeth.

"No chanting or any of that magic mumbo-jumbo," she insisted, though her aggressive stance did little to hide the desperation in her eyes.

"That's not needed for this to work."

"I have to stay in the room with you."

"Absolutely."

"If I say you leave, you leave."

It was Jasmina's turn to hesitate, but the arguments that ran though her head were pointless.

She nodded.

"Fine," Miriam sighed. "Do what you have to do."

Rushing into the room, Jasmina took Gerry's hands and was immediately transported into a battle scene. Looking around, she saw a line of Roman soldiers, their shields on the ground, bows up and ready to fire.

"Release," she heard herself shout, and then felt dumbstruck as she watched fifteen arrows streak into the packed crowd of soldiers barely a hundred yards from them.

She tried to shout to her other self, but the lack of response made it clear she was only an observer, as she had been with Remmy. It was then she heard a faint voice screaming in the background. She wanted to look around for whoever was screaming, but realized the voice was not coming from outside his body, and it was a voice she recognized.

"Gerry?"

"Jasmina?" he cried, but so faintly his voice was nearly drowned out by the roar of the battle in front of her.

"Gerry! I'm here to help you. Where are you?"

"I'm inside this guy's head, but he doesn't seem to be able to hear me."

"Who is he, and when?"

"He's a Roman Legionnaire and he's reenlisted because he wants to die."

"He *wants* to die?"

"Yes, and we have to figure out how to make him want to live."

"What does this have to do with Remmy?"

"Remmy? Where is she?"

Jasmina's breath caught as the body she was in looked toward the village, and she realized what was going on."

"Gerry! Remmy's a member of this clan. She's a woman soldier."

"A what?"

"A woman soldier. She's probably fighting in this battle somewhere."

She felt a sudden sense of alarm and then heard Gerry sob.

"What is it?"

"This soldier and his troop attacked a large group of women soldiers only a little while ago."

"Where are the women now?" When Gerry did not respond, she shouted, "Gerry?"

A sense of despair nearly overwhelmed her, and her heart froze when he finally answered,

"They killed all but a few of them."

An immediate question popped into her head, making her feel nauseas as she resisted asking it, but couldn't help herself.

"Remmy?"

Another sob delayed his response. "I can't believe it!"

Darkness began to cloud her vision. "What?"

"I may be the one who killed her."

Chapter 11

Taking the leather straps from the slave, I looked at the unconscious woman with an arrow sticking from her shoulder. Her face was serene, but I knew that would not last as I carefully unhooked her bronze breastplate and threw it aside.

"The surgeon will surely not be available until morning," I announced to no one in particular, "and this stick is going to fester long before that." My attention briefly shifted to the slave. "Fetch hot water, wine and vinegar, and something to stitch up the hole in her shoulder."

After the slave bowed silently and hurried out, I returned my attention to the thin wildcat before me, not sure if she was a prize or a burden. Though confused by my thoughts, I reached down and ran my rough fingers over her soft cheek. A thin white scar ran down the side of her cheek, but her silken skin reminded me of what I had lost. I tried to remember my wife and son as they had been in life, but could only dredge up the memory of their mutilated bodies.

After a moment, I shuddered away the mental images and focused on the arrow. She wore only a thick leather jacket over a wool sweater. The jacket presented an immediate problem, as the arrow protruded through it.

Pulling out my knife, I scored the shaft about halfway down and snapped it off, trying as I did to avoid doing more damage than I already had. She flinched when I did so, but did not wake.

That will not last, I thought while lifting the jacket over the arrow stub, and slipping it off. Under her sweater was a light tunic of finely woven cloth that showed me that this young woman was not a pauper. The colors were as bright as the blood staining the left part of her chest.

Removing the tunic revealed a strip of cloth wrapped around her chest, presumably to keep her not-so-large breasts from bouncing. Quite naturally, I found the sight exhilarating, but then something happened that struck me as totally strange. Instead of removing the cloth and admiring her breasts, as any lusty man might do, my attention drifted to her face.

The strap binding her long hair had come undone in the fracas, and reddish-blond curls now framed a thin, angular face as pale and beautiful as the goddess Diana. Lust created a noticeable transformation in certain parts of my anatomy, and I found nothing wrong with it. She was a beautiful woman, and my slave. Using her as I wished was one of the perks of being the victor.

Yet, I could not bring myself to further undress her, short of removing her sandals. I was not surprised to find a hidden sliver of hardwood, sharpened at the tip and just the right size for shoving into the throat of an unsuspecting opponent. Holding up the wooden knife, I was struck by the intricate carvings in the handle. Though it was small, I could make out a snake, a bull, and some strange lettering.

Surprised that I was letting myself be distracted by her and the things she possessed, I tossed the weapon aside and returned to the task at hand. After throwing a wool blanket over her lower body, I used leather straps to bind her hands and feet to the cot. As I finished, I heard footsteps and turned to see the slave arrive with the requested supplies.

Motioning for him to wait, I turned back to the girl, knowing that what I had to do next would bring a violent response from her. Unable to think of any other way to do it, I wrapped a strap of leather around my hand, pressed it against the broken end of the arrow, and shoved. The tip sliced through flesh until it came out the back side.

Her eyes opened wide as an angry scream erupted from her. Before she could do more, I grabbed the tip and pulled the shaft from her shoulder. Her face distorted as every muscle contracted from the pain. Fighting against her bonds, she howled angrily, her lightly covered breasts jiggling violently as she reacted to the agony. In an instant, this once calm, beautiful woman changed into a biting, spitting, and I am sure, cursing tigress that both surprised and excited me. Though she lay half-naked in front of me, my attention was on her face as she swore, cursed, and undoubtedly debased my parentage, my manhood, and my very existence.

It mattered little, because the more she fought; the more she struggled; the more she swore; the more she verbally abused me…the more I was drawn to her.

I do not know how long I watched her, the mere thought of her filling my brain with a pleasing sensation I had not felt in what seemed like a lifetime. When exhaustion caused her to collapse back onto the cot, I picked up the wine jug, wetted a clean rag, and started to clean her wound.

Her presence so intoxicated me, I noticed nothing else around me for some time until I realized her attention was no longer on me, and that someone was calling my name.

"Optio."

A soldier stood in the entrance of the tent, and I knew from the spit-and-polish shine on his armor that he was the *centurio*'s clerk.

What is he doing here?

Any legionnaire knows that Rome's army is obsessed with recordkeeping. Legions of clerks record every aspect of our lives: the size of our legions, the names of every soldier, how much we eat, how much we march, how much we sleep, and how much we fart. These clerks are technically soldiers, but are exempt from digging trenches, building fortifications, pushing carts, or pulling guard duty while they speedily, monotonously, and minutely document every tiny detail of our sorry and violent lives.

This loathsome clerk was probably counting the tits on my new slave.

She has the required two, I thought angrily as I pushed the woman down, and modestly threw a blanket over her, but true to her nature, she sat up and sent the blanket to the floor.

My eyes still on her, I shook my head while the clerk announced, "You are to report to the *centurio*."

A nasty comment was stopped by those magic words.

I straightened. "I am on my way."

Despite his exalted position as an *immunes*, *optio* is just high enough above him to make any insubordination a punishable offense.

After he saluted and left, I rewetted the cloth with wine and again pressed it against her wound, eliciting more howling, spitting, and unintelligible name calling. Any other time, I might have enjoyed such a spirited exchange, and even joined in.

"Enough!" I shouted, and to my surprise, she went immediately silent. "I will dress your wound and you will be quiet as I work."

Even more surprising, she blinked, and I suddenly realized she understood what I was saying.

"You are loathsome pig!"

The realization of what she said filled me with such unexpected emotion I wanted to take her in my arms and kiss her. In actuality, the feeling was much stronger than that, and the cloth and jug nearly slipped through my fingers before I snapped back to reality.

No one keeps the *centurio* waiting.

Fighting unwilling muscles, I moved to the entrance and summoned the nearest soldier.

"Watch this woman," I ordered. "This slave will tend to her, but you are not to let anyone else come near her. Is that understood?"

"Yes, *Optio*," he barked in response.

Moving back inside, I passed the cloth and jug to the slave. "Clean and bind her wounds, and then get a blanket over her. Otherwise, one guard will not be enough to keep the whole camp off her."

His eyes wide, the slave merely nodded and took the offered objects.

I did not wait for more of a response, but as I hurried from the tent, I puzzled over my feeling for this foreign woman. After all, she was a primitive Gaul. Like dogs, their men probably lift their legs to piss on trees, if they bothered to lift their legs at all. What could I possibly have in common with her?

I had plenty of time to deliberate over this as I marched across the bridge and hurried the hundred or so paces to where the *centurio* was organizing his siege efforts.

"*Optio*," he announced after I saluted. "The enemy has already tried to sneak soldiers out at the locations you pointed out earlier." He pointed at thirty men in formation behind him. "As you also suggested, our scouts have discovered that soldiers from the neighboring village are gathering to come to their aid."

"How many are there, *Centurio*?"

"Less than one hundred, but they are poorly organized. Take these men and wipe them out to the man."

I snapped a salute. "Yes, Sir. May I make a suggestion?"

"I will hear it."

"I would advise killing all but one of them, Sir. Then, after a thorough interrogation, I would send him into this village. It would seriously dampen their morale to know their expected reinforcements will not be coming."

Showing no emotion, he gave me a simple nod and waved me on. Saluting, I hurried to the men and ordered them to march.

As we moved out, my thoughts kept drifting to my new possession, though I felt a twinge of guilt envisaging her in such a lusty way. She was a beauty, a tigress, a woman soldier, and though the last item was disconcerting, it did not decrease my desire to have her.

Deep-seated training quickly won out over lust, and I focused on the upcoming encounter, setting a brisk pace to get through the forest before the enemy reinforcements.

When we approached the edge of a small valley, I stopped the men and listened to reports from my scouts. At their insistence, I moved to a vista within the wood that allowed me to watch the approaching enemy without their seeing me.

Two things became immediately apparent: First, as reported, the enemy were poorly organized, their men spread out across the valley floor in small clusters with no obvious scouts. They must have assumed we were too few in number to send a contingent to meet them.

Second, and somewhat more important, there were far more than one hundred.

Standing in a cluster of trees at the entrance to the valley, I took in the situation. The valley varied from five hundred to a thousand paces wide, with clusters of brush scattered along the floor. The sides rose up sharply, and were thickly covered with trees and brush, but were useless as cover for an ambush because the thick brambles made passage difficult at best.

For their part, the oncoming soldiers -- and I am being generous in calling them that -- were lightly, if at all, armored, and their weaponry was as varied as I could ever imagine. Most of their trained soldiers had probably gone to join the fight against Caesar. Those remaining were not professional soldiers, but then these savages had little understanding of such things, so it came as no surprise.

I picked a path down to the valley floor that kept a thick cluster of brush and trees between us and the enemy until we were in position to face them at a point where the valley floor was narrowed by a small outcrop of rock on one side and dense brush on the other. It was the most defensible location I could hope for as the narrowness of the space made it difficult for all their soldiers to attack us at once.

I was pleased with how quickly my men hurried to the contact point, and organized into three rows of ten. It was my opinion that as soon as these Gauls saw us they would run for the hills.

A small contingent of about twenty-five enemy soldiers were marching down the center of the valley towards us, but they stopped as soon as we appeared in their path. Unlike their comrades, these Gauls were wearing simple, one-piece breastplates; carrying spears, swords, and bows; and marched in formation. Their bare arms were heavily tattooed, faces painted with bright colors, and legs bound in leather leggings.

One of their number -- a broad-shouldered hulk of a man, wearing an elaborate horned and feathered headpiece -- held up a hand and all of those close to him stopped. As we continued to march toward them, the leader walked several steps ahead of his men and stared at us for a long moment before bellowing something I could not understand.

Another of his number stepped from the formation and called back to those straggling behind. The valley erupted into a roar of shouting, screaming, and angry cries as the rest of their members raced to catch up and form into disorganized clusters behind them.

Sizing up the situation, I turned to the closest legionnaire.

"Go to the *centurio* and tell him we are facing a larger group than anticipated. Twenty-five of their number are armed and well organized, along with another two hundred or more of mixed heritage and skill level. We will delay them as long as we can, but their numbers may give them the advantage."

As the enemy continued to stand, I looked around at the bramble "guarding" our left flank. While there appeared to be no obvious paths through it, there were undoubtedly lesser trails made by animals that someone familiar with the terrain might know.

The Roman fighting formation is second to no one in its effectiveness, and if I had a full *centuria* under my command we would easily wipe out this rabble. With only twenty-nine men, I could not hold formation if forced to fight on two fronts at once. If enough of the enemy got behind us, we were done for.

I grabbed two more men from the back of the formation.

"Go into the brush. Listen for enemy soldiers trying to attack our flank. If you can, use bows to take them out. If not, report back to me."

"Yes, Sir!"

As they ran off, I mentally wished them luck, and was turning back when a shouted command from the enemy's leader sent most of the armored soldiers into a single row across our view, their bows at the ready.

"Raise shields!" I commanded as a hail of arrows were launched into the air.

The first volley missed us entirely, but most of the next round thudded into shields and the ground around us. While it might seem our best bet was to charge into the enemy, I knew that was exactly what their leader wanted. Out in the open, we could easily be surrounded and slaughtered. In this narrow draw the advantage was ours. Ever so slightly, to be sure, but still ours.

The twang of a bow string on my left made it clear that time was not on our side.

We stand here or be lost!

I was struck by the absurdity of that thought. I had rejoined with the hope of dying in battle, and here was my chance. Since the day I joined the Legion it had been drummed into me that death in battle was the highest honor. I no longer a wife, child, or a home to go back to. My only life had been the legion, all my life-long friends had been here. Where else would I choose to be when I die?

But a nagging voice in my head kept insisting that I save my savage captive who will, in all likelihood, slit my throat as I sleep. Despite my reservations about her, for the first time in recent memory, I did not want to die.

I was drawn back to the period just four years after my discharge, when death was all I could think about. The images of my small farm smoldering in ruin, my wife's tortured, headless body, and my son hung up like a gutted sheep. I should have killed myself right then, but more than twenty-five years of service embedded in me the need to fight for my life and would not let no let a dishonorable suicide join them in the afterlife. In the end, the only logical solution brought me here, looking into the faces of over two-hundred crazed Gauls. It was the perfect solution for a man looking for death, but I knew it had to be an honorable death. The gods would know if it were otherwise.

Then that new voice slithered into my head, and made me want more.

You have to protect her!

After shaking my head to banish the voice, I looked out at the gathering enemy, their numbers seeming to grow with each passing moment. I felt sweat dribbling down my cheeks, the antsy jerking of muscles as I tightened and relaxed the grip on my spear.

Even if we take a stand here, we are not likely to survive this, I insisted to unnamed gods while scanning the threatening mob before me.

You can figure out a way to make it. I know you can!

Then you are a bigger fool than I.

I took another look around to see if our situation had changed, but the enemy still held their positions, raining arrows down on us, and shouting what I assumed were damning insults. Our only advantage was the narrow space we were in. If the enemy did not have an easy path through the brush on my left, we could hold them.

Their leader was tall: easily half-a-head above the next highest, and broad shouldered. His simple, unpolished breastplate seemed to glow in the sunlight as he leaned on his spear, ignored the pandemonium around him and stared at us.

Though he did not move, I sensed that he was aware that time was on my side. He had surely seen the runner I sent and would expect reinforcements at any time. Just the same, he also knew how far we were from the village, and how long it would take a Roman contingent to get here.

He was soon approached by thick-bodied warrior, naked to the waist, tattoos covering most of his exposed skin, wearing long colorful trousers, and carrying a broad ax with a face the length of my arm. The leader kept his eyes on us while the newcomer ranted, stabbed his ax in our direction, and waved his free arm.

After a moment, the leader gave a curt nod and the warrior ran half-a-dozen steps in our direction before throwing his arms into the air and howling like a speared lion. Almost instantly another sixty or seventy warriors -- dressed and painted much like the first, or even naked except for a loin cloth -- roared their response as they ran toward him.

Without waiting for the others to catch up, the first warrior sprinted in our direction, his unorganized troop running in rag-tag formation behind him.

I actually felt relief when they reached the halfway point because the rain of arrows stopped.

"Those fools," one of my men muttered as we all watched the oncoming mêlée.

"Shields down! Tight formation," I commanded. "Third row. Bows at the ready."

At this point I could clearly see the faces of the men coming at us, and smiled when I saw that most of them were already breathing hard. It stood to reason that these were citizen soldiers who spent their time farming, not training for hours on end as we did. These fools had already run hundreds of paces, and the bulk of their fighting strength was spent.

"They are winded," I shouted as the lead warriors reached firing range. "First two rows duck behind your shields. Third row commence firing."

There were only ten bowmen, but when each arrow found a welcome home, the remaining attackers skipped a step before continuing their charge. They were easily fifty paces away when the second volley had a similar deadly effect on their numbers.

Three of those at the head tripped on their own feet and went down, and the sudden loss of those in the lead made the others slow. Seeing this, the original lead warrior turned and bellowed angrily and urgently waved them forward. Unfortunately for them, as he was turning to continue his charge, an arrow speared his throat, and the sight of him staggering along as the two men beside him went down with arrows in their chests, made the remainder of his troop stop entirely.

The seventy were now forty, and after another volley, nearly thirty. Those still standing were breathing hard, and when their adrenaline rush changed to terror, they turned and ran, their legs barely carrying them away as my men continued to bring them down until only about a dozen made it back to collapse in front of their leader.

Though some distance away, I could see the look of disgust on the tall leader's face. I would have killed all of them right then to show what happens to cowards, but he simply waved a hand and his subordinates hauled them away. I could also see those standing beside him giving him the kind of looks that say, "Maybe we should leave this mad dog in peace."

Ignoring them, he marched several paces in our direction.

"Front rows up, shields at the ready," I commanded. "Rebius."

"Sir," responded the only man in my company who understood the savage's language.

"Do you know anything about this leader?"

"Only that his name is Ardal, which I believe means *high courage,* and that he has some military training."

"Training? With our army?"

"No, Sir, but it is said he fought with their rogue leader, Vercingetorix, who has given Caesar much trouble."

"Those around him do not seem to share his confidence."

"What can you expect from farmers?"

"Let us see what his resolve is."

Though we had cut their number by a considerable amount, my heart still raced as I moved into the open.

"Ardal," I shouted. "My name is *Optio* Marcus Aremus. Send your farmers back to their fields. Already too many of your sheep will be missing their sleeping companions. Why should more suffer the same fate?"

"I would if I could, Roman," he bellowed back in respectable Latin, "but my dogs are hungry for Roman entrails, and I am not of a mind to deny them."

"They had better settle for their own, because peasant farmers stand no chance against the best of Rome."

"We shall see about that."

Turning to his left, he spoke to a red-faced man, but was interrupted by screaming. I turned around to see half-a-dozen men running down from the wood directly behind us. At first I thought this was a clever move on his part to delay us long enough to get troops behind us, but quickly realized the screaming was not from attacking warriors, but terrorized peasants.

"What are they saying?" I asked my translator.

He hesitated for a long moment, his expression stern, eyes locked on the approaching men.

"I think they are saying, 'They are coming,' over and over again."

"*They* are coming? Who are..." I looked back at Ardal and his many companions. "Our soldiers are coming?"

Though Ardal and his twenty-five soldiers stood their ground, the rest of their company looked decidedly uncomfortable. Thirty of their number had been slaughtered by our small contingent. They were surely wondering how they would fare against a larger group of Romans. From their expressions it was obvious that Ardal's confidence was not shared by all who followed him.

"Archers! Take out those fleeing behind us."

The zip of released arrows was all I needed to know the cowards fleeing their village were dealt with.

I turned back to the force we were facing and shouted, "Ardal. Your neighbors have paid a high price for their resistance. We will soon batter down their walls and burn their houses to the ground. Are you ready for the same?"

Though the commanders around Ardal looked at him anxiously, their leader did not take his eyes off me.

"We will pay a high price no matter what choice we make, Roman," he finally bellowed. "Maybe it is you who should run back to the protection of the feral dogs you call countrymen."

I shook my head.

"They did not teach me how to retreat, so I must stand and kill all who come at me. Give us your best, clumsy farmer. The crows will dine on your carcasses this day."

Ardal turned to his commanders, pointing to each in turn and giving orders. To their credit, some of the commanders glared right back at him, nodding as he spoke, and then hurrying back to their men. Others kept looking our way, their nervousness obvious by their jerky movements, and the indecisive way they moved toward their troops.

As they were organizing, I took a quick assessment of my own resources. Though each of my men were deadly with their bows, a man can only carry so many arrows, and many of those were already sticking from the bodies of the first group to attack us.

"Strip to battle gear," I commanded. "Last row keep your bows, gather as many arrows as you can carry."

The men sloughed off their packs, shedding anything they would not need, and tossing the lot behind us.

"Forward twenty paces."

We marched clear of our gear, confident that we would stand and fight to the death.

"Perimeter guards return to the unit."

Within moments, the two men I had sent out appeared from the brush on either side of us. I knew what the enemy would try to do. This was their home territory, so it stood to reason that Ardal's men knew how to get through the thick brush on our left. My only hope was that by the time they worked their way through, we would be fully engaged with their frontal assault.

I looked forward to see a group of about thirty men hurrying toward the brushy side of our position.

"Tight formation."

I looked down at grass browned by the dryness of the season. Scanning the thicket, I saw more brown in the brush than green, and it occurred to me the dry leaves would tell us when the enemy was approaching.

Then I realized what else dead leaves might do.

"Scouts," I called. "Grab your flints and set fire to the brush."

Without hesitating, the men ran back to their gear, grabbed the needed equipment, and disappeared into the brush.

When I looked at Ardal again, it was obvious he was waiting for his men to get into position before ordering the rest forward. While the twenty-five men under his direct command stood at attention and in nearly-presentable order, the rest were embarrassing to watch as they struggled to form proper rows, their menagerie of weapons held in every possible fashion, their angry commanders rushing to and fro yelling, pointing, pushing, and shoving.

I was thankful for the delay, and heard the crackle of burning brush long before Ardal finally moved to the front of his men. My scouts were just returning when the Gallic leader waved a hand over his head and shouted for the attack to start.

"Raise shields!" I commanded as enemy arrows appeared in the sky.

The formation, known as a *testudo,* or tortoise formation, was our best protection against an aerial assault. The front row of soldiers lifted their shields up to just below their eyes while the next row held their shields over their heads, and forward so they also covered the first row. The remaining two rows did the same, creating a box of shields that no arrow could penetrate.

Smoke was wafting across our view as the enemy roared and began their charge. When the path ahead of them narrowed, the undisciplined farmers were pushed into the brush on one side and loose rocks at the base of the opposite cliff face, making many of them stumble and fall. Those who remained on their feet staggered toward the center, pushing into others, tripping when toes slammed heals, creating even more confusion as their ranks were pushed out of shape.

Ardal's men kept their formation, using their elbows and hips to keep the stumbling farmers out of their way, but even they must have felt unsure of themselves when our figures became ghost-like in the thickening smoke.

Screams in the brush made some of my men look around.

"Eyes forward," I commanded.

Despite the smoke, it was not hard to know where Ardal's men were because of all the shouting and complaining of the confused civilian soldiers.

As the smoke thickened, the accuracy of their arrows decreased. I watched the approaching soldiers merge with the smoke until they were no more. Moments later I realized the enemy arrows had stopped coming. "Shields down. Front row, fire at random."

The ten men in the front row dropped their shields and knocked arrows, listening carefully before releasing their deadly missiles into the smoke. The screams of men confirmed the skill of my archers.

When my men finally ran out of arrows, I pulled the unit back into formation and watched as a light breeze brushed my cheek. The smoke slowly cleared, and no one was more surprised than I to see weapons, shields, pitch forks, scythes, and hammers littering the ground. The only troops remaining were those loyal to Ardal.

The big man's expression was one of shock as he looked around the smoky field and realized his ten-to-one advantage had been reduced to an even match.

"Surrender, savage," I shouted.

The big man's face hardening even before my translator finished speaking, he straightened as his men protested my insult.

"Rot in Hades, Roman," he declared before heaving his spear and rushing to follow it.

His men mimicked his action, throwing light spears as they ran behind him.

I could hear many swords slipping from their sheaths before his running men held them high and bellowed. The sight might have terrified simple-minded farmers, but my men held their positions.

The spears were easily slapped away by shields or simply avoided, and this presented an opportunity I had been wanting for a long time. The voice in my head was now only a faint whisper as I hefted my *pilum*, its heavier weight feeling good in my hand as I noticed the flash of sunlight off its razor-sharp tip.

"Forward," I commanded after moving to the front line. "Throw *pila*."

Though the enemy's line was starting to become uneven, years of strict training kept us in perfect formation as we rushed forward as one and heaved our spears. The *pilum's* heavy weight keeps us from throwing it very far, and that meant the Gauls could not recover from our *pilum* strike before we crashed into them.

I immediately pulled my shield up against my left shoulder, timing my move so I could throw my entire body into it the instant I made contact with an enemy soldier.

All along our front line, my men were now running at full attack speed. Since they mimicked my move, most of the front line of enemy soldiers were knocked onto their backs. Instead of stopping to finish them off, however, we kept going and left that task to the row behind us.

The ensuing clash of armor and weapons was loud and invigorating. Though my men blocked their strokes with shields and stabbed up with their swords, the Gauls put up an impressive defense with Ardal himself fighting in the middle. From the way his men fought, it was obvious they had been trained by someone who had been in our army. A typical barbarian usually holds his shield close to his body and tries to slash down with his sword. This sort of move leaves much of his body exposed. A Roman soldier keeps his shield in front and stabs up.

When one of his men went down in front of him, Ardal charged into the gap, slamming his massive body into the first soldier he met, taking advantage of his greater weight to stop the man in his tracks before stabbing at his throat. Thankfully, he missed, but only because my man fell backwards. Before the unfortunate legionnaire could be massacred, I jumped into the fray and blocked his downward thrust.

"Third rank! Cover the flanks," I commanded while blocking Ardal's stabbing move and slamming him with my shield.

He staggered back only a step, but recovered so quickly I barely had time to avoid his slashing sword. In retrospect, it would have been easy to slack off just a little bit and let Ardal finish me off, but years of fighting to survive were impossible to dismiss, and I matched each blow with my own.

The fight devolved into a mêlée, but I had no intention of fighting these barbarians on their own terms.

"Keep ranks close," I bellowed after forcing Ardal back with a stab to the stomach.

I pulled the sword up, nicking his forearm, but Ardal took no notice as he swung his shield at my face before slashing at my own belly. The sword struck my armor to little effect, and exposed his right bicep. My stab was quick and effective, but though his sword fell from his hand, a hard blow with his shield sent me staggering back. The sudden distance between us gave me half-an-instant to assess the situation. It appeared that nearly half of Ardal's original force was now out of action, and my own men were starting to encircle those still standing.

Though they fought valiantly, Ardal's men were no match for my troopers, and one-by-one they fell to the endurance and precise movements of experienced soldiers. Ardal and his few remaining men were soon surrounded, but they showed no interest in surrendering.

I, on the other hand, wanted this chieftain as both a captive and an example to the others in his village.

"Capture him," I howled loud enough for even the distant gods to hear.

Having recovered his sword, Ardal glared at me for an instant before he charged forward and hammered me with his shield, his sword nearly knocking mine from my grip. Bellowing, he stabbed his blade at my head and as I ducked the stroke, he nearly bowled me over with another blow with his shield. I caught myself, and barely blocked his attempt at decapitating me, but I was off balanced and the impact against my sword sent me to one knee. Before he could follow up, one of my legionnaires hit him from behind with the butt of his sword and sent his limp body to the blood-soaked ground.

Two screams yanked my attention from his unconscious form to see the last two of Ardal's men fall off swords and land next to their leader.

The sudden silence was almost deafening, and it was a moment before I could hear my men's heavy breathing over my own. Like each of my men, I instinctively scanned the area for more attackers, and seeing none, suddenly realized how tired I was. The fight left us all stunned, but after a moment one of the men gave a long and exhilarated howl and it spread like a contagion through the ranks until we were all shouting, whooping, and celebrating our victory.

The cheering was short lived, and after it stopped, I felt disconnected with myself, as though I were out of my body and experiencing the world for the first time. As smoke continued to billow around us, the space near me came into sharp focus with the acrid smell of burnt wood mixing with that of spilled blood and urine. I heard indifferent birds chirping overhead, the crackling of fire, my men's heavy breathing, and the rubbing of the overlapping metal plates in my armor as I moved.

Shaking my head to regain focus, I took two quick steps away from the others and looked back to assess the situation. Eight of my own were dead, and three wounded. I would say that was not bad, considering that over sixty enemy corpses littered the battlefield.

"Company halt," a voice commanded behind us.

We all jerked around to see the perfectly arraigned formation of Roman soldiers, their leader standing in front.

Though my body was weary, and I knew my men were as well, I commanded,

"Legionnaires form up at attention."

The leader of the newly arrived troop hurried to me, saluting as he stopped.

"*Optio*. We were told you were outnumbered five to one."

I nodded without smiling. "More like ten to one, but we chased most of them off, and what remains will provide carrion for the birds."

"No captives?"

Pointing at the unconscious Ardal, I shook my head. "He was their leader. Take him to the *centurio*."

The trooper waved a hand at a subordinate. "Bind him and deliver him to the *centurio*." After the man snapped a sharp salute and hurried off, he turned back to me.

"The *centurio* ordered us on to the next village. If we hurry, we might get there before they have stripped everything and vanished into the hills."

Though I nodded in agreement, I was surprised by an insistent voice in my head.

Leave these poor people be, and get back to Enid.

The absurdity of the thought produced an involuntary laugh. "Is this a joke?"

"*Optio*?" the subordinate asked, his expression confused.

It was only then I realized it was not he who had made the ridiculous comment.

My mind suddenly in turmoil, I turned away to give myself a moment to regain my composure.

Pointing up the valley, I said, "They do not have a serious army left to defend themselves, but we should not delay."

"Yes, Sir!"

After arranging for the care of our dead and wounded, I formed up the nearly forty-five men now in my company and marched them at military pace down the valley, sending the usual scouts forward, and keeping an eye out for ambushes.

When we finally came to the village, I found it to be as heavily fortified as the previous one, but this time the front gates were wide open.

"It looks like they are welcoming us in," the leader of the second troop announced.

I shook my head, growling, "Never trust a smiling Gaul." After looking over to see his puzzled look, I pointed at the town. "Send ten men through the wood to the back. They are not to let anyone leave by that way."

Though the puzzled look remained, he knew better than to challenge me. "Immediately, *Optio!*"

When the men were on their way, we continued on. As we approached the open gates, our scouts came out with two old men in tow.

"Greetings, great Roman warriors," the taller of the two announced through my interpreter. "We welcome you to our humble village."

"You sent soldiers against us as we approached. That was a strange way of showing your welcome, and it cost us Roman lives."

"Please forgive our misguided transgression, great Sir," the old man pleaded while bowing. "We did not want to do so, but Ardal is a brute of a man and forced our people to attack you."

That's good, the annoying voice in my head announced. *Now make them pay a fine and get back to your camp.*

I gave my head a sharp shake to rid it of this pestering demon before glaring down at the old man.

"Someone must pay for this."

The man shook his head. "But I am told you defeated Ardal and his soldiers. What more can you want?"

"Bring me the commanders of your army."

After listening to the translation, the old man stared at me dumbly for a moment before realization seemed to dawn on him.

"Why do you not take me instead, oh great Roman? It was I who advised my people to follow Ardal's lead."

Moving to the old man, I started to walk past him and the old man was turning to follow my path when I pulled my right hand across my chest and swept it out, slamming the back of my fist into his jaw.

A loud *NO!* was shouting in my head, but not loud enough to drown out the distinct crack of a neck bone as his head jerked around and his body slowly spiraled to the ground.

The second elder cried in anguish, his eyes bulging, mouth gaping, hands stretched out as though to catch his dying companion.

"Listen to me," I bellowed loud enough to regain his stunned attention. "Either bring me the commanders of your army or I will burn this stinking hovel to the ground along with every dog-humping savage in it."

After listening to the translation, the old man jerked a nod and started to leave.

"And rest assured, old man," I added. "If I find that the men you send out are not the true commanders, or that any one of them is missing, I will take no less revenge on this village. Am I understood?"

His whole body shaking, the old man nodded quickly and staggered toward his village. I watched him for a moment before turning back to look at the legionnaires standing in formation behind me. It was only a few moments before I heard screaming coming from the far side of the village, and knew that sending ten men around to that side had effectively backed up my threat by keeping them from escaping.

I pointed at my second-in-command.

"Five men on the eastern border and five more on the west. Bows at the ready. Shoot anyone who tries to escape. Ten inside the front gates to make sure they do not try to lock us out."

"Yes, Sir," he responded sharply before turning to relay my orders.

Looking toward the village gates, I tamped down the voice in my head, shrugged off the easy victory, and waited for my captives to be delivered.

Chapter 12

Remmy!

The thought made Jasmina's eyes jerk open, and blinding light forced her to close them again. Holding a hand above her eyes, she squinted into the light, unable to stop herself because her heart was thudding and her head felt like it would explode if she did not move.

Pushing herself into a sitting position, she quickly looked around at...nothing. After her eyes adjusted to the light, she recognized the beige curtain surrounding the bed and remembered she was in a hospital.

"Remmy?" she cried while struggling to get out of the bed. While she fought with the covers, Miriam pushed the curtain aside and moved to her.

"Miriam," she pleaded while rubbing her eyes. "What happened? Is Remmy OK?"

Gerry's mother shook her head. "Yes, I believe so. She became very agitated just after you fainted, but finally calmed down again."

Pressing her hands on the bed to steady herself, Jasmina gave her head a shake. "How did I get here?"

"You were holding Gerry's hands and you just fainted."

After looking around the room again, Jasmina nodded. "Gerry told me he killed Remmy. He felt so sure about it, I...I...guess I blacked out."

Miriam nodded as well. "I wanted to call the doctor, but Alvin said that's exactly what you didn't want, so we put you up on this bed and have been watching to see what happens."

"How long have I been out?"

Miriam shook her head. "Close to an hour, I think."

"An hour?" she exclaimed. "Has anything happened during that time?"

Miriam shrugged. "Gerry got restless for bit and then he settled down." She held up a finger. "Oh, and he mumbled something. I think it was 'Get back to the girl.'"

Jasmina shook her head. "He's found Remmy."

"He's dreaming about her?"

Seeding Miriam's confused expression, Jasmina shook her head again.

"Miriam," she said firmly while swinging her legs over the edge of the bed. "This isn't a dream. Gerry and Remmy have been transported back into the bodies of a man and a woman in Roman times. Gerry's kind of like a corporal, or sergeant in the Roman army and he's captured Remmy's counterpart."

"Remmy's a man?"

Jasmina shook her head. "No. She's still a woman, and that is definitely not good for her."

"Why would it be worse?"

"The Romans weren't particularly gracious in their treatment of captured enemy soldiers. Sadly, they treated women warriors even worse."

"Lord in Heaven," Miriam gasped, "are you saying my son has…"

"No," Jasmina cried, her hands up, palms out. "He captured her and brought her to his tent. She's wounded, and he was tending her when his *Centurio* called him away to fight. The problem is that if one of the other soldiers find out she's there before he gets back, that soldier might decide to take his own form of revenge on her."

The fear on Miriam's face made it clear she understood what that meant. "What do we do?"

Jasmina pushed herself off the bed, standing unsteadily, and feeling grateful for Miriam's hand gripping her arm.

"I've got to get back to Remmy."

"What can you do?"

"If she's unconscious, I have to wake her up and warn her."

The room swam as Jasmina tried to walk towards the door, and she waved her right hand through thin air, trying to grasp something to steady herself. Just before she toppled over, Miriam grabbed her hand and moved close.

"Alvin?" she called. "Didn't I see a wheelchair somewhere?"

"There's one in the hall," her husband called as he poked his head around the edge of the curtain surrounding Gerry's bed.

"Well get it. We've got to save Remmy."

Jasmina felt Miriam gently push her aside as Alvin rushed past them and out of the room. Seconds later, he was back with the requested transportation.

"Stay here with Gerry," Jasmina said to Miriam as she settled into the chair. "And try to get him moved to Remmy's room. This will be a whole lot easier if I'm not being shuffled from one room to the other."

Miriam nodded. "Alvin will take you to Remmy. I'll page the nurse."

Jasmina nodded and relaxed into the chair as Gerry's father started to push her from the room. To her surprise, a hand on her arm stopped them.

"Please," Miriam pleaded, her expression desperate. "Find a way to bring them back."

Chapter 13

Pain in her shoulder woke Enid, but it was someone tugging at her clothes that made her open her eyes.

Still groggy from the opiate she had been given, it took her a moment to realize she was looking at a ruddy-faced man as he pulled her by the knees toward the lower end of the cot on which she was tied. Since her hands were bound to the sides of the cot, the move pulled them up to her shoulders. She screamed from the pain as the man spread her legs and started fumbling with something under the pleated skirt of his uniform.

"No reashon for the *optio* to have allll the fun," he growled drunkenly. "A man'sh got to show theesh shavagesh their place."

She shook her head in dismay as his underclothes fell to his ankles and she suddenly realized what he was planning to do.

The young witch's voice in her head screamed in panic, but she was not about to let this stupid brute foul her without making him pay dearly for it.

"Wha…" he started to cry as she shifted her butt to put weight on her left foot. He was still holding his erect member when she brought her other foot up hard into his crotch.

He bellowed like a stuck bull as she kept the pressure up and jerked her foot back. Grabbing his crotch, he started to bend at the waist, but she brought her knee up to slam his forehead. The first blow simply countered his forward motion, and left him standing over her. Ignoring the pain in her shoulder, she dug her heels into the bottom edge of the cot, shoved herself as far back on the cot as she could go. In one swift motion, she yanked her knees to her chest and hammered both heels against his shoulders. The howling brute fell backwards onto the floor, his body curled into a fetal position as he groaned and retched from the pain.

Pushing herself up on the cot so her arms were no longer in a cramped position, she pulled her knees up as far as she could in preparation for his next assault. It took him only a moment to recover, and while still bellowing, he rose unsteadily, his face beet red, hands over his crotch, body doubled over.

"You poxed whore," he groaned. "I'll cut you from ass to throat."

One hand over his throbbing testicles, he pawed through the clothes at his feet as two other soldiers entered the tent, their swords at the ready. A quick assessment of the situation made it clear what had happened.

"What is the matter, Quintus?" the taller of the two laughed. "Is the *optio*'s bitch too much for you?"

Enraged by the newcomer's laughter, Quintus unsheathed his dagger and turned toward Enid, his eyes red with anger, and probably too much wine.

"Watch what I do to troublesome whores," he announced, though still doubled over as he moved toward Enid.

Shoving his sword back into its scabbard, the taller soldier rushed up to grab Quintus by the shoulders.

"Hold on there, Friend," he cautioned. "It is one thing to poke the *optio*'s slave girl because it will not affect her value at auction. On the other hand, that will not be the case if she is dead. Am I right?"

"Hands off me, Lucius," Quintus cried as he struggled to break free. "She nearly castrated me."

"Yes," Lucius countered. "But if you kill her, the *optio* will probably tie a box full of hungry rats to your privates, and if you are lucky, they will not still be attached to you. Is that what you want?"

Quintus looked up at him, his face contorted by both rage and pain. "And what do I get out of it?"

"Think on this, my friend. You can find dozens of whores anywhere you go, but once you lose your testicles, those women will be of little use to you. No?"

Quintus rolled his round head in Enid's direction, his face scrunched up as she imagined his slow mind working through his options. After a long moment, he straightened slightly, sheathed his knife, pulled his drawers up, and hobbled out of the tent.

After he was gone, Lucius waved at the other soldier.

"You were left to guard her?"

His face flushed, the soldier nodded. "I only took a moment to run to the latrine. Quintus promised to watch her while I was gone."

Shaking his head, Lucius waved the man out. "Leave her to me, OK?"

The soldier's attention went briefly to Enid before he faced Lucius and gave a curt nod. Without another word, he left.

Lucius also looked at Enid.

"I think, little one, that you are going to be far more trouble than you are worth." Smiling grimly, he shrugged. "Ah well. That is a problem for my friend, Marcus. Is it not?"

Chapter 14

"That takes care of this region," the *centurio* announced as I watched captives being taken away from the towns we had captured. "We control this area for Caesar."

"What are we to do next?" I asked, dreading the possibility of peace as it offered so few opportunities for death.

"I have been informed that our *Imperator* is going to Rome to celebrate a triumph, and we are going with him to guard the booty."

"Rome?"

"Have you ever been there?"

"Yes, *Centurio*," I snapped. "I was born there."

"Then you will get a chance to reunite with family before we are reassigned. How does that strike you?"

I felt my head shake, but that annoying voice in my head was not sharing my discomfort at returning to my former home.

"I will go where my legion takes me, *Centurio*," I said with little enthusiasm.

Thankfully, it did not really matter what I said, as his attention was already on a cluster of legionnaires gathering around a naked woman.

"Then clean yourself up," he said before hurrying off to chastise the men, not for abusing the woman, but for possibly damaging sellable merchandise that might contribute to all of our endowments.

I watched the goings on for a moment, but quickly lost interest. I was in a disturbing limbo: wanting to die, and not wanting to. Shaking off the puzzling contradiction, I spent a few moments giving orders to my men before finally turning the task over to the other *optio*.

While walking back toward my tent, I looked down at my armor, not surprised to see it covered in drying blood and gore. New recruits are often sickened by the mess hand-to-hand fighting makes of their clothes, but you soon get used to it. The problem is, if you do not clean it off quickly, the blood stains cloth and corrodes metal. I swear I spend more time cleaning armor than I ever do fighting in it.

I stopped at the river to wash as much blood as possible from my armor and skin, discovering as I did the numerous cuts and bruises I received in the fight.

It did not come as a surprise. In fact, it was expected. I was just glad to find that most of the blood was someone else's.

Carrying my gear to the tent, I moved inside to find my newly acquired slave curled up on her cot, her eyes wild, bound wrists bloody. The slave I left with her had a serious bruise on the side of his face, and was holding his side.

"Greetings, *Optio*," he called anxiously as I entered.

"What in all of Hades happened to you?"

Waving a hand at Enid, he gingerly shook his head. "It was not her, *Optio*. Another soldier came in, and when I moved to stop him, he…roughed me up and threw me out."

"How? I left a guard."

"He went to the latrine and had another take his place."

"Who?"

The slave winced and looked away. "He goes by the name of Quintus. I do not know his family name."

I looked at Enid and saw the bruises forming on her thighs.

"He will not need a family name once I am finished with him," I growled.

"With respect, *Optio*, I…"

He stopped, mouth open, hand partially raised, as though he suddenly realized that a slave could not ask of me what was on his mind.

"No one abuses my property," I growled.

"If I may, *Optio*. He paid a high price for his indulgence." He motioned toward Enid. "She gave him a good, hard kick where he makes his bread, if you understand my meaning. If I am not mistaken, he will not wish to be doing any walking or heavy lifting for a good while."

Despite my anger, I could not help the smile that formed on my face. "Then I swear by Jupiter, he shall get plenty of both."

I started to leave, but stopped to look at the woman. Her angry expression made it clear that she did not differentiate between Roman soldiers.

We probably all look alike to her at this point, but there is little I can do about that.

"You shall be avenged," I was surprised to hear myself say before hurrying out.

It was only as I made for the camp's common area that I realized how absurd my last statement must have sounded to her. I am an enemy soldier. What did she care what one Roman did to another?

You are all dung-eating mongrels to her, the voice in my head chastised. *She is just waiting for you to come back and rape her yourself.*

It is not my habit to rape slaves.

It doesn't bother you that you just wiped out her village, killed most of the people she cares about, and enslaved the rest?

We are at war. That is the consequence of losing to a superior enemy.

And what if your general decides to make peace? How would you treat them then?

"*Optio*," a soldier called as I entered the common area. "The *centurio* has summoned you."

I stopped and faced the man, his armor smeared with blood that was obviously not his own. The sight made me look down at my half-clad body and realize that my revenge would have to wait.

I wanted to sigh, but that might be interpreted as a sign of disrespect for the *centurio*, so I swallowed my anger and snapped,

"Tell him I will be there as soon as I put on my armor."

"Yes, Sir!"

Hurrying back to my tent, I stripped off my wet tunic and threw it across the small space. I made a point of not looking at the woman as I grabbed a fresh tunic and pulled it on.

"I am called by the *centurio*," I growled at the Greek while picking up the segmented upper-body armor still dripping from its dip in the river. "If that soldier returns, go directly to the guard on duty and have him escorted to the cells by my direct order."

"Yes, *Optio*."

I looked at the slave: a Greek with olive skin, large brown eyes, long curly hair, and an unmanly figure. I had never much cared for Greek slaves, finding them generally untrustworthy, and devious. However this one had a determined look that implied he was glad to participate in my revenge.

"I will return when I return," I said while pulling on my arm guards and marching to the entrance. "See that my goods are well taken care of."

I watched him bow in assent as I hurried out, wondering if I would ever see the Gallic woman again.

Chapter 15

Feeling lightheaded and disoriented, Jasmina pushed herself from the wheelchair, thankful that Alvin was there to take her hand.

"I can't believe how unsteady I am," she complained while grabbing the rail attached to Remmy's bed.

"Are you going to be OK?" Alvin asked.

Gripping the rails with both hands, she nodded before turning to face him.

"You need to get Gerry moved into this room so I can connect the two of them together."

"Do you think that's wise?"

She shook her head. "No, but it is necessary. At present, Gerry has more control over his former self than Remmy, and Enid is determined to kill him the first chance she gets."

"Enid? Who's that?"

"That's the woman Remmy is connected to."

"How do you know she wants to kill Gerry?"

"There isn't time to discuss the minute details of what I know. Just find Gerry's doctor and get him moved. I'll try to help Remmy gain control of Enid's body, but that might not help unless Gerry has the ability to set her free."

Alvin shook his head. "I'm not sure what difference this can make. After all, these people are in the past. Gerry and Remmy can't change that."

Jasmina took in a deep breath as she struggled to clear her head. While slowly letting the air out, she turned to Gerry's father.

"Actually, they can. I'm not yet sure what they are supposed to do, but it seems very important that they make it to Rome."

"But why?"

Leaning more heavily on the railing, she shook her head. "There's this...spirit, if that's what we can call him, which I call the *Tsabbat*. It seems he can travel through time and he's hell bent on altering human history as we know it."

"How do you mean?"

"He started by making sure Elizabeth and Phillip didn't have children."

"Are they the ones we met when Gerry was a college freshman?"

She nodded. "Their eldest son, who was to be named Phillip Robert Augustus Montgomery, would have enlisted in the Foreign Service in 1913 and gone undercover to thwart the attempted assassination of Archduke Franz Ferdinand of Austria."

"Ferdinand? He's the guy who started Word War I."

"No," Jasmina corrected. "His assassination was used as an excuse to start the war. If it hadn't happened, the First World War might have been nothing more than a minor skirmish in Europe between the Germans and the French, and the Japanese would probably have limited their fight to the Chinese."

"Thou millions of lives would have been saved," Alvin said with a nod, "it would have totally altered us as a nation."

"Not only that, but if Europe had remained stable, Hitler might never have gained control of Germany, leaving us with decades of peace instead of war."

"A peace that could be manipulated by the *Tsabbat* to change our world."

Taking Remmy's hand, Jasmina felt a shudder run through her body. "And now the *Tsabbat* is up to something in Roman Italy. We have to find out what it is and stop him."

"But how?"

"Gerry and Remmy are there for a reason, and it is our job to help them discover it and provide whatever they need to succeed."

"Is he supposed to stop an assassination?"

Jasmina shrugged. "Caesar was a tyrant, but he planted the seeds for Imperial Rome, and as brutal as our history books make the Romans out to be, a stable Rome meant a stable Europe. Much later, after the collapse of the Roman Empire, Europe went into hundreds of years of decline. If Imperial Rome never happened, who knows what might have become of European society."

"Yeah, but Caesar *was* assassinated."

"Only after being given unlimited power by the Roman Senate and establishing the idea of emperorship in the minds of the Romans. But that isn't the whole picture. Julius Caesar paved the way for the next emperor, Augustus to rise to power by making him his heir, which gave him wealth and influence he might never have acquired. If that had not happened, the Roman Empire might have self-destructed as individual factions fought for control and left all of Europe in the dark for a thousand years."

Alvin shook his head. "If he had died sooner, we might not even know his name today."

"Even worse, the *Tsabbat* might use a human intermediary to take over and rule in his place. I'll bet you everything I have that the *Tsabbat* would make sure *his* guy wouldn't be assassinated by those senators."

Turning abruptly, Alvin hurried to the room's only door, looking back as he reached it to wave at Jasmina. "I'll find Miriam and see what progress she's making."

Taking another deep breath, Jasmina leaned against the bed railing, and gripped Remmy's hands. She immediately found herself in a small tent with a swarthy looking person slumped in a chair across from her. As far as she could tell, he was asleep, but when she struggled to rise, she felt the pain of her wrists and looked down to find herself tied to the bed.

Remmy! Where are you? she asked, and felt surprise when the young woman jerked her head back and looked around. *I'm not here to hurt you,* she assured Enid. *I only want to find my niece.*

Be gone witch!

I can't, Enid. We have to work together to save you.

You cannot save me. If I do not kill this Roman pig, he will surely end my life, and I will be grateful for it.

But if you die, your children will not be born.

Fool! I have no children, and you can be assured, no Roman dung heap is going to foul me.

You must listen to me. Remmy needs your help.

Remmy? What kind of name is that?

She is not a Roman.

Is she the weak one who has been testing me? You should tell her to be silent. I need my mind clear to prepare for my escape.

You can't escape. You have to help Marcus stop an assassination.

Who will be killed? Another Roman pig? I will gladly do that for him, after I cut his throat.

He isn't going to kill anyone, but if you help him, he might be able to grant your freedom. You could go home.

My village is destroyed, my people enslaved. I have no home to return to.

They why are you trying to escape?

Jasmina felt confusion mingling with Enid's anger as she hesitated. She looked at the sleeping slave, his head forward, a soft snoring coming from his partly opened mouth.

Desperate to free herself, she scanned the tent for what Jasmina knew was the umpteenth time until she spied a metal shaft sticking out from under a pile of equipment. Rolling off the cot, she pulled it over her head and moved as silently as she could to the object.

Her eyes on the slave, she carefully kicked it free of the other equipment, and smiled when she realized it was the soft iron shaft that would be a tip for a *pilum*. As she looked the weapon over, she realized it would serve her in two ways. First, it was long enough to reach from one of her bound hands to the other. Second, the tip of the shaft was sharp and could cut the rope.

She looked back at the slave contently snoring in his chair, and struggled to hold back a derisive snort. Leaning to her right, she brought the cot down so her right hand could grab the metal shaft.

The slave grunted and snorted loudly, making her look quickly to see he was still asleep before turning back to her task. The rod was barely long enough to reach across the cot, and she could only apply a little pressure to the sharp end to cut the rope. Since the cot kept her hands a fixed distance apart, she was forced to stab at her bindings, and that meant she cut herself nearly as much as she did the rope.

Jasmina wanted to cry out from the painful cuts, but Enid refused to let a single sound come from her mouth as she continued to stab at her wrist until the binding started to separate.

Get off, you donkey's ass, Enid thought angrily as she continued to work at the rope. *All...most...theeerrrreeee.*

"Yes," she gasped with relief when the cot fell away from her left hand.

Unfortunately, the unbidden outburst woke the slave, and she turned to stare at the gasping Greek.

Don't kill him, Jasmina pleaded, and to her surprise, she heard an even weaker voice cry, "Don't."

"No, you cannot," the slave protested as he held his hands up, palms out. "They will kill you."

Grabbing the spear shaft with her left hand, Enid quickly cut her remaining wrist free and pushed the cot away from her.

"You scream, I kill" she growled in broken Latin.

"You do not understand," he cried. "They are cruel to runaway slaves. It is not dying you should fear, but what they do to you before you die. I have seen unspeakable things. I know."

"Worry not, coward," she said while shifting her hand on the spear shaft for a better grip. "They kill me only. I never surrender to degenerate Roman whores."

"But what of me?" he gasped, the pitch of his voice high with terror.

"You I no kill."

His head jerked from side to side, his eyes wide with fear, mouth pinched so tightly the lips were white.

"If you escape, they will treat me no differently." He gasped in a desperate breath. "You must kill me now." When she hesitated, he spread his arms, and added, "Please!"

His arms still outstretched, he dropped to one knee, and dipped his head to expose his neck. Uncertain of what she should do, she initially held up the spear shaft, but could not bring herself to do it.

You will be condemning him to a gruesome death, Jasmina protested as Enid continued to hesitate.

Though she had no problem killing enemy soldiers, this unarmed slave was an entirely different matter.

"No," she finally announced while backing toward the tent's entrance. "That is your problem. I must go."

He jerked his head up, his dark eyes revealing his desperation as he cried, "No! Please!"

Ignoring his protests, she turned quickly and bolted for the exit, but had taken only two steps outside when a sharp pain brought immediate blackness.

Chapter 16

"Oh my God! Not again."

The exclamation forced Jasmina's eyes open and she looked up to see Alvin staring down at her.

"What happened?" he cried as he and a nurse's aide worked to get Jasmina to her feet.

"Sit her down over here," he added while nodding toward a chair at the foot of Remmy's bed.

Though she wanted to resist, Jasmina was still struggling to reorient herself when she felt her legs bump into the chair.

"You just rest here and I'll get the doctor," he said as they lowered Jasmina into the chair.

"No," she protested while struggling to sit up. "No doctor. Enid has been attacked, and I apparently was knocked out with her."

"Who's Enid again?"

Jasmina pointed a shaking finger at Remmy. "The woman whose body Remmy is trapped in."

"Trapped? What do you mean?"

Giving her head an unsatisfying shake, Jasmina finally collapsed back into the chair.

"Remmy and Gerry have a mental link with two people in ancient Belgium. Remmy's person is called Enid, and she is a native of what the Romans referred to as Gaul." She waved a hand at the doorway. "Your son is in the body of a Roman soldier whose legion is fighting in Gaul during the time when Julius Caesar commanded the armies there."

It was Alvin's turn to shake his head and look lost.

"I don't...I...You can't seriously think..." He gave his head another shake before his eyes narrowed and he pursed his lips. "What have you done to my son?"

The accusation made Jasmina jerk upright. "I haven't done anything to your..." Her mouth still open in preparation for the next word, she looked at Remmy. "That's it."

"What?"

Rising from the chair, Jasmina moved quickly to the side of the bed, taking Remmy's right hand in hers.

"Remmy...I mean, Enid is unconscious."

"What do you mean?" Alvin asked anxiously. "How do you know?"

Jasmina jerked her hands away from Remmy's. "I don't think Gerry and Remmy are in this to take over their counterpart's body. They seem to be acting as conduits for me...or maybe us to participate in whatever is happening."

"Who are you talking about?" Miriam asked as she marched into the room.

She moved up beside her husband before they both faced Jasmina.

"What do you mean, us?" Alvin asked.

Jasmina shook her head. "We all have psychic healing powers. It's just that in some of us they are more developed than in others, just like you'd see in athletes."

"Are you saying *we* can also connect to our children's past lives?"

"And in doing so, possibly your own."

Miriam grabbed her husband's arm, as though the answer to what she was going to ask would be a shock she could not tolerate on her own.

"You mean, we have past lives too?"

"Everyone does," Jasmina responded. "We just need a way to connect to them."

It was Alvin's turn to grip his wife's arm. "You're not serious?"

"I very much am. These young people need our help, but even if I have both of them in the same room, it's going to be damned hard for me to juggled two lives at the same time. One of you has to step up and take part."

Jasmina watched as Alvin and Miriam looked at her with wide eyes, and partially opened mouths. Each, in turn, started to ask a question then stopped before words came out. They finally gave each other questioning looks, before Alvin straightened and turned to Jasmina.

"I'll do it."

"Alvin," Miriam protested. "You can't be serious."

Looking down at her, he set his jaw and nodded. "You're damn right I'm serious. Our son is in danger, and if this is what it takes to save him then I'm going to give it a try."

"But surely the doctors can..."

"The doctors are clueless," he interrupted angrily. "And after what I've seen Jasmina do in the past, I'm going to take a leap of faith and follow her lead."

"But…but…" Miriam stuttered as she looked from her husband to the bed with the sleeping Remmy. "What if you're wrong?"

"We're not giving him strange potions, Miriam," Jasmina insisted. "All we're going to do is take their hands and see what comes through."

Gerry's mother looked at her husband. "And what if he sees nothing?"

"Then we're no worse off, and we'll have to deal with it."

"Whoa, Miz Jasmina," the young EMT cried as he pulled Gerry's bed into the room. "We meet again."

Though he looked familiar, Jasmina was confused by the greeting.

"Oh, sorry, Ma'am. I'm Robert, the EMT who rode in with you and your niece in the ambulance."

"Oh yes, Robert. I remember now, but what are you doing here?"

Robert shrugged. "My ambulance gig is great, but it doesn't pay squat. I make up the difference by working here as an orderly."

"Oh my, what luck," Miriam said sarcastically, but the barb was lost on Robert.

"It's totally in the stars, Ma'am. I was destined to see you again."

"Good to see you too, Robert," Jasmina said while motioning to Remmy's bed. "Could you push Gerry up beside her, please?"

"Glad to do it!"

After moving the existing bed out of the way, Robert guided Gerry's into position then stepped back to let the nurse hook up the necessary monitoring devices and hang his IV. When done, she turned to Alvin and Miriam.

"He's still stable, but I'm sorry to say there has been little change."

"Thank you, Nurse," Miriam said with a calm control Jasmina was sure she could not have managed.

After the nurse left, all three turned to stare at Robert.

"Oh yeah," he said self-consciously. "I just wanted to see if there was anything else I could do to help."

"Thank you for your concern, Robert," Jasmina said politely. "But we need some time alone with them."

Nodding, he started toward the door. "Sure. I totally understand, but if you need anything, call the nurse's station and ask for me. When I'm not on the ambulance, I'm always hanging around here."

"We'll do that."

Before the door closed, Alvin turned to Jasmina. "What do I do now?"

"Just take his hands, close your eyes, and tell me what you see."

Moving to the side of the bed, he gripped his son's hands, clamped his eyes tightly shut, pinched his mouth, held his breath, and waited.

After a long moment, he gasped, "Nope. Nothing."

"You're sure?" Jasmina asked.

"He might be sleeping or something, but no, I'm getting nothing."

Hesitating for a long moment, Jasmina turned to Miriam. "It's your turn."

Shaking her head, Miriam took a step back. "No. I can't do something like this. It's…it's…I would need to speak with my priest first."

Moving quickly to her, Jasmina grabbed her shoulders.

"Miriam, there is no time. We have to act quickly or one of them is going to die, and if they do, we have no way of knowing how that will affect Gerry and Remmy."

"What will happen to us, if *we* are still connected to them when they die?"

"Are you willing to risk your life for your son?"

"Of course. What kind of question is that?"

Jasmina stabbed a finger at Gerry. "Then this is no different. If you can help him, you must."

"But what can I do? I don't know anything about Roman soldiers."

"I do," Alvin blurted loud enough to make both women jerk around to look at him. "Or at least I know something about them. Maybe enough to help." He looked at his wife. "We can work together to figure it out."

Jasmina nodded. "And my husband, Tim will be here soon. He's a history professor. Between the two of them, we should be able to deal with whatever they're facing."

Looking indecisive, Miriam folded her hands together and bounced from one foot to the other. "I don't know…"

"Miriam!" Alvin shouted angrily. "Just do it. We'll work it out as we go, like we always do."

She looked slowly from her husband to Jasmina and back before wringing her hands and turning toward her son.

"It probably won't work anyway," she said as she slowly reached down and took Gerry's hands.

When her eyes closed, she gasped at the sight of fifty Roman soldiers lined up in front of her, the daytime sun made their brilliant red uniforms glow, polished metal armor glitter, and their hot, perspiring bodies stink.

"Lord in Heaven," was all she could think to say.

Chapter 17

I pushed a clump of brush aside and stared across a small valley to where the rock rose almost vertically from the ground. Though there was no one in sight, the ground clearly showed that quite a bit of traffic had gone in and out of the three caves across from me.

"Did they have scouts?" I asked.

"No, *Optio*," the scout responded. "I have been watching them since we took their village. They only come and go a few at a time. It is hard to say how many are inside."

"Any other caves in the area?"

"Three others, but they are shallow and unoccupied. We have already rounded up thirty women and children who tried to hide in the forest. As far as we can tell, these are all the rest from the village."

"Are there soldiers in there as well?"

The soldier nodded. "Maybe twenty or so."

"Do those three entrances lead to separate caves, or just one?"

"We noticed that the same people seem to move from one entrance to the others, so I think they are separate."

I turned back to look at the troopers standing amongst the trees, sunlight filtering through the canopy above to make them nearly glow. The sight elicited a sense of surprise I could not explain.

A woman's voice cried, "Lord in Heaven," but a quick look around revealed no one nearby but Roman soldiers. The situation was alarming, but the men were waiting for orders, so I ignored the comment and turned to my second.

"Put ten men on each side of the caves to catch any who might try to escape. The rest of the men are to line up in front, swords ready, shields in a row. Let them see how hopeless their situation is."

The men moved quickly into position as I motioned for the interpreter to follow me up to the front of the line and easily within hearing range of the caves. Before speaking, I looked back at the straight line of soldiers, their steel helmets glistening in the sunlight, their red and gold shields forming a single wall as wide as anyone inside the caves could see.

What are you planning to do? The female voice demanded.

The voices were becoming both confusing and annoying. I have been a loyal Roman soldier for over twenty-five years, and could not understand where this was coming from. In addition, it was also irritating to have them interrupt my concentration.

I will do my job as I have been trained to do it.

Leaning toward the interpreter, I said,

"All you inside, hear my words. I am *Optio* Marcus Remus. We have defeated your soldiers and have your caves surrounded. Your men are captives, but most survived and wish to be rejoined with you. If you come out willingly, none of you will be harmed."

Moments later, an arrow smacked the roof of one of the cave entrances before bouncing off the ground in pieces. A second arrow embedded itself into the base of a legionnaire's shield.

"It appears they rejected our offer, Sir," the interpreter stated.

Let my son go! the female voice demanded.

I gave the space around me a quick glance before focusing on the task as hand.

"Archers! Send a dozen arrows into the largest entrance. Aim for them to pass just under the top of the entrance."

"Sir!" a dozen voices responded as one before I heard the twang of bow strings as the buzzing arrows flew to their targets.

Someone inside screamed in pain, but I was beyond caring. The enemy had a position of strength, since we could send no more than two men abreast into the cave at one time. A direct assault would be costly, and I did not want to waste more Roman lives on these people. Whatever the slavers might pay for them, taking these people alive was not worth the lives of even a handful of my soldiers.

"Octavius," I called. "Did you bring that supply of sulfur we found in the last village we took?"

The named soldier hurried forward. "Yes, *Optio.*"

"Get it," I ordered while walking back toward the wood and motioning for the interpreter to follow. "I have a special task for you."

Chapter 18

Her head throbbing, Enid slowly opened her eyes, unsure of where she was until the sounds of the Roman camp reminded her. Lifting her arms, she was surprised to find her hands unbound, but as she arose, a tight metal collar around her neck stifled any hope of escape.

"I knew you would be trouble, little one," Lucius Cornelius said as he rose from the only stool in Marcus' tent. "If I were not such a good friend to Marcus, I would have let you suffer the consequences of trying to escape, but he deserves better. Don't you think?"

Turning, she glared angrily at the soldier, before snarling, "You should have let me die. I will not make good slave."

Smiling, Lucius nodded. "I quite agree, but then, many a recently-captured person has said that, and some of them have done quite well as slaves. A few have even earned their freedom." He pulled a blade of grass from between his teeth and smiled grimly at her. "However, I fear you will not be one of them. Am I right?"

"Then kill me and be done."

He barked a laugh and rose. "Not me, little one. Marcus is my friend, but he is also my *optio*, and has ordered me to protect you, so that is what I must do. You know?"

"Why you always end statement with question?"

Lucius shrugged. "Does it bother you?"

Gritting her teeth, she slowly shook her head. "I care not one way or other."

Laughing again, Lucius walked to the tent's entrance before looking back at her. "I think it bothers you quite a bit. Am I wrong?"

"Stupid dog!"

"Oh my," he said sarcastically. "Does that mean you want to slit my throat as well?"

"I not need reason to kill Romans. We are mortal enemies."

"Correction, little one," he said while moving close to her. "You are a defeated mortal enemy, and that makes you a servant of Rome. If you do not want to die a horrible death, you should remember that. Do I make myself clear?"

"Come closer, Roman," she snarled. "I scratch your eyes out."

He took another step closer, and she tried to stand to take him on, but the chain attached to the collar around her neck stopped her halfway up. Still crouching and off balance, she was helpless to respond when Marcus reached in and pushed her back onto the bed.

"If you continue to make trouble, I will bind your hands and feet. The Greek has done a good job of tending to the wounds on your wrists, but I would guess they are still painful. Are they not?" She spat at his face, but he easily dodged it and laughed. "I do not envy the task my friend has taken on, but in the end, I am afraid he will have to kill you. Am I right?"

Enid glared at him, unwilling to agree with anything he said, even though she was sure he was right on that point.

When he left the tent, she grabbed the chain binding her to the ground and yanked on it. The effort made her wrists ache, but she continued to tug on it as her eyes followed the chain down to where it was attached to a rod hammered into the ground. When she squatted and tried to pull it free, the rod did not even wiggle. Unwilling to give in, she pulled and pushed on it until her back muscles cramped, but could not work it free.

You have to cooperate with Gerry, a young female voice insisted.

"Where are you?" she cried in her own tongue while looking around the tent. "Show yourself."

I can't. I'm inside your mind.

"What Roman rubbish is this? I alone rule my mind."

Well, right now I'm trapped in here with you, and you have to listen to me.

"I do not! You are a witch controlled by my captors. I will never do as you say."

I'm not a Roman. I am trapped in your body and my boyfriend is in Marcus'. We are here to save your life.

"Rubbish! If you wish to help, strike this Roman mongrel down and let me escape."

I don't have super powers. I can't will things to happen. I can only try to reason with you and convince you that the capture of your town was a significant historical event, but someone is trying to alter the future to make all the deaths that happened here insignificant.

"What are you saying?"

This is the last battle for the Roman takeover of Gaul. From this point on, you have hundreds of years of peace, and many of your people will be returned to your homeland to continue to develop it, not as warring tribes in constant turmoil, but as a unified people who eventually become the countries of France and Belgium.

"How can you know such a thing?"

Because, in my time, it has already happened.

"Impossible. No one can know the future."

I know the future, because I am in the future.

"How is this possible?"

I can't explain it, but...

She stopped when Lucius returned, looking around as though searching for something.

"Who are you speaking to?"

Still squatting next to the cot, she turned her entire body in his direction and glared in silence.

After a moment, he shook his head and sighed, "Are all you Gauls stark raving mad?"

When she still did not respond, he scanned the space one more time before adding, "We will be leaving for home soon. I cannot tell you how happy it will make me to be quit of this place once and for all. Would you like to see Rome, pretty one?"

Here is my proof. Ask him if the war is over.

Closing her eyes, Enid remained silent.

Ask him!

"Are the Roman soldiers leaving our land?"

Lucius barked a laugh. "Not for a very long time, little one, but Marcus and I are going to guard you and the rest of our booty. Gaul is now firmly under the Roman hand and our *imperator* is going back to celebrate a Triumph. Glorious. No?"

"That cannot be true. My people will never surrender."

Lucius laughed again. "And yet they have. Now it does not matter whether we leave you here or take you with us, from this point forward you are a servant of Rome. What do you think of that, Savage Woman?"

She lunged at him, but the short chain stopped her with a choking jolt as she grabbed air and struggled against the unbreakable bond. His laugh only angered her more as she struggled, and she was not surprised when he lurched forward to deliver a powerful blow to her forehead.

The impact sent her back to crash into the cot, falling over it and onto the ground. She tried to rise, but the room swam, her balance so disrupted she fell crossways onto the cot. Flailing her arms and legs in vain, she struggled to sit up, enraged by the sound of Lucius' laughter as he sauntered from the tent.

I will castrate that degenerate, dung-eating slut, exploded in her head. *And then I will cut out his blackened heart.*

Killing him will not help us, the young woman cried. *You have to work with Marcus to stop them from changing history.*

Finally regaining her balance, Enid pushed herself up until she could sit on the edge of the cot. After a quick look around the room, she shook her head.

Maybe your idea is the correct one, she finally said. *I must make them believe I will be a good slave.*

Yes, the young woman agreed. *Then you and Marcus can save the future.*

I care nothing for the future, little witch, she growled. *I want only to turn those two into food for dogs.*

Chapter 19

"Archers at the ready," I commanded as three pairs of my soldiers moved quickly along the face of the hill toward the cave openings, their hands full of smoldering packages.

Each team held a bundle of hot coals wrapped in moss and leather. When they were in position, I motioned for them to open the leather covers and pour sulfur over the hot coals. The men pulled their heads back as the acrid fumes billowed up.

"Fire arrows," I commanded.

As soon as the arrows passed their position, the three teams rushed in and heaved their bundles into the caves. Each bundle contained a vial of flammable oil, and a flash of light confirmed the spilled oil had ignited.

I felt an unexplained nervousness as yellow smoke billowed from the caves. Screams floated out with the smoke, and though it should not have, my anxiety increased when my men cheered the accomplishment.

You shouldn't be treating these people like this!

What would you have me do? They are obstinate.

What do you expect? You're trying to enslave them.

It is the nature of war.

It doesn't have to be.

It does. The centurio has commanded and I must obey.

Are you a slave as well? You sure sound like one.

I am a soldier and proud of it.

"*Optio*," the *decanus* called. "They are coming out."

It was only then I realized I had been looking at the back of my shield, and lifted my eyes to see coughing women and children staggering from the caves. At first, only a few came out, but gradually the numbers increased until there was a steady stream.

"Gather them up," I commanded, and a pre-designated group of soldiers rushed forward to herd them away from the entrances.

As I watched the line of captives march by, I suddenly realized that the only males were children.

"Where are their soldiers?"

The interpreter ran up to a cluster of women and spoke briefly to them before rushing back to me.

"They will not come out, *Optio*. They choose to die, rather than surrender."

You can't let them die.

And what would you have me do? Risk valuable legionnaires in a vain attempt at bringing them out alive? Their choice has doomed them.

You're an animal!

And you are a very strange woman. Leave me alone.

Turning toward the cave, I watched the last few stagger out, collapsing to the ground as they choked on the foul air. Two fainted and were dragged away. Another three tried to run, but were grabbed before they got far. After them, no more came out.

Shaking my head, I hesitated a moment more before turning to my second. "Station a contingent of men to watch. When the air is clear enough, go in and recover what valuables and weapons you can. Leave the corpses to rot."

"Yes, Sir," he snapped with a salute before I turned to follow the captives.

You should give them a proper burial, the woman in my head insisted.

"I do not bury my dead enemy," I responded, realizing too late that I said it out loud.

"*Optio*?" a soldier next to me asked. "Was that an order?"

"No," I snapped back to cover the embarrassment of my blunder. "Get these slaves to the internment post and secure them."

"Yes, Sir. At once."

He ran ahead, shouting at and pushing the struggling captives. I felt ashamed of my concern for them, and my unreasonable wish to call my soldiers back and order them to release the captives.

Why am I having such strange thoughts?

That has to be Gerry's influence, the woman's voice announced. *He has to be mortified by what you are doing.*

Who is this Gerry?

His soul has been joined with yours in the hope of helping you with your mission.

My mission? The centurio has said nothing of another mission for me.

There is a plot to change history by assassinating your general, and it is your task to stop it.

You cannot change history. It is a man's mission to make it.

Well, there is an evil man who wants to make the future fit his design, even if it is detrimental to the rest of us.

I felt my eyes roll before I looked ahead to see the line of captives being led to their uncertain future.

I know of two who wish to shape our future to fit their own needs.

Caesar and Pompeius Magnus?

Indeed, but I care not of what Pompeius Magnus does in Rome. I am a soldier and proud of it.

But will he alter history?

Both of them already have, and if I were a betting man, I would say one of them will do even more and eliminate the other.

Caesar?

You read my mind, Witch. That gives you an unfair advantage.

But a third party is planning to assassinate Caesar before he could do that.

Why does your foolish statement make me anxious? I care not for who kills whom as long as my pay comes regularly.

You lost your wife, didn't you?

Leave my past out of this.

But your past is clouding your future. You must look beyond it.

My past is my future. I will die soon and my family will be restored to me. I wish for nothing else.

What about Enid?

Who?

Your new slave.

She will bring a tidy sum. I care nothing more for her.

If you are going to die soon, why do you care how much you make from selling her?

Slapping the rod in my hand against my thigh, I used the shot of pain to banish the woman from my head. Her argument was for nothing. I will die in battle because that is what I must do to assure my entry into the Elysian Fields where my family is surely waiting for me. While marching on, I instinctively reached down to feel for the gold coin sewn into the hem of my shirt. This coin is special because it will pay Charon, the ferryman for my ride over the River Styx.

If I died alone, with no one to provide the coin, I could tear it out and shove it into my mouth, assuring that it would accompany me on my journey. Nothing was being left to chance, except the date of my death, and I was growing weary of the wait.

Chapter 20

"Oh my God," Miriam gasped as she stumbled back from Gerry's bed, her hands covering her face. "My son is trapped in the body of a monster."

"What did you see?" Alvin asked anxiously as he rushed over to steady her.

"This evil man killed a group of people because they would not come out of a cave."

"Why wouldn't they come out?"

"The Romans wanted to enslave them, and when they refused to come out, he filled the cave with sulfur smoke. Those who stayed were suffocated."

"Who is this guy?"

When Miriam lowered her hands, the tears on her cheeks glistened in the greenish-gray light of the hospital room.

"He's a Roman soldier. I don't know what the date is, but he's evil and Gerry's stuck in his body."

"Ancient Rome?" Jasmina's husband, Tim asked as he entered the room.

"Yes, I think so."

"Then that sounds about right for a Roman legionnaire."

Looking surprised, Miriam and Alvin jerked around to face him.

"What sounds about right?"

Tim shrugged. "It wasn't at all uncommon for victors – whether Roman or otherwise -- to treat their captives cruelly. It didn't seem to matter what they did, it was considered justified because they won the battle."

"That doesn't make it right!"

"No, but you have to consider the context. Such things were expected, and if this guy didn't do them, he could be punished as well."

A loud gasp behind them, made Miriam and Alvin turn to see Jasmina leaning against the rail along the side of Remmy's bed.

"This is not going to be easy," she nearly whispered.

Miriam pushed away from her husband and moved closer to Jasmina. "What is yours like? I can't even begin to reason with this man. He thinks I've bewitched him."

After wiping her sweaty brow, Jasmina shook her head. "We have to keep trying to get them to work together."

"Even though they want to kill each other?"

Jasmina moved to a chair and collapsed into it. "I get the sense that though they can hear us, it is our children's emotions that come through strongest to them."

"What do you mean?"

Jasmina wiped her face again and took a deep breath.

"When Enid was preparing to escape, the slave watching her begged for a quick death. At first, she was going to do it, but the idea must have repulsed Remmy so much, Enid changed her mind and spared him."

"So our children are influencing them?"

"It is a slow process, but yes, I think they are."

"But you have to be careful here," Tim insisted. "They must not move too fast. These people had their own set of morals. They did lots of things we in the twenty-first century find repugnant."

Miriam looked from Jasmina to her husband before turning her attention back to Tim. "What do you mean?"

"If Gerry's soldier is too compassionate, he might be seen as weak and indecisive. His superiors would have punished him for wasting time trying to wait those people out, and if he had tried to attack the cave, his own soldiers might have turned on him for needlessly endangering their lives."

"You can't possibly agree with what he did?"

Tim shook his head. "No, but we also can't expect them to behave exactly like we would."

Rising from her chair, Jasmina took her husband's hand. "Our goal here isn't to change the past, but to stop it from being changed. To some degree, we have to focus on that and leave the rest to history."

Miriam collapsed back against her own husband. "I'm not sure I can do that."

Her head shaking, Jasmina faced Miriam.

"Your son's life may depend on it," she stated firmly. "This isn't a time to be squeamish."

"But I…"

"Don't play the religious card here. You either step up and help or get out of the way and let me handle it."

"You can't do this alone. You said so yourself."

"Probably not, but it will be even harder with you confusing things by trying to force Christian morals onto this soldier. Christianity won't even exist as a force in this region for another four-hundred years. We need to focus on finding whomever is trying to change the past and stop them. Do you understand?"

Her eyes wide with shock, Miriam stared blankly at Jasmina for a long moment before she swallowed hard and jerked a nod.

"What should I do?"

"Marcus and Enid have to stop trying to kill each other because one of them will eventually succeed and our plans will be squashed."

"Will their deaths affect our children?" Alvin asked.

Sighing heavily, Jasmina looked at the two sleeping forms before turning back to Gerry's parents.

"I don't know for sure, but we have to assume it will. The last time Gerry connected with someone, he got a cut each time the other person did. Remmy screamed when Enid received an arrow in the shoulder, and was quite agitated when that soldier tried to rape Enid."

"Someone tried to rape her?" Alvin asked, his eyes wide.

Jasmina held up both hands. "Another soldier intervened, but the point is, unlike last time, both of our children are mentally linked to their past selves full time. If that girl dies, I'm not sure Remmy will survive it."

"And Gerry?" Miriam asked anxiously.

Jasmina sighed. "I'm afraid he is equally at risk."

"But why?" Miriam whined. "What has my son done to deserve this?"

"I'm sorry. I don't know for sure why they have been pulled into this, but I do know that we foiled an attempt by this entity, which I call the *Tsabbat*, trying to help his human puppet become emperor of China, and quite possibly leader of the entire world. For some reason, it seems this entity can't interfere with our lives directly, but through intermediaries it just might be trying to trap Gerry and Remmy in these bodies to stop them from interfering in whatever plans it now has."

"And we think it is to kill Julius Caesar?" Alvin asked.

"Actually, I think it is," Tim answered as he looked from one person to the other. "It is the most significant thing someone could do at this time in the history of western civilization."

Miriam barked a laugh. "But that wouldn't alter history. He *was* assassinated."

"Yes," Tim conceded. "But that was later. If he is killed now, before he makes his famous march on Rome and plants the seeds of imperialism, Imperial Rome might never have happened, and that would dramatically alter the development of both Western Europe and the Far East."

"How?" Alvin asked.

"If the Roman Empire had remained a republic it might never have grown large and powerful enough to conquer all the territory it did. Imperial Rome was a stabilizing influence on much of this area for hundreds of years. They spread a common language and culture throughout the region, established a system of government and laws. In addition, the emperor Constantine was responsible for establishing Christianity as the church of the empire and his descendants made it into a worldwide super power."

"That's all well and good," Miriam said, "but how does this help our children?"

Jasmina shook her head. "I'm not yet sure, but Tim's right. Julius Caesar is the most likely candidate for assassination."

"But what do I do right now?"

Letting out a long sigh, Jasmina looked at her niece and shook her head. "We need to reconnect to their hosts and do our best to get them to cooperate. Hopefully, Gerry and Remmy can help."

Miriam shook her head and sighed. "I'm not sure how much of him I can take."

A tear dribbled down her cheek as she looked at Gerry to see he was no longer sleeping quietly. His face was twitching, eyes jerking back and forth behind his eyelids, mouth twisting and distorting as though he was struggling to say something, but afraid to let it out.

Moving quickly to her son's side, she took his hands and leaned her face close to his, but when she closed her eyes, she was walking through an open field with corpses lying randomly across it.

"Though he would rather bite off his tongue than say so," Lucius was saying as they looked down at the bodies. "I think the *centurio* was impressed with how you dealt with these savages. Why else would he have sent me to fetch you?"

"I was only doing my job," Marcus responded. "He probably has another task for me."

"He's going to take you with him to Rome. I'm told we will be acting as Julius Caesar's personal body guard. Could it be that we are blessed by the gods?"

"Where did you hear that?"

Lucius shrugged. "One hears things. It may be truth, it may be fantasy, but would it not be exciting if it were true?"

Marcus did not answer, preferring to keep his disappointment to himself. How was he going to die in battle if peace ruled this land?

Think of Enid. Is she not worth living for?

Quiet witch! I will not be disloyal to my family by lusting after a savage woman.

She's a warrior like you. Surely the two of you have more in common than you're willing to admit.

Though he wanted to fire back an angry response, he had to admit the witch had a point. The woman was a tigress, and he did find that arousing. On the other hand...

He stopped, forcing Lucius to jerk around when he realized his friend was no longer by his side.

The wench may come in handy yet, he thought.

What do you mean?

She wants to kill me. I just need to let her.

Chapter 21

She waited on her cot, though truth be told, the collar around her neck meant it was not really a choice.

What are you doing? the older witch asked.

Enid did her best to keep her mind blank in the hope the witch could read nothing from it, but as the silence dragged on, she could not stop herself from answering. Even so, she didn't have to tell the witch everything.

I am biding my time until my master comes back.

Are you still going to kill him?

No. The Romans have conquered my people. We must make the best of it and learn our place.

Remmy? Can you hear me?

Enid held her breath and focused on keeping the young witch from speaking.

We are in agreement, your young witch and I. We speak with one voice now.

I'd still like to speak with her, if I may.

There was a long pause before Enid chuckled quietly to herself.

She chooses to speak through me.

I find that hard to believe.

Believe what you wish. She and I will do our best to serve this Roman and earn our freedom. There is nothing else to discuss.

There is much to disc....

NO! Be gone, Witch.

Expecting an argument, Enid tensed, but her mind remained quiet. Quiet, that is, except for the faint echoes of the young witch's screams. Would she ever shut up?

Footsteps outside meant someone approaching the tent.

"We are pulling out at first light," Marcus announced, his voice growing clearer with each word, implying he was heading for the entrance.

Must do this right. He will not believe me if I give in too quickly.

"Have the men pack up the tents we will not be using tonight. We will have parade at sunrise. The *centurio* will keep it short. He wants to get out of here as much as we do."

The Greek rose from his chair, gasping in relief when he realized who was speaking. Marcus hardly noticed him as he entered, but the bruise on Enid's face caught his eye immediately.

"What has happened here?"

Enid said nothing as she watched the slave prostrate himself on the ground. "I was helpless to defend her, *Optio*.

She looked at Marcus, surprised to see his hand on the hilt of his sword when the young female's voice declared,

He's obviously as much a victim as you are. Why would Marcus want to kill him?

Not bothering to answer, she watched Marcus glare at the Greek, his right hand gripping and releasing his sword.

"Why are you still alive?" he asked.

Still prostrate, the slave shook his head wildly. "I fought him with all my strength, but I was no match for a legionnaire, *Optio*. He would have killed me, if it had not been for your friend, Lucius."

Marcus looked again at her, and to make a good show of it, she leaned forward to strain against the metal collar, snapping the chain taught. Despite her aggressive stance, she felt confused by how protective he was being of her.

What does he care about a captive he is going to sell?

Looking angry, Marcus jerked his attention back to the Greek, opening his mouth to speak, but stopped when Lucius entered the tent.

"Why did you not mention this to me?" he asked angrily.

"And what would you have done?"

"I would have cut his balls off!"

The statement seemed to startle Lucius. "What has happened to you, my friend? Only a day ago, you were calling her lot savages who ate their young, and now you defend her?"

Enid was surprised to see the muscles in Marcus neck tense as his face darkened with rage. She was certain that if it had not been for his long years as a disciplined soldier, he might have struck his friend.

"She is my property, and I will not have her damaged."

"And what of Quintus?"

"He is the one?"

Lucius nodded. "Would it not be best to deal with him in an appropriate manner? One that would not get you executed?"

She saw another flash of confusion on Marcus' face as he gasped in a desperate breath and gave his head a sharp shake.

"I will deal with Quintus in a way that will not put me in the gallows."

Lucius sighed. "I am glad to hear it, my friend. May I know how?"

Marcus' laugh came out more as a cough. "You will learn soon enough." He turned to the Greek. "Go away and speak of this to no one."

When the slave started to leave, Marcus shouted, "Wait!"

Enid felt her body jerk as Marcus moved close and pointed at her wrists. "What happened to her?"

"It was her own doing, *Optio*," the slave moaned. "She fought so hard against her bindings it rubbed off most of the skin."

"And yet," Marcus observed as he pulled down the metal collar around Enid's neck, "there is no damage to her here."

The slave gave her a momentary look of surprise, but she pretended to ignore him as she sat passively even though every muscle in her body cried out to attack him.

"She has been a changed person since the attack, *Optio*. I do not know what brought it about."

Lucius barked a tense laugh. "I wonder. Has she come to realize that not all Romans are in need of gutting?"

"Only a fool would think that," Marcus snapped back, though Enid detected the sound of surprise in his response. "I...she..." He paused, his fingers still on her collar, but to her surprise, she was no longer thinking of attacking him. "It is probably a blow to the head she must have received in the struggle," he finally said, his fingers lightly brushing the tell-tale bruise on her left cheek. "It rattles the brain and slows a person's thinking." He bent over until his head was level with hers, a move that made her uncomfortable in a way she had not expected. "After she recovers I am sure she will be as troublesome as ever."

Feeling a smile form on her lips, she immediately suppressed it, and though it lasted only an instant, she was sure Marcus saw it.

I am still dangerous, Roman dog, she thought. *Which of us will kill the other?*

Pulling back from her, Marcus turned to the slave. "Use your renowned potions to heal her injuries and make her presentable." He looked back at her, his expression implying he was gauging her attitude from the micro moves of her body. She felt naked, and embarrassed, the sudden warmth in her skin eliciting the hint of a smile from him. "The slavers will give me twice the money if she is uninjured."

"By Jove," Lucius cried. "Quintus will give you ten-times the amount for a night with her, do you not think?"

Turning quickly toward his friend, Marcus scowled. "What I will do to that rabid mongrel will give me far more pleasure than any amount of gold."

"Marcus?" his friend asked cautiously. "This is just a common slave girl. Why all the anger?"

Stabbing a finger at Lucius, he growled. "Because I am *Optio*, and no soldier under my command abuses my property. My rank demands respect, and if I let this offense pass, what kind of leader would I be?"

His attention jerking from his friend to the woman and back, Lucius bowed his head. "And that is why you are *Optio*. Is that not so?"

"That is so," Marcus stated adamantly before he turned and stomped from the tent.

While the remaining two men watched Marcus leave, Enid let out a soft sigh of relief. She could face death in any form, but the feelings she was having made her sweat in all the wrong places.

This is your doing, witch! she thought as the two men looked at each other before also leaving the tent. *Let me fight this demon on my own.*

You're falling in love with him, aren't you?

Never!

Liar!

She clenched her fists so tightly the nails dug into skin, bringing enough pain to blot out the witch's ranting.

Lifting her hands to her face, she rubbed the blood on her cheeks and forehead.

I will kill this Roman and as many of his comrades as I can. By my brothers I swear this to be true!

Chapter 22

Storming from the tent, my first impulse was to go straight to Quintus and cut his throat. Maybe castrate him first then hack off each of his fingers and toes before ending his worthless existence.

Do you want to die in disgrace? the young voice asked.

This is your doing!

I didn't bring about this attack on her.

No, but you made me care enough to get this angry. I should sell her to the slavers right now.

You will get more for her in Rome.

It may not be worth the trouble she will cause.

Wait a minute. If you are so set on getting yourself killed, why do you care how much she will bring?

The haunting voice had a point. My mother was dead, father unknown, and my siblings detest me. My wife's family disowned her when she defied their wishes and married me. If those cretin sluts get anything from me, it will be a fist in the face.

My property will go to my brothers in arms. They are the only family I have.

And what of your general? A woman's voice asked. *Would you be doing your brothers a favor by letting Caesar be assassinated?*

The question surprised me, but when footsteps pulled my attention in that direction I saw Lucius' confused face and was flooded with conflicting feelings that both did and did not involve him.

"Are you following me?" I asked accusingly.

Lucius shrugged. "You are not yourself. What would you have me do?"

"I am fine. Just leave me be."

"What of Quintus?"

I shook my head. "The Legion has been my life since I left that squalid deathtrap my mother called home. I tried civilian life, but it displeased the gods, and they punished me."

Lucius bowed his head slightly, but thankfully said nothing.

"I know how to make a man suffer without it coming back onto me. He will learn his lesson and live to fight another day."

"The *centurio* would have him whipped. No?"

I smiled, and seeing Lucius' reaction, knew it reflected my angry mood. "He will not be so lucky."

I walked away, knowing my friend would fret until he knew what I had done. It was good that his stomach grumbled for a while. If Quintus had damaged the *centurio*'s property, he would not only have had him whipped, but also the person who was supposed to watch over the property.

Though I said no more, Lucius continued to follow. Out of frustration, I stopped and waved him away.

"I need no escort."

I could see his mouth opening as though to protest, but after giving him a scowl that matched my sour mood, the mouth closed without an utterance.

I continued alone to find Quintus sitting in front of his tent, his head down, tunic dusty as though he had fallen several times on his way there.

"At attention," I commanded. "*Optio* in camp. Quintus step forward."

The announcement brought his head up, his face painted with confusion until his befuddled brain realized what was happening. He slowly rose and stared at me with obvious trepidation. He tried to stand straight, but his obvious hangover was causing him quite a bit of pain.

"What is your command, *Optio*?"

I pointed at a corner of the encampment wall that was uncharacteristically truncated.

"In the morning you will build a fortification wall out from that corner one-hundred paces."

"Who will be assisting me, *Optio?*"

I looked at the men standing nearby, their anxiety obvious.

"You need no help, Quintus," I stated.

I knew he wanted to protest that the area was swampy, the mud knee deep, with huge biting flies that swarmed on the men so badly the *centurio* ordered them to abandon that area and truncate the corner of the enclosure.

"Yes, Sir," he shouted as I glared at him, hoping he would protest, even just a little, so I could add to his punishment.

"You will start at daybreak, only coming back into the compound for meals. Is that understood?"

"Yes, *Optio*."

I snapped a salute, which he answered. "Get a good night's sleep, Quintus, and do not forget to grease yourself up well or those flies will make short work of you."

"Yes, *Optio*."

My eyes swept the crowd around me, and I saw smiles and nudges. It was obvious word of Quintus' offense had spread quickly around the camp, and now everyone would also know of his punishment. The only problem was, I had no intention of stopping there.

Despite what he tried to do, the young voice stated. *He didn't succeed. What you are doing is beyond the crime.*

Did you see their faces? I asked.

Faces? Whose?

The other soldiers. They knew what he had done as well and were waiting to see what my response would be. If I do not make his punishment obvious and painful, they will not respect me, and my role as leader will be destroyed.

I hardly think it would come to that.

Then you are an ignorant fool. When we are in battle, the men turn to me for leadership, and expect me to be even more aggressive than they are. If they think I am weak they will hesitate, discipline will suffer, and we will cease to be an effective fighting unit. I will be risking their lives as well as mine.

You're not serious!

Oh yes I am, little daemon. It is a fact of war and a reality you had better come to terms with or we might both die in the next engagement.

But you want to die.

His statement dredged up that buried anger again, and to control myself, I slapped my thigh hard with my staff.

I will die a soldier's death, at the hands of my enemy, not be humiliated by a spear in the back from a member of my own troop.

I suddenly realized I had not moved, and when I looked around, I could see the men staring at me. Had this conversation taken a moment, or had it been longer?

Tell them you are thinking of something.

A leader never asks for forgiveness from his men, nor does he have to explain himself.

Jerking around, I marched back to my tent, saluting sharply when necessary, ignoring anyone else as though I were lost in my thoughts.

Rushing into the tent, I found the Greek slumped on a stool, but he jumped up when I burst in.

"Optio," he cried. "How may I serve...?"

"Out!"

He hesitated only briefly before giving a quick bow and hurrying from the tent. He didn't merit a second glance as I moved to the woman.

"What is your name?" I growled, and though my anger was not intended for her, it was there and had to boil out regardless of who was in its path.

She rose up as far as the chain would allow, the sound of it snapping taut pinged in my ears.

"Enid Pergo, of the Nervii."

I felt myself glaring at her, and the fact that she did not cower seemed to dissipate my anger.

I pulled out my knife and pointed it at her neck.

"Hold still, Enid Pergo, of the Nervii," I stated. "I am going to unlock your collar."

The look of surprise on her face made me want to smile, but the feeling passed quickly when her expression turned cautious.

"I am not going to kill you, and if it was my intention to rape you, I would not need to remove the collar."

Her head slowly shook, but her eyes were never off mine. "Then what?"

I lowered the knife and shrugged. "You can run, if you wish, but I doubt an unarmed Gallic woman would get far. I can assure you that they…" I pointed outside. "…will do far worse to you than I, but that is a choice you must make."

"I would rather die than be a Roman slave."

I nodded. "You must do what you will, but I ask one thing of you before I let you go."

Caution returned to her face.

"Yes?"

Her response stopped me, and I suddenly realized I had no idea what that one thing was. That was, until the young voice in my head answered for me.

"Listen to what I have to say."

She was silent for a long moment. "That is all?"

I stared at her, feeling dumbfounded until I felt myself nod.

"I must have your word as a warrior," the young daemon in my head added.

"And you will set me free?"

I shrugged. "I will release you, but cannot guarantee your safety if you leave."

She shook her head. "I am aware of the risk."

"The choice is yours."

"And what if I kill you?"

"Just give me your word that you will hear me out first."

I am sure the woman was as dumbfounded as I.

What are you up to, daemon?

You want to die, don't you? Give her a knife and fight with her.

I am not stupid. That would be suicide.

And suicide without honor will keep you out of heaven?

Absolutely.

Then I guess you had better be very convincing.

"I give you my solemn word as a warrior of the Nervii."

Her response shocked me and brought my focus back to her. Even then, it took me a moment to regain my wits before I reached up and used the tip of the knife blade to unlock the collar.

To my astonishment, I then flipped the knife around and extended the butt to her. Her eyes cautious, mouth agape, she hesitated for a long moment before she clenched her jaw and slowly reached up to take it.

The knife in hand, she stepped back and pointed the blade at me.

"I could kill you now."

Sensing that her statement was more a question than a statement, I simply nodded.

"But I have the word of a warrior of the Nervii."

Her chin jerked down, eyes squinting, as though she were fighting with herself over the promise. I was impressed with how quickly she nodded and lowered the knife, but did not relax her grip on the weapon.

"Romans lie. How are you different?"

Her question was legitimate. Many times I had stretched the truth to achieve my own ends, whether against an enemy or on a personal level.

I waved at the entrance. "Leave if my words do not ring true."

My statement seemed to puzzle her, and I am sure she was wondering what kind of perverse trickery I was up to. I had to suppress a laugh because I was wondering the same thing. The voice in my head was no longer "speaking." Instead, I was experiencing feelings so strange it was as though I had taken a hallucinatory herb and was outside my own body. After all, what soldier in his right mind would give his weapon to a captive enemy and set her free?

Only a suicidal one.

Chapter 23

As the tip of Marcus' knife blade moved close to her neck, Enid's mind went on full alert. There was little she could do. Though her hands were free, she was chained to the ground. If she tried to attack him, the chain would stop her, allowing him to pull out of reach and then jump back in to slit her throat.

He won't hurt you! the witch in her head screamed.

Unable to do anything else, she was determined not to cower in the face of death. Her hands remained by her side, head up as she watched the blade moved down until its tip touched the collar around her neck. She felt him push the blade against the metal then twist it several times. No one was more surprised than her when the collar clattered to the soft dirt floor at her feet, but the surprise turned to near panic when he flipped the knife around and presented the butt to her.

After waiting a moment to make sure this wasn't a trick, she grabbed the weapon and pulled back into a defensive posture.

"I could kill you now," she stated, though her panicked mind wanted her to shout it and dive into him, blade slashing.

He did not react, other than nodding. "But I have the word of a warrior of the Nervii."

His statement created an internal conflict that made her chin snap to her chest.

Yes, she thought angrily. *I have given my word, but you are still a Roman pig.*

A part of her wanted to seize the moment, and make it hers by killing him. Another part -- a part that was foreign to her -- made her muscles freeze.

Putrid dog though he is, I swore an oath, she thought before lowering the knife, but kept a tight grip on the weapon.

"Romans lie. How are you different?"

He hesitated briefly before waving a hand at the entrance. "Leave if my words do not ring true."

To her surprise, he turned his back to her. Her muscles were so taught she feared they might cramp as she looked at the brightly lit opening for a long moment, all her instinct urging her to strike this man down and run for her life, but she could do neither. Her indecisiveness both confused and enraged her, and she fought a wordless internal conflict for a long moment before turning back to him.

"I am not sure why I am doing this," he finally said as he sat on a stool and looked up at her. "It goes against everything I believe in, if you must know the truth."

She struggled to keep her face neutral as her internal struggle raged, pitting fight against flight. This Roman's problems were not hers, but before she could decide, another thought occurred to her. If she were free to move about the compound, she could help her people escape. As her plan began to form, she realized his attention was not on her. She followed his gaze to a small shrine next to the entrance.

"What is that?" she asked suspiciously.

Though his mouth opened slightly, he hesitated a long moment before speaking.

"It is a shrine in the memory of my wife and son."

"They are dead?"

He nodded slowly, his eyes still on the shrine. He held that pose for a long moment before turning toward her.

"A voice in my head," he finally said, "tells me you can help me, and therefore help yourself."

"Why would I help you?"

"Because your country has been conquered, and if it is to have a future, you must learn to live with that."

"I have told you. I would rather die than live as a Roman slave."

"Then maybe there is a way you can live as a Roman citizen."

"What is the difference?"

"Because if you are dead, there is nothing you can do to help your people."

"I do not wish to help my people live under Roman rule."

"That is no longer a choice. The battle for Gaul is over."

"You underestimate us, Roman. We are a far from defeated."

His head shaking, he gave her a weak smile. "I would guess you are talking about Vercingetorix of the Arverni?"

"He is a great leader. If we had not been fighting with you, our soldiers would be with him now."

"And many would be dead. The rest prisoners."

The shock of his statement stopped all thoughts for a moment before she snapped her head from side to side. "That cannot be. His soldiers are disciplined and well armed, and we are told they outnumbered your legions by two to one."

He sighed, his head still shaking. "As did yours here, and what was the result?"

"This cannot be true."

"And yet, it is," he responded while rising from his stool. "I do not tell you this to gloat over your loss. I mention it only because there is a chance you can make something good out of it."

She shook her head while glaring at him. "My people have been humiliated and many are dead. What good can come from that?"

"With your leaders in chains and your armies disbanded, Gaul needs the protection of Rome, but if Rome also falls, this entire region will be vulnerable to takeover."

"I live to see the Romans brought to their knees."

"Even if it means someone far less accommodating will rule over you?"

"We will enslave them, not the other way around."

"Not if you fight as poorly as you did against us. The Germans are a violent race, and much more savage than your people. I might have raped and enslaved you. They will gut and eat your children."

"They are not that bad."

Shaking his head while returning to his stool, he turned to give her a smile. "You have not seen what I have. They are much worse."

Don't argue! The voice in her head argued. *Think of freeing your people.*

The statement made her hesitate. The desire to kill a sworn enemy clashed with the newfound idea of freeing her leader and renewing the fight. Gripping the knife, her bloodlust rising, she felt uncharacteristically indecisive until reason brought her up short.

I must protect my people.

Still holding the defensive position, she sucked in a breath and asked, "And what would you have me do?"

As though he had not seen the internal conflict playing out on her face, Marcus leaned forward on his stool and pointed at the knife in her hand.

"Decide if you are going to use that or not."

Chapter 24

"Oh my Lord," Miriam gasped as she lurched back from Gerry's bed.

Jerking awake from a partial doze, Alvin jumped up from the chair he had slumped into and staggered to his feet.

"What is it?"

"They're either going to kill each other or fall in love," she answered while shaking her head. "At this point, it's a tossup as to which way it will go."

"No," Jasmina announced as she straightened and moved toward her. "Our children are getting through to them. I know they can make them work together."

"Why on earth would you think that? That Roman isn't acting as though my son is involved in any of his decisions."

"He gave her the knife, didn't he?"

"Yeah, but he wants to die, and he's just giving her the chance to do it."

Jasmina gave her head a sharp shake. "No. That's not right because it would be a dishonorable death, and that won't get him what he wants."

"What do you mean?" Miriam asked angrily.

Tim moved up beside his wife. "To a Roman, suicide is a sin unless it is for a good cause. If he's seriously committed to seeing his wife and child in the afterlife, that's not going to work for him."

Miriam glared at him, demanding, "So what does he want?"

Tim shrugged. "I think Jasmina is right. Gerry and Remmy are affecting these two in ways they don't realize. It's a delicate situation, and they have to be careful, but if they can keep the emotional pressure on, it just might work."

"But I feel so helpless because I can't hear Gerry when I'm connected to this guy. I mean, sometimes this Roman's thoughts are a one-sided conversation, as if I'm hearing someone talking on the phone, but I don't know what Gerry might be saying, or even if it is my son."

"Can Gerry hear you?" Jasmina asked.

Looking thoughtful, Miriam slowly shook her head. "I'm not sure."

"He must know the woman is Remmy, or he wouldn't be trying to get Marcus to cooperate with her."

"That's probably true, but how do we know if we're actually having an effect on them?"

"I don't know," Jasmina answered. "This girl has been resistant to everything I've suggested. If I say I want something, she seems to go out of her way to do the opposite, but she eventually seems to come around. That could only happen if Remmy heard what I wanted her to do and put pressure on her in a more subtle way."

"But how do we communicate with our children without letting their hosts know what we are up to?"

Closing her eyes, Jasmina rubbed her hands together for a moment before answering. "We don't need to hide our intentions. If we state them, Remmy and Gerry will hear and do their best to make it happen." She shrugged. "It's not perfect, but it might just work."

Miriam pushed a lock of brown hair from her face and nodded. "I get what you are trying to do, but it's a pretty big leap to trust in something you can't actually test."

Sighing, Jasmina looked at Miriam. "You believe in the good works of God, don't you?"

"Yes," she answered cautiously.

"Have you or anyone been able to actually test to see what the best form of communication is? I mean, can you actually say, 'I want this to happen' and see it come to pass?"

"Sometimes," Miriam said uncertainly.

"But even then, you aren't sure of the result or timing when a request is made."

"Sometimes God just says no."

"Yes, but you pretty much have to figure that out on your own. There's rarely an obvious sign that tells you He will or will not agree to your request, and that's what we're dealing with here. We just have to trust that our children will hear what we say and respond as best they can."

"And what if we are wrong?"

The question brought a sudden quiet to the room, and it was a long moment before Tim responded.

"We'll watch what happens, and adjust as needed."

Jasmina walked back to Remmy's bed. "And a little praying might be called for."

"I most certainly will do that," Miriam sighed. "Like I've never prayed before."

Chapter 25

Gerry Patterson. Gerry Patterson. Gerry Patterson.

My body was gone, and being in a disembodied state was so surreal that the only thing keeping me from losing it was repeating my name over and over. I just kept at it until I started to gain perspective on my situation, if *perspective* was the right word.

It felt like I was floating in a black void, with bolts of energy racing past me like cars on a busy expressway. After a time, I realized these "cars" were thoughts, and managed to connect with them. It was confusing at first, until I realized this was happening at a conscious level below what we think of as language. Once I figured that out, I began to understand what was going on.

I was no longer Gerry Patterson, not in the physical sense. Maybe mentally as well because my mind was merging with a Roman soldier, but it's not as straightforward as you might think. We weren't sharing common thoughts. We were two individuals in one body, and though we kind of had an insight into the other's thoughts, there was still a problem of communication.

It wasn't a language barrier, as our minds intersected at a level below language, where feelings, smells, emotions flew around like angry bats in a dark cave. Although he was happy in his job as a soldier, age was sneaking up on him, taking away his endurance, sapping his strength, and though he put up a good front, I could tell his chosen life was taking a toll on him. And then there were all the painful memories of a bad childhood and the more recent deaths of his wife and child.

At first, I didn't try to talk to him. I just hid inside his mind, watching, learning, and waiting to see what I was doing here. I mean, this guy's life was tame. He marched, practiced, dug ditches, built walls, and worked with his men. The normal day-to-day routine of a Roman Legionnaire was pretty dull.

And then there were exciting spells, with lots of energy expended, and orders thrown about like blasts from a rapidly-firing weapon. His adrenaline ran high in the middle of a fight and despite the threat of serious injury or even death, he was at the top of his game. But when he wasn't fighting, such sadness prevailed that I wondered if my host wasn't bipolar. At times like these, his defenses were down, and I could inject my own thoughts and feelings into his mental stream, but because we were so different, I had to be careful, because his reaction was often quite strong.

But now there was a sense of calm, like you feel right after a hard rain. My host was looking at a short, thin, very beautiful woman, her blond hair short, blue eyes glaring at him, tanned face and brown leather dress smeared with mud and blood, and a red-stained bandage covering her left shoulder.

I wonder if she will do it? Marcus was thinking.

Do what? I asked.

At first, sensing Marcus' thoughts was really confusing, because they were so intense, I wasn't sure they were mine or his. And then, when I began to realize what was going on, I started paying closer attention to what he was seeing and thinking. I have to tell you, that was a serious shock: hand-to-hand fighting, physically killing a person, ordering the enslavement of women and children, murdering those people in the cave because they were simply inconvenient. It was hard to deal with.

I also came to understand that my host also heard my thoughts and felt my feelings. Like it or not, we were starting to merge into one person, and I had to think that considering how he lived, such a transformation might be dangerous. A Roman soldier has to be tough, aggressive, and unflinching when it comes to killing. It was something that I, a modern American teenager, would not want to be. Oh yeah, I dream about being a super hero, even imagine myself as tough enough to take on someone like Marcus. But the truth is, if a person were to come at me with a weapon, I'd run or dive for cover.

A recent thought of Marcus' sums this up well: *What you are and what you wish to be are two different things.*

I was surprised by how quiet Marcus had become. His brain had been running up and down an emotional flag pole since I first connected to him, but now he was just staring at this girl, looking from her determined face, to her small breasts, and down to her narrow waist. He was thinking she was much thinner and less buxom than the others, but I also sensed a hint of arousal in him. No. He wasn't going to ravage her. He was waiting for something.

What am I going to tell her?

The thought was surprising because of the intense desperation I sense along with it. By this time, I had been communicating with him for several days. To my surprise, he wasn't all that alarmed to hear my voice. I suspect he has been arguing with an internal voice he refers to as *the Daemon* for some time and simply thinks I am him.

What do you mean?

This is your doing, Daemon. I am not so foolish as to hand my enemy a weapon and wait for her to attack me.

But you're showing her you want to make peace.

After we destroyed her village? Are you mad?

Maybe, but if she wanted to kill you, she would have done it by now.

He lifted his eyes to look at her again, and could see the uncertainty on her face.

I think she wants you to convince her that killing you is a bad thing.

I have no idea what you are talking about.

I felt him stand, his muscles taut as he saw her react defensively, but did not lift the knife from where its blade rested on her thigh.

"I…know what you are feeling…right now," he said hesitantly.

Her face hardened, eyes slitting, lips pinched into a narrow line, the knife coming up slightly.

"Not possible."

Sighing, he turned his attention to the small shrine by the entrance. "Five years ago, I retired to a small farm south of here in the Aquitania region, near the coast. I married a woman I had lived with for some time, and we settled in to work on our little patch of green in the warm climate so typical of southern Gaul.

"We already had a child, and I will tell you I had some difficulty adjusting to a life without the constant regime of army discipline."

"You grew soft," she stated, though the disdain Marcus expected was absent.

After a pause, he jerked a nod, and I felt his face flush. "There is nothing so demanding as the life of a legionnaire. It took me some time to get used to sleeping every night with a woman, or talking with a neighbor about something other than fighting, marching, or the next construction project our *centurio* had in mind for us."

To his surprise, she nodded slowly and lowered the knife again.

"You are soldier," she said knowingly. "Was such a life too strange for you?"

He shook his head. "It was at first, but I got used to it, even grew to like it."

"Until?"

"A rebel group of Tarbelli tribesmen attacked us one evening, just before dark. I was in the forest, gathering wood when they razed our village, and killed everyone in sight. I came back to find my home in flames, bodies everywhere."

"Your wife and child?"

He jerked his head left and then right before turning away. After a moment, he wiped his eyes and looked at her again.

"So you see, I do know what you are going through.

He could see puzzlement on her face for a brief moment before she scowled at him.

"You were the invaders. They only fight for land that is theirs by right."

His head shaking, he glared at her. "And I re-enlisted the very next day."

She glared back. "You want revenge."

He held her angry gaze for a long moment before looking toward the shrine.

"I am a soldier," he said softly. "It is not up to me to say who I fight, or when. I do what I am told."

"And when your leaders say attack the Nervii, the most feared warriors in all the land, you jump at the chance."

He moved quickly to her, his fisted hands clenched by his side.

"When your commanders told you to prepare for battle, did you ask where or when?"

She shook her head, but still did not lift the knife. "To defy them would be treason."

"And even as young as you are, I am sure you have seen enough fighting to fill your belly with a want for something better."

She pointed at the collar at her feet. "This is better?"

His attention jerked to the collar for a long moment before he met her eyes again.

"Before we came, you fought with your neighbors almost constantly, but Roman rule will allow you to live normal lives, without the threat of attack. You may hate us now, but in time you will thank us for giving you peace."

She spat at his feet. "You have enslaved us. What good is peace, if we cannot return to our farms and rebuild our lives?"

Marcus shook his head. "Many will be returned once the land has been secured. We only need to…"

"Ha!" she cried, the knife coming up again. "You lie! Your greedy slavers will never give us up. Your own people will take our land, steal the fruits of our hard work, and let the rest rot until there is nothing of us left. Admit it!"

"No," Marcus responded, though I knew he was lying.

"Then what of the land you were given, huh? From where did it come?"

I felt his head shaking. "The land was abandoned."

"Was there a house on it? Did animals graze in fenced fields? Did you have to dig a well for your water?"

"Yes. No, but..."

"Someone made those things, and they are now either dead or a Roman slave. Do not lie to me about sending my people back to their homes, Roman. You have no intention of doing so. Am I right?"

Marcus froze, and I felt immediately afraid as Enid pointed the knife at him. To my surprise, I sensed no fear in him.

She is holding the knife wrong, he thought. *She is making a point with it, not threatening.*

"Your leaders will be taken to Rome," he responded softly, without anger, "along with whatever booty has been accumulated, but the rest of you are to be returned if you will only swear allegiance to Rome."

"Which we will never do!"

I felt tightness in his throat as his head shook. "The choice is theirs, not yours."

She lowered the knife again, her face cautious. "What do you mean?"

"You were the leader of your troop, were you not?"

Her back straightened, feet snapping together as she glared at Marcus. "I *am* leader of my troop."

He nodded while shrugging. "Then you are coming with me to Rome."

Chapter 26

Enid wanted more than anything to lunge forward and slit the Roman's throat, but her muscles would not permit it.

What are you doing to me, Old Witch? she protested angrily while glaring at Marcus as he slumped on his stool and stared at her, his expression relaxed and expectant.

You do not want to attack him.

I want more than anything to kill this slobbering shit!

To save your people you must pretend to work with him.

I would rather lie with a rabid dog than help this Roman pestilence.

Please listen, the voice pleaded. *With the Romans in charge, the Gauls had hundreds of years of peace and prosperity. It is Roman rule that keeps the Germanic tribes from rolling in and taking over. The Germans only want your land, and will completely wipe out your people before they can reorganize to defend themselves.*

"You lie, Old Witch. My people have survived for generations without Roman help. We will carry on for another thousand years."

Even the mighty Roman army cannot completely control the Germanic tribes. What chance would your people have against them?

Invaders are invaders. We fight for our homes. We will prevail.

Like you did yesterday?

The question perplexed her, and she hardly felt the knife pressing against her thigh as she watched the Roman's eyes once again move down her body. He had done that earlier just before he told her she was to be taken to Rome, undoubtedly to be humiliated before their people and then sacrificed to one of their perverted gods.

I must escape and free as many of my people as I can.

You are one woman against hundreds of armed soldiers. That puny knife will be of little help.

As much as she hated to admit it, the old witch had a valid point.

She dropped the knife and scowled at Marcus. "Then that is where I will go."

His mouth opened briefly, but he quickly recovered. "I have your solemn oath that you will not try to escape?"

She looked briefly at the knife now sticking up from the ground next to her foot before nodding. "I swear by *Sucellus*, and his holy wife, *Nantosuelta* that I will not try to escape while in your possession."

"And you will not try to kill me?"

Must I agree to that? she thought.

Yes! The witch snapped.

"I will not try to kill you, as long as you do me no harm."

She watched warily as the Roman nodded. "I do so swear."

To her the conversation was ridiculous. Romans lied as a matter of course, so why was she making promises to him?

He isn't lying about this, the witch insisted. *He honestly needs your help.*

How would you know?

The laugh she heard was not what she expected from a witch, old or otherwise.

Because I am an old witch, and you would be wise to listen to me.

She wanted to defy her, to wait for this Roman to turn his back so she could snatch up his knife and put it to good use. However, deep-seated superstition nagged at her. One did not cross old witches, especially one powerful enough to enter a person's thoughts.

Are you a slave to these Romans? she asked.

No, Enid. I am a free woman. I only want to help your people survive.

She looked up to see the Roman looking quizzically at her.

"What is your plan?" she asked.

His head shook. "I do not have a plan, except to follow my commander's orders."

"And those are?"

"To escort our *imperator* to Rome."

"*Imperator*? You mean the one called Caesar?"

He shrugged. "Me and about four-thousand other soldiers. Our two *centuriae* will join Caesar's favorite legion, the Tenth *Equestris*. Our job will be to guard the plunder and prisoners."

The sudden discovery stunned her.

Julius Caesar. I will get the chance to kill that Roman mongrel and free Vercingetorix. Now that is a cause worth dying for!

"I will accompany you?"

He nodded. "I cannot keep you in my tent on the campaign trail. You will stay with the other slaves until we get to Rome."

"I am to be sold?"

She was surprised to see him shrug. "No. My wife's sister..." His face showed a hint of pain as he paused briefly. "...gave us a slave when..." Despite her desire to kill this Roman, the second pause made her curious. "The slave died, and you will replace her."

"But your wife's family you hate."

He nodded. "Most of them are beneath contempt, but her youngest sister is the one exception. You will do well with her."

The thought of being anyone's slave was repulsive, yet she was surprised by her next question.

"But what of your farm? Will you not return to it?"

His eyes unfocused, he slowly shook his head. "I no longer have a farm."

"And my duties?"

He shrugged. "You will do whatever she tells you to do."

She bristled when his statement revived memories of the horror stories she had heard about the Roman's treatment of slaves.

"I will not be sold on street like common whore!"

Her outburst brought him out of his thoughts, and when he looked at her, there was surprise on his face.

"She is a good person, and would never prostitute a slave for money."

"It is said such things are common in your Roman cities."

Shaking his head, he let out a long sigh. "It is not illegal, but selling slaves for sex is not encouraged." He waved a hand at her. "You have my word, she will not use you in this way."

"Then how will I be abused?"

"My wi..." She was surprised by the pain that distorted his face as he choked on the word. "I would guess you will help with her children."

"And what of your child?"

He turned away so quickly she thought he was going to rush from the tent, but he did not move except to lift both hands to his face. After a moment, he straightened, but did not look at her. Moving slowly to the shrine, he gently ran his fingers over two small statues.

"My son died along with my wife."

She was suddenly flooded with unexpected feelings that brought tears to her eyes. Now thankful he was not looking at her, she blinked twice before swiping at her eyes.

"I will do my best to serve them."

To her surprise, she was not sure if it was a lie or the truth.

Chapter 27

Peering at his laptop's screen, Tim pulled his lips to the left side of his face, absentmindedly chewing on the inside of his cheek as his fingers flew across the keys.

"What are you looking for?" Alvin asked anxiously as he shifted his attention from Tim to Jasmina and finally to his wife, her hands gripping Gerry's, eyes closed, lips tight, head tipped back.

"Something to tell us what happened after Caesar's conquest of Gaul."

Both men were silent for a moment before Alvin asked, "How is this going to change our situation?"

Tim looked at him, his expression confused. "What do you mean?"

Alvin pointed at Miriam. "She told me this isn't like those psychic connections you read about. Miriam is actually inside the head of the man our son is connected to. How is that possible?"

A scowling Tim shook his head. "Jasmina can give you a better answer, but it has to do with spirits from another universe. Most people don't even have a clue that these spirits exist, but my wife, and apparently yours as well, can connect with them and share their experiences."

"But this Roman guy died a couple thousand years ago. How can they connect with a dead guy?"

Tim scratched his head. "This is well beyond my area of expertise, but there is a theory that the future and the past already exist, and are just one infinite line that we can only see a narrow slice of."

"A theory?" Alvin said skeptically.

Chuckling, Tim shrugged. "It's the closest thing we have to explaining what's been happening."

"And how does this help our wives and children?"

"If we can figure out when assassination attempts might be possible, we can give them some idea of what to watch for."

"Caesar was killed in Rome. We know who killed him and where."

Tim shook his head. "Not this time."

"What do you mean?"

Taking a deep breath, Tim let it out slowly as he turned toward Alvin. "Apparently, someone has figured out how to manipulate past. Minor changes made thousands or even hundreds of years in the past will transform our reality into something completely different. It will most likely be a world where this…uh…*Tsabbat* creature is in control."

Alvin looked briefly at his wife and son. "Do we know anything else about this creature?"

Tim turned back to his laptop's screen and shook his head. "Just that whatever future it has in mind won't be pleasant for us."

"So what did you find out about Caesar?"

"He stayed in Gaul for several years after it was conquered, and fought many battles during that time: some in Germany, some in England, and again in Gaul." Sitting back, he interlaced his fingers at the top of his head and sighed. "There are too many opportunities to choose from."

"So what do we do?"

Tim shrugged. "He had an elite guard protecting him from assassination, and Caesar himself was a master at self-defense, so it had to be someone who could get past his defenders and put their general off his guard."

A gasp from behind pulled both men around to look at Jasmina, her eyes wide with fear.

"What?" Tim barked anxiously as he rose from his chair.

"I know who can," she whispered while moving from Remmy's bed.

"Who?" Alvin nearly shouted.

"Enid."

"Are you serious?" Tim protested. "There's no way a recently captured slave girl is going to be allowed to bring a weapon to within striking distance of Caesar."

"She will if she is with Marcus."

"Marcus?" Miriam gasped as she jerked away from her son. "What about Marcus?"

Jasmina faced her. "He is a pawn in the plot to assassinate Caesar."

"How?"

Looking at her husband until he shook his head, she turned back to Miriam. "I'm not sure, but we have to watch for something, anything that will bring Enid in contact with Caesar."

Miriam jerked her attention from her husband to her son before announcing, "I'll tell Gerry. Maybe, if we work together, we can make sure that doesn't happen."

Nodding, Jasmina faced her own husband and smiled weakly. "If only it were that simple."

Chapter 28

"*Optio*," Lucius called as he entered my tent. "The *centurio* has summoned you."

The announcement brought a strange sense of fear, and I found myself looking at Enid and wondering what was going to happen to her.

"Where is he?" I asked as automatically as my next breath.

"By the *Porta Pratoria*."

A summons by the *centurio* was never a casual thing, and despite my concern for Enid, I grabbed my helmet and hurried toward the front gate with Lucius close behind. I felt only half myself, and as such, was torn between my duty and my unexplainable feelings for my new slave.

The *centurio* was berating an unlucky soldier as I approached.

"*Optio* Marcus reporting as ordered, Sir!" I announced when he paused to take a breath.

He pointed at the soldier. "Back to your duties, and this time, try not to cut off anyone's fingers."

The soldier turned sharply and marched away as the *centurio* turned to me.

"By Jupiter," he swore. "I lose more men to sheer stupidity than the enemy has ever taken in battle."

"Another digging accident, Sir?"

His head shook slowly. "If a man is so clumsy with a spade, how can I ever trust him with a sword?"

Knowing the question was rhetorical, I kept silent. After a couple of heartbeats, the *centurio* turned to me.

"We have a change in orders," he stated. "Rome is not offering our *imperator* a triumph. It seems that politics will keep him in Gaul a while longer."

A dozen questions popped into my head, not the least of which was what would become of Enid. Yes, the *centurio* had given her to me, but that didn't mean she could remain in camp. I had to find a place to keep her or when the *centurio* found out, -- and in this tightly knit camp, he *would* find out -- I would be whipped, and undoubtedly demoted.

"What will we do with the captives?"

There goes my mouth again, blurting out what was in my head instead of obeying protocols.

To my relief, the *centurio* did not seem to pick up on my blunder.

"They will be delivered to the slavers." He waved a hand dismissively. "What they do with them, I do not care."

I struggled to breathe, feeling a panic I would not normally feel over a captured enemy. Even more surprising, I wanted to protest the deplorable abuse of those poor people. After all, they were only defending their homes.

As though sensing my distress, the *centurio* turned to scowl at me.

"Be on the lookout, *Optio*," he growled, expressing more than his usual scowl. "I hear that some of our men are keeping female slaves in their tents. We do not want the men fighting over sex partners, do we?"

"No Sir!" I responded more loudly than intended.

Looking away, he nodded. "Put together a patrol and do a sweep of the camp. Roust out any you find and deliver them to the slavers. We move out in the morning."

"Yes, Sir."

Without another word, he marched away, shouting as he pointed his wooden switch at a soldier slouching against his shovel, but my preoccupation blotted out his words. If I could not find a place to keep her, Enid would have to be delivered to the slavers. She was good looking, strong, and I would get a hefty price for her.

Then why are you so desperate to keep her? shouted in my head.

Why indeed?

I started marching toward my tent, but stopped when I realized that would not do. I had been given an order, and my personal needs would have to wait. I was struck by how desperate I suddenly felt, and was at a total loss of what to do when I spied Lucius leading a small group of men past the gate.

"Lucius," I called, and when he started walking my way, added, "What are you doing with those men?"

Saluting, he used hand signals to command the men to stop. "We are going to practice our sword work."

"I will take them. The *centurio* has ordered me to organize a sweep of the camp for captives being held in the tents."

His eyes widened. "All captives?"

"That is correct," I said, staring at him intently and hoping he was as smart as I gave him credit. "*All* captives are to be gathered up and delivered to the slavers. We move out in the morning."

Without batting an eye, he asked, "Will you be leading the patrol clearing out the captives, *Optio*?"

It was all I could do to keep my expression neutral as I looked toward the south end of the camp. The furthest from my tent.

"I will start over there. Spread the word to the men that they are to start preparing to move out and make sure the mules are ready to be loaded in the morning."

His back to the men, he smiled at me. "I will do so at once, *Optio*."

Muttering for the men to follow me, I hurried away, almost certain my friend could hide Enid for me, but that did not take away the ache in my gut. I should not have been feeling anything for this captured savage, and it irritated me that I was. I did not want a future. My only wish was for an honorable warrior's death so I could see my family again in Elysium.

Maybe he will do me a favor and fail, I thought while marching the men to the starting point.

Chapter 29

Her arguments with the witches made Enid want more than anything to hit something.

Her bladder aching, she peeked from the tent, and looked around to see the area around her devoid of legionnaires. Marcus had already dressed her as a man and snuck her into the nearby latrine several times, so she knew the way.

"I am a captive, but not a troll," she muttered while pulling one of Marcus' shirts over her leather outfit and quickly crossing the distance to the empty latrine.

Moving to a trough of water, she splashed her face and arms, rubbing off the dirt and blood. Her shoulder still burned like the fires of the sun, but she gritted her teeth and endured, unwilling, even in this private moment, to show her weakness, lest it overwhelm her and deprive her of the opportunity to kill the hated Roman's general.

You can't kill him, the old witch protested.

To banish her, Enid splashed cold water on her face before pulling off her clothes to do the same for her entire body. Staying close to her clothes, she remained alert for the sound of anyone approaching.

As her body dried, she took a wet cloth and wiped blood and sweat off her leather clothing and then put them on still wet.

You have to help us stop Caesar's assassination, the younger witch pleaded.

"I will gladly die to free my people of that plagued monster," she muttered while pulling on her top. "Without him to lead them, our warriors will cut them down like wheat."

He wasn't there when your village was taken.

She spit on the ground. "We were mostly farmers, old men, and children."

And how many of your warriors survived the last battle against Caesar?

The question made Enid stop.

"I do not know what became of them. I suspect most were killed or captured."

"And what have we here?" a deep, guttural voice asked from behind her.

Enid jerked around to gawk at Quintus' round head and ruddy face, but what surprised her even more was the many bite marks on his face, neck and arms. His clothes were wet and muddy as though he had just waded through a swamp.

His malicious glare made her fighting instincts immediately kick in, and she faced him, knees slightly bent, hands forward, eyes scanning the space nearby for a weapon, and finding none.

Anything can be a weapon, her commander's voice echoed in her head as Quintus pulled out a long knife and took several steps toward her.

While keeping eyes on him, she spotted a basin at the corner of her vision. Though he was half-again heavier than her, Quintus stopped when she took a quick step toward him. She took advantage of his hesitation by grabbing the wooden basin and heaving it at him. Though the experienced legionnaire easily ducked out of its way, the momentary distraction gave Enid enough time to quickly close the distance between them.

The overconfident soldier's laugh was cut off when she slammed both fists into his face. Reacting instinctively to the assault, the soldier brought the knife around to stab at Enid's neck, but she threw her shoulder into his chest, knocking him backwards. As he struggled to regain his balance, she continued pushing until his foot snagged something and he went down.

Unfortunately, his knife was behind Enid, and as Quintus fell back, its blade sliced into her left shoulder.

"Gaaahh!" she cried while scrambling over his body.

Slamming her left foot into his crotch, she tried to lunge in the direction of the open doorway, but her foot snagged in his clothing. Loosing her balance, she fell forward, her knees thumping against his chest. Under normal circumstances, she might have escaped, but Quintus was a well-conditioned Roman legionnaire, and though he howled like a wounded bear, he reacted quickly.

Looking back, she saw his knife moving toward her ribs, and pressed her body against his. Her waist now at his face, she tried to slam his head with her fists, but could not manage enough force to do more than annoy him.

The knife blade cut into her right side, slicing a shallow groove just below her ribs. Screaming, she tried to roll into his right arm in a vain effort to limit his use of the knife, but he was too strong, and in a flash, the fingers of his left hand were wrapping around her neck.

With one strong tug, he pulled her down his body until they were face-to-face, then slammed his forehead into hers. The impact stunned her, and before she could react he smacked her again, nearly knocking her unconscious.

She felt herself being rolled off as Quintus swore more Roman curses than she knew. When she tried to rise, she was roughly shoved back to slam her head on the wooden floor. She felt a tug on her top and then it was gone. Another tug on her leather skirt, and from the coolness on her skin, knew it was also off her.

"Oooo I am going to have fun with this Gallic slut," Quintus was saying as he yanked her legs apart and she heard him grunt when his knees thumped against the dirt floor.

Her head still spinning, she tried to rise and take a swing at him, but her fist bounced off solid muscle. When she tried again, Quintus swore and then something solid smashed her face, sending her to the edge of consciousness.

She tried to fight her way back, to continue the struggle, but her vision grew darker and darker until all she could hear was her attacker's distorted voice. She groped at his waist in a feeble effort to prevent the coming violation, stopping only when her fingers wrapped around something long and hard.

She gripped the shaft and pushed, surprised that it seemed to move farther than she anticipated, but before she could do more, another blow slammed her head against the wood floor.

Chapter 30

Jasmina jerked back from her niece, gasping in shock as Remmy screamed. She looked up to see both men jump to their feet and move toward her, but Miriam stayed focused on her son.

"Miriam!" she shouted. "You have to warn Gerry. Quintus is attacking Enid."

Tim immediately changed direction to grab Miriam's shoulder and give it a sharp shake.

"What are you doing?" Alvin demanded.

"She has to warn Gerry!"

"What?" Miriam cried, her eyes wide.

"Marcus has to get back to Enid now," Jasmina shouted. "She's being attacked."

Looking stunned, Miriam slowly shook her head. "He can't. His commander has ordered him to search the camp for captive women. He can't very well stop doing that to run off and protect a woman he's not supposed to have in his tent."

"Then what can we do?"

"He sent his friend, Lucius to hide her. Hopefully, he'll arrive in time to stop the attack."

"That's no good," Jasmina protested as she moved away from Remmy's bed. "If Lucius and Quintus fight over the girl, she will be exposed. Then Marcus will have no choice but to sell her to the slavers."

"But Quintus knows about her, so that's already happened."

Jasmina shook her head. "I've been connected to Marcus long enough to know that strict military discipline will keep Quintus from going over his head. The only way he can expose the girl is to do something that would force Marcus to punish him. Then the centurion would have to be told why he was being disciplined."

"Connect to him," Tim added. "He has to get there before the fight gets out of hand."

"And what is he going to say to his men?"

"He doesn't have to say anything to them. He's their superior, and in the Roman army, that's all that matters."

"It won't make any difference," Miriam countered. "He's still caught in a quandary over the woman. He can't discipline Quintus for attacking her without exposing his own indiscretion."

"He can if he gets there while Lucius and Quintus are fighting."

"But how will that help?" Jasmina asked.

Tim shook his head. "The centurion won't care why they fought. His only concern is that these men work together as a unit, and if Marcus deals with them, he won't bother getting involved."

"But what if Quintus blurts out his reason for being attacked."

"This guy is a brute, but he's not that stupid. If he plays the victim, he will look weak. Not something a leader wants to see in his men. He'll keep his mouth shut or face even harsher discipline."

Jasmina's eyes jerked from Alvin to her husband to Miriam. "Get back in contact with Marcus and tell him what is going on. He has to get to Enid as soon as he can or she may well be killed. Even if he hasn't developed an attachment for her, she has to be worth something financially." She shook her head when Miriam's eyebrows rose. "I know what he's been telling himself, but from the way he's been acting around Enid, I think he's falling in love with her."

Nodding, Miriam grabbed her son's hands, but to everyone else's surprise, she jerked back, pulling her hands to her chest.

"Oh my God," she cried.

"What is it?"

"It was like an electrical shock." Moving close to her son again, she slowly lowered a hand to touch him, but jerked it back before she made contact. "Why is he doing that?"

Looking down at Remmy, Jasmina hesitated briefly before putting a hand on hers, sighing with relief when she found her skin cool, but not shocking. Sighing again, she gripped her niece's hands tightly and closed her eyes.

"Wake up," she pleaded. "You have to defend yourself."

Her mind still filled with darkness, she started a mantra, "Wake up Enid. Wake up Enid. Wake up Enid." Repeating it again and again until she felt a leg bump her thigh. Jasmina flinched when her head suddenly throbbed with pain, and she felt Enid's disorientation as the young woman opened her eyes to see the double image of Quintus kneeling between her legs. She felt Enid's head shake as the girl struggled to clear her vision, and the brain fog from her recent beating.

"Come on, old dog," Quintus pleaded, his eyes on his crotch as he massaged his limp member. "Don't fail me now."

Jasmina knew that at any other time, Enid would have laughed at his masculine failure, but right now it was all she could do to get her scrambled wits about her.

Feeling cold, she looked down to see her clothes had been cut away, and she lay naked in front of him. It took her several heartbeats to realize that in his distress over his inability to perform, he was not holding her down.

Get out of there! Jasmina shouted.

Finally finding something she and the old woman could agree on, she jerked her feet up, and started to push herself away from him. Quintus reacted quickly, slamming a hand into the middle of her chest to knock her to the floor.

"Damned witch," he shouted angrily. "You put a hex on me." Grabbing his large knife, he pointed it at her face. "Take it off or I skin you alive."

Though she knew a powerful witch could interfere with a man's libido, she had no idea how it was done. Even so, she was certain this brute would not believe her.

Make him think you can, Jasmina insisted.

She felt the young woman's hesitation, and her certainty that the suggestion was absurd. She also realized Enid was still reeling from Quintus' abuse, but to her relief, she did not hesitate long.

"I will," she gasped while struggling to control herself, "if you release me."

Quintus moved the blade closer to her face. "Maybe I will slice off that pretty little nose of yours. What do you think of that?"

Spasmming stomach muscles flushed the haze from her mind. Keeping her eyes on Quintus, she did her best to mask her fear.

"Disfigurement makes a witch even more powerful, Roman," she stated with a calmness she definitely did not feel. "If you think your little *soldier* is having problems now, wait until I shrink it to insignificance."

Though the knife stayed close to Enid's face, Quintus' eyes showed he was taking her threat seriously.

"Remove the hex first," he more pleaded than demanded.

Realizing she now had the upper hand, but only if she did not show fear, Enid slowly shook her head. "What kind of witch would I be if I removed it while you were still between my legs?"

The shaking weapon meant Quintus was undergoing an internal fight between his anger and fear. It was all Enid could do to maintain a stern expression as the knife hovered next to her left cheek. The moment dragged on, getting more dangerous with each passing minute until Quintus squeezed his eyes shut, and grunted like a constipated cow.

Though the threat also had her heart beating hard, Jasmina stayed silent when she sensed that Enid was trying to think of alternatives. She felt Enid's hand slide slowly across the floor, and both women were surprised when it bumped into something hard. Not sure what she had, and afraid to take her eyes off her attacker, Enid wrapped her fingers around the object. Only when she had a full grip on it did she realize it was the handle of knife she had pulled from Quintus' clothes just before he knocked her unconscious.

In addition to carrying a sword, every Roman soldier had two knives. One was large and used in battle for slitting throats and stabbing. The smaller one was a utility knife, employed when the larger one was too cumbersome to be useful. Once Enid had a good grip on this smaller knife, her arm muscles tensed in preparation for bringing it up to her attacker's neck.

The knife near her nose shook as she mentally counted down in preparation for her move.

Five. Four. Three. Two.

She shifted her body ever so slightly in preparation: tensing leg muscles, tightening stomach, bicep hardening as she counted the last number and…

Grunting angrily, Quintus jerked back, his face a mixture of fear and loathing as he rose to his feet, his underwear still around his ankles.

"Take it off!"

Despite her years of training as a citizen soldier, Enid could feel her hands trembling. To hide it she pressed them to the floor and pushed herself into a sitting position.

She pulled the knife close to her thigh, realizing that her small blade would be useless against his larger one unless she could take him by surprise.

"When I am safely clear of you only," she insisted, hoping that Quintus was too upset to hear the quavering in her voice. "Pull up drawers and leave. When you are gone, I remove hex."

Quintus glared at her for another long moment before angrily sheathing his knife. Enid slowly rose as he pulled up his drawers and tied them off. She tried to pull her leather vest around to cover her breasts, but it was too badly damaged to be of any use. Without taking her eyes off him, she tossed the ruined top aside and pulled on the tunic Marcus had given her.

"How do I know you will keep your word?" Quintus asked accusingly, as though he were now the victim.

Gripping the small knife by the blade, she held the hilt out to him. After he took it, she glared at him.

"Because, unlike you, I am honorable woman." Though it was a struggle, she kept her face stern. "Hex take time to wear off, but all be normal by morning."

He pointed the blade at her. "Why should I believe a savage?"

She pointed at his crotch. "Is that not proof enough?"

Quintus stood for a long moment until the sound of footsteps outside seemed to shock him awake. Shoving the knife into its sheath, he raced out the entrance.

It was all she could do to keep from collapsing as she turned to follow his progress only to see Lucius appear in the entrance a moment later.

"What are you doing here?" he demanded angrily.

Surprised by his aggressiveness, she pulled the tunic tight against her body and glared at him.

"That pig tried to rape me," she growled.

Her statement stopped him, and he looked at the departing Quintus.

"Tried?"

When he looked at Enid, she nodded. "He have...problem."

"By Jupiter. You hexed him?"

"I think your Jupiter not look favorably on that one."

Shaking his head, Lucius did not even try to hide his amusement as he moved closer to Enid.

"You have become a liability. No?"

Enid suddenly longed for the knife she had given Quintus.

"What you mean?"

"We are not going back to Rome for a long while, and the *centurio* has banned all but a few slaves in camp. Without a plan for dealing with you, Marcus will have to deliver you to the slavers. What do you think of that?"

"So?" she countered. "I stay with them until time is right."

Lucius shook his head. "The slavers will be leaving for Italy soon. If you go with them, you will not be coming back to Marcus."

"And what will become of me?"

"I am sure some very rich, very ugly, and very old man will pay handsomely for a beauty like you. Don't you think?"

"Hunh," she grunted. "Maybe I slit my own throat."

"You have a point, pretty one," he said while moving back to the entrance and looking out, "but if you do not like that choice, start thinking of an alternative, and quickly."

Chapter 31

This is so seriously unreal, I'm having trouble telling where Gerry Patterson ends and Marcus Aremus begins. I can tell you, he's nothing like me. There is no way I'd ever be able to kill someone as callously as this guy does. Of course, that's the world he lives in. If he wasn't this brutal, he'd most likely be dead by now.

As such, I'm afraid to try to exert much influence on him. Of course, at times, it hasn't been a choice. When he thought about selling Remmy, uh, I mean Enid to the slavers, I couldn't very well sit back and let him do it now, could I? On the other hand, he lives by so many unbreakable rules, I'm afraid that my butting in will get him beaten, demoted, or worse.

I've tried making suggestions, but he most often ignores them. Even so, I can't let him lose Enid. I heard my mother telling him it was important to keep Enid close, so that means Remmy is connected to her, and I'm pretty sure we're together for a reason.

I can hear Mom's voice, but I don't think she can hear me. I've no idea how she got connected to Marcus, but right now all I care about is doing what I'm supposed to do and get out of this guy's head. Maybe I'm just a wuss, but there have been plenty of times, if I had been in my own body, I'd have thrown up or passed out.

I try to think about my previous past-life experience connected to a Han Dynasty soldier, or the one before that with an abused woman in late 19th century England. The Han Dynasty soldier had to fight, but I wasn't as connected to him as I am to this guy.

Marcus is a focused man on a mission: to die honorably in battle. As far as I can tell, my job is to make sure he doesn't. At least not before he stops the premature assassination of Julius Caesar.

At times I feel at one with the guy, like right now as we march through the camp, searching soldier's quarters for hidden captives. Despite the front he is putting up for his subordinates, he can't stop thinking about Enid. Will Lucius get to her in time? Even if he does, will she go with him? Where will he hide her? It will have to be outside the camp, but if so, will she run away?

I didn't need the distraction, but I couldn't stop worrying about Remmy. Her fate is linked to Enid's, and that means if she tries to run away and is caught,

Remmy will experience the same abuse and humiliation as Enid. As much as I didn't want to think about it, being connected to Marcus made me fully aware of how the Romans treated their captive women. You don't convert a captive into a submissive slave by being nice to them. If she is taken away from Marcus, her future is grim.

"*Optio*," a soldier called as he snapped a sharp salute. "We have searched this entire section of the camp and found two captive women."

I could feel Marcus give a sharp nod, but he also felt a sense of angst. Or was it me projecting my own fear onto him?

"Have two men take them to the slavers. They can join up with us as we search the next section."

"At once, *Optio*," the soldier responded with another salute before he did a quick spin and marched back to a small cluster of men holding two struggling women.

A legionnaire next to one of the women, gave her a backhand that sent her to the ground. Both women screamed as she fell. The first tried to jump back up, but was knocked down again. When she stayed down, the soldier barked a command at the second woman. At first, she did not seem to understand him, but when he held up a fist and shook it at her, she went silent and lowered her head.

"Brutus. Ansio," the soldier who had spoken with Marcus called. "Take them to the slavers and get back here as quick as you can. We will move onto the next section. Bring the money to the *optio*. He will deliver it to the *signifer*."

I knew from my short time in Marcus' head that the *signifer* was the unit's standard bearer, he was the only legionnaire who wore an animal skin like a cape with the animal's head covering his helmet. Most importantly, the *signifer* managed our *centuria's* pension money.

Strange combination, I thought.

Brutus grabbed the woman on the ground, roughly yanked her up, and gave her a shove. Caught off guard, she managed two steps before falling again. The soldier picked her up again and slapped her hard on the butt before pushing her in the direction of the slaver's camp. The second woman grabbed her arm and tried to help, but the first shook free and turned to glare at her captor. The defiance cost her another fist in the face that sent her sprawling. As she tried to crawl away, Brutus grabbed a handful of her hair and yanked her up again, holding her only long enough to regain her footing.

"We're not likely to get much for that one," a soldier next to Marcus complained. "Why do these Gallic women have to be so troublesome?"

It was a good thing I wasn't in control of Marcus' body because I'd have knocked the man down and kicked him for treating that woman so brutally. I could tell my anger confused Marcus because he shifted uncomfortably and turned his attention away from the women.

"Let's move on," he commanded. "The camp will be packing up soon. Our time is short."

Frustration made me want to scream, but as much as I abhorred this violence, I also knew that this wasn't the 21st Century, and protesting this outrage would only cause problems for Marcus. As much as I hated to admit it, I needed him to be at least an *optio* if I was going to have any chance of saving Julius Caesar's life.

No longer able to see the women, I was preparing to shout out that Marcus needed to get back to Enid when an electrical shock surged through me.

What is happening? I cried.

What is it now, Daemon? Are you also offended by our treatment of that slave?

You don't feel that?

The intensity of the sensation increased as he stabbed a finger at a nearby tent.

"Two of you start here and work down this row." He pointed at the next row. "The rest of you, two to a row. Hurry. We have little time."

Moving with the first pair, he asked, *What is it I am supposed to feel?*

An electrical shock.

What is 'electrical'?

How do you explain electricity to a man whose world totally lacks any trace of it?

It's kind of a buzzing feeling that makes your muscles spasm.

Never heard of that.

The intensity of the sensation increased, and I felt a loss of connection with the future. The place in my…head where my mother's consciousness had been was now totally empty and that sent me into a panic.

Jasmina? Mom? Where are you?

"Who are you talking…" Marcus stopped when he realized he had spoken out loud. *What are you talking about, Daemon?*

The buzzing changed with his shift in mood, and it was obvious he was in a very foul one.

You want to get back to Enid just as much as I do, I said.

The statement made him stop, and at the same moment the level of buzzing energy spiked. As the sensation intensified, I struggled to maintain focus.

You know I'm right!

His steps were now stilted, like he was fighting me for control, his thoughts wordless and angry. He looked around as if to gauge the progress of his men, and decide if he had enough time to sneak away, but in the next instant it no longer mattered.

After another step, the buzzing totally stopped, and in that stretched-out instant between total chaos and total calm, it hit me. I could now feel the weight of his armor on my shoulders, staff in my hand, and helmet on my head. Stumbling, I felt his sandaled feet pressing onto the ground, the bottom of his kilt slapping against bare legs, and muscles tightening as I steadied myself.

I was no longer in Marcus' head.

I was Marcus.

"Oh my God," I gasped and looked around to make sure there was no one close enough to hear me.

What is happening?

I almost fell over with relief at hearing his question.

"Marcus. You and I are sharing a body, but I am dominant now. You have to help me get back to Enid and stop her being sold to the slavers."

The centurio has given the order. I cannot disobey.

Panic tightened my chest as I saw the men reaching the end of the row of tents they were searching.

"What do I say to them?"

Tell them to move on to the next row.

"But I don't speak Latin."

What do you speak?

"English."

Anglich? What is that?

I remembered from history class that during this time England was still held by the Celts. The English language didn't exist in 51 BC.

"It is the language of wizards. None of your people will understand it."

I understand you.

"Yes, but that is because we are sharing thoughts."

So what now?

It was then I realized that when he spoke there was a different tempo, and though I understood what he was saying, it felt strange.

"Say the words and I will try to mimic them."

How will that help?

Looking around, I was surprised to see Marcus' men heading my way.

"Just do it."

Keep searching. Back soon.

I noticed the sensation again and did my best to emulate it while motioning to the approaching men.

"Keep searching." I pointed at Marcus' tent. "Back soon."

My legs went wobbly when the men bobbed their heads and continued on. After releasing a long breath, I remembered what I was here to do, and took off, wanting to run, but knowing that would only attract attention.

I had no idea what to do once I got there, or how to communicate with Enid. After all, it would be pretty obvious something was wrong if I had to pause to ask Marcus to say a phrase for me.

Halfway to the tent, I realized I didn't need to worry about words because Marcus and I shared a consciousness. Latin was now a part of my consciousness. I only needed to use it, and that was where the strange sensation came in. When I was thinking in that way, I was thinking in Latin.

Focusing on the sensation, I started saying, "The rain in Spain lies mainly in the plain."

I kept repeating the phrase while focusing on the feeling, finding that with each iteration, it was easier and easier to do. Surprisingly, I also realized that I could think in Latin as well.

"*Imbrem in Hispania consistit in campo.*"

A nervous laugh escaped as I neared the tent. With no other recourse, and feeling sweat beading on my forehead, I walked up to the guard Marcus had posted there.

"You are relieved," I said with as much authority as I could.

"Yes, Sir," he responded without hesitation.

Knowing I couldn't just stand outside the tent looking hesitant, I charged through the entrance to find Enid glaring at me.

"I kill you now," she growled, her knife inches from my throat.

Chapter 32

After taking a sip of tea, Miriam looked at her son and froze.

"He moved," she whispered.

His magazine dropping from his lap, Alvin jumped up. "He what?" When Miriam did not respond, he turned to see his son lying quietly on the bed. "Are you serious?"

As his wife continued to stare at Gerry, Alvin slowly approached the bed while shifting his attention from one to the other and back. He was nearly to Gerry's bedside when the young man jerked into a sitting position, eyes wide, muscles tense, his hands up as though he were prepared to fight off an attacker.

"*Ubi sum ego!*" he cried.

When Alvin stepped back, Gerry scanned the room before grabbing the bed's side rail and leaping out. Landing in a slight crouch, his hands at the ready, he faced a shocked Alvin and demanded, "*Quod genus Daemonum vobis?*"

"Oh God," Alvin gasped.

"Careful," Miriam warned. "That's not our son."

"What do you mean?"

"Gerry doesn't speak Latin. This guy is now Marcus."

Glancing at her, Alvin returned his attention to the young man. "How do you know it's Latin?"

"*Ubi sum ego!*" the young man demanded.

Miriam shook her head. "He just said, 'Where am I?' Gerry wouldn't know to do that."

They all froze for a long moment before Marcus turned his attention to the room's only door. Seeming to realize what he might do, Alvin moved between him and the door, both hands in front of his body, palms forward.

"Please stop," he pleaded. "You don't want to go out there."

"*Qhid?*" Marcus asked, his expression puzzled.

Though he did not understand the word, Alvin could tell from Marcus' expression that he understood him.

"You know what I am saying?"

"*Ego intelligo.*"

Shaking his head, Alvin could only stare at him, his mouth open, hands still up.

"I understand *you* as well, Roman," Miriam said with a determination that made Alvin turn to look at her.

"You do?"

Without taking her eyes off Marcus, Miriam nodded. "We've been connected for the better part of a day. Somehow, we've learned each other's languages."

Still in a fighter's crouch, the Roman shook his head. "*Non certus sum possum.*" He looked at Alvin then back to Miriam. "No sure I am that this be possible."

"It *is* possible," she insisted, "but you need to calm down because we can help each other."

Still shaking his head, Marcus' expression changed from confused to angry. "I know not how you do this, but go back I must."

"We didn't do this," Jasmina announced as she hurried around Remmy's bed to stop only a few feet short of Marcus.

His aggressive demeanor vanished upon seeing her, and he pulled back, his hands now up as though trying to push her away.

"*Ego autem mortuus sum? Quis enim es tu?*"

Jasmina shook her head. "No. You are not dead, but your general, Julius Caesar may soon be if you don't help us."

He hesitated for a long moment before lowering his hands. "How know you this?"

"There's no time to explain. We have to move quickly or the person now occupying your body is going to die."

After another pause, Marcus' face turned suspicious again. "You try trick me. This no Hades." He slapped his chest with both hands. "I not dead."

"*Fatuus!*" Miriam shouted. "Do you think we brought you here to play games?"

Mouths agape, Jasmina and Alvin watched Miriam hurry around the bed to stand in front of Marcus, her fist clenched in front of her.

"Yes, I called you an idiot because your petty problems are like dust to us. We have bigger fish to fry."

He gave Jasmina a questioning look before focusing on Miriam. "Bigger fish? *Quid?*"

"Your general -- the one you call *Imperator* -- is about to be assassinated before his time, and we brought you here because you were too slow to realize how important Enid is in helping you stop them."

His eyes went wide at the mention of his captive's name.

"She is slave only. I sell her."

"No," Miriam insisted. "You have to keep her with you."

"No possible."

"It is no longer your choice," Jasmina countered as she moved closer to Marcus, but motioned to Miriam. "Her son now controls your body and he's in charge."

"But if he defy *centurio*, he die."

Miriam jerked a nod. "Then you have to help us make sure he doesn't die."

Marcus shook his head. "I tell you. No possible."

"Well, with your years of experience in the army, you're the one to do it. If you don't, both you and my son will die."

Without speaking, Marcus continued to shake his head.

"How will you account for your life in front of the three judges, Roman?" she shouted angrily. "Will they look kindly on your mistreatment of a poor woman, or will they see you as a brave warrior who had no fear of even the gods when asked to do good? Your family awaits you in the Elysian Fields, but you won't get there this way."

Marcus shook his head. "What gods are you who abuse me even after I die? I am good soldier. I make all needed sacrifices."

"Well, that's not how it looks to…"

"What in Heaven's Name is all the shouting about?" a nurse protested as she rushed into the room. She stopped as everyone turned toward her, her eyes searching every face until she stopped on Marcus. "And who is this?"

Miriam moved a step closer to Marcus. "This is…well…my son."

Looking at Marcus again, the nurse shook her head. "I don't think so. Your son's hair is blond. This man's is much darker."

"I no be her son," Marcus argued. "I am *optio* in Legio Eleven Claudia. I fight for might of Rome!"

Though briefly taken aback by his statement, the nurse recovered quickly. "You don't say."

Marcus jerked a nod. "I do say. It is truth."

"He's delirious," Miriam said with a hint of panic in her voice. "You need to sedate him."

"No!" Jasmina protested. "If you put him to sleep, we lose the connection to Gerry."

"It's not going to happen anyway," the nurse chimed in. "I'm not giving anyone anything without a doctor's order, so let's forget the sedating thing." She turned again to Marcus and pointed at the tube attached to his arm. "We need to get you back into bed before you yank out that IV."

Marcus shook his head. "I no need bed. I need clothes. Where my *arma*? How you say, soldier's clothes."

"He thinks he's a Roman legionnaire," Miriam announced conspiratorially to the nurse. "He's obviously having a bad reaction to something you're giving him."

The nurse shook her head. "We're not giving him anything but saline."

When she pointed again at the IV tube, Marcus seemed to notice it for the first time. Without hesitating, he grabbed the tube and yanked it from his arm.

"What you do to me?"

Holding her hands in front of her, palms out, the nurse insisted, "It's just a saline drip to keep you hydrated, Sir. It won't hurt you."

"You are witch," Marcus growled as he tossed the IV tube away. "Take away your curse and return me to my people."

Moving only her head, the nurse looked at Jasmina. "What is he talking about?"

Jasmina shook her head. "He's confused. He thinks you are…"

"Hey Dude!" a different male voice greeted. "What's all the fuss about?"

Everyone turned to watch Robert, the EMT rush into the room, but his eyes were on Marcus.

Their attention shifted again when Marcus shouted, "*Dis gratias! Gaudeo te.*"

Gasping at his declaration, Miriam turned to Robert.

"Why is he happy to see *you*?"

"You understand him?" Robert asked as he stopped beside the nurse.

"Don't avoid the question."

He shrugged. "Maybe I look like someone he knows."

"And maybe you *are* someone he knows," Jasmina said as she moved next to Miriam.

He hesitated, as though trying to make a decision, and then nodded.

"Maybe I am."

Chapter 33

"You must listen to me," Enid shouted, her chin down, eyes angry, mouth stretched in a thin line. "Your mother. No longer she speaks to you."

I hesitated, not because I knew Marcus' mother was long dead, but because her knife was only inches from my throat.

Even so, I had to ask, "What do you mean?"

Lowering the knife as she turned away, Enid swore in her guttural language before looking at me again, her face distorted with confusion.

"This is *caothach*…how you say…madness!"

"What are you talking about?"

Snorting angrily, she shook her head as though there were bees in her hair. When she looked at me again, her face was so distorted I hardly recognized her.

"The witch in my head begs for me to say your mother can speak with you no longer. She say you call her a *daemon femina*. I know not what this means."

For a long moment my thoughts stopped.

Mom! shouted in my head. *She's trying to reach me.*

What struck me was the sudden silence that followed the thought. I knew I was now in control, but hoped Marcus was still in there somewhere.

"Enid. You have to tell her…"

I stopped when Enid jerked her head up to look at me, her expression both angry and puzzled. It took me a long moment to realize I had just spoken in English.

Something had changed, and it took me several heart beats to realize that the only thoughts I now heard were my own. I sucked in a quick breath when it was clear Marcus and I hadn't just switched places in the same body.

Marcus was gone altogether.

Chapter 34

"Are you Beauregard?" Jasmina asked Robert expectantly. "Or more precisely, were you the spirit who occupied the dog that saved Gerry's life in his first past-life connection?"

"What she say?" Marcus asked, his attention on Robert.

After looking from one person to the other, Robert shrugged. "Maybe that's not the priority here." He nodded at Marcus. "Our mutual friend cannot leave this room. He is a two-thousand-year-old man who has no experience with our twentieth-century world.

"I no two-thousand-year-old man," Marcus bellowed as he dropped a shoulder and charged forward.

Robert tried to react, but he was not fast enough to avoid Marcus' fist as it hammered his gut.

The other three people froze as the EMT flew back to land hard on the floor. Before anyone could even cry out, Marcus slammed through the door and stopped.

As Miriam, Alvin, and the nurse rushed to Robert, Jasmina followed Marcus.

"You must not leave."

Spinning around, he tried to scowl at her, but his wide eyes made it clear he was also afraid.

"What is this place?"

Shaking her head, Jasmina held out both hands. "I will explain it all to you, but you must come back. Please!"

"No! I will find my unit. I must do my duty."

"You won't find your people out there, Marcus. If you come back inside, we will work together to get you back to them."

"How you do that?"

She looked back at the foursome to see that Robert was now sitting up, but still gasping for air.

Marcus pulled back when he saw me. He thinks...

"I am a very powerful witch, Marcus," she said while lowering her chin and trying her best to look confident despite her racing heart. "I brought you here and I can send you back. Trust me when I say it is not something you can do on your own."

After taking a quick look around, Marcus returned his attention to Jasmina. "I must go back now."

She took a deep breath.

Don't let him see your nervousness. Be confident. Positive.

"Not right now. There are things we must do before that can happen."

What things? Hopefully he won't ask, because I have no idea.

"What things must you do?"

Jasmina's mind froze for a long moment before she heard someone grunt behind her.

"Marcus! Dude," Robert gasped. "You seriously have to chill, man. Jasmina has it under control."

Hesitating, Marcus jerked his attention from Robert, still bent over from the attack, to Jasmina, staring at her with an expression she found hard to read.

"What have you under control, Witch?"

You can't hesitate!

"You have to believe me," she said as calmly as she could. "My only desire is to stop an assassination attempt on your general. That is why you are here."

"What I can do? I know of no one who would kill my *imperator*, except half Gallic tribes, but their armies are defeated. They no longer are threat to us."

"What about Pompey?"

"He hides in Rome. He never attack Caesar with six legions at his back."

"But does he need to take on Caesar's legions when a vial of poison or a quick stab in the back will do the trick. Not every general is killed in battle."

"Many times it has been tried. Guards of Caesar fiercely loyal, and the gods give him gift to read intentions on any man's face."

"A lot of good that will do him," Jasmina muttered.

"What? Now you can see future?"

Jasmina laughed. "In your general's case, I can. He will not be going to Rome. At least, not for a couple of years. His next move will be to invade England."

"But those not my orders. Our legion accompanies our *imperator* to Rome for triumph. In morning we move out."

"But that's not possible," Miriam cried, her eyes jerking from Jasmina to her possessed son. "We know he doesn't..."

"Wait!" Jasmina barked, her eyes locked on Marcus. "This is it."

"It?" Miriam asked anxiously. "What it?"

"This is where history changes. The *Tsabbat* is making his move."

"How do you know?"

Turning toward Miriam, she shook her head. "Our history shows that, at this time, the Roman Senate turned down Caesar's request for a triumphal march through Rome, but what if someone intercepted that refusal and replaced it with a different message."

"To what end?"

She turned to Marcus, whose sour expression made it clear he already understood the ramifications of the move.

"It is long way to Rome. If my *imperator* believe he is returning hero, his guard, it will be down."

Jasmina nodded eagerly. "And there will be many opportunities to assassinate him."

"Hoc nefas est!" Marcus growled. "Who would do such a thing to our greatest general?"

Tim moved up beside Jasmina. "The one who would gain the most would be Pompey."

His head jerking from side to side, Marcus barked a laugh. "Caesar is no such fool!" He shouted while grabbing for the hilt of a sword that was no longer there. Realizing the weapon was missing, he looked briefly at his left hip before adding, "Many try, but only their widows left to mourn them."

"This is a daemon with powers beyond any your general could imagine. Not even Caesar can defy the gods."

"If god take mortal form, he can."

"But he stands a better chance of surviving with our help," Jasmina countered.

"But what I can do? You take me from there." He swept a hand at his surroundings. "I no can help from here."

Jasmina shook her head. "We have not taken…" Suddenly seeming to realize what she must do, she nodded. "We brought you here so that one of our own can occupy your body. It is vitally important that we move quickly, and you weren't cooperating."

Though Miriam gasped, Marcus kept his attention on Jasmina.

He laughed. "Your imposter will be undone."

"I don't think so," Jasmina said as she pulled a small mirror from her purse and turned it toward Marcus. "As you can see, we didn't bring your body here, just your soul."

"You try to deceive. Such as this cannot be done."

"And yet, there you are, looking at yourself in the mirror. Is that face yours?"

He stared at the image for a long moment. The hair color and eyes were like his, but the face was very different. He turned to her and jerked a no. "What witchcraft is this?"

"The kind that will get you killed if you don't cooperate," Jasmina insisted. "No matter what happens, you have to believe we have your best interest in mind, and that of your general."

"And if I no do as you say?"

She shrugged. "Then your general's assassination will start a chain of events that will probably plunge Rome into a dark period from which it may never recover."

"You lie. To Rome this cannot happen."

"Are you willing to take that chance?"

Tearing his eyes from the mirror, Marcus looked at each of his three companions. He looked at the mirror again, turning it over to see...what, he wasn't sure, but this had to be a trick.

When Jasmina coughed, he turned to look at her. Her clothing was different, in fact everyone's was. He looked around the room again, seeing tiny lights but no flame, objects with strange writing in their surface that mysteriously changed as he watched it.

This has to be the work of the gods, he thought before nodding.

"I am yours to command."

Chapter 35

"I do not understand," Enid said, her expression still both angry and curious.

I've got to speak Latin!

My mind froze. This wasn't going to work if I kept babbling on in a language that hadn't yet been invented.

Mom? Are you there? I stopped briefly to listen to the terrifying silence in my head. *No. She's not.*

Panic stopped my breathing, and it was a moment before I regained focus. Thankfully, it did not take long to find the sensation I had earlier, merge with it, and speak.

"Do you understand me now?"

"Why shouldn't she understand you?" a deep voice asked from behind me.

I turned to see a smiling Lucius. My first reaction was to suck in a sharp breath, but Lucius' attention had moved to Enid, and he didn't seem to notice my reaction.

"She doesn't speak our language well," I finally blurted.

Lucius shrugged, his eyes still on Enid. "She spoke it well enough to me. Is that not correct, little flower?"

I was still at a loss of what to say when I remembered that I outranked Lucius. Even if he was Marcus' friend, I did not need to explain myself to him.

"What are we to do with her?"

Turning to face me, Lucius shrugged. "I found a caravan leader amongst the camp followers who is willing to keep her for you."

Something left over from Marcus told me I should pretend I didn't care. That was going to be a tall order.

"They will take good care of her?"

He nodded. "The leader might want a little 'personal' time with her, if you will allow it, but otherwise, they'll keep her until you can return her to camp."

Looking at Enid, I nodded as well. "Give him ten denarii for his trouble, but he keeps his hands off her."

Though my attention was on Enid, out of the corner of my eye, I could see Lucius jerk around to look at me. I'm not sure how Marcus would have felt about this, but I had no intention of prostituting Enid, and therefore Remmy. In our history class, we learned that very few Roman citizens actually forced their slaves into prostitution, but among Legionnaires, who were forbidden to marry, female slaves were generally thought of as currency, to be used, abused, and even spent as needed. Few soldiers would consider actually spending money to protect them.

But even Lucius knew better than to challenge me.

"Yes, *Optio*."

I struggled to contain a sigh of relief.

"I must return to my duties."

I marched through the entrance, but stopped just outside to suck in a desperate breath, and wonder what I was going to do next. Protecting Enid had been my primary goal, but now I was faced with the overwhelming challenge of pretending to be a Roman legionnaire: a brutal soldier, willing and able to kill on command. It is one thing to read about life as a Roman soldier, but quite another to actually live it.

"I am so totally screwed!"

Steeling myself for what I knew would come next, I marched back to where Marcus' men were searching the tents. When I arrived, a Legionnaire was wrestling a woman out from under a heavy blanket. The man lost his grip on the woman, and as he tried to regain his balance, a knife appeared in her hand. In one swift move, she slashed his arm, knocked his helmet off, and brought the blade back to cut his cheek. Seeming to ignore the pain, the soldier tried to grab her wrists, but she was too fast for him. Breaking free, she was preparing to deliver a fatal thrust when she screamed and looked down to see the tip of a sword sticking out of her chest.

As she sank to her knees, the soldier behind her yanked his blade free, lifted it over his head and brought it down on her neck, severing the head from the body.

I froze and fought the urge to throw up, but that was something I could not do because I was an *optio* in the Roman army, and had to think of this horror as "business as usual". Thankfully, all the men were watching the headless corpse fall to the ground as a shudder of revulsion ran though me and I swallowed hard to keep my stomach in check.

"What happened here?" I demanded with as stern a voice as I could muster. Stopping next to the corpse, I focused my attention on the man with the sword.

The trooper bent down and wiped his blade on his victim's leather tunic before he spat. "This slut cut Aremus, and would have killed him had I not done her."

Bile rose in my throat, forcing me to swallow hard.

I turned to Aremus. "Have the medico stitch you up." After waving at a pair of troopers watching from a safe distance, I pointed at the corpse. "Clean this up, and then continue the search."

All three barked, "Yes, Sir!", and hurried to do as told. Moving my shaking hands behind my back, I turned to the legionnaire who had killed the girl.

"I will help until they come back."

Feeling faint, I let the others get slightly ahead of me, and as we moved from tent to tent, fought the tears welling in my eyes. That woman might have been someone's mother. Or worse yet, she might not yet be a mother and her untimely death will mean her line of descendants stops here, and a whole lot of people in the future will disappear because their many-times-great grandmother was never born.

Wiping tears from my face, I moved to the next tent. When I pulled back the flap, I was shocked to see a young girl, no more than ten-years of age, huddled in the far corner, her brown eyes wide, mouth tight, arms across her chest. From her clothes, it was obvious she had not been a combatant, and from their torn and tattered condition, that she had already been badly abused by one or more of the tent's occupants.

Feeling a sudden rage, I turned toward the troopers, but they were already two tents ahead. When I looked at the girl again, her hands shaking as she crouched in the far corner of the tent, I couldn't make myself move toward her.

Should I leave her here?

Every bit of me screamed to take her away and hide her like I had done with Enid, but there was no way I could manage that without Marcus' men seeing me. My head felt like it was going to explode when I realized I had to act as Marcus would or my future and the futures of everyone I knew would vanish.

Opening my mouth, I started to call for a soldier, but only a pathetic squeak came out. I couldn't sacrifice this young girl to save myself. My eyes on her, I finally figured out what I would do, and was preparing to shout an order.

"*Optio,*" the *centurio* announced from behind me.

I was so focused on the girl, I hadn't heard him approach and jerked around to see him marching in my direction. Shocked by the sight, it was all I could do to pull myself together and hammer out a salute.

"Yes, Sir."

Only after he stopped in front of me did I realize I was still holding the tent flap open. His eyes turned in that direction, and his scowl grew even deeper.

"How many of these have you found so far?" he demanded.

Feeling tears welling up again, I dug fingernails into flesh and forced myself to hold it together.

"Five, not counting this one," I answered. "One had a knife and had to be killed." I wanted desperately to add, "But this one is only a child", but kept my mouth shut.

It was only then I realized there were five men behind the *centurio*. Without hesitating, he waved one forward.

"Deliver this waif to the slavers and come right back." The *centurio* turned to me. "You have cleared all the tents for the first *centuria*?"

Unsure where the boundary was between the two centuries, I waved back at the area I knew had been covered.

"All of these tents are cleared of captives. I will have my men working double time on the rest."

Without comment, he gave a curt nod and moved on. Though still standing at attention, I watched the girl being dragged away and felt a horrifyingly guilty sort of relief. I hadn't been forced to give the order to deliver her to the slavers. Even so, I hoped her situation would be better with them than with the abusers who originally captured her.

"I'm not sure I can do this," I muttered anxiously while wiping tears from my eyes. "I need Marcus, or this is going to end badly."

I looked around to see the two who had hauled the dead woman away making their way back. I desperately wanted to run after the *centurio's* soldiers and save that little girl.

"Shit!" I cursed under my breath. "Shit! Shit! Shit!"

The outburst did nothing to temper my cramping gut, but it returned my focus enough to remember why I was here.

Sucking in a deep breath, and letting it hiss through my teeth as I exhaled, I moved away from the tent and headed toward the approaching soldiers, desperately struggling to regain my composure before we met up.

"Help me, Jasmina!"

Chapter 36

"What are you going to do now?" Miriam whispered angrily. "I didn't know people could swap bodies like this."

Her face grim, Jasmina shook her head. "This isn't the norm." She shook her head again. "Hell, nothing about this is normal, so I'd say from this point on anything goes."

"So what are we going to do?"

"I am open to suggestions."

"Ha! You're the expert in this woo-woo-voodoo stuff. Burn incense, invoke spirits, sacrifice a sheep, I don't care, just get my son back."

Jasmina shook her head. "I don't do *this* kind of *stuff*, but even so, the stakes are much higher than the lives of our children."

Her heart aching, Miriam briefly turned to watch Marcus speak with her husband before she looked again at Jasmina. "There is *nothing* more important than the life of my son."

"Normally, I would agree with you, but if we don't figure out why this is happening and stop the assassination of Julius Caesar, you, your son, all the rest of us, and our way of life may vanish into a history that never was."

"What do you mean?"

"Haven't you been following what I've been saying? We exist because of a series of events that kept our ancestors alive long enough to create a line that presently includes us. One change in events anywhere along that line might result in one of our ancestors not being born, or dying before their children were. If the *Tsabbat* manages to kill Caesar before he actually died in our timeline, the America we now know will probably never happen."

"That's ridiculous," Miriam protested as she again looked at her husband and Marcus. "You can't change the past."

Both women's attention was drawn to a nurse entering the room, a release form in her hands, but before she reached Marcus, the woman vanished.

Miriam gasped and did a quick spin to face Jasmina. "What the hell just happened?"

Eyes wide, Jasmina slowly shook her head. "Gerry or the *Tsabbat* may have done something to get that woman's ancient ancestor killed. We are somehow exempt, but as far as anyone else is concerned, that nurse never existed."

"This can't be happening."

Jasmina watched as another nurse entered, a piece of paper in her hand and headed toward Marcus. "It is, and if we don't find a way to contact Gerry, more people will disappear."

"But how? That Marcus person is no longer connected to him, is he?"

"I don't know for sure. Maybe we should ask him."

Moving to the young man, Jasmina extended a hand, which he took. Placing another hand on top of his, she smiled.

"We need to know if you are still connected to the one now occupying your body."

"You do not know?"

She shrugged. "As I am sure you know, witchcraft is not always an exact science. I need to see if I can connect to Gerry."

"Gerry? *Quis est iste?*"

"Gerry is the warlock now occupying your body. It is important that we stay in contact with him."

"Without me you cannot?"

Jasmina felt her chest tighten, unsure as to what a Roman thought a witch could and could not do. "Since the two of you have swapped bodies, it makes sense that you would have the strongest connection to him."

"And for this my hand you must hold?"

Freeing a hand, she took his other. "Actually, I need to hold both of them, if I may."

He shrugged. "I will permit it."

Closing her eyes, Jasmina saw flashes of a sickly young woman whose hard life aged her beyond her years; the brutality of hand-to-hand combat; colorful military parades; women conquered not by force, but by seduction; and finally a brutal scene that brought on such an intense feeling of heartbreak and grief, she jerked back, gasping as her eyes popped open.

"Oh my!"

"What is it?" Miriam demanded. "What did you see?"

Still in shock, Jasmina kept her eyes on Marcus for a moment before she sucked in a breath and said,

"I understand why you want to die."

Chapter 37

"Continue the search, and be quick about it," I demanded before the two soldiers were close enough to see my tears.

"Yes, Sir," they fired back, their pace increasing as they headed toward an unsearched row.

On the plus side, the Gallic war was now over, so it wasn't likely I'd have to kill anyone. On the other hand, I was totally disconnected from Marcus and my mother. Though I had a fairly good idea how a Roman solider should behave, the incident with the young girl made it clear there were some things I just could not do. And yet, if I was going to survive, I had to. In addition, I needed to get to Caesar and warn him, which in my current situation wasn't looking too likely.

"This is total crap," I muttered while following the soldiers down the rows.

It took less than an hour to go through the remaining tents, and to my relief, we didn't find another captive. Quickly dismissing the men, I hurried back to Marcus' tent, distressed to find it empty of everyone, even the Greek slave who normally occupied a stool on the far wall. I had the overwhelming need to find Enid, because she might be my only connection to Jasmina.

"*Optio*?" Lucius called from outside.

Feeling angry that I was in a dangerous situation with no easy answers, I pushed through the opening, and faced him. I started to ask where Enid was, but stopped when I saw a small contingent of legionnaires behind him.

"Yes?"

When he looked confused, I realized that my response had been in English. Before speaking again, I searched for the feeling I had earlier.

"What is it, Lucius?"

He hesitated briefly before responding. "Should we tear down the auxiliary tents after supper?"

Though Marcus might think it a simple question, I hesitated, having no idea how to answer.

"If I may, *Optio*," Lucius said when I still had not answered. "The men will not need the supplies from those tents until we arrive at our new destination, don't you think?"

I stopped a sigh of relief and answered, "Take the tents down now. One less thing to worry about in the morning."

"Yes, Sir," he snapped and hurried away.

I wanted to call him back and ask about Enid, but kept my tongue. Instead, I walked around the camp, both to orient myself with the place and to try to get my head into my new role. I had many of Marcus' memories, so I knew that there were two *centuriae*, about 160 men in this encampment. Normally, each *centuria* was led by a *centurio*, but one had been killed recently and not yet replaced. This was because though a common soldier like myself could easily be promoted to a lowly position like *optio*, *centuriōnēs* were appointed by the Roman Senate, and that was a very long way away.

Our *imperator*, Julius Caesar could also promote someone in the field, and he often did, but since the war had only just ended, there was much to do to get the army back in shape. After all, the last few battles had been costly in terms of lives lost, but also in the number of *centuriōnēs* killed. I doubted he would do anything until he had a chance to sort out his surviving army. That meant a replacement *centurio* wasn't probably going to be coming soon. Until then, I, a lowly optio who would normally be at the back of the formation keeping the men in line, would now be leading eighty men. I wasn't sure I was up for it. I'd never thought of myself as a leader. I just wanted to go to school, get an education, and hang out with my friends,

I desperately needed to connect with Jasmina.

Chapter 38

Angry beyond reason, Quintus barged into the leather tent set up by a camp follower to slake the legionnaires' thirst after a long day of marching. A doe-eyed girl approached him, but his mood was so sour, he pushed her away and sat at the first table he could find in the dim light.

Before he could shout out an order, a shadow of a figure moved up to his table.

"Greetings, Legionnaire," the man said with a voice that was so ingratiating, even Quintus hesitated. "May I buy you a drink?"

His mood was so bad, the only response Quintus could think of was to slam a fist into the man's face. However, that changed when the doe-eyed girl approached with two bowls of wine.

"If you are the great soldier I think you are," the stranger continued, "we should share some wine and talk for a bit."

Quintus' attention shifted from the thin man to the girl and back before he took a sip of the wine, surprised to find that, not only was it quite good, but it had not been heavily diluted with water as was the custom of most innkeepers.

"I'm Quintus Fluvius Flaccus," he finally growled. "What is it you want?"

Seeming to ignore his question, the pale-faced stranger lightly tapped his forefinger on the side of his nose and smiled.

"My good man, Quintus," he said softly. "I am told you are an exemplary soldier, but not appreciated by your superiors."

Straightening on his stool, Quintus glared across the table at the man's narrow, pinched face, but kept a firm grip on the bowl of wine. It wasn't his habit to spurn free drink or women.

"May I join you?"

Quintus thought of blowing him off, but it occurred to him that this man might supply more than one bowl of wine. *Might he also add a woman to the mix?*

Quintus took another long draught of the wine before blurting, "No sweat off my ass."

The stranger's smile was crooked and seemed to have a bit of a sneer to it. In fact, Quintus was pretty sure this dandy thought himself too good to be in the company of a measly soldier.

So why are you here? he asked himself as the man sat.

"I am wondering if you might be interested in a...little proposition?"

What is his accent? Thracian? Southern Italy?

He wanted to ask the question out loud, but snarled at him instead.

"What'd you want?"

"I am told you are not well treated by a certain *optio*."

It wasn't just the look of this man that put Quintus off, it was his attempt to intrude on something he thought of as private. Though he and his brothers-in-arms privately degraded their superiors every chance they got, it was considered bad form to say such things to civilians. It wasn't that Quintus didn't appreciated this man's generosity, but his scrawny, almost emaciated body made it clear he had never been in the army. He even doubted this disgustingly thin person could lift a *gladius*, let alone fight with one, and therefore, he could never understand what it took to be a legionnaire.

"I get along well enough."

"Ah yes," the man said knowingly. "I am sure you are a fine example to the men you serve with, but I understand that is not the opinion of an *optio* by the name of Marcus Aremus. It seems he has very much taken a dislike to you. In fact…" He leaned closer and lowered his already faint voice, "…word is he plans to make the rest of your army career a complete misery."

The tenseness in his stomach countering the casual wave of his hand, Quintus took a drink and laughed. "That will blow over. It always does."

He tensed even more when the stranger scowled and shook his head. "I do not think so, my friend. He seems quite taken with his new female slave, and is unhappy with how you treated her."

"I was just having a bit of fun," Quintus protested before taking another deep draught from his bowl. "I didn't damage the goods."

Though his eyebrows were raised, the stranger nodded eagerly. "I agree. I agree. Yes, my friend, you have been unreasonably punished for something that is your right as a legionnaire. I can fully understand why you are upset with him."

The suggestion made Quintus look at his wine bowl, which he found to be empty. He wanted more wine, but was hesitant to ask. Even the thought of sharing his feelings about his fellow troopers or the much-hated officers seemed treasonable.

As though reading his thoughts, the stranger waved to the doe-eyed girl for a refill. Waiting for her to come, Quintus had time to think about the unjust abuse, the pain, the humiliation Marcus had brought on him. Like it or not, he slowly but surely began to agree that this wretched weakling had a point. The thought sloshed around in his brain with the undiluted wine, and it did not take long for the alcohol to prevail.

"You got that right," he finally said while nodding. "That woman was plunder, just like the rest of 'em, so by right, she's as much mine as his."

"But, of course, my friend," the stranger said soothingly as the doe-eyed girl poured more wine into Quintus' bowl. "Any fool can see that."

"You got that right," he repeated dully, "but it don't do to fret over it, 'cause there's nothing I can do about it."

When the stranger did not respond, Quintus looked over to see a pencil-thin smile on his narrow face.

"What?"

The man shook his head slowly. "I think there might be a way to get revenge without risking retribution."

Not really sure what *retribution* meant, Quintus stared at him for a long moment before asking, "What do you mean?"

"What I'm saying is that there are ways to deal with this *optio* without your superiors ever knowing about it."

Quintus squinted at him. "There are? What would that be?"

After looking around the room, the stranger leaned close. "Would you like to be *optio?*"

Huffing angrily, Quintus pressed the wine bowl to his lips and noisily slurped in a long draught. Finally lowering the bowl, he swallowed and stabbed a finger at the stranger.

"The *centurio* didn't so much as say it, but that was to be my job before Marcus come in and took it." He looked around cautiously before leaning close to the stranger. "I'd bet a month's wages that a bag of coins traded hands to make that happen."

"Quite likely," the stranger agreed conspiratorially, "And even worse, I am told he gets twice the pay for half the work, correct?"

"Right enough."

"Doesn't sound very fair, if you ask me."

Quintus glared at his companion. Even when sober, he was an angry man, but in his present state, his few inhibitions faded to nothing.

He rose unsteadily from his stool. "I think I'll gut the bastard and be done with him."

"Oh no, my friend," the stranger said soothingly as he rose and put a hand on Quintus' shoulder to push him back onto the stool. "I know a far better way to get what you want."

Incensed by being so easily manhandled, Quintus tried to grab the man's arm, but the stranger was faster than he looked and his hand found only air.

"What could be better than that?"

The stranger smiled. "Why don't you have another bowl and we can talk about it."

Barely able to put two thoughts together, Marcus' mood changed suddenly at the suggestion, but when he waved his arm wildly to get the innkeeper's attention, he swept everything off the table.

After looking at the debris on the floor, he parroted, "Why don' we have another bowl and talk about it."

"Yes," the stranger responded, his grin now much broader, his bony hand motioning for the innkeeper's attention. "Why don't we?"

Chapter 39

Taking Marcus' hands again, Jasmina steeled her mind against the nearly overwhelming grief, and forced herself to search for a connection with Gerry. The images she received were confusing: partially in the present and partially in the past. Faces flashed in her mind, some angry, others affectionate, some she recognized, most she didn't. She wanted to scream when she not only saw but felt blood flowing over her hands. People were bumping into her, their hands flying at her face. She pulled back to avoid a fist, lost touch with Marcus, and returned to the present.

"My God," she gasped as she staggered away from him.

"What is it?" Miriam cried while grabbing Jasmina to steady her. "Did you find him?"

Jasmina shook her head. "No," she croaked. "The connection is twisted; everything is jumbled. I can't follow it."

"Well, that's not good enough," Miriam shouted angrily as she pushed Jasmina aside and grabbed Marcus' hands.

"What is this?" Marcus asked when he found himself face-to-face with Gerry's mother, her mouth set in a thin line, eyes glaring at him.

"Hold still, and don't get any funny ideas," she demanded before closing her eyes.

Though she was also assaulted with Marcus' thoughts and feelings, her own anger and fear helped her push past them to see a dark space filled with flashes of images that moved so fast it made her nauseous.

"Stop thinking, Roman," she shouted, her eyes still closed. "You're filling your head with nonsense and I need to find my son."

"*Aegre fero,* dear lady."

"Don't say you're sorry! Work with me here."

"*Et ego. Etiam.* I mean to say, I try. Yes."

"Then clear your damned mind and let me work."

Though looking surprised at her aggressiveness, Marcus did as told.

To her dismay, Marcus did such a good job that Marion found herself being sucked into a blackness more intense than anything she had ever imagined. She tried to pull back, but felt her hands pulling away from Marcus'. Clamping them tighter, she steadied herself and tried to probe the darkness, but found nothing. Even the sounds of the room around her were gone.

Despite her near-death grip on Marcus' arm, she had the overwhelming sense that she was falling. The sensation continued for an indeterminate amount of time, and just as she was preparing to break her connection with Marcus, her vision was suddenly filled with light. Stunned, she looked around at the Roman camp as sounds filled her mind: hammering, men talking, squeaking wheels, and even the hushed sound of a slight breeze rushing past her ears. The smell of disturbed earth filled her nostrils as tent stakes were pulled from the ground, accompanied by the stench of sweating men, mule dung, doused fires, and a nearby latrine ditch.

"Gerry! Lord in Heaven! Is that you?"

"Mom? How did you find me?"

Feeling tears dribbling down her cheeks, she was glad their communication was only mental, because her throat was spasmming as she fought the urge to cry.

"I'm connected through Marcus, and he's in your body."

"Yeah," Gerry responded. "Well, you've got to figure out how to get him back here. I'm way out of my league."

"At least we're connected again. Marcus can help you until we get him back into his body."

"But where is he? I don't sense him at all."

"Don't worry about that now. If you need to know something, I can ask him."

"Then ask him this: we're moving to a new location. I'm supposed to organize the tearing down and packing of the camp. How is that done?"

"Let me ask."

"Wait?"

"What is it, Son?"

"If you leave, how can I be sure you'll come back?"

Miriam took a deep breath, not only to help her relax, but because she wasn't sure she knew herself.

"As God is my witness, I will return to you. No one can stop me from doing that. OK?"

"Yeah. I guess."

She hesitated for a moment before she broke contact with Marcus and opened her eyes. His face was questioning when she looked up at him, but when he opened his mouth to speak, she cut him off.

"They're preparing to break camp and move out. What do you do to make it happen?"

He froze a moment, his mouth open, eyes flicking from her to Jasmina and back until he smiled.

"It is simple, no?" he answered enthusiastically. "The men, they do this many time. It like second nature. My job is to keep after lazy ones."

"But how is it organized?"

He shrugged. "Each group of eight fighting men is a *contubernium*. They share one tent and are responsible to tear it down, collect other gear, and pack on mule. When they do that, you move each *contubernium* to other places to pack up what need it. What we no take, we burn so locals not use against us."

"But what do you take and what do you leave?"

He laughed. "Not to worry. If we cannot build it, we take. Otherwise we burn. Simple, no?"

"But how will Gerry know...?"

"Miriam," Jasmina interrupted as she put a hand on her shoulder. "Gerry must have some of Marcus' memories. If he just takes the time to look around, he'll know what to do."

When she jerked a nod, Jasmina pointed at Marcus. "Now take his hands and connect with Gerry. I'll make contact with Remmy and see what she can do to help."

Miriam nodded again and looked up at Marcus, his eager, almost come-hither smile making her uncomfortable. After all, this was her son's body, and the thought that another man might be inside it and having lecherous thoughts about her was disturbing.

A shiver running through her body, she steeled herself against the unsettling feelings and grabbed Marcus' hands again. The feeling of falling was briefer, but no less disorienting. When it stopped, she gulped in air, tightened her grip even more and opened her eyes. Her senses filled again with the sights and smells of the Roman camp.

Even though she'd already seen it once, the sight confused her so much she nearly forgot what she had been told.

"The men are organized in groups of eight," she blurted when the memory returned. "I can't remember what they are called, but they all sleep in the same tent. Once they're done packing up their tents, send them to gather up anything else they will take."

"Wait," Gerry said excitedly. "I remember this from class. They only took what they couldn't build at their new destination."

"That's right. Walk around the compound and see what needs to go and order the men to pack it up."

She felt his head shake. "I think I'm getting a sense of what to do."

"Then trust those feelings, no matter what your brain tells you. The more you connect with his memories, the better your chances of surviving."

"But I have to get back to Enid."

"I assume you know that Enid is Remmy, or at least that's who Jasmina says she's connected to."

"Yeah, I kind of figured that part out. How is she doing?"

Miriam shook her head, and quickly realized that Gerry could not see her doing it.

"We don't know. After Marcus appeared in your body, we've been so busy with him, we lost contact with her. Jasmina is trying to reconnect now."

"Let me know, will you?"

"Absolutely."

She felt her son take a deep breath and let it out slowly.

"Listen, Mom," he said with such authority she immediately wanted to resist. "I've been thinking about this situation, and there may be some things I have to say, and even do that...well, they aren't going to be what..."

"...a person in our day-and-age would do?" she finished when he hesitated.

"Yeah, and it is going to be really hard for me to do that with you...here. You know?"

"I'm not leaving you!"

She felt a sense of irritation, and knew it was not coming from her.

"You really, like, have to. I can't do this with you watching me."

"But son, what about..."

"No, Mom! I'm serious. It has to be this way."

Though she wanted to protest, she felt his certainty, and though it went against everything she knew, she felt herself nod.

"How will we contact you?"

He paused for a long moment. "What time is it there?"

She hesitated, not sure if she knew the answer, when it suddenly popped into her head.

"About nine-fifteen in the evening, I think."

"And it is early morning for us, so I'm guessing it's about six or so. Talk to Marcus and see if they get regular breaks, or lunch. If so, figure we are about nine-hours ahead of you. I'm going to be on the march for most of the day, but if you connect with me, I should be able to move off by myself to speak with you."

"But what if you need me in the meantime?"

He paused and she felt a moment of uncertainty followed by determination.

"I'll just have to make do with what I can get from Marcus' memories."

"I don't know, you've never had to deal with…"

She barked in surprise when the connection was suddenly broken. She opened her eyes, surprise to see a burly black man dressed as a nurse, a cotton mask over his mouth and nose, green latex gloves covering his hands.

"What's going on?" she demanded.

The man's attention was initially on Marcus, but when she spoke, he turned to her. "The doctor's on his way and you'll need to go out of the room until he's done examining the patients."

"I will not," Miriam insisted. "He's my son and I'll stay."

"Sorry, Ma'am," a tall, thin man wearing green scrubs, and a stethoscope around his neck announced as he hurried into the room. "This is looking more serious than we originally thought."

"How do you mean?" Jasmina asked as she moved up beside Miriam.

Facing her, the man nodded. "I am Doctor Hiram McFaddan. I work for the CDC and specialize in new viral strains."

"The CDC? What do you have to do with Gerry and Remmy?"

He shook his head. "We believe their symptoms match those of a new, and thankfully rare disease we call The Walking Sleeper." He waved a hand dismissively. "It's part of the *Flaviviridae* family of viruses."

"I've never heard of it."

Doctor McFaddan shook his head. "Thankfully, few have, but as luck would have it, I was in the hospital when they were admitted. The case is strange, so I was asked to look into it." He motioned to Marcus. "When he woke up believing he was a Roman soldier, I knew immediately that this matched a case I only recently dealt with in northern Florida. Though that was the first known case in the US, it is a growing problem on the European continent."

Jasmina shook her head. "I don't think these two are infected with anything, doctor. They're just in a trance."

Instead of responding to her statement, Doctor McFaddan turned to Marcus.

"Quam operor vos sentio?" he asked.

"Bene," Marcus answered, "sed etiam confusum."

"Just like the others," the doctor muttered.

"What do you mean, 'Just like the others'?" Miriam demanded.

The doctor shook his head. "I asked him how he was feeling, and he said..."

"We know," Jasmina interrupted. "He feels fine, but he's confused. I understand Latin, but how in the world did Miriam's son suddenly start understanding and speaking a dead language he had never spoken before?"

Shaking his head, the doctor gave them an embarrassed smile. "I don't have a good explanation for it. The only theory that comes close -- and believe me, ladies, this is really reaching out there -- is that we all inherit memories from our ancestors that are deeply encoded into our cells, and somehow, this virus releases those memories." He shook his head again. "It's a stretch, but at least it's better than that past-lives mumbo-jumbo the spiritualists are trying to sell."

Jasmina's cough brought Miriam's attention briefly to her before she looked back at the doctor.

"My son isn't just remembering this ancestor, he's become him." She pointed at Marcus. "He doesn't even know me."

"Then this is further advanced than I thought, and we have to move quickly, before it is too late."

"Too late?"

He scowled. "I'm sorry, I didn't mention that of the seven known cases in Europe and the US, none the patients survived more than twenty-four hours after the ancestral memories took over their brain."

"Survived? You mean..."

"I am sorry to say, ma'am, but all of them died. We think the virus eats away at their brain cells and before their body can react, the brain just...disintegrates."

"Disintegrates??" Miriam squeaked. "What can you do about it?"

Doctor McFaddan shook his head. "We don't yet have a cure, but I'm thinking that if we can put the victims in a deep sleep, it will slow the progress of the disease and give us time to come up with a cure."

"But Gerry believes he is in grave danger in his past life. We need to stay in contact with him to help him survive."

"It's all an illusion, Ma'am. A trick of his mind."

"I don't think so," Jasmina insisted. "Gerry saw a woman get murdered -- a murder that might not have happened if Marcus had been in charge -- and moments later a nurse in this very room vanished."

Doctor McFaddan turned to Miriam. "Did you see this, Missus Patterson?"

Miriam hesitated, her eyes jerking from her son talking quietly with the male nurse, to Jasmina and back to the doctor.

"Not exactly. I was next to Jasmina and heard her cry out. When I looked at where she was pointing, there was no one there."

As two more men wearing scrubs entered the room, McFaddan motioned for them to approach Jasmina.

"It looks like you are also infected, Missus Maxell. We'll have to isolate you as well."

"What?" Jasmina protested as the two nurses took hold of her arms. "You can't do that."

"I'm afraid I can, Ma'am," the doctor said as the men forcibly escorted her from the room. "And in the end, I'm confident you will be glad I did."

When she was out of sight, the doctor turned to Miriam. "How are you feeling Missus Patterson?"

Shocked by what just happened, it took Miriam a moment to collect her wits, and when she did, it was obvious to her that something was not right about this man.

"I'm fine."

"Can you speak Latin as well?"

Terrified at the prospect of being separated from her son, she looked at him briefly before answering, "No, but my son also speaks English. I can still communicate with him."

Doctor McFaddan shook his head. "Not possible, Ma'am. We have to get him away from others and I am afraid that you and your two other companions will be quarantined in this room until we are sure you are not infected."

The doctor waved at the black nurse to get his attention and then nodded. It was then that Miriam saw the syringe in the nurse's hand. With only seconds to decide what to do, she grabbed a metal bedpan from a nearby counter and swung it at the doctor's head.

"Marcus!" she screamed as the metal tray rang like a bell. "They're going to drug you. RUN!"

Before the doctor could react, Miriam hammered his head again, knocking him to his knees. She looked over to see Marcus grab the nurse's wrist, push it away from his body before slamming his forehead into his opponent's.

The impact made the nurse stagger, but he quickly recovered and again tried to stab the needle into Marcus' neck. True to his training, the legionnaire dodged the weapon and brought his fist up into his stomach. When the man doubled over, Marcus slammed the back of his head and sent him to the floor.

Only then did Miriam realize the doctor had grabbed her bedpan and when she tried to resist, he yanked it from her grip. She screamed when his left hand smacked her face, knocking her down. Her vision blurred, she struggled to tell up from down, but before she could recover the doctor's blurry form filled her vision. As she held up her hands to defend herself, a body crashed into the doctor.

Unable to rise, she flailed around for something to grab onto, and was crawling toward Remmy's bed when strong hands grabbed her under the arms and yanked her to her feet. She started to resist until she realized it was Marcus.

"Show where we can go?" Marcus demanded.

"Go?" Alvin asked.

"We must leave now, before others come back. There is great danger."

"But what about Remmy?" Tim asked. "We can't leave her here."

Now fully recovered from the ordeal, Miriam looked around the room. "The wheelchair. Load her into it."

As Alvin ran to the wheelchair, Miriam patted Marcus on the chest.

"I'm OK now," she said. "You can let go."

Without hesitating, he released her and rushed to Remmy's bed. Scooping her up, blankets and all, he carefully lowered her in the wheelchair.

"What about Jasmina?" Tim asked anxiously,

After waving for Alvin to the wheelchair, Marcus scanned the room.

"I need weapon."

"No!" Miriam protested as she moved to a closet next to Marcus' bed. "Let's do this without hurting anyone." She handed him a stack of neatly folded clothes. "We'll worry about getting you dressed after we're safely out of here."

They hurried out of the room into a hallway full of people, though no one seemed to notice them.

"Help!" someone shouted from down the hall. "I'm being kidnapped!"

"Oh my God," Tim cried. "That's Jasmina."

Marcus dropped his clothes on Remmy's lap and grabbed Tim's arm.

"Come. We get her."

Stumbling as Marcus pulled his arm, Tim quickly caught up.

Her eyes on the men, Miriam hesitated for only a moment before pointing in the opposite direction.

"Get Remmy to the car. We'll be right behind you."

Alvin jerked his attention from the elevators to her. "But what if…"

He stopped when she turned and ran after the two men.

Chapter 40

After hardly sleeping the night before, I arose early and walked a complete circuit around the wooden fence that defined the boundaries of the camp. Tapping Marcus memories, I knew it was called the *castra aestiva* or summer camp. It was not as substantial as it might be if this had been for an entire legion, having only tents, rather than wooden structures for buildings. Fewer spaces were set out for administration purposes, since we had no *legate* or *tribunes* in our company. However, the eight-foot fence around the perimeter was enough to keep roaming bands of barbarians from sneaking into our tents at night and massacring us.

I was walking as much to get used to my uniform as to orient myself. I tightened my chin strap to counter the extra weight of the crest on my helmet and then struggled to manage the *optio's* long staff. Though Marcus' body was used to this equipment, my brain was not and it took time to adjust.

Halfway across the camp, I saw the *centurio* urinating into an artificial stream created when the camp was laid out, and was glad that Roman armies put a high value on sanitation to prevent disease. I then looked at the main gate where friendly locals would normally be gathering to sell us food and supplies. However, on this day, none were allowed close to the camp to avoid the possibility of a surprise attack while we were preparing to move out.

By the time I returned to my starting point, the *optio* of the other centuria approached with five men in tow. Though I knew we were both *optio centurionis*, meaning we were chosen for our position by our respective *centuriōnēs*, my *centurio* was the man in charge, so I technically outranked this one. Even so, I, more than anything, wanted to sneak away and hide when I saw him.

"Optio," the other man said after he stopped and saluted. "With these men I will start packing the extra stores and weapons. I see you already had a contingent tear down the mess tent. At this rate, we should be ready to move out by mid-morning."

Hesitating several heartbeats to make sure I was speaking Latin, I returned the salute. "Good work, *Optio*. It is good to impress the *centurio* once in a while."

My opposite laughed. "But not too often, eh?"

Though my own laugh felt forced, the other did not seem to notice as he immediately marched past me.

"Well," I muttered when the others were out of earshot. "That went well enough."

"*Optio!*" Lucius called as he approached. "Quintus is still drunk from last night and will not get up from his cot so his tent can be packed. What should we do?"

Quintus' name produced a surprising flare of anger. "Throw him into the watering trough. If he drowns, we'll all be better off."

Struggling to contain a smile, Lucius jerked a salute, did a quick spin and marched off. I started to follow, but stopped after only a couple of steps. A feeling that solidified into a memory told me that if I were there to see Quintus' behavior, I'd be forced to punish him and a drunk soldier might spout off about Marcus keeping Enid in his tent. I knew the *centurio* had given her to Marcus, but that wasn't a good reason for defying protocol. Camp discipline demanded it, especially from the *optio*.

Turning to my right, I spied the *centurio*'s tent in the middle of camp, but instead headed toward the rows of tents occupied by my men. Along with Quintus, a third of our number had been relieved of duty the night before. I was sure that drunken brute wasn't the only one of their number suffering from overindulgence.

Over the next hour, I rousted a dozen hung-over soldiers and had the bulk of the men's tents and supplies lashed to their respective mules. I then organized the men into their usual *contubernium* and sent them off to help tear down the rest of the camp. It felt empowering to be obeyed so unquestioningly. I kept expecting someone to challenge me, like my mother would do whenever I tried to think for myself. I was starting to enjoy this role when the *centurio* called me to his tent where the other *optio* was already standing at parade rest.

"Status report," he demanded after I saluted.

"We will be ready to move out within the hour, Sir." I answered.

Instead of looking at me, he scanned the camp. "I will lead the first *centuria*, and you will take the second. *Optio* Scaeva will bring up the rear."

"With respect, Sir," Scaeva stated, the rest of his statement was implied and understood, even by me.

The *centurio* turned to face him. "I realized that with the loss of your *centurio*, it is traditional for you to take the lead of your *centuria*, but I need you to stay in the rear while my *optio* covers our middle. This is still hostile territory, our men will be stretched out on this march and it is important no one lags behind. I am counting on you to do that."

Without looking at me, he snapped to attention and barked, "Yes, *Centurio*!"

As though that ended the conversation, the *centurio* turned to me. "I have acquired horses from the natives and will need a *contubernium* to act as scouts. Pick out your best riders and get them ready."

Though the order made my heart race because I had no idea which soldiers could ride well, I also snapped to attention and saluted. "Yes, *Centurio*!"

"Are the slavers still with us?"

I had no clue, and when I hesitated, *Optio* Scaeva responded, "No, Sir. They left at first light yesterday. They wish to move quickly before the locals regroup from their losses."

The *centurio* looked in the direction we were headed. "With women and children in tow, we'll no doubt catch them before day's end." He shook his head. "It is no matter. Have the scouts keep a lookout for our next encampment. Once there, six can stay and secure the location while the remaining two return to guide our engineers to it. Get the engineers marching with two *contubernia* now so they will have the area surveyed and begin construction before the first of our troops arrive to help them set up the perimeter."

"Yes, Sir," we both said at the same time.

"Dismissed."

As we marched away from the *centurio*'s tent, I looked at my opposite, totally unsure as to what I should do next. I mean, could Roman Legionnaires ride horses? Did this man hate me for being placed over him in the ranks? To my surprise, it really didn't seem to bother him.

"If I may, *Optio*," he finally said without breaking stride. "I have two *contubernia* of excellent riders. I will send one of them to be the scouts."

I was about to respond with *That would be so cool*, but thankfully stopped myself before the words slipped out. "Yes. An excellent idea."

Without further comment, he changed direction and marched away. I slowed and took a deep breath.

Marcus? Where the hell are you?

Chapter 41

Still in hospital gown, Marcus moved quickly through the crowd, making it hard for Tim to keep up. Catching up with the men holding Jasmina, the soldier did not hesitate.

"Aaahhh!" he cried as he used both hands to hammer the man holding Jasmina's left arm.

As his opponent fell, Marcus pushed Jasmina in the back, her sudden forward motion throwing the remaining man off balance long enough for Marcus to land a roundhouse punch square on his jaw.

When Jasmina started to fall along with the second man, Marcus wrapped an arm around her waist, lifted her off her feet, and headed back the way he had come, passing Tim so quickly, the poor man knocked an orderly to the floor as he struggled to change direction and follow.

"Sorry about that," he shouted over his shoulder.

When they caught up, it was Alvin who asked, "Where's Miriam?"

Marcus looked back down the hall. "She follow us?"

"She certainly did."

"I didn't see her," Tim announced, "but then, I wasn't looking for her."

Marcus turned to see Miriam's blond hair in the crowd. When the people between them moved aside, he saw Doctor McFaddan firmly gripping her arm while she ineffectively struck him with her free hand. Marcus started running, his bare feet barely making a sound as he sprinted down the hall, his eyes on the man holding a woman with whom he felt a strangely-distorted familial connection.

Unfortunately, before he could reach them, Miriam looked in his direction and screamed. The action brought the doctor's attention around, and when he realized what was happening, he reached his right hand into his jacket and pulled out something black. Pushing Miriam away, McFaddan straightened his right arm and pointed the thing at Marcus.

Unaware of what a pistol was, Marcus continued on his collision course as the doctor leveled his weapon and squeezed the trigger. However, before the hammer released, Miriam slammed a fist into his arm, pushing the weapon aside as it discharged. The resulting explosion in the confined space stunned Marcus, but his many years of battle experience did not abandon him. Dropping to all fours, he bounced off the floor and was on his feet without missing a step. Though he was running, he was still far enough away to give the doctor time to wrap one arm around Miriam as he re-aimed the weapon.

"Stop," McFaddan shouted.

"No!" Miriam screamed, her cry pulling the doctor's attention to her only briefly, but it was enough to allow Marcus to close the distance between them.

Marcus jerked to his right, the gun discharged and its bullet tore through the fleshy part of his upper arm. His adrenaline levels were so high, Marcus hardly registered the injury as he plowed into the doctor, sending the two airborne for a brief moment before the doctor's head slammed to the floor.

His senses acutely alert, Marcus heard the gun sliding across the linoleum even before he and the doctor stopped moving. After making sure his opponent was unconscious, he looked up to see the gun bump into a pair of feet. A hand reached down and picked it up.

Miriam was pulling on his arm, her voice a hallow echo, and so frantic he could not understand the words. He tried to shake off the strangeness of the echoing sounds around him, as though he were under water. He looked up at the man lifting the gun from the floor, but unlike the doctor, this man held it loosely, his hand gripping it in the middle, and not by what appeared to be the handle.

"Go," Robert's distant voice insisted.

Before he could process what was happening, Miriam yanked on his arm, and he rose to face her. When she threw her arms around his chest and hugged him, his first impulse was to push her away, but to his surprise, his arms automatically wrapped around her.

"There is no time," Robert was saying. He continued speaking, but his words made no sense to Marcus.

It was Miriam who pulled back and motioned for him to follow her to where the others were waiting at what appeared to be a door. He looked the other way to see a crowd of people staring at him, the press of bodies hiding the two he had previously knocked out. He started to look down at the doctor again, but Miriam's insistent yanking on his arm brought his attention back to her.

"You're bleeding," she cried.

Only then feeling the sting of pain, he looked at his arm to see a small stream of blood running down to his elbow.

"It is nothing," he finally said as his hearing returned to normal. "We must go."

He looked again to see all his other comrades except Jasmina had vanished. She was standing in the now-open doorway waving them forward.

"So the gods also fight in heaven," he muttered while following Miriam.

Chapter 42

"Hello, my friend," the silky voiced stranger called softly as Quintus sat on the edge of the watering trough. "How are you faring?"

Shaking off water that trickled down his face, Quintus rubbed his aching temple and glared at the man as he moved to sit on a nearby barrel. "Your wine is a fickle bitch. She gives much pleasure then wakes me with a kick to the head."

The stranger chuckled. "Ah yes, you did drink quite a bit last night. The innkeeper was supposed to add water to lessen the effect, but alas, he did not."

"That's not funny," Quintus snarled as he squinted at the stranger.

"You are right, absolutely, but I did not come here to discuss your drinking. Rather, I bring an opportunity."

"What are you talking about? We move out within the hour."

Nodding, the stranger smiled. "And that is where your opportunity lies, my friend."

His head throbbing, Quintus shook it slowly. "I don't follow."

"Then I should tell you that a small raiding party will be attacking your *centuria* somewhere in the hills ahead, and it is quite possible your *optio* will be killed in the skirmish."

"He will? How could you know this?"

The man's smile grew as he pointed a long, slender finger at Quintus. "Because you, my friend, are going to be the one who kills him."

His statement made Quintus freeze, his slow mind struggling between his desire to eliminate the loathsome Marcus Aremus, and his strong dislike of the idea of killing one of his own.

When he did not respond, the stranger asked, "Did you not say this *optio* had stolen your chance for promotion, your chance to double your pay?"

Grunting in the affirmative, he nodded.

"And who is to know which sword does the killing during a skirmish?"

Quintus squinted angrily at him. "They will if no other blood is shed."

"Then you have to make sure to show them what a hero you can be. You can do that, can't you?"

Enraged by the challenge, the soldier stood quickly, but the pounding in his head kept him from lunging at the man.

"I'm a better legionnaire than Marcus Aremus will ever be. You mark my words, he could never…"

The realization of what he was saying made Quintus stop.

"I can best him without killing him," he growled.

"That goes without saying," the stranger said soothingly, "but if he lives, you do not get the woman."

The soldier's eyes widened briefly before squinting again in disbelief. "She has been sold to the slavers. The *centurio* ordered it. The *optio* is not foolish enough to defy him."

The stranger nodded. "And yet, he has." The stranger smiled when Quintus' eyes' widened again. "Do not worry, my friend. She is now in my hands, and I will make her a gift to you, *if* you eliminate Marcus Aremus."

"But why do you want the *optio* killed?"

Shaking his head, the stranger rose from his perch. "Trust me when I tell you, my friend, this is something you do not want to know."

Quintus cocked his head to one side, his expression curious. "Why?"

The stranger waved a hand dismissively. "Just think of how you will enjoy being *optio* and having that woman all to yourself, to do with as you please and leave such petty issues for me to worry about."

Chapter 43

Stressing over what to do during the long march back to the Legion headquarters turned out to be a waste of perfectly good angst. The men knew their duties. After all, these soldiers had done this many times. That did not mean I was completely in the clear. Though Gaul was now a conquered land, it was still a hostile one. Not all tribes had fully surrendered, and small bands of rebels were a constant threat. I might still have to fight for my life, and I wasn't sure I could do that.

My initial plan for the present was to simply follow the example of the other *optio*, but that plan didn't work so well. In this hilly country, an army this large can't march in battle formation. Because of the narrow roads available to us, the best we could do was four abreast, and much of the time, we were single file, stretched out nearly a mile from the leading *centurio*, to the last of the camp followers. Because of this, I saw neither the *centurio*, nor the other *optio* until we arrived at base camp that evening.

Before we left the next day, there was a long wait while the *centurio* took care of last-minute business, and I took the opportunity to go to an area inside our *castra* called the practice field where many posts remained. Only a few of the head-high, hacked, scratched, and battered posts still stood, most having been cut off about waist high as soldiers practiced their sword work and built up their upper bodies.

I found the best of those remaining and went to work, being tentative at first, but finally realizing my newly acquired muscles knew what to do and letting my body's automatic reflexes do the bulk of the work. I slashed, stabbed, spun, and hammered until my sword sliced all the way through, sending the tattered top thumping to the ground. I had been so focused on my task, I was totally caught off guard by the whistles and shouts of the men gathered behind me.

Both embarrassed and filled with bravado, I put a foot on the fallen chunk of wood and held my sword up in victory. The men gave a raucous cheer in response, but went suddenly silent when the *centurio* appeared among them.

"Not enough to do, *Optio?*"

Sheathing my sword, I snapped to attention and saluted. "We are packed and ready to march on your order, *Centurio*."

Without so much as a nod, he responded, "I will lead the first *centuria* now. Keep the men moving. No gaps in the line. No slaves among the men."

"Yes, *Centurio!*"

Without further comment, he turned and marched away. Grabbing my staff, I hurried to the gathered men already making faces at the *centurio*'s back, and chuckling among themselves.

"Go," I barked. "You have your orders."

Many of them glanced at my staff before hurrying off to their units. I was preparing to follow the departing men when Lucius called to me.

"*Optio*. I have just returned from the camp follower's encampment. Your slave girl is gone. What should I do?"

"What?" I cried, feeling my heart nearly seize at the idea of Remmy being alone in this crazy land. "I thought your man could be trusted."

"He says she escaped while he slept. Maybe it is not his fault?"

"It is," I said as I turned to march in that direction, but stopped before I even took a step. The *centurio* was preparing to start the army moving and I needed to be there to organize things as the men formed up behind him.

I turned back to Lucius. "Find her, even if you have to gut that bastard."

Lucius shook his head. "But what of my unit?"

"You are on an errand for me. Catch up with me when you can."

Lucius hesitated only briefly before he marched off. As I watched him go, desperation clamped my chest.

She promised not to escape. She promised!

The desire to follow Lucius was overwhelming, but my job was to be an example to the men under my command, and a bad example could not be tolerated.

Turning quickly, I nearly ran to where the men were gathering and found the *centurio* instructing the scouts. Moving quickly up behind him, I stood at attention and waited until I was acknowledged.

After the scouts left, he turned to me. "The next camp has been located and the engineers have been dispatched to prepare it for our arrival." He waved at the troops milling around behind me. "Move them out, four abreast."

My head spinning, I hurried as the *centurio* moved to the *immunis* who would march in the lead with him.

"Four abreast," I commanded to the milling crowd as I approached. "Prepare to march."

To my relief, the men quickly formed the column, but not everyone moved as fast as I would have liked...or more precisely, as fast as I thought

Marcus would have wanted. Thankfully, I only needed to point my rod to get them moving.

I felt a mixture of relief and stress upon seeing Lucius returning. I stepped away from the column to give us some privacy as he stopped in front of me and saluted.

"She was nowhere to be found, *Optio*."

"You asked the merchant again?"

He nodded. "He told me she had been very cooperative the night before, and insisted that he had done nothing to harm her. Though he tied her to the bed before going to sleep, when they awoke this morning, the ropes had been cut and she was gone."

"Did you see signs of a struggle?"

"None, Sir."

"Do you think this merchant is lying?"

Lucius shrugged. "He seemed quite sincere and scared when I questioned him."

I turned away, wanting more than anything to take a handful of men back to the camp and tear it apart. Somehow, I knew she wouldn't be there. My stomach ached at the thought that this guy might have killed her during a rape attempt, and dumped her body in a shallow grave. I was hoping against hope that he had sold her to one of the slavers who left the day before.

At least she would still be alive.

Chapter 44

Remmy awoke in total darkness. After blinking several times to make sure her eyes were open, she still saw nothing in the blackness. The hard, erratically rocking floor under her told her little about where she was. Her last memory was of talking to her aunt, and then... She struggled with the bizarre memories, the flashes of images: a man she felt a strong attraction to, yet hated; another, uglier brute she wanted to skin alive; and a Greek she pitied.

She did not even try to move for several minutes until the floor painfully slammed her head, eliciting a cry of pain and flooding her nose and mouth with dust. Disoriented, she struggled to figure out where she was, and it took a moment to calm down enough to think it through. The floor continued to buck and shift, but it was the constant rumbling beneath her that finally made it clear where she was.

I'm in a cart and it's moving.

She looked around, searching for any source of light that might give her perspective -- a sense of where she was -- but there was darkness everywhere she looked.

When she tried to lift her hands to rub her aching temples, she felt a coarse rope tightening around her wrists as it stopped her. Trying again, she realized that both her hands and feet were tied. Suddenly overwhelmed with a desperate need to be free, she tried to sit up, but something coarse synched around her neck. When she tried to reach up to pull off the noose, the rope around her hands tightened again and her feet were pulled upwards. Several more attempts made it clear the rope binding her hands was also tied to her feet, and she could not lift her arms above her waist.

The sensation brought a flash memory of a rodeo cowboy roping and tying up a calf, only this time she was the calf, and there wasn't likely to be anyone around to untie her. Or, at least, not anyone she wanted to be around when she was untied.

Slavers!

She felt a flash of anger that made her strain against the bonds, but the struggle only tightened the noose, cutting off precious air. Lying back, she felt it immediately release.

She tried to call out, but a wad of something filled her mouth, the sudden realization nearly making her gag.

This can't be happening!

Another sharp jolt stopped the gag reflex. She clamped down on the rag which focused her mind as she lifted her head and stared into the dark corners of the confined space for something, anything to help her escape. Panic gripped her chest even tighter when she saw nothing except her own body and the ropes that bound her.

It was only when she lowered her head to the cart's floor again that she felt the leather strap covering her eyes.

Blindfold! Get it off!

Pressing her head against the floor, she tried to push the strap up, but it just slid over the smooth wood. Unwilling to give up, she tried again and again until her head rolled up on the rope running from her neck to the cart's deck. It was coarse enough to create the friction she needed to move the strap, but it also scraped her cheek, bringing a stinging pain.

She hesitated only briefly before trying again, gritting her teeth against the pain until the blindfold slipped up enough for her to see light streaming through many tiny holes in the crudely woven cloth covering her rolling cell.

After a tense moment, she was again jolted by the cart, and that took away some of the panic. Regaining her senses, she first struggled against the rope on her wrists, but it was so tight she could barely move them. Her fingers told her that her captors had not only wrapped a rope around her wrists, but then ran another rope over that one and between her wrists, cinching the rope as tight as could be done without totally cutting off circulation. Even so, she strained against her bonds, only stopping when she could no longer stand the pain of the coarse fiber digging into her skin.

You're not going anywhere, Sister, she thought, but before she could do more, the cart stopped.

Voices speaking too low for her to understand, drifted in, the urgency in their tone making it clear something was wrong. She wasn't sure why, but she knew slavers would not have to speak softly because during this time their abhorrent practice was legal, even sought after.

How do I know this? History class. Right. The Roman army enslaved their enemies.

If that were true, it meant her captors were not interested in selling her into slavery, and she could not imagine any scenario in which that was a good thing.

Chapter 45

As the elevator descended, Marcus struggled to maintain his balance. When it stopped he quickly shed his hospital gown and pulled on the pants he had been given. When Alvin handed him a T-shirt, he held it up.

"What say this?" he asked while looking at the brightly colored T-shirt displaying a rearing white unicorn with blood running down from its horn, around its eyes, and splattering its chest and forelegs.

Alvin shook his head. "It's some rock band named, *More to the Point*."

"I no understand."

"You probably don't have such mythical creatures in your time."

Marcus shook his head. "I think *Imperator* Caesar describe something like this he see in Germania, but I not see it."

A chime filled the carriage and to Marcus' surprise, the doors swept open. The legionnaire hesitated until Alvin hurried out and motioned for him to follow. Marcus quickly pulled on the shirt and cautiously peered out.

"Let's go, Roman," Alvin shouted as he pushed Remmy's wheelchair down the hallway. "We have to get out of here."

"Where all the people go?" Marcus asked as he looked around.

"What people?"

"The ones outside room when doors close."

"What peop...Oh," Alvin nodded knowingly. "We're on a different floor." He pointed at the ceiling. "Those people are now above us."

Marcus looked up, confused.

"We just rode down in an elevator." Alvin said then shook his head. "I know you don't know what that is, but..."

"Elevator. Yes. I have heard of such things," Marcus said, his eyes still wide as he looked at Alvin. "So where we go now?"

When Alvin pointed at the main entrance, Marcus charged ahead, his hands in front of him as he prepared to push the double doors open. As he drew near, they slid aside, making him stop in his tracks.

"*Quid est hoc?*" The soldier cried as he shied back.

"Move along!" Alvin shouted as he rushed past. "I'll explain all this later."

Being a man of action, Marcus quickly followed, but as he passed through the opening, he searched for an explanation as to why the doors moved without anyone there to do it.

"Surely, this is home of the gods," he muttered.

"And some of those gods are nasty creatures," Alvin responded while trying to ignore the harsh look his wife was giving him. "So let's get out of here."

"I hope they don't block off the parking garage before we can get out," Jasmina said as she and Tim caught up with them.

"Without our car, we don't stand a chance," Miriam insisted.

Since a building blocked the street just outside the entrance, it terminated in a tight, horseshoe turn that allowed cars to turn around without having to stop. To make better time, they cut across the end of the horseshoe on their way to the parking garage. They were only halfway through when Jasmina moved ahead of Alvin and waved him toward the sidewalk.

"There's a van coming our way," she announced. "Get Remmy onto the sidewalk."

He cut right and pushed the wheelchair in the direction indicated as the van raced around the sharp turn, its tires squealing as the driver leaned out his window.

"Missus Maxell," a familiar voice called as the van slid to a stop.

"Robert!" Jasmina cried while rushing to open the van's side door. "Thank God the cavalry is here!"

"We've got to hurry, Ma'am," Robert exclaimed as he jumped from the van. When Alvin started turning the wheelchair around, Robert held up a hand, palm out. "You'll have to leave the chair."

Before Alvin could argue, Marcus scooped Remmy up and carried her into the van.

His eyes wide, mouth open, Robert watched him disappear from sight before exclaiming, "Wow, that dude's fast."

Waving a hand at the others, Jasmina shouted, "No time for this. Get inside, quickly!"

Doing a one-hundred-and-eighty degree turn, Robert took two steps before stopping in his tracks.

"Oh shit!"

After guiding Miriam into the van, Jasmina looked back to see McFaddan coming through the main door.

"Stop!" he shouted as he stabbed a finger at them.

"Let's go!" Jasmina countered while jumping inside and pulling the door closed.

Robert climbed in, revved the engine and burned rubber as the doctor and his three associates raced after them. Everyone but Robert stared out the back window to watch the foursome grow smaller and smaller.

"This isn't over yet," Jasmina sighed.

"Not by a long shot," Robert added as he looked at her in the rearview mirror.

"What do you mean?" Tim asked from the passenger seat.

"Haven't you already figured it out?"

When Tim shook his head, Robert turned to Jasmina. "Surely you know, Missus Maxell."

Jasmina nodded. "They weren't really with the CDC."

Looking forward again, he gave an exaggerated nod.

"Not by a long shot, Ma'am," he repeated solemnly as the van squealed around a corner. "Not by a very, very long shot."

Looking over her shoulder again, she saw no cars pursuing them, and returned her attention to an anxious Marcus clutching Remmy as though doing so would keep him from flying off into space. Though she knew this situation was probably terrifying for him, there were more urgent issues to deal with.

"We have to make contact with Enid."

Marcus turned his attention to the woman in his arms, and to his surprise, she opened her eyes and glared at him.

"Who are you?" she demanded.

"Remmy? Is that you?" Jasmina asked.

Pushing away from Marcus, the woman looked at Jasmina and scowled. "That voice! You are witch who haunt me!"

"Enid?" Marcus asked.

She slid off of Marcus' lap, and dropped into a squat, seeming to take no notice that she was wearing nothing more than a hospital gown.

Her attention jerked from Marcus to Jasmina and back. "What you have done to me? Where is this place?"

When Marcus did not answer, she looked out of the van and realized things were zooming past her at breakneck speeds.

"*Is hanc magiam potest?*" she screamed as a bout of vertigo made her grab the back of the front seat and turn her attention to Jasmina. "I am bewitched!"

"No," Jasmina responded before leaning toward the front. "Robert? Find a side street and pull over. I think these two are getting car sick."

Without comment, Robert nodded and the vehicle slowed. Moments later, he pulled into a side street, and stopped the van.

Seeing the pair in front of her were seriously disoriented, Jasmina held up both hands, palms out.

"Listen. I know this is all very confusing, but you have to believe me. We are here to help you."

Though it was obvious she was struggling to keep panic in check, Enid defiantly jerked her head from side to side. "I no need help of witch."

After taking a quick look around, Jasmina asked, "Does anyone have a mirror?"

When everyone, but the two newcomers shook their heads, Robert reached up, yanked his rearview mirror off its mount.

"Don't know how I'm going to explain this to the insurance company," he said while handing it to her.

"Thank you," Jasmina said before turning to Enid. "You know what a mirror is, so I am going to show you something that will be a big shock."

Considering what Enid was going through, Jasmina wasn't surprised to see the puzzled look on her face, which turned to shock when she saw her reflection in the mirror.

"What is this?" she gasped then shook the mirror at Jasmina, demanding, "What is this?"

Struggling to remain calm, Jasmina pointed at the mirror. "It is just a common mirror. You and…" She pointed at Marcus. "…and Marcus have been transported into a different…world. An existence beyond anything you could…"

Enid was temporarily fixated on the mirror, but at the mention of Marcus' name, she turned to gawk at him. "You are the Roman?"

His expression cautious, body tense as though prepared for her to attack, Marcus nodded, then glanced down at his new body.

"I am he."

"You are nothing like him."

His smile tentative, he nodded. "Nor are you."

Eyes wide, mouth open, Enid slowly rotated her head to look around the van before peering out the window at a world she could never have imagined: mowed lawns, concrete sidewalks, smooth-sided houses with large windows, and cars in the driveways.

"What is this place?" she whispered.

Sighing, Jasmina turned her attention to Enid.

"Oh dear. That will take a little time to explain."

Chapter 46

"That cocky little shit," Quintus muttered as he slogged along beside his comrades.

The declaration left him frustrated because he was not sure if it was intended for the dark-haired stranger or Marcus. His hate for Marcus was fully justified. The man had taken his job as *optio*. A job Quintus knew was rightfully his.

"Give me just one chance. One chance," he growled. "I'd pound that son of a donkey's ass into a bloody pulp."

On the other hand, he also felt anger towards that slick-talking bug of a stranger who had the audacity to ask him to betray a fellow legionnaire. You didn't betray a brother...unless, as the slimy weasel so aptly pointed out, he betrayed you.

That was no excuse...and yet...it was.

No it's not! he chastised himself.

But the punishment he inflicted on you, the stranger's voice echoed in his head, *your humiliation. That was unforgiveable.*

No!

He had no right to treat you that way for what you did to the woman. She was plunder, and as much yours as his.

He is optio.

But is that how a good leader treats his subordinates?

The memory of slogging through the mud, biting flies, the stench of rot, the baking sun. Even though he smeared that stinking mud over his body, it quickly dried and flaked off, exposing skin to the burning sunlight and biting flies.

You deserved better! the stranger's voice echoed in his head.

The fly bites stung for some time, but now they itched like Pluto's fire.

I didn't deserve that.

You are a better soldier, Quintus. Marcus is obviously jealous of you.

You think so?

I know it is so, and that is not how a legionnaire should behave. Especially not an optio, a leader of men. Such an unworthy individual will get you killed. You have to defend yourself, and your fellow legionnaires. You have to eliminate this threat.

Quintus struggled with the suggestion, but he also knew the stranger had a point. Marcus had to be eliminated, but his stomach ached at the thought of doing such a thing. The punishment for killing an officer was severe: brutal beating, humiliation in front of your *centuria*, and then tied into a bag with a half-dozen poisonous snakes and thrown into a lake…in full armor.

A man would have to be mad to listen to that weasel of a stranger. Let someone else kill him!

He marched on, his anger growing as the weight of his two *pila* dug into a puss-filled bite on his shoulder.

Or maybe not.

Chapter 47

Sick with worry about Enid, I marched behind the first *centuria* and in front of the second, plodding along at a mind-numbing pace with no iPod to distract me.

Where can she be?

When Lucius had returned to say Enid was gone, I almost abandoned my post and ran to see for myself. My stomach ached from guilt, but I knew the punishment for desertion was death, and a brutal death at that. The brutality didn't matter as much as the thought that if I died, the world I had unwillingly left would disappear forever. I had no choice but to keep up the charade, get the army marching, and hope against hope that I could do whatever I was sent here to do.

My only consolation was that the last time I connected with a past life, all the injuries I suffered disappeared when the Chinese merchant's plan failed. According to Jasmina, once the merchant actually started executing his takeover, he created a new timeline with a different future. When his mission failed and he was sucked into a time vortex, all that he did vanished. That left me undamaged physically, but the memories of all that pain and anguish remained, along with the trauma of being kidnapped three times, and the fear of being sliced open while still conscious so a crazy person could get the blood from my living liver. I have to say, it took me some time to get over that!s

And if the world returned to "normal" the last time, I had to hope the same thing would happen this time. Even though we would remember what we had gone through, at least there would be no residual physical damage. Wherever Remmy was now, she would be returned to me if I saved Caesar's life.

Please let it be so, I prayed to whoever was out there listening.

The last two past-life experiences changed me. How could they not? The soldier I connected to in the last adventure gave me some experience fighting, but I also remembered that An-Chi and Mei-Xiu had planned to marry. Unfortunately, I knew An-Chi would not survive the next battle he was to fight, and that changed my relationship with Remmy in both a mental and physical way. Life was simply too short to be hesitant. We weren't yet living together, but I hoped to change that very soon.

I stepped on uneven ground and stumbled, which brought me back to the present. Embarrassed, I took a quick look around to see we were passing through a narrow opening in a forest, the sides of our path cluttered with frequent patches of brush. The men ahead were slogging on, many with their heads down, blindly following the soldier in front, their minds in their own magical world.

Feeling suddenly alarmed, I looked around, only by chance seeing a flash of light in the wood. When I focused more intently on that location, I saw movement and then many shadows slipping from tree to tree.

My brain froze, but my mouth took on a life of its own.

"AMBUSH!!"

As though possessed, I dropped the many pounds of gear I was carrying, grabbed my helmet from its cord hanging around my neck and pulled it on.

"Form up!" I screamed while freeing my shield from its cover before scooping up a pilum and charging toward the movement. As the men rushed to organize themselves, a roar of countless voices seemed to come from every direction.

True to their training, the men did as I did, and were ready in seconds. Unfortunately, the enemy descended on them like rabid dogs, spears embedding themselves in chests, arrows flying.

With a roar, I threw my pilum, gripped my shield and had a sword in my hand within three steps. The force of an ax bouncing off the shield, briefly throwing me off balance, but my well-conditioned body regained its footing. After two more strides, a screaming, blue-faced maniac burst from a nearby bush, his huge sword overhead, body leaning forward as he strained every muscle to get up to speed. Changing direction to head right at him, I pulled my shield up, leaned my shoulder into it and plowed into him. His sword went flying as air exploded from his lungs. When the impact straightened him, I brought my own sword up from below and into his belly clear to the hilt. He didn't have time to scream before I reflexively twisted the blade and pulled it out in a slashing move that opened him right up.

While my Gerry Patterson brain struggled to deal with the horrific violence, my Marcus Aremus body reflexively pushed him over backwards and charged on.

Though the attack had been sudden, and quickly executed, it was not well organized. The enemy were running out of the wood in no particular order or grouping.

Finding no one else close to me, I turned to see the leading men in the following *centuria* were starting to organize, but were not being attacked.

"Sound the alert!" I bellowed. "Form up and prepare to defend yourselves."

Their gear already on the ground, the men quickly pulled on their helmets, grabbed their weapons and ran towards me. Hearing footsteps behind me, I jerked around to see a blue-faced attacker, naked but for a loincloth, spear in one hand, long ax in the other.

Having no more spears, I remembered the *centurio's* instructions to the recruits just before Marcus had been promoted.

Strike hard and fast!

Sucking in a breath, I brought my shield up above my shoulder and turned sideways with my sword at the ready. Though the shield would protect me from a spear, this position gave me the added advantage of being able to throw my shoulder into the shield if he got close enough to make contact. Seeing my defensive pose, the Gaul tossed his spear aside, grabbed his ax with both hands, and bellowed like a speared cow.

I knew I had to take this man on in order to survive, but at that moment that bellowing warrior looked deadly, and despite what I knew, my brain was screaming for me to run like hell. Thankfully, my body was still in charge, crouching slightly as it prepared to charge at him, knowing that the man with the greatest momentum would win in a head-to-head collision.

It was then I fully realized there were two of us in this fight. Me, with my mind in one big knot, thinking *I gotta get out of here, NOW!* and Marcus' body seeming to relish the moment, springing from foot to foot, squeezing and relaxing my hand on the sword's hilt, never letting me take my eyes off the oncoming attacker. He seemed to be waiting for something, his head nodding slightly in rhythm with the attacker's footfalls.

In the next instant came the horrifying realization that if I didn't clear the screaming terror from my head and join the fight, we were going to die a brutal death. I took a deep breath, and tried to get in rhythm with my new body.

Do or die! Do or die! shouted in my head during the seconds it took for the attacker to close the distance between us.

"Do or Die!" I screamed as I lurched forward to the attack.

Chapter 48

A man's heavy breathing startled Remmy, and it was all she could do to keep her eyes closed and pretend to be sleeping.

"She's still out," someone said in Enid's native tongue, but with the strong accent of the southern Gauls. "We must move quickly. He will be here soon."

She heard the cover being stripped the rest of the way off and struggled to keep her eyes closed as hands groped her body, lifting her up and out of the cart. Her kidnappers did not appear to have noticed the leather band over her eyes was no longer covering her right eye. With her head resting on one of the arms holding her upper body, she carefully opened that eye just a crack to see the cart slowly moving away.

Or are we moving?

Footsteps beneath her confirmed it was the latter, and a moment later the light dimmed and the man carrying her unceremoniously dumped her on a dirt floor.

"Bar the door and keep watch," a high-pitched, voice ordered.

Footsteps moved away from her and a closing door dimmed the light even more.

"The client has not yet arrived," the high-pitched voice announced as his companion's footsteps drew closer again.

The second let out a grunt. "This one is a beauty."

She heard one man move even closer to her, his breath hot on her face. "Maybe we should entertain ourselves until he gets here."

"No," the first protested angrily. "He said she is to be unharmed. That is what the drug was for: to stop her from fighting us."

The second laughed. "I promise, I'll only spread her legs and do my thing. It won't leave any lasting damage if she's asleep while I do it. Who would ever know?"

"I don't think that is a good…"

"Oh shut up with your good ideas," the second mocked as he moved toward her feet. "It will only take a moment. There might even be time for you to have her. We both win."

There was a long pause before the first responded, "But how will you do it with her legs bound up like that?"

"That's easy. I just untie them. She's asleep, so what's it matter."

Tugging on at her ankles made Remmy want to open her eyes and scream, but the sensation of the plug of cloth in her mouth almost gagged her. It was all she could do to keep her stomach in check and her body relaxed as though she were really asleep. A moment later, additional tugging on her wrists almost forced her eyes open.

"Why are you untying her hands, Eno?"

"Stop being such a worrier, and watch the door."

As footsteps moved away from her, Remmy peeked out and saw the second man drop a satchel and then untie his tattered robe and strip it off, standing naked at her feet. He was a scruffy, thin man with splotchy pale skin and scruffy brown hair and beard that had not been combed in, probably ever.

When he dropped to hands and knees, she looked down at his satchel with a knife hilt poking out from a small pocket on the side. As he started to crawl forward, she hooked a foot on the satchel and tossed it toward her right hand. Her fingers instinctively wrapped around the hilt and she yanked the long blade out and slashed at his throat.

Reacting quickly, the attacker screamed oaths as he jerked out of range. Finding herself free, she yanked the rag from her mouth, rolled over and tried to stand, but he was on her back before she could fully straighten. After the two of them hit the floor, she saw his right hand reaching for the knife, and without thinking, brought the blade toward the arm wrapped around her throat and pulled hard until it dug deeply into his flesh. Howling like a crazed banshee, he fell off her back, his warm blood dribbling across her skin.

Knowing she could not hesitate, she jumped up to see her attacker gripping his wound and crying in protest,

"Ahhh! That bitch has killed me!"

Her attention quickly turned to his partner, who, despite his high-pitched voice, was quite stout and better armed. His red beard and hair were also unkempt, but his robe was clean and un-patched, his movements more like a soldier than his companion.

Staying where he was, he slowly pulled out a long, curved sword and glared at her.

"You don't want to be doing that, little one." He held up the sword menacingly while pointing at her knife with his other hand. "I'm thinking my stinger is more deadly than yours."

She looked from the shining sword to his determined face and felt her heart sink.

Struggling not to let out the sigh of defeat making her lungs ache, she dropped the knife and nodded toward his groaning partner. "He was going to rape me."

Smiling, the soldier shrugged. "The spoils of war."

"But you didn't capture me in battle. I was kidnapped."

He shrugged again, his expression not changing. "Makes no difference to me."

A whimper from his comrade made the soldier glance his way. Remmy looked as well and was shocked by the amount of blood pooling around him.

"You need to do something, or he'll bleed to death," she protested, not sure why she suddenly felt so much concern for a man who tried to rape her only moments earlier.

The soldier did not move, but continued to flick his attention from her to his partner until, with a pleading whine, the injured man dropped his arm and slowly fell onto his back.

"Guess that means I get to keep all the money," the soldier said flatly before turning his attention to her and pointing his sword. "Take two steps back and sit."

After glancing longingly at the knife, she squatted.

"All the way down, with your feet and hands in front of you."

After she complied, he stared at her for a long moment before walking up and kicking the knife across the room. Sheathing his sword, he picked up the cord and squatted at her feet. She winced when he roughly cinched the rope around her ankles.

After he bound her wrists just as tightly, he laughed. "I know I wasn't supposed to do any damage, but you have been such an uncooperative person, you leave me no choice."

Uncooperative? Remmy thought. *A big word for a common soldier.*

"Where did you get your education?"

Smiling knowingly, he rose, walked to the door and opened it a crack to peer out.

Still looking out, he said, "I'm not a green recruit, but then, I'm guessing neither are you."

"Why are you doing this?"

Without hesitating, he answered, "Money." A gruff laugh followed the statement before he looked at his dead partner. "And thanks to you, a nice bonus to boot."

"My people will pay you more."

He laughed again. "*Your* people are no more. The Romans have seen to that. Everything you used to have is now theirs to do with as they please, and I am certain none of them would part with an ounce of it to free your skinny ass."

She opened her mouth to respond, but stopped when he pulled the door open and the sound of footsteps echoed in the empty room. A moment later a thin man with a pinched face swooped into the barn, his eyes falling immediately on her.

"I see you have lived up to your part of the bargain," he commented flatly, as though he was stating the obvious. His attention shifted to the corpse. "Your partner did not fare as well."

For the first time since the stranger appeared, the soldier said, "That has no effect on our agreement. You hired me, you pay me, as agreed."

"Oh yes," the stranger responded almost gleefully as he reached into his cloak. "As agreed." When his bony hand reappeared, Remmy immediately recognized the silver pistol in it, but the soldier's eyes were blank when the stranger held it up to display it. "This pretty little thing would be priceless in this time, but the part of it that I'm going to give you is also worth a king's ransom. The only problem is…" he said while taking aim. "…it won't be of much use to you."

Remmy cried out as three loud pops echoed off the walls of the barn. The startled soldier stood for a long moment before his eyes glazed over and he flopped onto his back.

"Pity," the stranger said sadly as he buffed the shiny weapon with his sleeve. "I probably should have had him carry you out to the cart before I snuffed him." He gave an exaggerated shrug. "Hindsight sucks, doesn't it."

Still unable to grasp what had just happened, Remmy jerked her attention from the newcomer to the soldier and back.

"If I am correct," the stranger said while holding up the pistol, "I'm guessing you know what this is."

Swallowing hard, Remmy nodded.

The stranger nodded as well.

"Then I've found the right woman."

Chapter 49

"Missus Maxell," Robert announced before Jasmina could answer Enid's question. "We've got to get going. Those guys, whoever they are, will be putting up roadblocks any minute now. Where are we gonna go?"

Running fingers through her hair, Jasmina gave her head a shake before looking at him.

"I hadn't really given it much thought," she answered. "We obviously can't go to our own houses."

"Maybe we could rent a couple of hotel rooms," Alvin offered, but then shook his own head. "Oh no. That wouldn't work. They could trace us through our credit cards."

"We also have to find another vehicle," Miriam added. "They surely got Robert's license plate as he was driving away."

"How about my sister, Susan's place on the coast?" Alvin asked.

Tim shook his head. "The less time we spend on the road the better. They're probably already moving to block major highways."

"Well, we have to move quickly," Alvin argued, "or we won't even get out of town."

"Drive south," Jasmina stated as she pointed at Alvin.

"Seriously?"

She nodded. "Yes, but stay off the freeway. I have a dear friend in Jefferson, twenty-five minutes south of here. If we do this right, they'll never find us."

"I'm not sure I know how to get there without going on the freeway."

"Don't worry, I'll tell you where to turn. This is going to work. I know it will!"

"Why we go?" Marcus asked.

"We can't let them catch us before we figure out how to get you and Enid back home."

"Then we fight them like men, not hide in bushes like cowards."

"He is right," Enid added. "I will not run either."

When the van started moving, Marcus tried to rise, but hit his head on the ceiling. Confused, he looked up, but jerked his attention back down when Jasmina put a hand on his arm.

"Listen, you have to trust me," she said more calmly than she looked. "You're in a strange place, occupying someone else's body. We live by a different set of rules than you are used to, and if you violate those rules, we may never figure out how to get you back to your own time."

Marcus' response was cut off when the van accelerated. The sight of the world racing by threw off his balance and he sat down hard on the seat.

"How does this wagon go so fast?" he asked.

Jasmina shook her head. "Just think of it as magic, and leave it at that. I'm hoping you won't be here long enough to understand even if I did explain it."

When he started to turn green, Miriam pointed toward the front of the van. "Look that way. It is less disturbing because you can see where we are going."

After Jasmina motioned for Enid to sit beside Marcus, she stared out the front window for a moment before looking at him again.

"You are skinny," Enid said.

Looking at her, he shrugged. "As are you."

When she scowled, he shrugged again and looked ahead, but when Jasmina turned around to look at Enid, the expression on the girl's face was one of confusion, not anger.

"Are you OK, Enid?"

The puzzlement vanished as she jerked a nod. "Yes. Why would I not be?"

"You just look confused, is all. I'm wondering if you are feeling anything from your former self."

"How is this done?" she demanded angrily. "How do I know what is happening to the real me?"

Jasmina shook her head. "I'm not sure you can, but you might. When we get to a safe place, I want to connect with you and Miriam can connect with her son. Together we can see what is going on and try to move things along."

"But why can I not see for myself?"

"I don't know for sure, but it appears that your body is acting as a conduit to the past. I'm just hoping this switch of bodies hasn't broken that connection."

"And if it has?"

"Then I suspect a lot of people will die needlessly."

Marcus looked at Enid in Remmy's body, his expression confused. "I do not know this woman."

"You don't know the body she is in, but the person inside is the woman you captured on the battlefield. Please trust me."

"Why trust you?"

She shook her head. "Because that man we escaped from wanted to do something bad to prevent you from saving your general from an early death."

"And if I do not believe this?"

"Then Gerry and Remmy will die, and you will be disgraced." She locked eyes with him, her expression one of unmovable determination. "I cannot believe that is something you want to happen."

Marcus gulped in a breath, his face showing the movement of the vehicle was getting to him. Jerking his eyes forward, he took another deep breath and sighed. "I have no choice but to help."

"Each of us has a choice, Marcus," Jasmina said. "And as a warrior, you have to know that the right choice is to defend your general."

He scowled at her. "This you say, but I know of no plot to kill him."

"Then we have to find it, and soon."

Chapter 50

When spears started flying, Quintus quickly found himself in an organized cluster of twenty-four of his fellow soldiers. None of them needed to think about their formation, for they had practiced this situation many times. Since they were being attacked from both sides, they formed up in two lines, back to back, shields up, spears in hand.

"Two steps forward," someone shouted, and each line moved in the direction they were facing.

Quintus took a quick look around. The blue-faced attackers were disorganized. Hard-won Roman discipline would easily win the day, but when he saw Marcus send an opponent to the ground, he made a split-second decision.

Get closer to him.

"*Pila* at the ready!"

Unaware, and not caring who was calling out commands, he lifted the weighted spear over a shoulder, picked out an opponent, and focused on the man's ugly blue face.

"Forward!"

Each man lurched forward at the same time, their pace exacting, their line staying in nearly perfect order. At four paces they pulled their *pila* back in one swift motion and four paces later, released a single combined grunt and heaved the heavy spears into the air.

The enemy were somewhat closer than normal, but that only improved the legionnaire's accuracy. Out of a dozen spears, only one missed its mark. Even though the first line of enemy was decimated by the assault, more came up behind them. Instead of stopping, the soldiers pulled out their swords and kept running, throwing their shoulders into their shields just before they crashed into their opponents and quickly dispatched them.

The enemy line dissolved, turning the battle into a hand-to-hand mêlée with every man for himself. In this situation, Quintus turned into a fighting machine, his vision expanding as much as his helmet would allow while his focus was on the person ahead of him. Though his opponents were powerful fighters, they were not well disciplined, and few carried shields large enough to be useful. The combination of his razor-sharp *gladius* and heavy shield gave him a distinct advantage despite the longer blades or heavy axes these savages were using.

The best weapon a legionnaire had was his muscular body, finely tuned and conditioned by the thousands of hours of training. The training not only kept him in top physical condition, but gave him actual experience fighting one-on-one in various situations. In fact, it was quite possible, he knew more about Gallic weaponry than the Gauls did.

He was so pumped up with adrenaline, he barely heard his opponent's scream when he rammed his *gladius* into his stomach, twisted the blade and yanked it out with a practiced slashing motion. So intent on moving on to the next attacker, he gave no thought to finishing the man off.

He'll bleed to death soon enough.

Surging past his last combatant, his heart thumping, arms tensed as he took two paces forward, he scanned the area for the next fighter, and to his surprise, found himself outside of the cluster of fighters, looking in. He was preparing to charge back into the fray when a voice stopped him.

"Hang in there. We're coming!"

Confused, he turned to see his *optio* running toward him while waving at a dozen or more soldiers and urging them to follow. The absurdity of the statement made him stop. Even if he ignored the first sentence, because it made no sense, the second was totally out of character for a leader of legionnaires.

A legionnaire fights as though his troop is the only one at hand. If outnumbered, reinforcements are welcome, but a warrior does not fight as though they are expected. That is for his leaders to determine. He fights until either the enemy is defeated, or he is dead. For a leader to announce that he is bringing reinforcements is almost as absurd as if he were to show up in the middle of a battle with flasks of wine to pass around.

As much as Quintus hated him, he knew that Marcus Aremus was an experienced soldier who knew how to lead men. Why was he acting so strangely at such a critical time?

Before he had time to even consider an answer, a half-naked Gaul pulled away from the fighting and ran toward him. He blocked the man's ax with his shield, but his opponent was quick and jumped sideways before his sword could disembowel him. Trying to react to the move forced Quintus to twist at the waist, and when he shifted his shield to compensate, another ax blow caught its edge and pushed it hard against his left shoulder, twisting his upper torso around even more.

As he tried to get his feet back under him, his opponent threw his own shoulder into his shield, and before he knew it, Quintus was on his back. A shadow crossed his face, and he looked up to see the near silhouette of his attacker, ax above his head. He jerked his shield up, but the crushing impact of the ax split it from top to bottom. The Gaul was preparing for another quick stroke when something crashed into him, his body suddenly gone and the ax flipping end-over-end until the blade embedded itself in the ground only inches from Quintus' right shoulder.

Discarding the useless shield, he quickly righted himself to see Marcus rolling off the Gaul, his *gladius* now sliding across the ground on the opposite side of his opponent. The howling Gaul was on his feet in an instant, a long knife in his hand, the crazed expression on his face accentuated by the many loose strands of hair floating around his head.

What kind of move was that? he wondered.

Though the *optio* was also quickly on his feet, he had not pulled out his own long knife in response to the Gaul's threat. In fact, he seemed to be acting as though he did not know he had one.

Has he taken a blow to the head?

Quintus was prepared to step into the fray, when the stranger's voice popped into his head.

Just think of how you will enjoy being optio and having that woman all to yourself.

He wanted Marcus gone, but something deeper inside would not let him stand aside when killing was an option.

When the Gaul moved to attack Marcus, Quintus rushed in and rammed his sword into the man's naked breast. Though he regretted the move as soon as he did it, his puzzlement grew even more when he saw the near panic on Marcus' face, his eyes fixed on the fallen soldier.

Other legionnaires began arriving, and soon the remaining Gauls were running away as fast as their naked legs would carry them.

"Wait!" the *optio* cried. "Let them go."

The men stopped, looking frustrated. Quintus had not tried to chase the escaping enemy, as he was hoping if everyone else was paying attention to them, he might have a chance to kill Marcus.

As the men returned, Marcus ordered them to search the battlefield for injured and dead soldiers. It did not take him long to declare that they had lost only three men, with half-a-dozen wounded. Normally, the *centurio* or *optio* would order the men to "clean up", but when Marcus failed to do so, they moved on their own to dispatch those injured Gauls who had not escaped, but it did little to raise their spirits.

As he moved around the battlefield, kicking at enemy corpses, Quintus watched Marcus seem to recover himself and start ordering the men to gather their gear and prepare to continue the march. A runner was dispatched to inform the *centurio* of what had happened, and a small contingent was assigned to take the wounded to the surgeon. For his part, Quintus sighed as he collected his equipment, but the stranger's voice would not stay out of his head.

He must be dead before you reach the legion.

"Yeah, yeah," he muttered to himself as he kicked the broken remains of his shield. "And who is going to pay to replace this?"

The opportunity is yours for the taking.

"Only if I don't get caught," he muttered while looking around to make sure no one was close enough to hear.

You will have two opportunities, my friend. Stay close to your optio and help him find the way to his lost family.

He had told the stranger he would think about it, but the idea was like sour wine. The bitter taste of it turned his stomach, but the more he drank the more he remembered the many injustices Marcus had abused him with: the biting flies, slogging through knee-deep mud, not letting him wash off the grease he'd put on before they left for a ten-league march that evening.

He was starting to see reason in the stranger's offer.

"Maybe," he said while moving toward his place in the column, "but only if nobody's watching."

Chapter 51

"Where did you get a gun?" Remmy asked as the thin stranger slipped it into the pocket of his robe.

The man laughed malevolently, and the tenor of it made her gut cramp.

"I think you know the answer to that, *Slave Girl*."

"No, I don't. I mean, I know I'm connected to a woman from my past, but I couldn't bring anything from the future with me."

The stranger started to open his mouth, but a sly smile closed it.

"Then leave that as a mystery for now. The important thing is that you know I can not only kill you at any moment, but have the resources to make your life a living hell if you don't cooperate with me."

Remmy did not have to fake the sudden flush of fear that froze her mind. When the stranger's smile grew, she also knew the fear reflected in her expression.

"What do you want?"

He pointed at her feet. "For starters, I'm going to unbind your feet and help you up. You are then going to walk out to my cart and climb in." He patted the pistol in his pocket. "I don't have to tell you that running is not an option."

She stared at him for a long moment before she jerked a nod. Nodding as well, the stranger pulled a knife from his belt, and while holding the other hand over the gun in his pocket, leaned down and sliced the rope binding her ankles.

Though terror threatened to overwhelm her, Remmy had been a British soldier in another past life, and that training seemed to help her get a grip on what was happening. Pushing the panic down, she rose slowly, her muscles tense, knees slightly bent. Seeing her pose, the stranger took several steps back and pulled out the pistol.

Pointing it at her knees, he scowled. "Shooting you in the leg will not reduce your value in the slightest, and as I have already shown…" He nodded at the dead soldier. "…I will not hesitate to do it."

She looked at the two corpses, flies already congregating on them, and felt panic overtake her again. Sucking in a deep breath, she returned her attention to the stranger and nodded.

"What will I call you?"

He huffed derisively. "Get in the back of the cart and lay down."

Trying her best to at least appear calm, she marched past him, but stopped when she saw two carts, side-by-side. Moving up behind her, he announced,

"The larger one."

Walking to it, she crawled in and lay down. After he appeared at the back of the cart, she saw him pocket the gun and pull out a cord. She thought of kicking him before he could tie her feet, but realized that unless she could knock him out, he would have the gun up and ready before she could be on him, and her hands were still bound.

She flinched when he cinched the rope and roughly finished tying the knot. When he was done, he walked out of sight. Curious as to what he might be up to, she rose enough to see over the cart's edge, and saw him removing the harness from the mule on the other cart. After slapping the beast's hind quarters and sending him on his way, he started to return to his own cart, but stopped halfway and looked back. After a moment, he returned to the other cart and removed two ropes from the back.

Remmy lay back down and looked around to assess her situation. Her hands were bound tightly, but that wouldn't stop her from rolling out when they got close to civilization again. He could claim she was a slave, but Marcus had not branded her, so it was her word against his. A sudden shadow made her look up to see the stranger lift up his ropes and point to her.

"Do not try anything."

After she nodded, he bent over the side and used one rope to tie her hands and feet together. Making a loop in the second rope, he put it over her head, cinched it around her neck and secured it to a hook in the floor of the cart.

"I will not put a gag in your mouth, but if you shout out, even once..." He pulled out his knife and held it to her throat. "...I will make you a permanent mute."

Swallowing hard, Remmy struggled against the fear that made her jerk a nod.

To her surprise, the stranger held up a leather water jug close to her mouth. "This is going to be a long journey, so you had better have some water."

When she hesitated, he tilted the skin, splashing water onto her face.

"Either drink or I dump it onto the ground."

She hesitated a moment before opening her mouth and letting him pour the water in, but after only a couple of swallows, he lifted it up.

"That's enough for now. Maybe I will give you more later, if you don't cause any more trouble."

Angry and frustrated, she asked, "If I can't speak, how will you know when I have to…"

He laughed and splashed some more water on the cart's bed. "As you can see, water runs right through the floorboards."

When she didn't respond, he tied off the mouth of the water skin and stowed it.

"Then we shall have a pleasant journey."

Chapter 52

Marcus and Enid were both decidedly green by the time the van stopped in front of the small house in Jefferson. Jasmina opened the side door.

"Come with me, and we'll get this sorted out."

Eagerly following her, they both sucked in a deep breath when back on solid ground, their stride unsteady as a couple of drunks.

"Stop," Jasmina ordered as she held up a hand in front of them. "Give yourselves a moment to recover. That ride couldn't have been easy for you."

"I'll hide the van," Robert announced while closing the side door, "and get some other wheels."

Turning to him, Jasmina shook her head. "No. You've done enough. If you get caught, you could lose your job."

His head shaking, Robert waved her off. "Ma'am, this is no time to worry about my job. I saw that nurse disappear, and if we don't get this sorted out, and soon, more people will vanish, and one of them could be me."

Jasmina nodded. "Good point." Turning to Marcus and Enid, she added, "Let's get you inside. The fewer people who see you here the better."

After Tim and Alvin lead the youngsters inside, Jasmina stopped in the doorway and looked back at Robert's van disappearing around a corner. The stress of the situation made her heart ache, and she hesitated a moment to gather strength before moving inside and closing the door.

"I have to believe that if Marcus and Enid are alive, so are Jerry and Remmy," she muttered while moving to the living room where the foursome clustered together.

"What do we do with them now?" Tim asked before anyone else could speak.

Jasmina shook her head. "What do you mean?"

"Well, these two are from the first century BC. The more they know about our time, the more they can influence their own in ways that wouldn't have happened if they had not seen what we have today."

"So we need to keep them from seeing any more than is necessary."

He nodded. "More than that. We have to make sure we don't talk about things they haven't heard of yet. More specifically, these two are soldiers." He looked briefly at the twosome settling in on the couch, and when he turned back to Jasmina, he lowered his voice to a whisper. "The Romans were leaders in military weaponry for centuries. Can you imagine what a gun or explosives would do to warfare in their time? They might still be rulers of the known world in this day and age."

Her expression grim, Jasmina nodded. "I hadn't thought of that."

He held up a framed picture of three people. "I just pulled this off the wall." He pointed at the picture. "This is some kind of archery competition."

"Of course. My friend and his wife compete all over the country."

Alvin nodded as he tapped one of the bows in the picture. "This compound bow was unheard of in Roman times. It can shoot farther and with greater accuracy than anything they had. It's not just guns and explosives we have to worry about. We've got to find pictures, magazines, flyers, and certainly equipment from any kind of competition and hide it."

"But they saw the van we were in. Surely that can be used as a weapon."

Alvin smiled grimly. "I may be wrong about this, but I've been watching them. It seems they do have access to Gerry and Remmy's memories, but only if they ask the right question." He guided her into the next room, out of sight of the others. "Take the van for instance. If I asked Gerry how to make the van go, he'd most likely say he puts the key in the ignition, puts it in gear and steps on the gas. It wouldn't occur to him to say anything about how an internal combustion engine works, or how gasoline is made, so if they don't specifically ask about those things, they aren't likely to pull up that memory."

She pointed at the picture in Tim's hand. "You mean that if one of us talks about a compound bow, and if Gerry or Remmy knows how one is built then Marcus or Enid will know."

He nodded. "That's the way it looks to me."

Jasmina's mouth dropped open as her eyes went wide with fear. "Both of our kids learned about gunpowder, gasoline, and lots of other things in chemistry class."

Tim moved to the doorway and looked back into the living room, his gaze on them as he spoke.

"Then we've got to tread very carefully with these two, or our world is going to change dramatically, and I dare say, not for the better."

Chapter 53

Seeing a legionnaire on the ground with a Gaul ready to finish him off, Marcus' body instinctively charged forward, my shield held up in front of me as I prepared for the inevitable impact. Within five paces of my opponent, I put on a burst of speed, slamming into the Gaul, his howling drowning out nearly everything else, including my own wailing scream.

The jarring whump of impact knocked us both to the ground. I quickly jumped up, as did my opponent, but he had his back to me. Quickly spinning, he brought his sword around and charged at me again, bellowing in his strangled language, his weapon rising as he prepared to split my head open.

Unsure as to what to do, I staggered back, lifted my own sword and prepared to block his stroke. I realized almost immediately that this was the wrong thing to do. His forward momentum added to the power of his strokes, while my backpedaling weakened mine.

His angry brown eyes terrorized me as I stumbled backwards, struggling to control my heavy sword.

I'm dead!

I watched the sword rise above his head and knew mine wasn't going to be there in time to stop it. Certain death was seconds away when the working end of a *pilum* appeared in the middle of his chest.

Without understanding, I watched in total shock as he gasped, spit blood, and fell onto his face. My stomach heaved as I stared at the fallen warrior, nearly letting my sword and shield drop to the ground, but before that could happen, the roar of charging legionnaires pulled my attention away from him.

Acting on instinct alone, my body turned to join them. The Gerry Patterson part of my consciousness was confused and disoriented, but the other part was supercharged with an adrenaline rush the like of which I'd never felt before.

As we crashed into the line of fighters, the men disbursed, taking on anyone not wearing a legionnaire's uniform. My own body was now fired up and in need of contact, so I looked around until I saw another legionnaire on the ground and about to be impaled by a Gallic warrior. I didn't know what else to do, so I lowered my head and charged right into the man. Upon impact my feet went out from under me and I crashed to the ground.

I instinctively jumped to my feet, and only then realized I'd lost my sword.

Shit!

Taking a quick look around, I spied my weapon behind my opponent. Panic froze my brain for a moment -- which in battle is far too long -- and before I could react, the Gaul had a knife in hand and was running toward me. The crazed blue face, the wild hair terrified me, and unlike last time, my body did nothing but wait for my command.

I'm a dead...

An instant before impact, the Gaul vanished from sight, and I was lost for a moment before movement on my right pulled my attention in that direction to see Quintus twisting his blade and yanking it from my howling opponent.

The bellowing suddenly stopped, the Gaul went limp, and Quintus straightened to scowl at me. I wanted to thank him, but my mouth wouldn't work, my stomach threatened upheaval, and my legs wouldn't allow me to turn away. I could see his right arm, chest and face were covered in blood, and that made the convulsions in my stomach worse, but he only hesitated a moment before charging into the next fight.

The men I arrived with quickly turned the tide of the battle, and the enemy were soon running away. I saw one legionnaire catch up with a limping Gaul and hack him down from behind. The assault was brutal, and did not stop even after the body was no longer moving.

"Let them go," I shouted, as the rest of the enemy were already too far away for our heavily-armored legionnaires to catch them.

Several men turned to give me puzzled looks.

"Regroup and get ready to move out," I commanded, though I'm sure the thought did not come from me. "We are falling behind the others."

Though the men looked dispirited, they did not argue, and I watched them move to complete their grizzly tasks before gathering their gear and forming up. The occasional cry of a wounded Gaul being dispatched made me cringe, but I knew this was the way things were here and the last thing I wanted to do was go against convention. In the Roman Army, a squeamish soldier was a disgrace, a hesitant leader dies.

As I watched the men doing what was certainly second nature to them, I was left with only one thought.

Please God, get me out of here!

Chapter 54

Though the army was soon marching again, the monotony of the walking was countered by the tension Quintus felt, both at the prospect of another attack, and his indecision over what he would do if another opportunity presented itself.

He twisted around to look back at Marcus marching alone between the two lines of men. In this narrow wood, they marched only two abreast, and that stretched the men out so that only a few could see the *optio* at any time. When they turned a sharp corner, he might even be out of sight of anyone in the troop. If the situation were right, Quintus could slip into the brush and ambush him at a place where no one else could see them.

No, he chastised angrily, *he's a clever fox, that one. He'd put up a fight and the others will be on us before I can get away.*

His mounting frustration, combined with a throbbing fly bite on his shoulder, inflamed his anger. He wanted more than anything to lash out at someone, and had not realized he was wordlessly vocalizing his frustration until he saw the puzzled look of the legionnaire beside him.

"What's your problem?" he growled.

Without comment, the other soldier shrugged and looked away. That only made him want to hit the man, but was restrained by the knowledge of the additional punishment the *optio* would rain down on him.

That bastard is out to get me, and he will too, if I don't get him first.

Continuing to plod on, he nearly groaned when he saw more light ahead: a sign they were leaving the wood. His opportunity had passed. There were no more places for him to hide.

When the path widened, the *optio* bellowed. "Form up four abreast."

Though the command was expected, Quintus swore. Marching in a denser formation made it easier for the men to form up when attacked. It also meant more potential witnesses if he tried to kill Marcus.

As they slowed to allow those behind to catch up, the *optio* stepped to one side of the column to call out orders. The move made Quintus even angrier because his tormentor was now further away, making it harder to attack him.

Swearing internally, he scanned the men around him, frustrated that he could see no way to get Marcus alone and earn his revenge and the promised woman. However, a chance look at the head-high brush behind the *optio* nearly made him call out. With great effort, he dampened his natural instinct and jerked around to look the other way. Even though there was no wind, the brush was moving ever so slightly: a sign that men were moving through it.

Marcus was between the men and the brush, his attention on the column, his loud bellowing drowning out any sounds behind him.

Quintus felt himself smile. *I might not have to do anything to get rid of this bastard. Let the Gauls do my dirty work.*

Fighting to resist the sudden rush of adrenaline, he started moving toward Marcus, but stopped after only two paces. He had no reason to approach the *optio*. Doing so would only raise suspicions, and if this was to work, he did not want to do that. For a long moment, his mind remained blank, his muscles tightening from the frustration until he remembered the *Nervii* arrows he had picked up after the last skirmish. He had only taken them as a keepsake, but now he realized it wasn't necessary to get the *optio's* blood on his sword.

If they fail to kill him, a Nervii arrow will do the job nicely.

Chapter 55

With a dusty blanket stretched over the cart, Remmy could not tell which direction they were headed, but from the harsh jostling her aching body was absorbing, the cart was moving at a good pace. The trip would have been monotonous were it not for the frequent sharp jolt that sent her sliding across the cart's narrow bed. The sudden move tightened the noose around her neck, making breathing difficult until she wiggled closer to where the rope was tied and released the pressure.

She tried to free her hands, but with both wrists bound tightly together, palms in, she could hardly even get the tips of her fingers to the knot at the back of her left wrist, let alone untie it. The painfully tight knots made her want to cry out, but she could not forget the sincerity in her captor's voice when he held the knife to her throat and threatened to cut her vocal cords if she spoke again. She did not think he was a surgeon, but had little doubt he knew how to do just that.

After a short time, she began to feel sleepy, which considering the dire nature of the situation, surprised her.

The water was drugged.

Though she fought against it, she gradually slipped into an unhappy dream world in which she had the overwhelming feeling she was naked and exposed, not to the eyes of men, but to the whole universe. Her hands and feet still bound, she desperately scanned the area for someone to help her, but saw only a cold, dark-gray mist that swirled aimlessly around her until ominous shapes began to appear, moving around her like a pack of wolves preparing to attack. At first, the shapes were indistinct and kept their distance, but after a time they started condensing into wolf-like shapes that flew at her only to vaporize just before their drooling fangs reached her flesh. More shapes began to coalesce into lions, tigers, hyenas, and men with vampire-like teeth, and swords protruding from their crotches.

Each time a creature attacked, the slashing teeth drew closer and closer until they finally dug into her skin sending an electric surge through her, the painful shocks getting worse and worse until she awoke with a start, disoriented and afraid.

Realizing that she was still in the cart, she jerked her eyes down to see she was still wearing the simple tunic Marcus had given her after Quintus had destroyed her leather uniform. Now fully alert, she was struck by how different things felt: the air was drier, no birds chirped, and it was quite warm. Listening, she heard the wheels of the cart crunching over hard ground as opposed to the softer grasses and duff they had been crossing.

Where are we? she wondered, but kept her tongue as she looked at the tattered covering above her, its appearance seeming to be even more threadbare than she remembered.

Her stomach cramped. *Something has happened!*

Numb with exhaustion, she fought the return of sleep, but the adrenaline rush lasted only a few minutes before fatigue regained control, its misty tendrils fogging her brain, and dissipating her anguish until she once again fell asleep.

She awoke again to the sound of someone calling out in a language she did not understand. From her connection with Enid, Remmy understood the language of the Nervii, and just enough Latin to carry on a conversation. She could also follow the dialects of most of the nearby tribes Enid had come in contact with, but the language this person spoke was totally alien to her.

The stranger replied back so casually this could have been his native tongue. A moment later the cart stopped and footsteps around her made it clear there was more than one person outside. Her captor continued to speak with the first person, but not a word made sense to her. It was as though they were not even from this planet.

Oh God, she thought as hands grabbed the side of the cart and a scratchy-voiced man asked a question to which the stranger gave a curt response. *Are these people with the Tsabbat?*

It shocked her to recall the black emptiness she felt when the *Tsabbat* attacked the person with whom she once shared a body. It was not just that this creature was pure evil, but it had its mind set on disrupting human history. Thankfully, another force that neither she nor Gerry knew much about was using them to disrupt the *Tsabbat's* plans. They had been too late when Gerry had been connected to a woman in late-19th-century England. He should have been there a decade earlier when her husband went off to the First Boer War. Because he was so badly injured they never had the child who would grow up to stop the assassination of Archduke Franz Ferdinand that lead to the First World War. However, he had later connected to a soldier in China during the end of the Han Dynasty. With Jasmina's help, he had stopped a power-hungry Chinese merchant from disrupting history and making himself emperor of the world.

As light flooded in, fear nearly overwhelmed her as the dark silhouette of a man stared down at her, his face close, but in the dim light his eyes were empty-black sockets, thick lips forming a malicious smile that made her feel naked again.

He is not the stranger!

The thought did nothing to relieve the tension squeezing on her lungs.

And now we're at it again.

The stranger barked a sharp command from his perch on the wagon's bench, and the glaring person pulled back and looked up, his lust vanishing as he tossed the cover aside, his tone submissive when he responded.

She felt the cart jerk as the stranger dismounted, but before she could get her lungs working again, he appeared on the opposite side of the cart.

"These men have other ideas as to how you should spend your time with us, but they will not dare touch you unless I tell them to." He gave an exaggerated shrug. "Maybe, if my original plan does not succeed, I might do just that."

From his gloating smile, Remmy knew feelings of vulnerability and fear were written across her face, and for reasons she could not explain, that made her angry. Scowling, she glared at him defiantly, but it was hard to hold that pose when he produced a knife and moved it close to her face.

"Hold perfectly still," he demanded as the fingers of his free hand slipped under the rope around her neck.

She sucked in a breath and held it as he lowered the blade to her throat, and only released it when he sliced the rope and pulled back. As she tried to guess what he was up to, the stranger grabbed her wrists and cut them free as well. When he moved to her feet, she opened her mouth to speak, but could not utter a word before he gave her a stern stare and pointed the knife blade at her.

"I will make it plain for you," he said flatly. "We are many leagues from anywhere, and the desert sun will melt your brain long before you see another person." He sliced the rope around her ankles, bringing a sudden relief that made Remmy gasp as he stabbed a finger at the ramshackle hut behind him. "You will stay in that shack until I come for you. These men will remain outside." She could not help cringing when he scraped the blade of his knife over the stubble on his face before waving it at the men behind him. "Understand, that only one of them speaks Latin, and he is unshakably loyal to me. He will keep the men in line and make sure they follow my instructions not to enter the hut for any reason. On the other hand, if you try to leave…just once, under any circumstances, they are free to do what they will." He laughed. "Short of killing you, that is."

She took a quick look at the dirty, scruffy degenerates gathering behind him, the lust on their faces making her heart race, stomach cramp, and it was all she could do to stifle the scream in her throat.

Do not show fear!

She almost laughed at the absurdity of the thought.

Far too late for that, she thought then said in as defiant a tone as she could muster, "And what will your client think of that?"

The stranger chuckled again. "My client does not care what condition you are in. As long as you are alive, his needs will be met."

It took several heartbeats for Remmy's mind to grasp what he was saying and another long moment for the next question to work its way to her lips.

"What...what does he want with me?"

His laugh was raucous and loud, as though she had told the mother of funny jokes. When he regained control, he turned to the men and shouted in their strange tongue, producing a chorus of laughter. Wiping his eyes, he waved over two of the men before turning to her.

"Ahhhh ha. That is the hilarious part," he chuckled as the men moved to the cart and yanked her from it. While they held her in front of him, the stranger nodded toward the remaining men. "I know very well what these men will do to you, if given the chance, but as for my employer's intentions..."

He laughed again, and she shuddered with fear when the men holding her laughed as well.

"I have absolutely no idea."

Chapter 56

"What is…?" Marcus started to ask as he pointed at the dark wide-screen television against the wall opposite the couch.

Jasmina quickly waved a hand dismissively. "We'll talk about that later, but for now, we need to make contact with our children to see if they are OK and to help them if we can."

His eyes on the TV, Marcus hesitated for a long moment before turning his attention to her.

"We also want to know what is happening with our…bodies."

Enid jumped to her feet. "I cannot sit and wait to die. We must attack while the opportunity is at hand."

"Attack?" Miriam asked.

"The ones who chase us," Enid responded insistently. "They know this land better than we do. We must attack now while we have the advantage of surprise."

"But we need weapons," Marcus added as he also stood. "And more men." He turned to Jasmina. "You must find us allies to take on this enemy."

"No," Jasmina cried. "Your usual tactics will not work in our time."

"Wait," Alvin called. "Maybe they will."

"What?"

He shook his head. "I don't mean swords or guns, but there are other 'weapons' we can use against them, like public opinion, the press, or even a politician or two."

It was Jasmina's turn to shake her head. "We can't make this public."

Barking a laugh, Alvin pulled out his cell phone, but before he dialed, he nodded to her. "No, but we can expose the guys trying to kidnap our children, and I just remembered something that makes sense of this."

"What is that?" Miriam asked.

"We need to contact the CDC."

"The CDC? But they're the ones who sent them."

His head shaking, he lowered the phone. "Voicemail."

He hesitated for a moment before motioning for Tim to let him use the laptop.

"I have another idea."

"What?" Jasmina asked.

Alvin typed commands on the computer and stared at the screen for a long moment before turning to her.

"Just as I thought," he said before rotating the laptop so everyone could see it. "If those guys had been with the CDC and believed Gerry and Jasmina had deadly diseases, they'd have quarantined everyone who had contact with us and worn protective clothing before even entering the room. When this doctor, Hiram McFaddan, told us his name, I knew there was something wrong, but at the time it was just a feeling." He pointed at the screen. "According to this news report, that guy died three months ago in a car accident."

"Oh my God!" Miriam cried.

Jasmina moved close to the screen and read it. "But this article doesn't name the victim. How do you know it is him?"

"I remembered because I have a cousin who works for the CDC in Florida and she e-mailed me when it happened. She was quite upset because she worked with the guy and he wasn't that old."

"But why doesn't this article list his name?"

Alvin shook his head. "That's the really strange part. When it happened, the local newspaper reported his name and the cause of the accident, but by the time it hit the AP newswire, his name had been removed. She only knew about the change because the revised article appeared in her paper the next day, and when she mentioned it at her office, she was told it was some kind of terrorist thing and she was not to talk about it until the FBI got it sorted out."

"And what happened after that?"

"She doesn't know. No one will talk about it."

"And now a dead man shows up in Oregon and tries to kidnap us."

Alvin's pocket chimed. After pulling out his cell phone and looking at it, his expression turned grim.

"I texted my cousin to see if she had this doctor's picture." He held the screen so Jasmina could see it.

The smiling face on the screen had ruddy cheeks, green eyes, and thin lips. Wavy red hair topped his head, making it clear this was not the same person.

"This is serious trouble," Jasmina sighed.

Chapter 57

I broke ranks, and moved to the side of the line of troopers to see they were drifting out of formation.

"Pick it up, slackers," I shouted, desperately hoping I sounded like a leader.

Tired and bored from the long day of marching, they responded slowly, and I was about to shout another order when I saw Quintus staring at me. He looked like a kid who believes he has gotten away with something, and I was pretty sure it had to do with me. I, or rather Marcus had humiliated him, and a bully always wants revenge.

But what could he do in front of all these people?

His attention shifted to something behind me and I sucked in a sharp breath when he smiled.

What is he...oh shit!

Knowing I could not sound the alarm based on a bully's smile, I moved toward the men coming from behind, calling for them to keep the pace and maintain formation.

Halfway to them, I turned to look at the brush lining the edge of the clearing. My stomach cramped when the tops of some tall plants jerked slightly. There was no wind and a quick about face revealed the same thing on the other side.

"Prepare for attack!" I bellowed. "Enemy on both sides."

Unneeded equipment crashed to the ground, helmets flashed as they were slipped on, shield covers fell away, and feet pounded the dirt while the men hurried into formation.

"Archers at the front. Prepare to fire."

While every legionnaire was competent with bow and arrow, it was my good fortune that some of the best archers in our legion were trained by Marcus and were nearby.

Since the attackers were coming from both sides, I used hand signals to wave half of the men to one side and the rest to the other. In seconds they were lined up in perfect rows.

Seeing we had time, I shouted, "Second row to the front, form up behind your shields."

As expertly and coolly as though this were an unarmed practice, the second row slipped between the archers, and knelt behind their shields, effectively protecting the archers from enemy arrows.

The savage hoard's ear-splitting scream did not fluster my men, but it almost made me drop my sword. Arrows buzzed through the air, thunking into shields, banging off armor, but by the time the enemy came out of the brush, a third row of legionnaires had formed behind the first two, and without a word from me, lifted their shields over the heads of the archers to protect them from above.

"Archers! Release!"

The men were like robots, their arrows zipping away with practiced regularity, sending the first wave of attackers to the ground. I continued to be surprised and hugely grateful for how little I had to do to keep these soldiers working in harmony. Unfortunately, though the attackers were falling by the dozens, more came.

I was happy that Marcus' commands came so automatically I didn't have to think of what to say.

"Cease fire! Front row up. *Pila* at the ready. Forward!"

A shout from behind made me turn to see a cluster of legionnaires coming out of the wood. Though running our way, they were already forming into battle lines.

I pointed at the closest group.

"Half of you cover the flank on this side, the rest over there."

The men did not miss a step as they changed direction and moved into position.

Seeing all was under control here, I hurried between the opposite-facing rows to the other side to see those coming back to help were already formed up and marching to cover the flanks on that side. The sight gave me a rush of exhilaration.

By the time I arrived, the two opposite-facing rows were meters away from engaging the enemy.

"Throw *pila*," I commanded.

Unlike legionnaires, the charging Gauls did not maintain even rows, meaning that some of the men in our line engaged the enemy before others. The mismatch threw our front lines out of order, and after the first impact, some Gauls broke through. Thankfully, the second row in the formation took care of them, but it didn't take a seasoned commander to realize that this would create confusion.

My exhilaration turned to panic when I saw men in the second row falling.

What do I do?

The words flowed into my head like magic.

"Hold formation!" I bellowed. "Tighten your lines."

To my utter shock, the command made a difference, but despair quickly returned when I saw a huge Gaul take out two legionnaires with the powerful swing of his oversized ax. The man was more than a foot taller than those around him, and built like a bull with thick, powerful arms and legs. Unlike his nearly-naked comrades, this one wore a bright brass breastplate, and helmet. As his return swing knocked another man down, he bellowed words that seemed to inspire the enemy. The Gauls pressed their attack and he followed them in, howling as he went.

I was struggling to think of what to do when he stopped, backed away from the battle line, and looked directly at me.

Ooop!

Nearly paralyzed with fear, I saw his head move slowly from side to side as though he had sized me up and found me wanting.

You can defeat him, the voice in my head insisted.

Say what?

Big men tend to be slow witted. He will charge directly at you and try to use his strength to defeat you.

And this helps me how?

Your advantage is intelligence and speed. Use them!

I tore my eyes from the giant long enough to see the enemy was now fully engaged with my men. There was little I could do to help them, except…

A primal roar jerked my attention back to the big man as he leaned forward and started running toward me.

He is yours now.

The air completely vanished from my lungs. *Are you shitting me?*

The huge man pointed his ax at me and I nearly wet my drawers when he bellowed like a gored ox.

I was searching for a place to hide when my throat roared, "*Pilum!*"

As someone tossed me his weapon, another legionnaire ran in front of this earth-shaking giant. With the weapon in hand, I was beginning to feel more confident, but my heart sank when the ax swung wide, and the legionnaire's sword and head flew into the air. Without skipping a step, the Gaul moved past the poor fellow before his headless corpse hit the ground.

I nearly fell down as well.

You must be quick and decisive.

Despite my overwhelming fear, Marcus' body seemed eager to fight. I knew then that I either had to work with it or die. Sucking in a deep breath, I started running, and only then realized that my legs were strong, arms eager, fist gripping the spear so tight it would not slip until I released it.

The middle of the chest, the voice demanded, but the Gaul's flashy breastplate made me unsure.

The head will be a faster kill.

The head is harder to hit. Go for the chest.

I held up the *pilum* and the giant did the same with his monster ax. My stomach quivered at the sight of blood running down its blade.

Son of a bitch!

I let my body charge forward, hefting the weighted pilum as I howled to vent fear. Bellowing in response, my opponent lowered his head, gripped his ax, and pumped his legs even harder.

Shit! Shit! Shit!

I couldn't close my eyes.

Shit! Shit! Shit!

I couldn't change direction.

Shit! Shit! Shit!

He seemed to grow in size until it seemed like I was attacking a mountain.

The mountain bellowed again, took three long strides while he hefted that enormous ax over his shoulder. The thick muscles in his right arm knotted, and his sweating face scrunched up from the effort he put into throwing his weapon. My *pilum* was suddenly over my own shoulder, and though I felt like a terrified kid in a runaway car, I strained every muscle to heave it and immediately dove to my right. It was like watching a slow-motion movie: the ax flipping end-for-end, its broad blade glistening in the sunlight, and my body moving far too slowly to get out of its way.

The blade slammed my shield and spun me around. Up and down blurred together until my face hammered dirt. The jarring pain of impact scrambled my brain, but my muscles worked automatically until I was on my feet again.

When my vision cleared, I saw my opponent had stopped, my *pilum* hanging from his breastplate.

Gotcha!

My mini-celebration was cut short when he reached around and yanked out his massive sword. Stunned, I unsheathed my own sword, but compared to his, it looked like a sewing needle. Though I expected him to fall, I watched in stunned silence as he grabbed the shaft of the *pilum* and hacked it off to leave the soft metal part of the shaft hanging from his chest.

HOLY SHIT!

Though his face was distorted with pain, he called out in his strangled Gallic tongue and beckoned for me to approach. I hesitated, hoping he would just collapse from blood loss, but after a dozen heartbeats, panic rose in my chest again.

Fall down, damn it!

I tried to back up, but my muscles wouldn't cooperate.

You have to finish this! the annoying voice demanded.

HOW?

Your body knows what to do. Just let it!

I was tired of the voice, but since running was not an option, I took a deep breath, and felt Marcus' natural reflexes waiting for me to give the order.

This is the stupidest…

Without finishing the thought, I pulled my shield tight to my body, gripped the hilt of my sword, and charged. With each step it seemed the Gaul's pain and rage increased. He gripped his sword with both hands and waited.

Shit! I won't even get close.

Throw your sword.

Seriously?

As I drew near, the Gaul lifted his weapon over his head, obviously intending to split me in two with a single downward stroke. However, just outside the reach of the great man's sword, I whipped my sword back, let my grip drop to the rounded pommel, and heaved it as though throwing a knife. A slight downward flick of the wrist sent it on such a flat line I lost sight of it until the blade embedded itself in his exposed throat.

The man's expression changed from expectation to wide-eyed shock as he took a step back, lowered his sword, and reached for the offending weapon. Still running, I pulled my shield up level with my shoulder, lowered my head, and crashed into him. It was like ramming a rock wall, but despite his massive bulk, the giant staggered back a step, tripped over his own feet and went down, already choking on his own blood.

The impact knocked me back, but I kept my feet as my opponent hit the ground. Though the giant was still struggling, I rushed up and grabbed the hilt, pulling the blade sideways as I yanked it out. I grimaced as the weapon's sharp edge sliced muscle and artery, spraying hot, sticky blood over my face and arms. I was so excited, terrified, repulsed, I barely felt it.

Though mortally wounded, the Gaul used his last bit of strength to hack at me with his blade, and in one powerful stroke, sledge-hammered my head with the flat side. My vision blurred, and I lost track of the ground until it battered me once again. My ears rang and head throbbed with near-paralyzing pain, but my battle-hardened body once again rose to its feet. Everything was a blur as I staggered several steps from my opponent. Finally regaining my balance, I shook my head to clear my vision, and stopped.

The silence was so complete I feared my hearing had been affected by the blow. Confused, I looked around to see that all the other combatants had stopped fighting and seemed to be waiting to see if I would remain standing, or fall from a mortal wound.

To my surprise, I was still holding onto my *gladius*, and before I could react, my right hand shot over my head, stabbing it at the sky while warm, crimson blood ran down its blade and dripped off the hilt. The sight brought a loud cheer from the legionnaires and sent my stomach into convulsions. Thankfully, the death of their leader seemed to take the fight out of the remaining Gauls, and those still upright evaporated back into the wood.

The threat now gone, I looked at the nearly decapitated corpse and was overwhelmed with a torrent of emotions.

I did that?

I swallowed hard to keep my churning stomach in check.

Keep it together!

The urgency of the thought kept me from throwing up as I continued to hold the sword over my head, slowly turning in a circle, my knees wobbling, mind blank, breath coming in desperate gasps.

After the men quieted down, I lowered my arm and realized they were forming up ranks, their eyes on a common point. Turning in that direction, I saw the transverse horsehair crest of the *centurio*'s helmet towering above everyone else. He marched at full step in my direction leading a contingent of soldiers with their shields up, *pila* at the ready.

Looking again at the defeated Gaul, I felt the thrill of victory colliding with the horrific realization that I had just killed again. Bile started working its way up my throat once more.

"Report!"

While the *centurio* and his men stopped in perfect unison, I swallowed hard, stood as straight as I could, and snapped a salute.

"Another attack by savages, *Centurio*," I responded while pointing at the unmoving giant lying only a short distance away. "They were led by this one. Once he fell, the others lost interest in the fight and ran."

The *centurio* hardly gave him more than a glance. "Injuries?"

Still struggling with the turmoil raging in my head, I hesitated.

"Six killed, thirteen wounded, most not seriously, Sir," Lucius announced from behind me.

Though I wanted to thank him for rescuing me, I instinctively knew that was not allowed in this army.

"Who killed this…freak," the *centurio* asked as he finally looked at the fallen giant.

"I did, Sir. He had taken out three of my men, and I was damned if I was going to let him do more damage."

Liar!

Shut up!

I thought the boast would be met with approval by the *centurio*, and was surprised to see him scowl as he stepped closer.

"You decided to show off instead of leading your men?"

The question shocked me, but after a moment of confusion I realized what he wanted to hear.

"The enemy clearly looked to him for leadership, Sir. Taking him out in man-to-man combat dispirited them. As soon as he hit the ground, they ran off."

The scowl softened, and I knew from Marcus' memories that was as good as a smile.

My relief was short, however as he turned and quickstepped to another of the fallen enemy.

"What in Pluto's Name is this?"

I looked at the body, my mind blank for a moment before I realized what I was seeing.

The man's face is painted blue!

"He's a *Pict*," I answered.

He turned to me. "I have heard of them in *Britannia*. What are they doing here?"

The Tsabbat! flashed in my mind, and I desperately wanted to tell him what was going on, but said instead, "I have no idea, Sir."

He looked at the corpse a moment more before shaking his head. "Maybe our *Imperator* will take them on next."

"If this is how they fight, it will not be difficult to conquer them," I said though I knew Caesar gave his best effort, but never completely controlled the English tribes.

"Bury our dead and get the men moving, *Optio*," the *centurio* commanded. "The less time we spend in this cursed place, the better."

"Yes, Sir," I barked with another salute, but he was already moving away.

"You were quite impressive, my friend," Lucius announced when the *centurio* was out of hearing range. "I am sorry to admit, I did not think you were up to the task. Did you?"

Always! the strange voice demanded.

The thought made me hesitate, but I quickly recovered and looked at him. I wanted to laugh at the absurdity of the situation, but bile rose again and only sheer will kept it down. When I finally opened my mouth to speak, it was someone else's words.

"A legionnaire is ready for anything. To not be is to die."

Chapter 58

A hard blow with his shield knocked the blue-faced opponent back a step, giving Quintus time to shove his sword into the tattooed chest. The man screamed when Quintus twisted the blade and yanked it out. Blood spurted from the wound, making it clear he had struck the heart. Not wanting to give the dying man a chance for a final strike, he brought his shield around and hammered the pathetic creature onto his back.

His senses alert, adrenaline coursing, Quintus turned away from his writhing victim in time to see Marcus running at a giant Gallic warrior.

"He's a dead man," he chuckled, but his rush of pleasure turned sour when Marcus impaled the big man with his *gladius* and then knocked him onto his back.

Frustrated and enraged, he looked away to see almost everyone, Roman and Gaul, watching the fight, their attention so focused they seemed to have forgotten about the battle.

He turned back to see the giant make a dying effort to slash at Marcus, only to slap him with the side of his sword. A collective gasp went up from the crowd as Marcus rolled once and rose, bloody sword in hand, helmet askew. His opponent's head dropped back, arms thumping lifelessly onto the ground as Quintus heard a mixture of gasps and sighs of relief.

When Marcus' sword rose above his head, Quintus turned to see all of the remaining Gauls running away, as though the loss of this one warrior decided their fate.

He spat on the ground. "These pigs are not worth the bacon."

A roar went up from the legionnaires, enraging Quintus so much that he considered using a Gallic arrow he had found to kill the damned *optio*. Everyone's attention was on Marcus, and surely no one would notice him firing it, but unfortunately, his kit was many paces away, mixed in with a jumble of others, and by the time he reached it they would be marching again.

"This bastard is nearly as invincible as Jupiter himself," he muttered while moving toward Marcus, bloody sword in hand as he struggled to think of a way to get his revenge without getting caught.

He stopped when the men went silent, and only then saw the *centurio*'s transverse headdress bobbing above the other's heads.

"Will the gods not grant me just one little chance?" he protested.

Seeing the *centurio* stop in front of Marcus, Quintus strained to hear, but both distance, and the sounds around him -- injured Gauls being dispatched, men in pain, the sound of rattling armor as the troopers hurried to get into formation -- blocked anything they might be saying.

Surely the centurio is praising him for killing that lumbering giant when it was all dumb luck, he thought angrily. *Anyone could have killed that oaf.*

After cleaning blood off his sword, Quintus returned to his dropped kit to find that a stray arrow had cut a three-inch slit into his leather shield cover.

"A pox on these savages!"

His muscles tense and ready to strike, he looked around for a head to crack open, and realized that most of the men had already collected their gear and were moving into formation. Seeing the other men of his *contubernium* were almost to their place in line, and knowing the punishment if he failed to join them in time, he scooped up the rest of his kit and headed toward them, deftly moving through the lines of soldiers until he reached his place. Dropping his jumbled kit, he started to rearrange it for the best comfort during the long slog ahead. He had done this many times, and quickly got his equipment settled, but that had no effect on his sour mood. He hardly noticed that those around him were also somber and quiet, but for a different reason.

A big part of a legionnaire's income came from booty. By order, anything gathered after a battle was to be given to the *centurio*. Valuable items were collected and stored with the baggage train, slaves sold to slavers, and the proceeds given to the *signifer* for safe keeping, to later be distributed to all the men according to their rank and seniority. However, a quick-witted soldier might pocket a handful of coins, or jewelry as long as no one was watching. These provided money for wine or whores, or both, if he was clever enough.

Unfortunately, during these last two attacks, the Gauls had been mostly naked, except for a few with bronze armor, and their weapons were either too crude or unwieldy for him to carry on top of his normal sixty-pounds of kit. That meant two engagements with no collectable booty. To further sour Quintus' mood, the *optio* had refused to die, even against that Gallic monstrosity.

"This means I have to do something," he muttered, but when a nearby soldier gave him a questioning look, he turned the conversation inward.

Maybe those pitiful arrows will serve a purpose yet. He glanced at his nosey neighbor to find his attention had drifted to something else. *Maybe I'll have to kill him too.*

The thought both repelled and excited him. He joined the army both because he liked to kill people, and he really had no choice. In Rome, under a different name, he had been a tough for an influential man, but liked his job too much. Men who were supposed to be roughed up, got a thorough beating. Those needing more of a scare usually ended up dead. With that sort of thing, he was quite good at making sure there were no witnesses to point a finger at him, but his powerful employer was growing increasingly unhappy with his way of doing things.

On top of that, women were also a favorite of his dark side. He had no concept of love. Sex was a man's right, and woe to the woman who resisted. However, when the daughter of a prominent senator accused Quintus of beating and raping her, he knew it was time for a change of name and occupation. He had not wanted to join the army, as he liked the decadent life, but being on the shit-list of such a prominent person reduced his job prospects in Rome to zero. Even worse, the toughs in smaller towns were family-centric, making entry into their groups a difficult and dangerous option.

You are my brother, he thought while glaring at his neighbor, *but if it comes down to you or me, Beetle Dung, it will be me.*

He glanced over his shoulder at the *optio*, his long staff, and helmet's front-to-back crest making him easy to spot, even if he had not been in the gap between the two *centuriae*. The sight made Quintus' stomach ache with a hunger that had nothing to do with food.

His pigheaded unwillingness to die is costing me, he thought angrily. *But not for much longer.*

Chapter 59

A shove in the back sent Remmy stumbling into the ramshackle hut. Her legs still stiff from being bound for so long, she struggled to keep her footing as the flimsy door slammed behind her.

"Keep a very close eye on her," the stranger announced as she regained her balance. "No one is to lay a hand on her as long as she stays inside."

He repeated the order in what she believed was the native language of the other men, and after his subordinate asked a question, the stranger moved close to the door.

There was a pause before a hand hammered the flimsy wood, stirring up tendrils of dust illuminated by light streaming through the many holes in the walls around her.

"If she steps one tiny foot outside this dung hole," the stranger shouted in Latin loud enough to make it clear this was for Remmy's benefit, "she is yours to do with as you please."

After again speaking in the other tongue, which Remmy assumed was a repeat of what he had just said, she sucked in a sharp breath when howls and whistles made it clear that those outside seriously wanted her to make the attempt.

When the footsteps grew fainter, she rushed to the door, straining to hear. To her relief, the men quieted when the stranger and his companion stopped a dozen or so paces away. In the silence that followed, she could just barely hear the two speaking in Latin.

"Just remember," the stranger warned. "She has the mentality of a warrior. If she does escape, she will certainly give your men a good fight. I don't need to remind you that delivering her alive and mostly undamaged will bring us ten-times the reward as otherwise."

"But who wants this sorry *sharmoota* so much."

She peered through a crack in the door to see the stranger walk to his cart and climb on. After picking up the reins, he looked down at his companion, his scowl obvious even from this distance.

"Keep your mind on the reward you will earn for delivering the goods unharmed," he said as he urged the mule on. "Leave that detail to me."

Remmy watched the cart until it disappeared from view before bringing her attention back to the leader of those left to guard her. It disturbed her that he was already staring in her direction, his gaze so intense she pulled back out of fear that he could see her through the door.

With nothing else to do, she turned her attention to the dark interior, but could hear the leader shouting at his men. The responses were mixed, with some barking a short, concise word while others spoke more casually, though from their tone, it was obvious that these men respected their leader. She just had to wonder if that respect was strong enough to hold up in a fight.

Scared and confused, she paced the room, her eyes scanning the mud-brick walls, with little more than spider webs keeping them from falling down. There was only the one rickety door, and a small opening high in the back wall she might be able to crawl through, if the wall didn't crumble under her.

It was early morning, but the poorly ventilated space was rapidly accumulating heat as the sun warmed its mud bricks. A quick look around made it clear there was no water, or even a pot to piss in.

"Obviously, whoever put me here doesn't plan to keep me long," she muttered.

Her aching bladder made it clear that however long it would be, she could not wait.

Returning to the door, she leaned against it and called, "Hello out there."

When no one responded, she called again. The sound of slow footsteps grew louder until she could once again see the leader.

"Probably the only one who speaks Latin," she muttered as he stopped several yards from the entrance.

"Be silent," the leader demanded angrily. "The sound of your voice excites my men. Too much of that, and I may not be able to control them."

"I need to pee."

There was a moment of silence, implying that even this hardened criminal was taken aback by a woman speaking of such things in his presence.

"So pee," he responded dismissively. "None of us can see you."

"There is nothing to pee into."

She knew from his bark of a laugh that he was not sympathetic.

"The Dark One made it clear that if you leave this hut for any reason, my men may do what they please with you." His feet crunched the rocky soil as he walked away, and added, "Pick a corner and do your business. It is of no importance to me."

He shouted something to the men and from the laughter, she knew he had shared their conversation, and no one else gave a damn about her situation.

Angry and humiliated, she took a step back, quickly shifting her attention from one part of the room to another before concluding that the only way out was through the door. As she was releasing a long sigh, the sound of a horn stopped her.

"What is it now?" she asked as she moved back to the door to peer through the widest of many gaps in the desiccated wood. Her heart nearly stopped when she saw each man pull out a small matt, unroll it on the ground, and kneel, all facing the same direction.

"Oh my God," she cried, her outburst briefly drawing the attention of the leader before he returned to his task. "They're Muslims?"

Chapter 60

"Any idea where they've gone?" Hiram McFaddan asked the two burly men standing at attention in front of him.

"No, Sir," the taller of the two responded sharply. "We've got a BOLO out on the van, but it hasn't yet turned up."

"Who does that vehicle belong to?" McFaddan asked, and when the first man shook his head, he turned to the second. "John?"

After glancing at his partner, John stiffened, and responded, "According to DMV records, the vehicle is a 1998 Chevy G2500 Cargo Van registered to a Vivian Parchenko of 121123 Pimento Street Southeast in Portland, Sir."

"Parchenko," McFaddan said thoughtfully, his eyes still on his subordinate. "That sounds Russian."

"Actually, Sir, her husband is an immigrant from Ukraine. He worked as a riveter in the shipyards until nineteen-eighty-six when he was killed in an explosion."

"Suspicious circumstances?"

The man jerked a no. "Not as far as we can determine, Sir. It was in a facility called the Swelty Island shipyard. Six people were killed by a natural gas explosion. They never really determined the cause."

"Could Missus Parchenko be helping our suspects?"

A smile flickered on John's face, but he quickly clamped it down. "No chance, Sir. She's ninety-two and uses a walker to get around."

"Family?"

"Only one son, Robert Parchenko, and he's kind of a flower child, Sir. We're trying to track him down now, but he's moved around a lot."

"Any chance he lives in Salem?"

John shrugged. "I don't have a current address, and he doesn't seem to own any property, vehicles, or have a valid driver's license. He's also never registered to vote, sought a job or assistance with any of the many government agencies in the area." The scowl on his face exposed a dogged determination. "If he's here I will find him, Sir, but he's definitely doing a good job of hiding himself. He might be using an alias."

"Have you spoken with his mother?"

John shook his head again. "Greg," he nodded toward his partner, "is going up to see her this afternoon. He'll get a photo of him that we can use to scan driver's license records. Facial recognition software will find him quickly enough."

"In the meantime, get back to the hospital and ask around. See if any employees suddenly disappeared today. It's highly unlikely this guy just happened to be there when they needed him, but he might have been on duty and decided to help them on a whim."

"Or he was in cahoots with them," Greg offered.

McFaddan jerked a nod. "Ask about that too. See if any workers showed up off schedule."

"Yes, Sir," both men responded sharply.

"We have to move quickly, gentlemen," he added. "Our CDC covers won't last long, and we must have these people in hand before the local authorities get suspicious."

"Yes, Sir," they responded again before turning sharply and marching from the room.

After the door closed, McFaddan turned toward the room's only window while using his index finger and thumb to rub his eyes for a moment before looking out at the busy streets of downtown Salem. His attention on the moving cars, he took in a deep breath, and was slowly letting it out when his phone chirped out a tune he was beginning to find irritating.

"Yes, Sir," he responded, knowing from the ditty who the caller was.

"You have them?"

He struggled to hold down another sigh, thankful his employer could not see his rolling eyes.

"No, Sir. We did have them, but an unknown accomplice helped them escape."

"How is that possible?" the gravelly voice demanded. "I was told the young woman was unconscious."

"Yes, Sir, but her boyfriend had completed the mental swap with the soldier and Marcus acclimated much faster than we thought he would. Even so, we still could have contained them, had it not been for an unknown third party who provided an escape vehicle. We're hunting him down now, and should have his location soon."

"Make it *very* soon," the voice insisted. "We managed to separate the Roman soldier and his lady, but I need the two in this timeline under our control before I can move forward. You *must* find them quickly."

"We are doing everything we can, Sir. If you wish to keep this from becoming public knowledge, we have to work within the very limited legal system these people have here."

"Yesss," the voice hissed angrily. "There is always some kind of roadblock to my plans, but you will overcome them, or I will make sure you and all your generations pay dearly for failing me. Do I make myself clear?"

A look of shock flashed across McFaddan's face, but even though his employer couldn't see, he quickly suppressed it. "Yes. Quite clear. We will have them soon."

"No," the voice growled. "I've heard that promise too many times. Give me results!"

McFaddan opened his mouth to respond, but before he could form a word, his employer disconnected.

"Yes, Sir," he sighed wearily as he once again looked out the window, this time no longer seeing the moving cars and people. His only thoughts were for the generations that might be wiped from history if he failed.

Chapter 61

After marching through a narrow valley, we entered a wide, flat area. Ahead of me, the first *centuria* was already reaching the newly built gates of our fort, its walls growing out from them. The newly-arrived men would quickly be dispersed to cut more trees and haul them to the new stockade, making it rise faster. By the time the baggage train arrived, the perimeter walls would be complete with posted sentries.

During the march, I had time to come to a sort-of understanding as to what is going on with me in Marcus' body. Though his active consciousness is gone, a part of him -- I think of it as instinct -- is still there, and I spent the time since the last battle trying to understand how it will help me.

For example: not long after we started again, a soldier started drifting out of formation. If it had been up to me, I'd have left him alone, figuring he'd eventually wander back in line. However, before I could even finish that thought, my body stiffened.

"Keep formation," I shouted.

Without looking back, the legionnaire quickly sidestepped back into line.

The event both excited and confused me, the conflicting emotions making it difficult for me to concentrate. I instinctively knew that a muddled brain would most likely get me killed and that scared the crap out of me.

Though I had gotten by so far by relying on the instinctive memory in Marcus' subconscious, those feelings seemed to be fading, which scared me even more. I was a Roman Legionnaire...a *real* Roman Legionnaire marching in a real Roman army. This wasn't some kind of Star Trekian virtual reality. The people were real, as were their swords and desire to kill. But it wasn't just that. There was another force that wanted me and Marcus to fail in our mission.

The whole situation was overwhelming, yet I couldn't let it get to me or I would literally not live this down. Showing fear would cause Marcus to lose the respect of his men, and there was no doubt in my mind that such a farce was going to be very hard to maintain.

I was so lost in my confusion, I had not noticed that the *centuria* in front of me had started changing formation. Up ahead, I could hear the *centurio* shouting orders, assigning tasks to each eight-man *contubernia*, sending several groups to help with wood cutting, another three to dig post holes, the rest to help with the trench others were digging around our new camp.

The men would stow their gear in the area inside the stockade assigned for trooper's tents. Each *contubernium* was assigned a space where their tent would be erected after the fort was completed. Until that happened, they would march off to perform their assigned duties.

After the first *centuria* had been dispersed, my task was to assign protection duties to the men of the second one. Those doing the physical labor could not do so in full armor, so the remaining troopers were needed to protect them from attack, should it be necessary. Thankfully, I could still tap into Marcus' memories and was surprised at how well he knew these men. While assigning duties, I instinctively knew which man in each *contubernia* was the *decanus*, -- roughly a sergeant in today's army -- and therefore responsible for the actions of the men in his group. If the men of his *contubernia* did not do their duty, he would be the first to be punished because my order was to be followed without question, and if he let the men slack off, it was on his back the whip would fall.

Seeming to forget their weariness from their long march, and two skirmishes, the men marched into camp, dumped their gear in their assigned spaces, and dispersed to perform their tasks. I am sure they were mumbling oaths under their breaths, but each knew the value of what they had to do, and I had no doubt they would do their best. After all, they had already been shown twice in one day that there were still roving bands of angry Gauls who would rather sacrifice their lives in hopeless attempts at retaliation than live under the yoke of Roman rule.

Once the men were gone, I moved into camp to stow my own gear. The smell of cooking drew my attention to the mess area where half-a-dozen hinds hung from a hastily erected crossbar, their meat adding the welcome taste of venison to our usually uninspired diet of bread, cheese, and salted beef.

But the smell also produced memories that had nothing to do with my present situation. I thought of my father barbequing in the back yard, family gatherings, the smoky campfires of our wilderness camping. The thoughts made me long for home, and even more than that, I worried about Remmy.

Where is she? exploded in my head, making my gut ache. *I have to find her!*

I was so lost in my thoughts I paid no attention to where I was going. Marcus' instincts must have taken over, because no one was more surprised than I when I suddenly stopped in front of a pile of gear. Blinking several times, I looked around to see ten more piles of gear in two rows next to mine: enough for one *centuria* of eighty men. Turning slightly, I saw another two rows of gear that must have represented the future sleeping quarters of the other *centuria*.

The sight brought on the sudden realization that though I was disconnected from Marcus, much of his instincts and memories remained. I was very thankful for that when it came to fighting, but it also meant I couldn't just take off and search for Remmy. My role had strict requirements and rules that had to be obeyed at any cost. If I was to accomplish my goal, I had to stay in this role and use it to stop Caesar's assassination. That meant keeping on task, not only at the risk to my own life, but even the sacrifice of my best friend.

That seriously sucks! shouted in my head as I dropped my gear in the designated space and looked around. *There has to be something I can do for her.*

A nearby flash of light caught my attention, and when I moved closer, I saw a small mirror had fallen from someone's pack. Picking it up, I automatically turned it so I could see my face. The sight was so shocking, I almost cried out.

Struggling to breathe, I lowered the mirror, took another look around to make sure no one was nearby before I held it up again. Pushing my helmet back, I could see Marcus' usually dark-brown hair was now dishwater blond, and his brown eyes, dark gray.

This is so totally bad!

Tossing the mirror back where I found it, I staggered away from it, but was so confused, I barely registered where I was going until I stumbled on a mound of gear and had to take a quick step to keep from falling over.

Looking around, I saw the men performing their jobs like well-organized ants, and no one was paying attention to me.

Maybe they won't notice my eyes, I thought while pulling the helmet back over my hair. *The men rarely look me in the eye...except maybe Lucius. Why hasn't he mentioned the change?*

Feeling lightheaded, I took several deep breaths to calm myself and looked around again.

Keep the helmet on at all times.

That wouldn't be hard, since we were in unsecured territory and always on alert. As the leader of my *centuria*, I should be ready to lead them into battle.

I need to talk to Lucius.

And say what?

Struggling with that thought, I looked around to see men cutting trees, dragging them to the fort, digging trenches, and carrying dirt up to build a mound on which posts would be lined up to create the fort's walls. The army would sacrifice nearly half-an-acre of timber to build this one fort, which was to be used for only one night then burned.

What a waste.

The absurdity of the thought almost made me laugh, because I knew it was coming from the mind of a twenty-first-century teenager, and this wasn't twenty-first-century Salem, Oregon. We were an invading army, and though the Romans had been victorious, it would be some time before a Roman could safely wander alone in this part of the world.

If I fail, everything I know will vanish and the reality that replaces it might be just as dangerous as where I am now.

The thought surprised me. Yes. If I failed, the world as I knew it would be gone forever, but even if I succeeded things might change. After all, Marcus wanted to die, and I stopped him from doing it. Enid might never have survived being raped and beaten when her fellow woman soldiers were overtaken by Marcus' men. What happened to the other women with her? I had no idea. If anything, Remmy and I have changed their lives forever. How will the continued existence of these two people affect the future?

And this stupid change in eye and hair color could totally fuck this up!

My mind in total turmoil, I marched around the camp and did what I thought Marcus would do: checking our perimeters, goading the men to work faster, making sure everyone was at station and prepared to defend us should it be necessary. I didn't need to be a legionnaire to know the *centurio* would want an update on how things were progressing. No matter how much the future had been changed, I had to do my best to see that things during this time aren't messed up even worse, so after canvassing the area, I sucked in a couple of deep breaths and marched to the *centurio*'s tent.

Here's the big test, I thought as I drew near and steeled myself for the task at hand.

"Permission to enter," I called out, not to the two guards standing at the entrance, but to the *centurio* within.

"Come," came the curt reply.

As expected, the guards did not even acknowledge me as I marched past them to find my superior leaning over a small but sturdy collapsible table covered with a single sheet of papyrus.

Just inside the entrance, I snapped to attention and waited for him to acknowledge me.

For a long moment, he kept his attention on the map inked onto the surface of the papyrus before finally straightening and looking my way. He had removed his helmet, revealing dark stubble on his close-cropped head. There was still a line on his forehead where the sweatband supporting his helmet pressed against it and the straight line of a scar ran at a sharp angle to his nose starting just inside his right eye, across the bridge of his nose and into his left cheek. I had to believe that the man who had given him that scar was a rotting corpse on some forgotten battlefield.

"Report," he commanded.

"The second *centuria* has been assigned their duties and the baggage train is preparing to unload. The camp will be ready by nightfall."

As a modern teen, I was expecting a complement for a job well done, but he didn't even smile.

"Tell the men to keep a sharp eye out. The natives have the advantage. We must be ready to take them on no matter where they come from."

Without further comment, he turned back to the papyrus which I took as a dismissal. Even so, I hesitated for a moment to make sure he wasn't trying to decide what to say next.

When he eventually gave me a questioning look, I stood at attention again and barked, "Yes, Sir!" before doing a quick about face and exiting.

This is getting worse, I thought desperately as I marched away from the *centurio*'s tent. *I've got to find a way to darken my hair then find Remmy and sort this out before Marcus is completely gone.*

Chapter 62

Frustration wrinkled Quintus' brow as he looked around the designated sleeping area inside the camp's walls. Around him, men were depositing their gear and hurrying to their assigned duties, making it difficult for Quintus to find Marcus in the milling crowd.

He was preparing to give up and follow the others in his *contubernium* when he spied Marcus coming from the *centurio*'s tent.

How can I make this work? he wondered as he watched the *optio* march around, urging the men on, checking out the growing wall, and thankfully not paying any attention to him. *That man has to die.*

Realizing he could not do it within the confines of the camp, primarily because the *centurio* would know it was a legionnaire who killed him. He also couldn't follow him around, as he and his fellow soldiers had been assigned to guard the wood cutters, and he had to stay with them or be punished for dereliction of duty.

Maybe someone will fall a tree on him, he mused wishfully.

As Marcus marched to where the soldiers assigned to guard duty were gathering, Quintus hurried to join them, all the while searching for an opening, an opportunity for a swift stab of his sword, or an unseen slash with a knife. He knew he could wipe off the blood and be at attention in seconds, if given the chance, but that was the difficult part: getting the chance.

"Guard at the ready," Marcus called out, his voice projecting less confidence that Quintus remembered. "Form ranks."

"Has he lost his nerve?" he mused on his way to join his comrades.

As he stopped next to the others in his *contubernium*, he was struck with an idea that appealed to him.

Gossip.

In every large group of people rumors often run rampant, mostly because people get bored and a bit of juicy gossip tends to liven things up. But in the army, rumors can be deadly, even if they are false.

If word spread that the optio has lost his nerve, someone else might do him in.

Smiling to himself, he marched along with his comrades while mentally working on a plan to start a convincing rumor without it coming back on him.

Maybe I will put the idea in the head of one of the immunes, he thought, referring to the non-fighting men who handle administrative tasks for each *centuria. They have little to do but gossip all day anyway.*

His mind made up, Quintus felt a new vigor in his walk, and smiled.

I will soon be an optio.

Chapter 63

Sweat dribbling off her forehead, Remmy shifted uncomfortably in the sweltering heat as shafts of searing afternoon sunlight pierced the gloomy dimness of her prison, baking the fragile walls and pushing the temperature of the room over one-hundred degrees.

"What time period am I in now?" she muttered to herself while watching the men kneeling outside her jail and muttering prayers as they bowed down until their foreheads touched the prayer mats. "I'm pretty sure there were no Muslims in the first century BC, so how did I get here, and are these guys really Muslims?"

Realizing that even if she asked them, the men either wouldn't or couldn't answer her question, she paced her confined, dimly lit cell in the hope of finding both a cooling bit of breeze, and an answer to her questions. Unfortunately, the dusty, confined space offered neither.

"Before I can do anything, I have to get out of here," she finally said while again peering through a crack in the hut's door.

As she pondered her limited options, she heard a faint grating noise, its constant droning bouncing around her mud-brick enclosure and muddling the sound so much she could not tell what it was. Peering out again, she watched her praying captors, until she realized their shadows were long.

"I can escape after the sun sets," she mused as she watched the leader seemingly lost in prayer until the strange sound was loud enough to draw his attention.

By that time, the sound lost its monotonous consistency, she noticed breaks in the slow, droning noise. It was then she realized she was hearing wooden wheels on the rocky soil.

"Is the stranger returning?"

After a few minutes, the leader rose from his mat, deposited his string of prayer beads on it and carefully rolled up the mat. Standing, he looked around, and Remmy realized the others were doing the same. As the sound grew louder, he wrapped a cord around the mat before passing it to a comrade and moving in the direction of the noise. Moments later, a small cart came into view, and Remmy let out a sigh of disappointment when she saw its fat, balding occupant.

The driver called out a greeting, and the leader responded in a way that implied he knew the man.

After the cart stopped, the driver heaved his bulky body off the seat, and clumsily lowered himself to the ground. The men chatted in their strange tongue as the newcomer moved toward the rear of the cart and threw back a dusty tarp to reveal something Remmy could not see, but it made the leader smile.

The other men, their prayer mats carefully stowed, approached the cart as well, and when the merchant held up a clay pot, most of them shook their fists over their heads and cheered. However, when one of the men ran to the newcomer, his hands outstretched as though to grab the clay pot, the leader barked a command and the man stopped.

Remmy felt her mouth drop open as the men went immediately quiet until the leader pointed at the cart, and while speaking again, motioned toward something outside her field of view.

"This must be a merchant delivering food and wine," she muttered as the men hurried in to grab cloth bags and more clay pots.

After the men disappeared from view, the leader tossed the merchant a small bag that made a metal-on-metal sound when he deftly caught it. After quickly depositing the bag into a pocket of his flowing cloak, the merchant seemed to ask questions to which the leader either nodded or shook his head.

"He's going through a shopping list for next time," she muttered.

Still speaking, the two men followed the others until they were also out of her field of view. The sight of the cart standing all alone made Remmy's heart race.

"I need to get on that cart."

Looking at the door, she realized that there was only a small rope attached where a door handle might be: good for pulling it closed, but not connected to whatever kept the door shut. Shaking her head, she stepped back and considered kicking it open, but quickly shook her head.

"Too noisy."

Instead of deflating her, the roadblock made her heart beat faster.

"I just need to find the key to…"

She stopped when her eyes fell on the rope hinges. The rope was fresh, and she did not have a knife to cut it with, so she turned her attention to the wood supporting the hinge, finding it desiccated and brittle.

"If I just had…" she muttered while looking around her small cell.

She became excited when her eyes fell on a rock that would have been too small to be of any use in trying to dig through the mud bricks, but its sharpened point would be perfect for chipping away at the dried-out wood of the door.

Scooping up the rock, she returned to the door and started to attack the upper hinge, but the sound of laughter stopped her. Peeking through the crack, she saw the guard sitting on the ground in the shade of a large bolder only ten feet from her door. She pulled back when he looked in her direction before turning his attention to the sound of the laughter.

Go play with your friends, she thought.

As though he heard her thought, the guard shook his head and squatted again in the shadow. While muttering dejectedly, he scooped up a stick and used it to scratch a circle in the dusty ground.

He held that pose for a long moment before looking in her direction again, pointing his stick at her and grumbling something. From the angry tone, she knew he was not only unhappy about not being able to party with his comrades, but that he almost certainly blamed her for it.

"Oh boy. Oh boy. Oh boy," she whispered anxiously while backing away from the door until her back bumped the far wall. "These are a bunch of angry, frustrated, and soon to be drunk men," she said while sliding down the wall into a squat, "and I'm the woman they blame for all their troubles."

Chapter 64

"We have to get out of here," Miriam insisted as she peered through a small gap in the front window's curtain.

Moving up beside her, Jasmina shook her head. "We're safe for now. There is no connection between us and this house. The only way they can catch us now is if we go outside and someone spots us."

"But we can't stay here forever."

Jasmina pointed back at Marcus on the couch and Enid in a chair opposite it, each pretending not to be watching the other, yet obviously doing so.

"We can connect with our children without fear of disruption. There is nothing the *Tsabbat's* people can do until they find us again."

"But they will find us," Miriam stated anxiously. "I feel it in my bones."

Jasmina nodded. "Yes, but by then it should be too late. Gerry and Remmy will have spoiled their plans."

"How do you know that?"

"It's a feeling I have, but we also have another problem."

"What?"

"They can sense our presence."

Releasing the curtain, Miriam jerked around to face her, her mouth agape, eyes wide.

"You mean the doctor and his people? How do you know?"

Trying to make her shrug look casual, Jasmina responded, "Because I can sense them as well. I wouldn't be all that surprised if you can too, you just don't realize it."

Taking a step away from her, Miriam held up a hand, palm out. "Wait a damned minute, Sister. If you can sense their presence, why didn't you warn us when they arrived?"

Jasmina shook her head. "I can sense the presence of many entities, and I didn't know who they were until the doctor grabbed me."

"How is that?"

After motioning for Miriam to accompany her to another room, Jasmina followed her in and closed the door.

"Think of it as recognizing someone's perfume. For the most part, you can only do that when they are close. Even then, you don't know if that person is good or bad just by the smell of their perfume. That comes when you interact with them."

"So they have to be close? How close?"

"In most cases, unless the person was particularly sensitive, they'd have to at least be in the front yard, probably at the door. A few drugs can enhance this ability, but their side effects are so bad, I'd never use them."

"But the people chasing us might."

Jasmina shook her head. "I don't know. Maybe."

"Which drugs?"

Moving back to the door, she opened it part way, looked at the young couple conversing in the other room, and sighed. "There have been studies that show the use of psychedelic drugs might enhance psychic abilities."

"Really? Have you ever done that?"

Jasmina shook her head again. "As I said, I'd never use something like that. The dangers far outweigh the possible benefits."

"But the people chasing us might not be so concerned about safety? You think they'd want to push this to the limit?"

Looking out the window again, Jasmina shrugged. "I don't know. Maybe."

It was Miriam's turn to look at Marcus and Enid. "So it doesn't matter where we hide. They'll find us."

"Possibly," Jasmina answered. "If we are going to succeed, we have to connect to Gerry and Remmy and move things along."

"That won't work," Miriam countered. "Gerry is out in the wilderness, miles from Caesar's camp. It could take him days to get to Caesar, and maybe longer to figure out how to stop the assassination attempt. He can't just go running around like Chicken Little, crying about the sky falling in."

"And we don't have that kind of time," Jasmina added as she motioned across the room. "We have to give Gerry and Remmy as much help as we can before we are separated. That's the best we can do."

She started to accompany Miriam across the room, but jerked to a stop when her companion did.

"What is it?"

"We don't have to just give in to them," Miriam announced. "There is something we can do."

"What is that?"

Miriam smiled. "I have an idea, but I need to know more about this psychic connection thing. What are its limitations? Can you control it? What I mean is, can you change your thoughts to hide from them, even if they are close?"

Jasmina shook her head. "It's not your thoughts, but a sort of energy signature you give off." While nervously wrapping a strand of hair around her index finger, she moved back to the window and looked out, feeling the sunlight warm her face. "I don't think it is something you can consciously change."

"But what if you became really excited or were in pain? I mean, your voice changes dramatically under those kinds of situations. Wouldn't the psychic connection change as well?"

Turning to face Miriam, Jasmina smiled. "You know, I hadn't really thought about it, but you're probably right. How can we test your theory, and if it works, what can we do with the knowledge?"

Smiling back, Miriam answered, "We might need to give these guys a distraction to get them off our scent."

"How do you propose doing that?"

Looking back at where Marcus and Enid were sitting, Miriam shrugged. "By screwing with the person chasing us."

Chapter 65

"*Optio* reporting as ordered, Sir," I announced while struggling to hide my surprise at seeing the other *optio* already in the *centurio*'s tent.

"Good," the *centurio* grunted as he straightened. "I have received word that our *imperator* has been called to Rome. The senate has awarded him a triumph and Caesar is eager to get there before they change their minds."

"We are at least a week's march from the Tenth Legion," the other *optio* announced, though I had no idea how he knew where they were. "If we set a good pace, we can cut a day off that time."

The *centurio* shook his head. "The Tenth Legion will be leaving in six days. We are to take a different route and will catch up with them…" He stabbed a finger at the papyrus map. "…here."

When the other *optio* moved closer, I followed suit. Unfortunately, most of what I saw meant nothing to me until I saw a rectangle near the line he had drawn on the map.

"We should be on alert, *Centurio*," the *optio* warned. "As I am sure you are aware, there is a *Belgae* town along our path. They may cause trouble."

Nodding the *centurio* looked at me, and I felt more afraid than when I had faced the giant Gaul.

"What say you, Marcus?"

For a long moment, my mind froze, and the more I tried to think of something to say, the blanker my mind became.

Finally breaking out of my fear-induced trance, I stepped up to the map and leaned over it. The closer look unfroze my brain. Unlike the topographical maps of my time, these were fairly simple. Rivers were shown with serrated edges, roads were simple thick lines, and mountain ranges were a row of bumps. To my surprise, I could actually read this darned thing, and I can't explain the sense of relief that gave me.

Of course, that still didn't tell me what I should say to the *centurio*, so I scanned the path we were going to take, and thought of Remmy.

Where is she?

That thought made me remember the baggage train and camp followers. Both were slowing us down and were vulnerable to attack. We had to defend the baggage, as that was our supplies

"They could attack from anywhere along this route, and we need to be more flexible and protect our supplies." Though it terrified me to do so, I knew it was required, so I straightened and looked into the *centurio*'s eyes. "We should send the camp followers and any unnecessary baggage on to where our legion is now camped, and interlace the remaining baggage train with our two centuries to better protect it from looters."

"But that will split our forces and make us even more vulnerable," the other *optio* protested.

Shaking my head, I pointed at the map. "It appears these valleys are wider than the ones we just came through, so we can march in a denser formation. In the last two attacks, we were marching two abreast and were still able to put up an effective defense. At four abreast we will be just as invincible."

But the Belgae will not be attacking us, a voice in my head announced.

"What?" blurted from my mouth before I could even think about it.

"*Optio*?" the *centurio* asked.

Pulling myself together, I straightened. "With respect, Sir, but by the stars, this feels wrong."

Everyone in the tent was silent for a long moment before the *centurio* said, "Continue."

I had to be careful here, or they would think I had lost it.

"I am only a common soldier, Sir, but I have heard that neither Pompey nor the Senate have any love for our *imperator*. If this is true, why are they bestowing such an honor on him?"

The *centurio* shook his head. "It is not for me to know the ways of those wily creatures."

"But what if he is being deceived, and the Senate did not issue that proclamation?"

Straightening to his full height, the *centurio* glared at me for a long moment.

"You have proof of this conspiracy?"

His question stopped me until I remembered that in history class we had discussed the superstitions of ancient people, and no one was more superstitious than the Romans.

"I had a dream," I stated, as confidently as I could. "I saw a great eagle land on a tree with a dead top, but the lower branches were still alive and healthy. As I watched, the top broke off and as the eagle fell, the lower branches slapped at him, keeping him from opening his wings to fly away. When he struck the ground, the lower branches dropped down to cover the eagle and smothered him."

Both men's eyes went wide.

"You consulted the Auger about this dream?" the *centurio* asked.

Knowing I didn't have to explain what the dream meant. Both of these men would know the eagle was Caesar, and the dying tree was Gaul. I nodded and stabbed a finger at the square indicating the *Belgae* village on the map.

"He told me that when we get to this village, there won't be a single able-bodied man in it."

Chapter 66

Munching on bread and cheese, Quintus leaned against the empty donkey cart and watched the *centurio*'s tent. Having heard the *centurio*'s summons while he and his fellow troopers were taking a dinner break, he had followed Marcus, careful not to let the *optio* see him.

"You don't have to be an officer to be clever," he mused before popping a piece of bread in his mouth.

The sun was already behind the western hills, but there was still enough light to see what was going on around him. A few remaining men were putting the finishing touches on the fort while others erected their sleeping quarters.

The merchants among the camp followers had been hawking their wares since they arrived in late afternoon, and were finally packing up in preparation of moving outside the stockade. At night, the enclosure was only for military personnel. All others fended for themselves.

But Quintus wasn't concerned with the merchants, camp followers, or even his fellow soldiers. He was only interested in eliminating *Optio* Marcus Aremus before they joined Caesar's Tenth Legion.

But how do I kill a man who slays giants?

Of course, he knew exactly how to kill such a man.

Sneak up behind him, stab him in the kidneys. If he doesn't bleed to death, the pain would so incapacitate him, there'd be plenty of time to decapitate him, and maybe cut off his feet so the centurio will think those savage Belgae did it.

"Quintus!" one of his fellow bunkmates called. "Unless you wish to sleep under the stars, come give us a hand, you lazy lout."

Sighing, he turned to see his tent-mates waving him over.

"How am I ever to become optio with such trivial tasks to weigh me down?"

Chapter 67

Remmy awoke, surprised that she had fallen asleep, and even more surprised that she could see nothing. Carefully looking around in the darkness, her eyes adjusted until she could make out amorphous shapes that made no sense until she realized it was moonlight coming through cracks in the hut's door.

She started when the door rattled, and quickly realized someone was unlocking it from the outside. Moving quickly, she put her hands down to push herself up and realized that she was still holding the small, jagged stone she had picked up earlier.

Not much of a weapon, she thought anxiously as she rose to her feet.

Tiptoeing to the right side of the door, she held up the rock, not really sure what she was going to do with it when the time came.

Wood scraped across the gravelly ground as the intruder slowly pushed the door open and moved inside. Remmy hesitated, unsure if she should attack this man without first knowing his true intentions. On the other hand, if he had a weapon, her only chance of surviving was to disable him before he could use it.

Silently drawing in a deep breath, she lifted the weapon over her head and waited for the intruder. Her heart froze as a moonlit figure slowly entered, and it took her another long moment to realize it was the merchant.

What does he want?

The thought made her hesitate as the figure stopped in the doorway, and appeared to squint into the space, as though searching for her.

Kill him now! Enid's voice demanded, as Remmy lifted the weapon as high as she could, hesitated for a fraction of a second before tensing her muscles in preparation of slamming the stone down onto his head.

"Remmy?" the man whispered.

Still holding her attack pose, Remmy gasped, pulling the man's attention to her, and in the moonlight she could see his eyes widen.

Strike now!

She froze, her eyes on the merchant's face, struggling to bring the weapon down, but unable to make her muscles work.

"Are you the one they call Enid?" he squeaked.

With a loud release of air, she stepped back and lowered her hands. "How do you know my name…er…names?"

Releasing his own sigh of relief, the merchant shook his head. "No time for that now. We have to go quickly before they wake up."

"But…"

"Follow me," he demanded and in a blink was out of sight.

Her muscles spasmming, Remmy hesitated for only a moment before peering out the door. Moonlight made the sleeping guard's dirty robe glow as he leaned against his rock. She sucked in a sharp breath when it occurred to her that he might not be sleeping.

"Sssst," the merchant hissed.

She jerked her attention from the reclining guard to see the merchant urgently motioning for her to follow.

Not knowing what else to do, she took off at a jog, catching up with her savior just as he was climbing into the cart.

"Did you kill them?" she asked as she prepared to follow him.

The merchant waved her back. "You walk for now." He pointed at the pathetic looking donkey. "The extra weight slows him down."

Dropping to the ground, she watched as the merchant turned the cart around and urged the donkey to hurry, but the poor beast barely made it to a trot.

Hurrying up beside the merchant, Remmy whispered, "You didn't answer my question."

The merchant shrugged. "The sleeping drug I gave them will only last about an hour. It is too dangerous out here to keep them asleep longer than that."

"Dangerous for whom?"

"For them, who else?"

"But when they wake up and find us gone, they'll come after us, and if this donkey can't make better time, they won't have far to go. The longer they sleep, the more of a head start we'll have."

He shook his head. "But this is dangerous territory, and if they are unconscious after the sun comes up, other raiders might attack them."

"But why do you care?"

After slapping the reins with no noticeable reaction from the donkey, he looked down at her. "That young man guarding you will play a significant role in this region's future. If he is killed or enslaved by another band of raiders, it may dramatically change how these people develop."

"And why am I here?"

"Bringing you here would also seriously disrupt the lives of those five people, probably having as devastating an effect as if I had killed them tonight."

"So why did you do it?"

Turning only his head, he scowled at her. "I didn't."

"You're not in cahoots with the stranger?"

He shook his head. "The stranger -- as you call him -- and I are not in...cahoots."

"Is he working with the *Tsabbat*?"

She was surprised by the tortured look of surprise on the merchant's face.

"Well...yes...and no."

"What does that mean?"

His mouth opened as though he was preparing to answer, but his expression implied an internal struggle that kept words from coming out. After a moment, he pulled on the reins and the cart came to an abrupt stop. As the donkey seemed to gasp what sounded like his last few breaths, he turned to her.

"It would probably be better if we weren't shouting at each other."

Squaring her shoulders, Remmy put hands on hips and glared at him.

"I'm waiting."

His head shook. "No. I mean, climb aboard so we can talk quietly."

She looked from the merchant's face to the gasping donkey and back.

"Your donkey looks like he is about to die of exhaustion. I don't think he can handle my extra weight."

The merchant chuckled. "Oh, he can handle you."

"Are you sure?"

Waving his hand impatiently, the merchant said, "Just get up here. We've only a short distance to go, but we have to get moving."

Spurned into action by his insistent hand waving, Remmy ran around the back of the cart and climbed up next to the merchant.

"And who the hell are you?" she demanded angrily.

He hesitated for a long moment before laughing. "I am just a delivery man, and my job is to deliver you back to where you were."

"That'll be a challenge. My body is from one time and my soul another."

He shrugged. "Let's start with fifty-two BC and see where that leads."

"And how do I get back to my own time?"

His eyes still on the path ahead, he laughed. "Maybe you should click the heels of your red slippers together three times and make a wish."

It took her a moment to place the reference. "How on earth does..."

Before she could finish, he slapped the reins again, and to her surprise, the donkey broke into a gallop.

Chapter 68

Her red hair stuffed under a broad-brimmed hat, sunglasses covering her green eyes, Jasmina pulled the collar of her coat up against the cool wind and followed Miriam through the Lancaster Mall parking lot to the main entrance.

"Miriam," she called as she hurried to catch up with her equally disguised companion. "What are we doing here?"

"You promised to trust me, and don't worry. You'll know in a few minutes. You did remember to bring that broach I gave you, didn't you?"

"Yes," she answered while holding up her right hand, "but why is it pinned to the inside my coat's cuff?"

"All in good time," Miriam laughed, though it was strained. "We're almost there."

Urgently waving Jasmina forward, Miriam jogged across the access road in front of the entrance and stepped up onto the concrete walkway, setting a brisk pace without running.

After they passed through the mall doors, they were immediately approached by another woman dressed very much as they were.

"This is sooo cool," Barbara Foltzman whispered excitedly when she was within earshot.

"What are you doing here?" Jasmina asked, her eyes on Barbara as Miriam looked around.

"Is everybody here?" she asked.

Barbara's floppy hat bobbed as she shoved a brown paper bag at Miriam.

"And I got the things you wanted."

"What things?" Jasmina asked.

Looking at her for the first time since they entered the mall, Miriam motioned for Barbara to hand the bag to Jasmina. "A change of clothes."

"What for?"

"I read an article recently that said our memories aren't fixed like we think they are. In fact, every time we call up a memory, we change it."

"Yes. I've heard that too, but how does it help us?"

"I'm thinking whoever this psychic person is, he or she has only made contact with you once, and even then it was for a short time, so they don't have a well-established memory of your psychic signature."

Clifford M. Scovell

"That's probably correct."

"I also remember that they only tried to kidnap you and the children. No one even gave me a passing glance."

Looking from Barbara to Miriam, Jasmina shrugged. "I wasn't aware of that."

Nodding, Miriam moved close to Jasmina. "So here's what I'm thinking." She pointed to the brown-paper bag in Jasmina's hands. "The clothes in that bag are identical to what Barbara and two other girls are wearing."

"And we found some auburn wigs that are, like really close to your hair style," Barbara added excitedly. "From the back, they won't be able to tell us apart."

"So what are you planning?"

"We're going to do a bit of bait-and-switch with them."

Jasmina's eyes bulged. "That crazy doctor and his friends? Are you serious?"

Miriam nodded. "Yes I am. Very serious."

"But there are at least half-a-dozen of them. How are you planning on keeping them at bay when they can surround us? They might even bring in the police."

"I don't think they'll bring in the police because I think they will view this as an opportunity to eliminate you quietly."

Looking around the mall, Jasmina nodded. "And it looks like they'll have no trouble doing that. This is too open for me to hide from them."

"It's not as open as you might think, or at least it soon won't be."

"And how will we know when they are here?"

Barbara laughed. "They already are."

"Where?"

She pointed toward the opposite end of the mall. "We saw them get out of their cars."

Jasmina shook her head. "How do you know who they are?"

Barbara laughed. "Two black Cadillac Escalades, dark suits, dark glasses. They might as well paste a sign on their foreheads saying, 'Fake Federal Agent'." She shook her head. "Anyway, now that we know who each of them is, we've got a person watching them. They're slowly working their way in our direction."

Taking another look around, Jasmina asked, "How many people do we have in here?"

Miriam smiled. "About two dozen of Gerry's high school classmates."

"But how did you set this up?"

"I just called Barbara. She was class president for two years because she is such a great organizer. I told her what we needed and she put it together."

"But how are you coordinating all the people?"

"You can thank my geeky friends for that," Barbara said, looking smug as she pointed at several points around the mall. "We put battery operated WiFi cameras around the place and tied them into the mall's free WiFi system. Then we set up a Skype conference call, so everyone can listen on their cell phones with earbuds." She laughed. "We're going to do a flash mob kind of thing when the time's right. With any luck, we'll have forty or fifty other people in on that, and then another dozen people positioned around the mall to 'accidentally' get in the bad guy's way at the appropriate time."

"Oh my word," Jasmina exclaimed. "I would never have thought of this."

Miriam let out a long breath. "Me neither. That's why I'm glad my son has creative friends."

"So what am I supposed to do?"

Smiling, Barbara pointed at a clothing shop behind Jasmina. "Go in there and put your clothes on. Once you're ready, we'll discuss how you're going to move through the mall. The idea is for you to let them see your face and then move away from them. When they come after you, we replace you with another person wearing the same dress, hat, and hair and get you out of here."

"And what will this accomplish?"

Miriam waggled a hand. "The idea is to confuse the psychic person tracking you. If he thinks he is chasing you, but it is really another person, the psychic will mix their mental signature with yours, creating an altered memory of what you were like. By the time they lose sight of you altogether -- actually, your replacement -- the psychic will have so many different images in his head they won't know the real you from a replacement."

"Meaning they'll be back at square one."

"Right."

"But what about…"

"Sorry, Missus Maxell," Barbara interrupted. "The bad guys are coming our way. You need to get your clothes changed, and quickly."

"Right," Jasmina acknowledged. "I hope this works," she added as Barbara guided her to the changing room.

Nodding, Miriam watched them move away, and when they were out of sight, she sighed, "Our children's lives depend on it."

Chapter 69

I'd never felt so much pressure.

The *centurio* had accepted my supposition, but it all depended on what we found when the army got to the next town. The men had not been happy about the stepped up pace of our march, nor being separated from the camp followers, many of which were family and lovers. If the men who fought against Caesar at *Alesia* returned to their town to await their conqueror's judgment, my "dream" was going to make me the laughing stock of the whole army. Even worse, nearly two hundred tired legionnaires are going to want revenge for making them work so hard for nothing.

A horn sounded, and everyone seemed to stop at once.

"*Optio*," a runner called as he approached. "The *centurio* summons."

Turning to Lucius, I ordered, "Have everyone fall out for a quick meal. Post guards as needed, and wait for my order."

"Yes, Sir," Lucius answered back, a questioning smile on his face.

Shrugging, I followed the runner at a jog, reaching the *centurio* just as two scouts approached.

"*Centurio*," the lead scout called as he saluted. "We found the village about a league ahead."

"Are there any men there?"

"There are none, Sir," the soldier responded with a hint of surprise in his voice. "The place has been deserted."

Without acknowledging the statement, the *centurio* turned to me, and it was only then I saw the other *optio,* along with several *decani*, all looking grim.

"No cooking fires," the *centurio* ordered. "We will not rest long. Our *imperator* is in danger."

We all saluted as one and turned in unison to return to our respective units.

"*Optio* Aremus," the *centurio* called. "A word."

I saw the other *optio* hesitate only briefly before continuing on his way.

"Yes, Sir!" I responded.

"We have yet to see what your insight might bring, but clearly the gods are showing you favor."

"Sir!"

"Have you any further insights into what the future will bring?"

Stifling a shrug, I turned to the lead scout. "How long has it been since the village was occupied?"

"Not more than a day, as some of the fires were still smoldering."

"Any indication that the enemy knows we are behind them?"

"Sir?"

"Did you see anyone ahead of you they might have left behind to watch for us?"

"No sightings were reported."

"And how far do you estimate it is to the legion's camp?"

"If they have not already left, three days."

Turning to the *centurio*, I said, "The enemy is confident they have surprise on their side, and we can turn that to our favor. If we maintain our current pace, we should catch up with them within two days. Once we have determined their strength, we can send a runner to warn the legion."

After the words were out, my brain remained empty, not another thought intruding on the blank slate my speech left behind. Rather than worry about where all of that had come from, I did my best to keep my face neutral and waited for the *centurio*'s response.

As if reading my blank mind, he gave a curt nod and said, "That will be all."

Though surprised by the curt dismissal, I couldn't help but see the near-smile on his face as he turned to address the scouts.

"Sir!" I barked before turning quickly around and marching back toward my place in line.

Maybe I'm getting the hang of this job, I mused while moving past row after row of solders.

I hadn't gone far before it struck me that though these men knew they would soon be in another fight for their lives, most looked relaxed: chatting and joking with their comrades, eating dried cakes and cheese, singing, playing catch. The incongruity made my stomach cramp.

And then again, maybe not.

Chapter 70

"There's got to be a reason we're marching at full step," Manius complained as he moved closer to Quintus. "What'cha wanna bet the Gauls have raised another army and Caesar's hurrying to get back to Italy before they catch up with us."

"Don't talk shit like that," Quintus chastised. "Caesar don't run from nobody. He knocked those savages down and spit on 'em. If they try to get back up, he'll cut off their collective balls and shove 'em down their throats."

"Yeah, well. That don't make my poor feet any happier, nor my bladder."

"Squealin' like a spoiled pig, you are," Quintus growled. "You don't have to stop walking to pee, just don't do it where everyone else is walkin'."

As Manius scooted sideways until he was out of the line of marching troopers to do his business, Quintus looked back and glared at Marcus.

"There's got to be a fight coming up, or we'd not be keeping this pace." Facing forward again. "That means I got another chance to earn my promotion and maybe some extra gold as well."

"What was that, Quintus?" Manius asked while still rearranging his gear. "What'cha goin' ta get?"

"Quiet down, fool," Quintus demanded. "I didn't say anything about getting wealthy. I was just mumbling to myself."

"And I want some of that."

"Some of what?"

"I ain't deaf. I heard you say gold."

"There ain't no gold. I was just wishin'."

"Now we're talking gold?" Manius laughed. "How much?"

"Will you shut up about this?" Quintus protested. "I don't want word getting around."

"What don't you want to get around?" Appius asked as he moved closer to the twosome. "Are you guys up to something? I want in too."

"No. We're not up to anything," Quintus responded angrily.

"Quintus is getting some gold and he needs our help to get it back to Rome."

"I don't need your help with…"

"I'm in!" Appius interrupted. "Who do I have to kill?"

"Who said anything about killin' anybody?"

Appius shrugged. "Why else would someone give you gold?"

"I never said anything about getting paid," Quintus countered, "and I also didn't say I was goin' ta kill anybody. Just forget about it! OK?"

"Can't," Appius insisted. "It's in my head, and there's no getting it out."

"Me too," Manius added.

"Donkey crap," Quintus shouted. "Don't talk to me anymore. I'm done with you guys."

"But we're not done with you, Quintus," Appius laughed. "Until you tell us what we can do to get all that gold."

"There ain't any gold!" Quintus bellowed, and when he suddenly realized what he had done, he looked around to see a dozen soldiers facing his way. "There is no gold," he insisted. "These guys have crap for brains."

The distraction caused some of the men to stumble on the uneven ground, and before they could regain their balance, Marcus moved up and shouted,

"Keep the lines orderly. Pay attention to where you're going up there."

Though the men grumbled, the interruption stopped all conversation, and Quintus hoped everyone would forget about gold. When the silence continued, he took a deep breath and let it out slowly, keeping his eyes ahead to avoid making contact with anyone around him.

"I'm not done with this," Appius whispered when Quintus was just starting to think he was in the clear. "You, me, Manius. We're in this together. You got that?"

Sighing, Quintus nodded. "Yeah. I got it."

"And another thing. Don't try to do us in. Whichever one of us survives will know it was you."

"Got it," Quintus said while thinking, *Unless I get you both at the same time.*

Chapter 71

"Where are we going?" Remmy asked as her hands gripped the seat of the bucking cart.

The merchant shrugged. "I don't know. Where were you when you crossed over?"

"What?" she protested angrily. "I was asleep and covered with a tarp. I have no idea where it happened."

Pulling on the reins, the Merchant called, "Slow there, Missile. That's a good girl."

As the cart slowed, Remmy asked, "Missile?"

When he seemed happy with the cart's speed, the merchant turned toward Remmy. "That is not a word in your language?"

She nodded. "Yes, but it usually refers to something that goes really fast."

Giving his shoulders a shrug, the merchant slapped the reins. "This donkey is so stupid she will walk right into a wall if I don't stop her." he turned to her. "That's what missiles do; plow into whatever is in front of them. Am I right?"

"Well...yes, but..."

"So what is your problem?"

After gawking at him for a long moment, Remmy shook her head. "Whatever. The important thing is we need to get me back to ancient Rome so I can help Gerry...er...Marcus with whatever he has to do."

"But you don't know where it was you crossed from that time to this."

"No, I don't. So what are the alternatives?"

The merchant looked ahead and lightly slapped the reins for a moment before pulling on them to stop the donkey. As the cart ground to a halt, he lowered the reins and turned toward Remmy again.

"You don't know how this works, do you?"

She jerked a no. "I don't even know what this is, so fill me in."

"Oh dear," he muttered. "That means you're outside the network."

"What did you say?"

"You're a volunteer?"

"A volunteer for what?"

His eyes went wide. "You're not working with the…"

The last word came out like grating static that was so irritating it made her pull back. Even so, she knew who he was talking about.

"You're with those people from that other dimension whose names we can't pronounce?"

The merchant looked wary. "How do you know about them?"

"One of them was in my body and almost got me killed. Then another time we found an ancient crystal that had thousands of them trapped in it and we helped them escape."

"We?"

"Well, yeah. Me and Gerry and my aunt, Jasmina. And now I'm in this woman's body and we've both been hauled off to who-knows-where by who-knows-who to do who-knows-what, and shit! All this confusion is pissing me off!"

Holding both hands up, palms out, the merchant pleaded, "Don't blame me. I'm just a delivery person."

"Well, who else am I supposed to blame, and how do I get my hands on the little shit's throat?"

She tilted forward, forcing the merchant to lean back so far he almost fell off the cart.

Though Remmy did not back off, he steadied himself and gasped, "I'm not sure how much I can explain to you." Lifting a hand, he motioned her back, and when she relaxed and accommodated him, he sighed and shook his head.

"There is much of this you can't understand, but you might think of us as a mental collective, much like a human brain only many magnitudes larger."

"The ones we met didn't act like they were part of any collective. They seemed to be pretty much working on their own."

Shaking his head, he waved her comment away. "We aren't mindless drones. Each of us is unique and independent, but we are constantly aware of the others around us, and normally we work as a collective unit, but these aren't normal circumstances."

"How do you mean?"

"Your universe is nothing like our own. It took us millions of your years to adapt enough to function at all, even longer to realize where we are and figure out what we needed to do to get back home."

"How many of you are there?"

He shrugged. "It's hard to tell. You see, we've been here millions of your years, and in that time, we have -- to use your terms -- reproduced."

Jerking back, Remmy threw a hand over her mouth and gasped. "There could be billions of you."

He nodded. "Most likely."

"And each one of you needs one of us to…what? Protect you?"

He nodded again, more quickly this time. "Without a corporeal body to anchor us, we will be swept away by the *Tsabbat* and lost forever."

"So, if there are billions of you, that means that a very high percentage of humans have an alien being occupying their bodies."

"Very high."

"But the souls that occupied me and my friends thought there were only a few thousand of you here."

"Yes, well, you see, we've been so busy in the more violent parts of this world, our people haven't had time to make contact with those on this continent. We only learned about you because two of your species made the jump to our universe."

"You mean, Long Gang and Toilet Face? They actually survived the crossing?"

He shrugged. "I don't know if they survived, but their transition was very disruptive for our collective. When they sent me to investigate, I found you."

"But I thought you were only a delivery boy."

He laughed. "I am. My job is to find you, or more specifically the body you occupy, and deliver you back to the correct time."

"But you said you couldn't do that unless you knew exactly where and how I got here."

He waggled a hand. "I can do it another way, but there are risks."

"What risks?"

He shrugged. "For starters, this body will most likely be destroyed."

"Destroyed? I'm not liking that one bit."

He waved a hand dismissively. "Your essence will survive, and in the process it will be pulled back to your original body."

"But then I can't help Gerry, er, Marcus save his general."

"Yes, and there is one other thing you'll have to deal with."

"What is that?"

"Enid will still be in your body."

"What will that mean?"

He smiled. "The two of you will have figure out how to share it."

Chapter 72

"How did you organize this so fast?" Jasmina asked Barbara as they peeked out of the dress shop to see a growing number of young people milling around the mall.

"It was really easy," Barbara laughed as she pinned the brooch Miriam had given Jasmina to a big floppy hat. "Since we had only a little time to put it together, I thought it best to create a flash mob."

"You did an incredible job. Do you know where Miriam disappeared to?"

"Oh, she went into the back where they have the computers to watch the web cams. She didn't want to take the chance they might recognize her from the hospital."

"Good idea," Jasmina praised her. "So what do I do now?"

Barbara moved close. "See that jewelry store across the mall?"

"Should I go there now?"

"Not until the bad guys get into position. They need to see you walking across the mall."

"Out in the open?"

Barbara smiled. "As soon as they see you, we'll start the music and people will be dancing, and running about."

"Do I go into the jewelry shop?"

"Nope," Barbara said as she pointed to another shop on the other side of the mall. "You turn left and go into the hobby shop four doors down. The first decoy will be there, and as she moves back out where they can see her, you go out the shop's back door."

"And what's out there?"

"A parking lot where your husband will pick you up and take you to the safe house. In the meantime, your "doubles" will lead them on a wild goose chase."

"I'm not so sure this was a good idea," Jasmina complained. "It's too risky. Someone might get hurt."

Barbara shook her head. "If you're right about what is going on, we're already in a lot of danger unless we can protect you from these people."

A smiling Jasmina said, "Barbara, I have to say, you are full of…"

Holding up a hand, Barbara touched an ear and nodded.

"They're almost here," she announced. "The music will start as soon as they see you."

"Should I go now?"

Barbara held up a hand, palm out as she listened to her phone. After a moment, she nodded and waved Jasmina forward.

Clutching her bag of clothes, she felt her heart racing as she nearly stumbled into the mall, her eyes scanning the crowd, ears straining for a shouted command she would not obey. In seconds, she spotted them: Doctor McFaddan, three other men in dark suits, and a short, black-haired woman wearing a full-length, navy-blue dress.

Her heart raced when McFaddan's face showed recognition. The shock was so great that when he tapped the woman's arm and pointed, Jasmina stopped walking, her mind in turmoil as she tried to remember what she was supposed to do next, and fought against the urge to abandon the plan and run away.

A blast of loud music brought her around just as the five people started moving in her direction. Realizing they were approaching fast, she continued on toward the jewelry store, and pushed her way into a cluster of people. Through gaps in the thickening crowd, she caught glimpses of McFaddan and the woman beside him holding her hands up by her temples, fingertips just touching skin.

STOP! exploded in her head, the intensity of it numbing her brain and halting her advance.

She tried to take a step, but it felt as though the woman was gripping her shoulders, keeping her from moving forward. She struggled against the sensation, lurching one foot forward, then the other, but each step was harder as though the woman was gaining control of her movements, and even threatening to take over her mind. Though she was able to use her own thoughts to resist the attack, it slowed her down too much and she was certain they would catch her. She was just about to cry out for help when one of the dancers did a quick spin, lost his balance, and crashed into the woman.

The woman's mouth opened, but her scream was drowned by the raucous music and shouting people. Now free, Jasmina gasped in a breath, and started moving again, heading straight for her first destination.

They're too close, shouted in her head as she quickstepped toward the jewelry store.

Steeling herself for the worst, she glanced back to see McFaddan had stopped to help the woman up, but the three men in suits were running her way.

"Change of plan!" she cried, her heart again thudding in her chest as she cut left and plowed into a cluster of dancing people, weaving past bodies, careening off hips and elbows as she tried to think of what to do.

"This is no time to panic," she shouted, more to get herself focused than for anyone else to hear.

Suddenly finding herself outside the crowd, she took a sharp right and skirted the mob, counting half-a-dozen quick steps before cutting back in. Hunkering down to make herself less visible, she continued her careening pin-ball path through the crowd until a cry on her right made her cut left. She wanted to straighten and run as fast as she could, but fear cramped her gut, and made her crouch down even more as she passed under flailing arms, zipped past twisting bodies, around twirling couples. Hoping she was still heading toward the jewelry store, she moved to the edge of the crowd and stopped when she saw the woman, her hands still fisted, strain distorting her face.

"All these mental images have to be overwhelming," Jasmina muttered as she watched the woman from the edge of the crowd and struggled to breathe.

Fearing the woman might see her, she started to pull back into the crowd until she heard a husky voice behind her cry out, "Coming through! Get out of the way!"

To her relief, mob members seemed to be resisting, shouting back defiantly at the suited intruders. At first she thought McFaddan's people were all around her, but soon realized they were on her left. Holding her breath again, she watched the woman scan the crowd one more time before moving right.

The shouting behind was growing louder, leaving her only one choice.

The hobby shop!

Bursting from the crowd, she ran full-tilt, her stomach in her throat, breath coming in gasps. It was all she could do to keep from looking back, her chest tightening at the almost certain thought that someone was about to grab her from behind. Over the loud music she heard a man shout, and knew they had seen her, but kept her eyes forward, and quickened her pace.

Be there, Barbara! Please be there!

The shop had a large display just outside its entrance, and she forced herself to slow down as she slipped behind it. Even then, it took every bit of willpower she had to keep herself from stopping right there and hunkering down.

Stumbling further into the store, she tried to look for Barbara, but her vision blurred as people, displays, and colorful merchandise mixed together in a streaked montage that nearly made her sick.

"Let's go!" a woman's voice shouted.

Her vision sharpening, she turned in the direction of the voice to see Barbara, her red wig and hat gone, one hand rapidly waving her toward the back and at the same time using the other to push an identically dressed woman toward the front.

Scrambling to the back counter, Jasmina heard Barbara shout, "You go right and I'll go left to slow him down."

Afraid to stop or look back, Jasmina rushed through an open doorway to find herself in a darkened space where gamers were gawking at the action on big-screen TVs as they punched buttons on keypads and took no notice of the gasping woman rushing past them.

There's a back door in here somewhere.

Moving quickly through the room, she scanned the dimly lit back wall, but it was covered from one side to the other with a black curtain, leaving no indication as to where a doorway might be.

She froze in place when Barbara screamed, "Hey! Watch where you're going, moron!"

Pulling the floppy hat off her head, she stripped off her coat and quickly rolled it up before rushing to a player in the far corner of the room.

"I need to borrow your cap for a moment," she announced while snatching the wool cap from the young man's head and pulling it onto her own. "Sorry, Dear, but there's a bad man after me, and I need to be invisible."

Seeming hardly interested in what was going on outside the screen in front of him, the lad shrugged. "Yeah. Whatever."

Even over the music playing outside, Jasmina could hear the heavy breathing as someone peered into the room. Holding her breath, she forced herself to face the screen, her ears struggling to hear what was going on behind her, as aliens were vanquished, cars blown up, and a castle vanished in a cloud of flame. Her hands shaking badly, she strained to hear over the noise around her, and when she could take it no longer, she summoned up the courage to look behind her, gulping in air when she realized the coast was clear.

After taking a moment to recover, she turned to her companion. "I don't suppose you know where the back door is?"

His eyes remaining on the screen, the kid nodded. "It's just behind that curtain in the corner, but it'll sound an alarm when you go out."

"Is there another way?"

Shrugging, the kid pressed a button on his controller and the screen froze. Rising, he moved to the corner and pushed the curtain aside. Jasmina gasped and started to move forward when she saw the doorway, but stopped when the young man held up a hand. Her heart raced as she watched him lift a small metal plate from a nail next to the door and hold it up.

"You need this to get out."

Puzzled, Jasmina shook her head. "How does it work?"

"The alarm only sounds when you use the bar to open the door," he explained while reaching behind the bar and pressing the plate against the door latch. "This way you don't have to do that."

He pushed, she heard a click, and the door swung open.

After quickly returning the metal plate to its nail, he turned to Jasmina and smiled. "You just gotta know the trick."

"Thank you," she said as she pulled the cap off and handed it to him. "You may have saved the world as we know it."

Smiling, the kid took the cap and put it on. "Yeah. Whatever."

Blowing him a kiss, she rushed through the door, her eyes scanning the parking lot in search of her husband's car. Just as she was starting to panic, it sped around the corner of the building.

"Oh God," she gasped as she waved needlessly to get Tim's attention. "If we don't end this soon, I'm going to have a heart attack."

Chapter 73

"*Centurio*," a scout shouted as he stopped in front of our leader. "We have spotted the enemy's rear."

Without changing expression, the *centurio* turned to face the men behind him.

"All stop. Tell the men to stand down. Post the usual sentries."

It had been two days since I made my prediction, and was surprised by its accuracy.

"How many are there?"

The scout shook his head. "I couldn't see all of them, but I'd estimate one thousand, maybe fifteen hundred. However, from the amount of damage to the ground, many more than that came through not long before them. Maybe two, three days earlier."

"And the Tenth Legion?"

"I sent my best runner around them to get word to the *imperator*. If they truly are a day's march further ahead, it will take time for him to get there and back, but at least the *imperator* will be warned."

"How far are we behind the enemy?"

"No more than two-hours march. If we get any closer, they will see our dust."

Nodding, the *centurio* waved a hand at me and my fellow *optio*. "Gentlemen? What do you think?"

As I looked at the path ahead and saw nothing but trees, grass, and sky, I wondered how quickly a man could run from here to the legion and back.

"Sir," the other *optio* barked. "Engage them now before they have time to organize."

Without comment, the *centurio* looked at me. I struggled to remember what Marcus had done when they took the Gallic village, and then it all came back to me.

"With respect, Sir, I disagree."

"Don't attack?"

I shook my head, absolutely stunned that I might be thinking like a Roman soldier.

"Not at this time. We don't know the strength of their forces, and if we attack now, it will alert them to our presence and take away the element of surprise."

"How do we coordinate our efforts with the legion?"

I suddenly realized he wasn't asking me about strategy. He knew what he was going to do, and was using this as an opportunity to test Marcus for a possible promotion to *centurio*.

"The runner will let *Imperator* Caesar know we are here. He will surely base his strategy on our presence and send his own runner back with instructions."

"What would you do?"

From the other *optio*'s expression, I could tell he also knew what was going on.

The giant!

Surely, by the time word of my defeat of the Gallic Goliath had worked its way to him in the rear, the story had been enhanced and distorted. As far as he knew, I had probably leaped sixty feet through the air, and snapped off the Gaul's massive head with my little pinkie.

Rumor is so much more exciting than reality.

"I would send more scouts to find their gathering place and try to determine their strongest positions. If we do not get word from the legion before they start their attack, I would wait until they were about to engage the legion and then attack whichever group looks the strongest."

"Why not hit the weakest divisions?"

"When the enemy realizes we are attacking them from both front and back, they will panic. If we destroy the strongest among them, the rest will drop their weapons and scatter."

I again gave the other *optio* a glance to find him nodding.

Jerking a nod as well, the *centurio* did not hesitate. "You will lead the second *centuria*. The *decanus* of your first *contubernium* can stand as your second."

Though Marcus would have expected this, it came as a shock to me. Primarily because it presented the perfect scenario for everyone: Remmy and I could go home once Caesar's assassination was avoided, and being promoted to one of the most dangerous jobs in the Roman Army, Marcus would have a chance to die bravely, and best of all, Europe would be unchanged, America would be discovered, and life would go on as before.

That would make everyone happy but Enid. If Marcus succeeded in his quest to die in battle, she would again be alone. The thought was a sad one, but before I could dwell on it, movement in front of me pulled my attention back to the present.

The fact that I did not respond was lost on the *centurio*. His statement was not a request, but an order to be carried out without question. While I was lost in my own thoughts, he had moved on.

But the *optio* had not.

"What are your orders, Sir," he asked crisply.

The *centurio* had given me a temporary field promotion, which would vanish once we merged with the legion. There was no question that his seniority kept him in charge, but I still had to respond to this man's question, and I was beginning to fear I wouldn't have an answer.

And then I remembered what we had discussed in history class.

"Have a sacrifice prepared and call up the auger. Let us see what he thinks of this upcoming engagement."

The man did not even blink at the order.

"At once, Sir!"

He did a quick turn and marched away.

"Shit!" I exclaimed while shaking my head.

There had to be some of Marcus still helping me decide what to do, but it was feeling more and more like he was fading away.

I took a deep breath and let it out, releasing an incredible amount of stress, realizing that by this time tomorrow, I might well be at the front of a Roman *centuria*, preparing to kill or be killed. If I survived, and Julius Caesar did as well, I could find myself home, but if I actually had to fight, the odds were not in my favor.

Remmy?

As we marched, I turned to Lucius. "Did you find my slave?"

After several steps, he answered, "There has been no sign of her."

"I know that, but what happened to her?"

He took a deep breath and let it out. "The merchant thinks someone kidnapped her for his bed. If that is so, it is most likely that she is dead."

"Dead?"

Whatever tension the deep breath had released was back again, and then some.

However, before I could think of what to do next, the *centurio* returned.

"Slow the men to three-quarter step and continue on for another hour. Unless the situation changes, I will have the scouts find us a place to stop so the men can stand down to rest. I want them as fresh as possible for this engagement."

My head swimming, it was all I could do to say, "Yes, Sir!"

Thankfully, he didn't wait for my response.

Remmy!

Her name screamed in my head as my mind seemed to totally separate from my body.

"No!" slipped from my lips.

"Sir?"

The question brought me back to the present with a bang. Well, at least the Marcus part of me, because Gerry Patterson was lost in a fog of grief.

Without my even thinking about it, my body turned to the *optio* and shouted, "Prepare to form up. Three-quarter step."

"Sir!"

I looked at the road ahead.

Will I die too? I could feel my head shake. *Do I care?*

And then I felt a tickle of anger at the back of my consciousness. Like lighting a match in a room full of gas, it exploded into my brain, and suddenly this tired body was energized.

"Lucius!" I shouted so loud the poor man nearly stumbled as he jerked around to face me.

"Yes, Sir, *Centurio.*"

Literally seeing red, I growled, "Take the lead."

"Sir!" he responded, his shocked expression doing nothing to calm my rage.

I'm going to make those bastards pay!

Jogging back along the line of men, I noted their curious stares, but didn't care. I had to be doing something. Had to be hitting something. Had to be creating carnage, and was sure from their changing expressions that the men could see it on my face.

You haven't seen anything yet!

The statement stopped me, and it was only then I realized how hard I was breathing. The men near me must have thought I was having a coronary, because some of their eyes were wide, expressions showing fear.

Another idea popped into my head.

Alone you might kill half-a-dozen. With the whole centuria behind you, that number will be in the hundreds.

I looked again at the faces marching past me, and something outside my experiences told me they weren't ready for this fight, because my strange behavior was eroding their trust in my leadership.

The biggest factor in any encounter is the confidence of the participants.
That was the voice of my self-defense class teacher.

If all other factors are equal, the one who most believes in himself will come out on top.

Believe in yourself!

The statement erupted again as a firestorm in my brain.

Believe in yourself!

I started walking along with the cadence of the syllables.

Be-lieve in your-self!

My shield being wrapped in its leather covering and strapped to my back, I couldn't pull it out, so I yanked out my sword and held it in front of my face.

Be-lieve in your-self!

The shining weapon fired me up in a way I had never felt before and that banished all my fears.

Be-lieve in your-self!

I quickened my pace, marching until I was in the front of the line, my attention on the blade in front of me, my mind repeating the new mantra.

Be-lieve in your-self!

"*Optio?*" Lucius asked cautiously as I approached him.

Lowering the sword, I glared, first at him then the line of men behind him. Curious faces peered out from under their load of gear, their curiosity not hiding their low morale.

"These Gauls want to ambush our *imperator*," I shouted, "and I won't have it."

The curious looks turned cautious.

Think like a centurio!

"These people are deceitful cowards. They surrender to us, but only days after our *imperator* has generously granted them clemency, they gather again to stab him in the back."

Though most of the men were still trying to understand what I was talking about, some shouted, "No."

My adrenaline levels in the stratosphere, I ran back down the line, my sword held high. "We're going to show these savages that Rome does not bow to anyone."

More faces turned angry.

"And if we show Caesar what good fighters we are, maybe he'll have us march in the first *centuria*."

Cries of, "Let's show him!" and "No one stabs our *imperator* in the back!"

"Are you with me?" I shouted.

"Yes!" about a third of the men responded.

"Are you with me?"

More than half bellowed, "Yes!"

"Are…you…with…me?"

Now almost all of them were shaking fists in the air and shouting, "YES!"

Someone started chanting, "Caesar! Caesar! Caesar!" and the rest joined in, their strides more determined, fists punching at the sky.

"Caesar! Caesar! Caesar!"

Moving toward the front of the line, I pointed my sword in the direction we were marching and needlessly shouted, "March forward."

The chanting continued as I moved up beside Lucius and continued to stab my sword, into the air like a drum major leading his marching band.

"Wouldn't it have been best to wait until we were ready to engage them?" Lucius asked.

I shook my head. "If I am to be their *centurio*, they have to accept me as such long before we engage the enemy."

"And are you ready to be their *centurio*?" he asked with a wry smile.

In my head I was shouting, *Hell no!* but thoughts of Remmy blew that away. Glaring at him, I answered, "There is no one more ready."

After a few minutes the shouting stopped. Flickering fingers of rage still tickled my consciousness as I sheathed my sword and marched in silence, wondering how long it would last.

An image of Remmy flashed in my head, her cute smile, gorgeous green eyes, flaming red hair. But just as quickly her expression turned fearful, as though someone were going to strike her down.

The rage returned. It was going to get me to the battlefield and after that…

I didn't really give a damn.

Chapter 74

"Caesar! Caesar! Caesar!"

Though Quintus pumped his fist in the air along with his comrades, he refused to chant the words as he fumed internally.

That arrogant cock is puffing up his feathers in front of the men. What a suck up!

His disgust increased when he looked around to see Manius and Appius mimicking the others: fists pumping, hollering their general's name as they jumped up and down despite the sixty-pounds of gear each was carrying.

"We're going to kill every one of them bastards," Appius shouted.

"We'll cover the battlefield with corpses," Manius added.

"Oh shut up you two," Quintus growled as he pushed Manius closer to Appius and whispered, "If we do that, we don't get paid."

The two gaped at him. "We don't?"

"No we don't!"

"We want the Gauls to kill our *imperator*?" Manius asked.

"But he's the best general who's ever lived," Appius added.

Snorting in disgust, Quintus shook his head. "Yes, we want to save our *imperator*, but not with Marcus at the lead of our *centuria*."

From their position in the back of the formation, they could no longer see Marcus, but Quintus stabbed a finger in his direction anyway. "He has to be taken out *before* we engage the savages."

The two men looked at each other briefly before giving Quintus clueless faces in stereo.

"Why is it we need to kill him again?" Appius asked.

"Yeah. Why?" Manius added.

"Why?" Quintus asked derisively, but the question made him stop.

He had never actually learned the name of the mysterious stranger who plied him with drink and the promise of promotion. Nor did he really know the man's reason for wanting Marcus dead. He only went along for the hope of sweet revenge.

How will I find you? he had asked just before he slipped into an alcoholic stupor.

Do not worry, my friend, the man had said. *I will find you.*

Until now that had been enough because he wanted to get revenge on Marcus, and the thought he might also get rich in the bargain just added to the allure.

"Because an oracle told me."

Appius seemed to accept his statement, but Manius wasn't so accommodating.

"Told you what, exactly?"

Quintus shook his head. "I don't remember all the words, but he told me if Marcus leads us into this battle, every one of us will be killed. If he don't, we'll wipe out these traitorous savages and be richer than that Greek King Midas."

Though Appius grinned like a punch-drunk hound, Manius remained cautious.

"Why would you be consulting with a…"

"Shape up, you three," the *optio* behind them shouted. "Save your gossiping for when we are resting."

"Sir!" the three shouted in unison.

Though they straightened and moved further apart, Manius kept his attention on Quintus.

"I still don't understand why…"

"Shut it," Quintus snapped, though he was inwardly glad they'd been interrupted. "You want to feel the sting of his rod?"

After walking for a few paces, Quintus looked over to see Marius still staring at him. Scowling, he kept his eyes forward and tried to pretend it didn't matter,

Who is this sewer rat to challenge me? He thought angrily, and felt even more irritation because he didn't have an answer to his own question.

A knife in the throat will be answer enough.

Chapter 75

"There's got to be another way!" Remmy protested as the merchant slapped the reins to get his donkey moving again. "I'm not sharing my body with anyone else, ever again."

"I'm open to suggestions," the merchant responded calmly, "but you hardly know how this works, and there simply isn't enough time to teach you even the most rudimentary aspects of the process."

She scowled at him. "And most of it is probably in your scratchy little language."

"I'm afraid so."

She snorted angrily. "Well, we have to think of something because I'm not staying here while Gerry is in trouble."

"Without knowing where you made the transition, there's very little chance we can…"

"Wait!"

"What?"

"Is this the same trail the stranger came in on?"

The merchant shrugged. "I'm not sure, but probably. There aren't many roads in this part of the world. Why would it matter?"

"Because his tracks would only start when we appeared in this timeline. Prior to that, he was in Northern Gaul, half-a-world and many centuries in the past."

"How do you know this time is that much later than the previous one?"

Throwing her hands up, she shouted, "Because I'm a history major." She stabbed a finger toward where they had come. "Those guys are Muslims and that religion didn't even exist before 600 AD. Even so, I'm guessing this time is much later than that."

He shrugged. "You're a very astute young woman, but I can't tell you exactly when this is."

Lowering her hands, Remmy glared at him. "Why can't you tell…Shit! We're going to come back to this time, aren't we?"

The merchant shook his head. "What do I know?" he protested. "I'm just a delivery…"

"You know far more than you're telling me," she interrupted, "and that implies you know that we'll have something to do here."

"That's not true. Things might get resolved long before you have to return to this place."

"I don't want to return to this place ever!" she stated adamantly. "At least not in this time period. I'm tired of living in the past. I'd rather just read about it."

"Then let's hope we can find the point at which you entered this time, or you and Enid are going to have to do the body-sharing thing."

Pointing at the donkey, Remmy ordered, "Get this beast moving then, because that's NOT going to happen."

Chapter 76

Taking one last look over her shoulder, Jasmina pushed through the front door of the house in Jefferson.

"Marcus? Enid?" she called. "We're back."

"Did it go well?" Alvin asked as he appeared from the living room.

Carrying a bag of groceries, Jasmina walked past the living room and into the kitchen.

"I think so. We definitely had them confused, but then so was I."

"We brought food," Tim announced as he followed his wife into the kitchen.

"Where's Miriam?"

Removing a bottle of juice from her bag, Jasmina put it in the refrigerator before facing Alvin. "She stayed behind with Barbara to see if she can find out anything about the lady chasing me."

"How are they going to do that if they don't even know her name?"

She shrugged. "I'm not really sure. They got plenty of images of her on the cameras they set up, but I'm not sure how you search for a picture on the web."

"They could do a search for psychics. Maybe she has a website, or something like that," Tim suggested.

"From my experience, if a psychic is worth her salt, she won't need to do any advertising. Word of mouth will get her all the business she needs."

"And you think this woman is the real thing?" Alvin asked.

Nodding emphatically, Jasmina sighed, "Yes. I'm afraid she is. She almost stopped me in my tracks, and if someone hadn't crashed into her, I'd be in their custody again."

"There is another witch pursuing us?" Marcus asked as he appeared from the living room with Enid close behind.

For a long moment, all the modern-age people froze, their eyes jerking from one of their group to another until Jasmina said,

"In a manner of speaking, yes."

"And she is as powerful as you?"

"That is a difficult thing to judge," Jasmina responded while looking at Alvin, "but she doesn't have our motivation."

"Motivation?" Enid asked, her own eyes moving from one person to another before she settled on Jasmina. "What people do you wish to conquer?"

Jasmina shook her head, but it was Alvin who answered, "We don't want to conquer anyone. We just want to get our children back."

"But they fight for a good cause," Marcus stated. "To save our *imperator*."

Alvin shook his head. "I wouldn't care one whit…"

"What he's trying to say," Jasmina interrupted, "is that we want to get our children back without sacrificing them to the cause. To that end, we need to reestablish contact with them so you can help."

Though Marcus seemed to want to say something, Enid elbowed past him and asked, "How can we help if someone here also wants us dead?"

"For the time being, we are hidden from those people, and hopefully it will give us enough time to…"

A rap on the door -- three knocks, one knock, three knocks -- interrupted her.

"That will be Barbara," she announced while hurrying to the door.

Barbara burst through without speaking, marching straight back to the group until she saw Marcus in Gerry's body. However, since just before the body swap Gerry's normally blond hair had darkened, and his blue eyes were now brown.

The sight made her gasp and stop, and gasp again at the sight of the blond-haired, blue eyed Remmy.

"Wow! You really have changed."

Quickly catching up to Barbara, Jasmina put a hand on her shoulder. "Where's Miriam?"

Her eyes still on Marcus, she answered distractedly, "Oh…yeah. She's parking the car around the block in case their people somehow tie it to us."

"Good idea. What happened after I left the mall?"

"Gerry looks different."

Nodding, Jasmina looked at him as well. "That's not Gerry anymore. His soul has been transported back to Roman times and this is the guy he swapped bodies with."

"They actually, like swapped bodies?"

"Yes, they did."

"And has the other guy changed as much as Gerry did?"

The question stopped Jasmina, and she looked at a surprised Tim.

"I hadn't thought of that. That would be a problem."

Tim nodded. "Marcus' world is filled with superstition and mythology. Such a thing might be viewed with suspicion."

"And how could Gerry do his job if everyone is keeping an eye on him?"

Jasmina hesitated for a long moment, a fist pressing into her chin, her eyes on the floor.

"There might be a way," she finally announced, "but I have to connect with him."

She looked up to see Marcus staring at her wide-eyed. "What you say?"

Jasmina shook her head. "You have to help me, Marcus. Your general's life may depend on it."

Without hesitating, he jerked a nod. "Tell me. What can I do?"

Reaching a hand toward him, she smiled grimly. "Prepare for the ride of your life."

Chapter 77

As we marched, reoccurring thoughts of Remmy pushed me from the edge of despair to the fires of rage again and again. In fact, I was just starting to fill with fiery-rage again when we marched over a low rise to look down at the Gallic army gathered in the valley below.

There were thousands of people down there and I have to admit, my vision filled with what initially looked like a chaotic mass of thousands, much like the floor of a basketball court after the home team won a big game. But I quickly started to see patterns, and after the initial shock wore off, I realized the group gathered in the field outside Caesar's fortified camp wasn't one homogenous army. The mass of bodies was actually a multi-colored collection of groups: one dressed in green, another in blue, two groups glittering as sunlight reflected off their metal armor, the rest wore the skin of whatever animal they revered. They didn't look like the screaming savages we had encountered earlier, but judging from the way they clustered around their own leaders, they didn't strike me as a cohesive whole either.

The sudden change in situation from quiet marching to facing such a large number of people who wanted to kill me, threw my mind into turmoil. I wanted to kill as well, to get revenge for Remmy, but there were so many. Fear and rage mixed violently in my head, making me sweat as my muscles seemed to tense and quake at the same time.

Finally recovering, I snapped my mouth closed, refocused on my need for revenge, and turned to the scout next to me.

"From where do these people come?"

He pointed needlessly. "I see *Allobroges, Helvetti, Nervii,* and *Leuci.* There are many other tribes, but those four are dominant. The *Allobroges* are probably the strongest contingent."

I was struggling to think of an intelligent question when my mouth started speaking for me.

"How many combatants, do you estimate?"

He shrugged as though I'd asked him how many pigs were in a slaughterhouse yard.

"Maybe ten thousand, and another thousand horse."

The mention of "horse" made my chest tighten, but it took the twenty-first century part of my mind a couple of heartbeats to realize the significance of what he said. "Horse?"

The sound of hoofs pounding the dry ground pulled my attention to the right.

I immediately regretted the decision to leave our bows behind. While my men were very proficient archers, the *centurio* had decided that we would dump all excess gear so that we could maneuver quickly, and he considered bows and arrows to be "extra baggage."

We came over the ridge in four rows of forty, taking up almost the entire ridge and making an impressive show for the enemy below. I was beginning to think this would be a straightforward attack when an arrow thudded into the shield of a man next to me. I hadn't considered that they would have horses.

Testudo! was my first thought, and though I wanted to voice the command, I checked myself. The usual defense against a barrage of arrows was to put up a wall of shields both in front and over the top of the men. This box-like formation -- Latin for tortoise -- is nearly impenetrable, but it also limits our mobility, and with horses approaching, we needed as much flexibility as we could get. Especially the ability to throw our *pila*.

But that didn't mean we had to stand here as open targets.

"Raise shields!"

Arrows stuck in or bounced off our shields. The shooting was sporadic, and I suspect their leaders were more concerned with what Caesar was going to do. So was I.

As soon as both *centuriae* were over the top of the ridge, a horn sounded, the north gate of Caesar's *castra* opened, and row after row of legionnaires marched out. A moment later the western gate also opened, and more men appeared, their armor glistening in the sunlight, the steady tromping of their united feet pounding out a rhythm that gave me hope, and surely hammered fear into the collective hearts of the enemy.

Both the horses and arrows stopped, and the enemy grew quiet, their attention no longer on us. They watched, and waited as one *centuria* came out each gate to be followed by donkey carts loaded with rocks and then something that had to turn that fear to terror: the *onager*, or as the Latin word clearly expressed, *wild ass*.

From history class, I remembered this weapon was most often used during a siege to batter the walls of forts with large rocks. Now they were going to batter the bodies of men, and the effect would be more devastating than being kicked by a wild ass.

Though I shouldn't have been, I was surprised to see a sudden burst of activity among the enemy troops. Some were holding up their weapons and screaming at the top of their lungs. Others seemed to be arguing among themselves: arms waving; mouths open; pushing and shoving; and at times, pointing to us. The ones I took for their commanders were rushing through the crowds, either howling along with their men, or lashing out with rods, shouting, and doing some pushing of their own.

The leaders of the arguing groups soon brought their men under control, but the message was clear. Not everyone wanted to fight, either because of their fear of us, or the simple realization that it was a hopeless cause, and each one of them knew the consequences of losing this battle. Caesar had been lenient to those tribes who submitted without a fight, or had withdrawn their troops after seeing the Romans were not going to be easily defeated.

My gut cramped when I realized that if the Roman's won this battle, Caesar would show no mercy for those who could not keep their promises. Every enemy combatant would be slaughtered, and I might be called upon to participate.

"Lower shields," the *centurio* bellowed. "Pila at the ready!"

Hesitating only briefly, the riders resumed their approach. After a moment of mind-blanking panic, I pulled myself together and counted heads.

Only about fifty.

The thought brought little relief. These men had probably been riding since they were children. I had been a legionnaire for only a few days.

My knees started to buckle, and it was all I could do to catch myself and keep walking. I hoped the men's attention was on the approaching horses because if they saw fear in me, one or more pila might find their way into my back.

I only barely heard the *centurio*'s command to charge.

"Forward at full pace!" I repeated, thankful my voice did not crack.

I could hear the men jogging behind me, but was afraid to look back for fear I might trip and fall. I was also worried they might see the terror on my face. In the past, Marcus' body had inexplicably taken over, and fought for me. I didn't feel him this time.

Where are you, Marcus?

I could feel tears streaming down my face as the sound of my plea echoed in the horrifying silence of my mind.

"Full charge!" the *centurio* bellowed.

Up until now, the men had not uttered a single sound. If the enemy could hear anything over their own screaming, it would be the stamping feet made as eighty men in each *centuria* marched in almost perfect cadence.

But now that we were only seconds from impact, a roar rose from the ranks.

"Throw!"

Each man in the first two rows hauled back their spear and heaved it with a combined grunt. Fifteen or twenty men and horses fell.

"All stop! Trade rows! *Equis* defense."

In the blink of an eye both *centuriae* stopped. The first two rows, except me, pulled back and were replaced with the third and fourth rows, their *pila* at the ready. As those horsemen still willing to attack us moved around their fallen comrades, the new first row of each *centuria* moved close together, hammered the bottoms of their shields to the ground, dropped to one knee and stuck *pila* in the gaps between the shields. The approaching horses now faced a solid wall lined with prickly spear tips. Since the bottoms of the shields were embedded in the soil they would be hard to move, even if the horse managed to get past the spear tip. Those who ventured close enough to try were speared by the men of the second row.

To my utter relief, only a few mindless twits tried and were quickly cut down. The others stood out of spear range and ineffectively lobbed arrows at us.

Not content to just stand there and let the enemy pick us off one-by-one, the *centurio* bellowed, "Forward, three-quarter step."

The front row rose, their spears at the ready, and though I'm sure every single man was as afraid as I, both *centuriae* marched as one. For their part, the Gallic horsemen shouted and shook their weapons at us, but kept their distance for a long moment before a horn blast pulled their attention back toward Caesar's camp.

"Full Charge!"

I was surprised by the *centurio*'s command, and nearly stumbled when I lurched forward to follow it.

"Full Charge!" I repeated, my sword suddenly in my hand, arm jutting out in front of me as fear made my head spin.

I tried to bring up thoughts of Remmy in the hope it might get my rage-thing going, but there was too much fear holding it down. I stumbled, righted myself and forced my legs to keep pumping as I shouted at the top of my lungs and watched the horses grow bigger and bigger.

They outweigh us by a ton each! exploded in my head.

"*Pila* at the ready!"

The *centurio*'s command made me realize that instead of crashing into the horses, we were going to spear the remaining riders, or bring the horses down to even the odds.

As though on cue, my rage burst from its fear-bound prison and shot out to every part of my body. I was suddenly invincible, wanting, needing, longing to take someone on as punishment for what I feared had happened to the woman I loved.

From what I was sure was previous experience with facing Roman legionnaire's *pila* attacks, the horses turned in chaotic order and trotted away. My relief was short, however, because as they split up, I saw a phalanx of green-clothed men with wicker shields and long swords running our way. We had just traded one form of death for another.

Fortunately, the sight did nothing to dampen the rage, and though I had no idea what I was going to do when I got there, I charged along with my men, heading directly at the green men.

It was during this rage clouded charge that something else pushed its way into my consciousness. I remembered the previous life I shared with An-Chi, a soldier in ancient China. When in hand-to-hand combat, he fought almost mindlessly, letting his finely-tuned instincts guide his movements. At times like this, he had no use for thoughts of personal safety, fear, family, and absolutely anything else that might distract him. Instead, he pushed them into some unused part of his brain until he was safe again.

Feeling a surge of strength in my legs, I gripped my sword and shield, shouted my rage, and bore down on the green blurs ahead of me.

They will pay for Remmy! howled in my head. *She will be avenged.*

Chapter 78

"OK, Marcus," Jasmina said as she pointed to the overstuffed, blue chair in the living room. "You sit here."

"What we are doing?" he asked warily.

After motioning for Enid to sit on the couch, she answered, "We need to connect with our children occupying your bodies in Belgium."

"Belgeeeum?" he said slowly. "What is that?"

When Jasmina did not answer, Tim moved into the room and said, "Trans-Alpine Gaul, which we now call Belgium."

"Oh," Marcus said cheerfully. "So you can get us back there, no?"

"That's right," Miriam said as she sat in a chair beside him. "We lost our connection to them after we escaped from the hospital, and we need to find out what they are doing."

"That I want to know as well. Can I speak also with them?"

When Miriam flashed Jasmina a questioning look, the latter woman shrugged.

"I don't really know, but I may be asking you some questions if he needs to know something related to your time."

He nodded. "I will do what I can."

After Marcus settled into the chair, Miriam reached over and took both of his hands in hers. She was immediately immersed in what appeared to her to be bedlam. Her heart raced as she felt herself swinging a sword, hammering with a shield, dodging blades and spears. Faces blurred before her eyes, but she was filled with overwhelming anger, fear, hysteria, and pleading. To her surprise, the faces were at one time young, and another old, their efforts feeble compared to the precise actions of her host.

She wanted to cry out, to find out if Gerry was OK, but was afraid to speak for fear of distracting him. She fought the urge to cry out when warm blood splattered her face, and the intense scream of a child filled her ears. The scream stopped abruptly, and before she could look down to see what had happened, an older face appeared in front of her.

Releasing Marcus' hands, she jerked back, her heart racing, hands pressing against her chest, sweat and tears running down her cheeks. Someone was shaking her, and it took a second to realize her eyes were closed.

Page 284

When she opened them, Marcus' anxious face filled her vision.

"Madam Miriam," he called. "Are you all right?"

She sucked in a deep breath, struggling to calm herself before her heart exploded. To her dismay, Marcus' hands on her shoulders flashed her to and from the past. One moment his face filled her vision, and the next she was close to an old man, his appalling look of shock as his eyes clouded over.

Throwing up her arms, she batted his hands away.

"Get back! Please!"

When he did not move, she pushed at him, but the move knocked her over instead. Laying on the floor, she covered her eyes, but the old man's face overwhelmed her, forcing her to open them to find Marcus standing over her, his face awash with confusion.

"I am sorry, Madam Miriam," he apologized. "I do not know what to do."

"No," she gasped, dizziness keeping her from rising. "I had to…it wasn't." She sucked in another deep breath and let it out slowly. "It's OK. Just don't touch me."

"What I do?"

"What is it, Miriam?" Jasmina asked, her touch not bringing the flashing images or surging emotions.

It was a moment before she could put words to the overwhelming images. She had to take several more deep breaths to clear her head and get her brain working again.

"It's OK," she finally said. "Well, no. It's not. Gerry's in the middle of a battle and it's ghastly."

"How did you know?"

Throwing her hands over her face, she gulped in another lungful of air. "It was the most horrific thing I've ever experienced. My son was killing people, and most of them were either old men or children."

"I know this might look bad to you, but…"

"NO!" Miriam screamed, her hands dropping as she pulled away from Jasmina. "My son is murdering old men and little boys. I didn't raise him to be that kind of monster."

"He's not, Miriam," Jasmina insisted while pointing at Marcus. "He is doing this killing, or rather he *did* this kind of killing, but it is in the past."

Pushing herself out of the chair, she staggered away from them, managing to reach the hallway entrance before turning back. "But how could my son do such a thing?"

Hurrying to her, Jasmina shook her head. "He isn't doing it. Gerry is incapable of killing someone. He's only along for the ride, just as you were."

Her attention jerked to Marcus and back. "But if Marcus is here, who else is doing the fighting?"

Jasmina looked at Marcus as well, holding his stare for a long moment before turning back to Miriam.

"This is not easy to explain, but when Gerry and Marcus traded places, a lot of who they are stayed in their own bodies." She pointed at Marcus. "He is a trained killer, but he can't bring himself to do that here because of Gerry's influence on him. Likewise, when Gerry kills in Roman times, it is really Marcus' instincts that are doing it, not Gerry himself. Please believe me. Neither of them has control over their subconscious minds."

After staring at Jasmina for a long moment, Miriam did a quick spin and marched for the door.

"I need to think this through," she announced as she opened the front door.

"Miriam," Jasmina called. "You really shouldn't…"

Her words were cut off by the slamming door.

Chapter 79

Gasping in air, I found myself bent at the waist, hands on knees, surrounded by corpses, my ears filled with the howling of the injured, and blasting horns. My vision blurred for a moment before I looked down to see the entire front of my body -- arms, legs, and torso -- was dripping in red, sticky, smelly blood. Try as I might, I remembered almost none of what had happened since we crashed into the enemy ranks. I could recall only snippets of blurry movement, echoing impacts, and agonizing screams.

Straightening, I looked around to see the men of my *centuria* were also tired, but they stayed in formation, their attention on what was going on around us. Looking further afield, I noticed we were an island in the midst of the Gallic forces. A small Gallic contingent was facing us, their shields up, weapons at the ready even though they made no move to attack us. I quickly realized that the bulk of the enemy turned their attention to Caesar's advancing army. The entire legion was now formed up, the siege weapons quiet as row after row of legionnaires marched toward the Gauls.

Apparently, we had cut a wide swath in the enemy's rear at the same time as Caesar's siege machines were doing their own grisly work, both of us keeping the Gauls distracted and confused until the legion could get into position. When the attack started, the Gauls pulled back, their leaders unable to keep them from doing so. Obviously, after the beating our small group had given them, most of the Gauls were executing a slow, deliberate retreat to stay just out of reach of Caesar's lines

Trap?

Maybe. The Gauls had done such things before. So had we.

We?

It surprised me that I was thinking like a Roman. This wasn't a history lesson where I could close my textbook when things moved too fast for me to follow.

I touched the sticky blood on my arms, and one thought filled my head.

This is real.

Bile burned my throat, and I fought to hold it down while looking around again to see the *centurio* standing his ground in front of his *centuria*.

Clifford M. Scovell

An experienced soldier would not throw up, I insisted as my stomach cramped. *But I just might.*

Turning my back to the men, I took several steps forward, trying to use movement as a distraction.

Don't throw up! Don't throw up!

When the feeling began to subside, I felt the weight of my sword, and tried to hold it up, but my fatigued muscles were not up to the task. I finally gave up when the blade was horizontal with the tip pointing away from me. This drew my attention to movement beyond, and I refocused to see a line of Gallic soldiers less than one-hundred-feet away. What shocked me was that many of them looked so young -- barely teenagers -- and nervous. Moving from face to face, I realized that this particular group was mostly young boys and old men.

If this is all the Gauls have left, there is no hope for them.

Frozen by the realization, I held my pose -- sword arm up, weapon pointing at the Gallic line -- unaware that it looked to the men in my *centuria* as though I was taunting them.

Behind me, the chant, "Caesar! Caesar! Caesar!" started, and I turned to see the men, their shields up, swords pointing at the enemy.

"Caesar! Caesar! Caesar!"

Again focusing on the Gallic line, I realized it was thinning without any effort on our part. Another scan of the battlefield showed lines of men moving into the wood beyond the meadow. When I again faced the Gallic line, it was gone, the last remnants having dropped their weapons and shields and rushed to follow their comrades.

In no time at all, the enemy ranks had thinned to leave only a few thousand soldiers to face Caesar's army.

The immediate threat now gone, my rage, my hatred, my lust for revenge vanished. Unable to even hold it up, I lowered the sword until its tip touched the ground, the bottom of my shield hitting a second later. I felt my body sag, and though I knew it wasn't allowed, I nearly gave in to the overwhelming need to flop down on the ground and sleep.

"March forward," the *centurio*'s voice shocked me out of my funk.

Looking back at my men, I saw them pull into tighter formation, but most of them were smiling. We had turned the tide of the battle. Though Caesar's legion would deal with those remaining, our two *centuriae* had shocked the enemy with our quick movement through their lines. My elation was muted by the realization that the Gauls we fought were not experienced soldiers. Against our well trained, highly conditioned legionnaires, it couldn't have been anything other than a slaughter.

Moving into my place in the formation, I marched with them while struggling with a boatload of turbulent emotions. I had killed out of anger, and fear, and because I wanted revenge. Whatever the reason, I had killed, and even though I had not chosen to be in this body, nor did I have a choice as to whether or not I was going to be in this fight, I still felt guilty as hell.

The *centurio* led us to a stream on the edge of the battlefield where the men could do a preliminary job of washing blood from their bodies and armor. Moving downstream from the bulk of the men, I was knee-deep in the stream before I looked down to see the water was bright red. My stomach lurched again, and knowing I wasn't going to keep this one down, I quickly moved to shore and into a small grove of trees. With the bile lurching up my throat, I didn't really have time to make sure no one was watching, and was barely out of sight before the entire contents of my stomach erupted from my mouth.

When the contractions stopped, I gasped in a desperate breath and leaned forward, hands on wobbly knees. My whole body was shaking, head spinning, but something pulled my attention to the left to see a pair of feet in Roman legionnaire sandals.

Working my way up the body, my eyes finally stopped on a face that made my chest tighten.

Quintus was leaning against a tree, his still-bloody sword in hand.

Chapter 80

They plodded along in the darkness, a single oil lamp the only illumination they had.

"I can't see the road," Remmy complained. "Don't you have anything brighter?"

In the dim light, she could see the ghostly image of the merchant's head shaking.

"A brighter light would attract attention. Those men have sharp eyes."

"And if we drive right over the tracks, we'll have to turn around and then they'll really catch us."

Pulling on the reins until the donkey stopped, he pointed at the eastern horizon. "The moon will be rising any minute. It will only be a sliver, but that should be enough light to see what is ahead, if you are on the ground."

Remmy looked in the direction he was pointing and back. "On the ground? But we have no idea how far it is to the jump-off point."

The merchant shrugged. "It is your only chance."

As she hesitated, Remmy noticed that the tops of the far hills were glowing gray-green. Looking in the opposite direction, she saw the brilliant tip of the rising crescent moon peeking over the horizon.

"We don't have a lot of time," the merchant insisted.

On the ground, Remmy moved in front of the cart and started jogging. With the jingling, rattling cart close at her heels, she set a steady pace, moving along the barely distinguishable trail in the dim light.

She estimated she had been running for close to an hour before her entire body started to tingle, the sensation growing stronger as she proceeded.

"Something's happening," she shouted without looking back.

"Yes," he responded calmly. "I feel it too."

Moments later, she saw the tracks of the stranger's cart vanish.

"Here it is," she gasped as she came to a stop, and was thankful to hear the cart stop as well.

Without getting down from the cart, the merchant motioned for her to move forward. "Go up to where they disappear."

Hesitating, she looked back to see him insistently waving her forward. Her body still tingling, she moved forward until her toes were in line with the end of the stranger's track. By this time, every cell in her body was humming.

"What is that?"

"The tingling?"

"Yes."

Instead of answering, he shook his head. "You are a witch. You know that, don't you?"

"Excuse me?"

He laughed. "It's not a bad thing. In ancient times, witches had real powers. Some used them for good, others did not. In the end, both sides became so possessive of their knowledge they refused to share it. Without novices to pass their knowledge to, the ability to control those ancient powers was lost."

"Are you kidding me?"

Sighing, he shook his head. "I'm not saying the power was lost. It still lives on in you and other women and men of your generation. It's just that eons of collected knowledge of how to use that power is lost to them. It's like having a really powerful car and not knowing how to unlock the doors."

Remmy shook her head. "But I don't...have any...I've never done anything magical."

He waggled a finger. "That buzzing you feel says you have the power."

Folding her arms tightly across her chest, Remmy shook her head. "But I don't feel like a witch." She shrugged. "I don't even know what that would be like."

Reaching into the folds of his cloak, the merchant pulled out a small book and tossed it in Remmy's direction. After picking it up and shaking off the dust, she squinted at the cover.

"It's in a strange language," she complained before looking at the merchant again. "How am I supposed to read it?"

Nodding, the merchant held up a finger. "Touch the cover with your right index finger and say, 'Reveal yourself.'"

Looking skeptical, she touched the surface and recited the incantation. To her surprise, the words morphed into English.

"The Book of Order?" she asked.

"With that book, you can help bring order to the world."

"How does it work?"

The merchant started to answer, but a shout from behind made him turn around. When he looked in her direction again, there was fear on his face.

"You have to go now."

"But how?"

"Face away from me and stand with your toes lined up with the point at which the wheel track vanishes."

Moving quickly, she stopped at the designated place and put her feet together. At this point the buzzing was so loud she could barely hear the merchant.

"As you take a step forward, say, 'Take Enid home.'"

"You're not serious."

"Do it!"

Lifting one foot, she leaned forward, reciting, "Take Enid home," and thrust her foot forward. As her foot touched down, the dark desert faded from view and she found herself in a large meadow in full daylight.

Her eyes being adjusted to low light, she had to squint for a moment before she could see she was looking at the back of a Roman army marching toward a Gallic contingent. Though she didn't know why, she had the feeling that the assassination attempt had failed.

"If that is so, then why am I still here?" she asked out loud.

Voices pulled her around to face a group of men washing blood off their uniforms in a stream, and she sensed a presence that she had not even realized was missing.

Taking off at a full run, she shouted, "Gerry!"

It was easily one-hundred yards to the stream, and as she approached, one-by-one the men stopped what they were doing and turned their attention to her. When she was nearly there, several men moved toward her.

"I am looking for Gerr..." She bit off his name and struggled for a moment to remember the correct one. She was nearly to them when it came to her.

"I am looking for Marcus Aremus," she called. "Where is he?"

Nodding, the largest of the soldiers looked around. "He is our *centurio*. He must be around here somewhere."

The man next to him jabbed a thumb over his shoulder. "I think he went into that wood to take a shit."

Without comment, she sprinted around them and ran to the trees.

"Marcus," she called. "Where are you?"

She had not gone far when she spotted him leaning against a tree, his eyes wide, hands waving.

An overwhelming sense of relief filled her as she ran toward him, but when she passed a large tree, a movement on her left barely registered before her world went black.

Chapter 81

Rushing out the front door, Jasmina found Miriam standing at the edge of the wide front porch, hands over her face.

"Are you OK?" she asked.

After a long moment, Miriam lowered her hands, and without looking at Jasmina, took a deep breath and slowly let it out.

"No, I am definitely not."

Moving up beside her, Jasmina kept her eyes on the street, watching for anything suspicious. "That had to be pretty bad."

"Oh yeah," Miriam sighed.

The two women stood quietly for a moment before Miriam asked, "How do you do it?"

Jasmina looked at her. "Do what?"

She pointed toward the house. "How do you deal with all of that?"

Shaking her head, Jasmina answered, "I don't." Turning her body toward Miriam, she added, "None of my other readings are nearly this intense. From the others I get snippets of feeling, or pain, or names, or other clues as to what they are experiencing, but nothing like this."

Tears streaming down her face, Miriam turned to her companion. "So why is it so different with my son?"

Jasmina shook her head. "I don't know, but I do know this: Gerry is a very smart, resilient, flexible, and intuitive young man. Whoever selected him for this had to know he was the best person to take on this kind of thing and survive."

"How do you know he's the first? Could there have been others?"

Jasmina looked at the street again. "You know, I haven't really thought about that. There may have been. In fact, now that I think about it, there may be others doing what Gerry and Remmy are doing right now."

Shaking her head, Miriam sobbed, "I don't care about any others. All I want is to get my son back in one piece, and that won't happen if he's always fighting in wars."

Her statement sent Jasmina's mind into turmoil, because her precious niece was in as much danger as Gerry. She glanced at the house, feeling a desperate eagerness to get back inside, but could think of nothing to say to convince Miriam to join her.

Wiping tears from her face, Miriam looked briefly at the street before turning back to Jasmina, her expression determined.

"Somehow, all of this seems to be centered on you. Nothing like this happened before my son started dating your niece."

"I don't think…"

"After this is over," she interrupted, "we're going our separate ways. You and Remmy stay away from my family. No more contact. No more of…" She looked up and waved a hand at the sky. "…whatever this is you do."

"Yes, but I don't think we can tell Gerry and…"

"I don't care if we have to move to New Hampshire, I'm keeping my son away from you."

Before Jasmina could respond, Miriam marched to the door. Her hand on the latch, she turned back and looked at Jasmina.

"Are you coming?"

Shocked by what had just transpired, Jasmina hesitated before answering, "Yes, I'll be along…"

Without waiting for her to finish, Miriam yanked the door open and marched inside.

Jasmina shook her head and sighed, "Could this get any worse?"

The sound of a car's engine pulled her attention back to the street to see a police car slowly moving down the block, the officer inside obviously looking for something or someone.

Rushing back inside, she closed the door and leaned her back against it.

"Maybe it can."

Promise of Victory

Chapter 82

The sight of Enid running my way completely took my breath away.

Remmy's alive?

Still gasping, I jerked my attention from her to Quintus standing with a tree between him and her.

"No. Stop," I tried to yell, but it came out hoarse and garbled. I held up both hands to stop her, but she didn't seem to understand. Her footsteps were heavy, and Quintus had no trouble determining the right moment to step out and knock her down.

"Remmy!" I croaked as she collapsed to the ground.

On wobbly legs, I ran to her, dropping to my knees beside her.

"Now ain't this perfect," Quintus declared, sarcasm dripping from every word.

When I saw she was still breathing, I looked up to see Quintus heft his sword, a malicious smile on his face.

"I've been trying to get rid of you since the *centurio* mistakenly made you *optio*," he announced, "but how was I going to do that without putting my own head in the noose?"

Looking at Remmy again, my emotions so overwhelmed, it took me a moment to realize that tears were flowing down my cheeks.

When I didn't respond, he laughed. "Now it looks like the gods are favoring me."

Not able to think of anything else to say, I gasped, "What do you mean?"

He pointed his sword at Remmy. "She's a fucking Gaul!" he exclaimed. "All I gotta do is stick my blade in both of you and then say I killed her after she killed you. Everyone knows this bitch is a fighter, and it was just a matter of time before she slit your throat. If you're both dead, who's gonna think otherwise?"

Out of the confusion in my brain, I suddenly realized what was happening. This grotesque bucket of snot was here to kill me, or rather, Marcus.

"Why would you want to kill Mar...er...me?"

"Because some dumb shit is willing to give me your job, that's why."

As if I wasn't confused enough, my mother's voice suddenly popped into my head.

Gerry? Are you OK?

I'm kind of busy right now.

Where's Remmy. Her aunt can't connect with her.

"How do you know he'll pay you if you kill me?"

Someone's trying to kill you?

Giving Remmy's shoulder a shake, I glanced down so my mother could see her.

Tell me she's not dead! Mom asked anxiously.

Not yet, but soon, if I don't do something.

Quintus took a step toward me. "That's not your problem now, is it?"

Remember last time when the Chinese soldier was unconscious and you helped me wake him up?

How could I forget? You almost died!

Help Jasmina wake up Remmy and quickly.

Not knowing what else to do, I pulled back from Remmy and stood. Without a weapon, there was little I could do to defend myself. I just had to hope I could stall him long enough for Jasmina to wake Remmy up.

"You really are an idiot," I stated.

The confidence vanishing from his face, Quintus gripped his weapon tighter and quickly looked around.

"You ain't foolin' me." He laughed, but it was decidedly forced. "If you've got no weapon, there's no way I'm gonna lose."

"Says you."

I tensed for his attack, but he took a step back instead, his eyes scanning the area again before they stopped on the unconscious Remmy.

Seeming to realize we were alone and there were no other weapons I could use, he smiled.

"That's right. I do say."

My mind blank, I started to move sideways, hoping I could outrun him in the dense forest, but instead of following me, Quintus looked down at Remmy.

"You leave, I cut off her head," he announced with a finality that stopped me. "Maybe I'll cut off other parts as well. I like hearing a woman scream."

As though my feet were anchored to the ground, I stopped.

"If I stay, you spare her."

As soon as the words were out, I regretted them.

"And you said I was the stupid one," Quintus laughed as he pointed at Remmy. "This one's got you by the nuts."

My chest nearly imploded as he lifted his sword and stepped toward me.

Jasmina? Hurry up!

Chapter 83

"What's happening?" Jasmina cried as Miriam sucked in a desperate breath and released Marcus' hands.

Marcus looked at her with a confused expression. "Like last time, I no see nothing."

"Remmy's been knocked out," Miriam announced, "and Gerry needs our help to wake her up."

All three turned to see Enid slumped in a side chair, her eyes closed, arms limp.

"God," Jasmina cried. "She's out as well." Jumping up from the couch, she waved for her companions to rise.

"Tim! Alvin!" she shouted then waited for the two men to enter from the kitchen. "We've got to form a circle around Enid and help Remmy wake up."

After Alvin and Tim pushed Enid's chair into the middle of the room, Alvin shook his head. "But we don't have a priest to help us."

Jasmina gave her head a sharp shake. "We don't need a priest. We just need to focus our thoughts while we hold hands. I'll talk you through it."

Once they were all in a circle, Jasmina said, "Everyone close your eyes and repeat along with me."

Jasmina nodded. "Remmy wake up."

"That's it?" Miriam asked. "You don't have a special wake-up incantation?"

Shaking her head, Jasmina looked at each face in turn. "There is no need for casting spells. We just have to reach her subconscious and get her mind working."

"Everyone ready?" she asked when everybody nodded. "Good. Let's get started."

"Remmy wake up," she said, and heard the others join in as she continued to repeat the words. "With determination," she insisted. "We have to get her attention!"

Her hand gripping Enid's, Jasmina closed her eyes, trying with all her might to sense Remmy's presence, but all she saw was darkness. After a long moment, she felt the stirrings of her niece's thoughts.

Don't get up, she commanded.

Her breath caught when she saw that Remmy was slowly opening her eyes. The first thing she saw was the legs of a man, the skirt of his legionnaire uniform making it clear this was a Roman soldier.

Can you see his face?

The scene tilted up until she could make out Quintus face, a self-satisfied smile on his lips as he spoke with someone behind her.

What made her heart race was that he was pointing his sword directly at her.

Chapter 84

Get him closer to Remmy!

I felt my body jerk in surprise at the exploding voice in my head. It wasn't just that it was loud, but there was a lot of fear and anger in it.

What the hell? I thought.

Just do it!

Fighting to keep myself from looking at Remmy, I slowly moved to my left, forcing the approaching Quintus to change course. Unfortunately, I had moved too far from Remmy to get to her before Quintus would get within striking distance. If I moved too fast, he would realize what I was doing, and if I ran anywhere else, his attention might turn to her and spoil whatever my mother and Jasmina had in mind.

I'm not going to make it.

Just keep going.

When I turned to look behind me, Quintus took a quick step closer, making me realize that his first concern was my not getting away. Remmy was only a prop to him: something to keep me in place long enough for him to murder me.

In response to his move, I took several steps back, struggling as I did to keep my eyes on his face. Convinced he would succeed, he stepped past Remmy and closed the distance between us. After all, in his eyes she was only a woman, not a real threat.

"You want to kill both of us, right?" I said in the hope my question would keep him focused on me.

At the edge of my vision, Remmy rose up behind Quintus, but the crackle of tinder under her feet brought him around. Though slow witted in most situations, this brute was a seasoned warrior, and that required quick reflexes and sharp battle instincts.

As Remmy lunged at him, he twisted and backhanded her knife blade away. Being in a warrior's body as well, Remmy ducked the follow up stroke aimed at her throat, but not his rising knee as it struck her chest and knocked her back. However, the move also left Quintus off balance, and when he stumbled backwards, I threw a shoulder into his side, eliciting a loud grunt from him.

Keeping my legs pumping, I tilted him over, but when we both hammered the ground, I lost my grip and we rolled apart.

I was quickly on my feet, but Quintus matched my move, his blade slashing toward my throat. Only Marcus' quick reflexes saved me as the razor-sharp edge hammered my helmet, sending me back to the ground. While I struggled to regain my feet, Quintus used his sword to force Remmy back. When his attention shifted back to me, I grabbed a handful of dirt and pebbles and lunged forward, throwing it at his face.

He quickly turned his head, and hammered his fisted left hand into the middle of my chest. The impact deflected my charge, sending me stumbling to one side, and though I stabilized myself, he was already bringing his weapon around so fast I knew it was going to bite flesh.

I threw myself backwards as the blade's tip cut a shallow slice in my left arm. My cry of pain was involuntary, but as the tip of the blade dug in, my body instinctively rotated along with it to minimize damage. The move left me leaning too far back, and before I could regain my footing, the ground slipped out from under me, I went airborne, and my world went into slow motion as the blade continued on its arc away from me.

"Haarrrumph!" exploded from my throat as I again hammered the ground.

I quickly rolled to see Quintus' glaring eyes looked on me as he lifted his sword over his head like a savage and prepared to split me from brow to balls. I desperately tried to dig in my heels, but the rotting leaves were as slippery as glass. That didn't stop me from trying as I watched the sword reach the peak of its rise, Quintus' face scrunching up from all the effort he was putting into the down stroke.

I was so focused on that blood-covered blade, I barely heard the high-pitched scream until Quintus' body jerked from an impact. Sword-over-head, he froze until a second impact shook his stocky frame.

"Yaaaa!!!" Remmy's scream finally penetrated my brain.

Quintus' body jerked two more times before the sword tumbled free and he toppled like a fallen oak.

Gasping desperately, I tore my eyes from the corpse, and looked up to see Remmy's face, her eyes wide, mouth clinched, skin flushed, breath coming in short gasps.

"My God," was all I could think to say as my eyes dropped to the bloody knife in her hand.

As though she had forgotten I was even there, her eyes jerked down to me, the look of surprise almost laughable if the situation hadn't been so intense.

"Gerry!" exploded from her with an exhale of breath. "Are you OK?"

Emotion overwhelmed me, stopping any response except a nod.

She's alive!

We stared for a long moment until Remmy's face turned questioning. It took me only a moment to catch up with her.

"Why are we still here?"

"Obviously," she answered. "We haven't saved him yet."

When Remmy extended a hand to me, I took it and rose on shaky legs, but it took only a couple of steps for my body's instincts to take over and regain some of my strength. That didn't mean the turmoil in my head was banished, but at least I stopped staggering like a drunken sailor.

As we approached the men, I signaled to Lucius, and when he approached I pointed back into the trees and said,

"Quintus tried to kill me. His body is in that wood."

Though his look was cautious, he nodded and signaled for two other men to follow him. As they hurried off, I turned toward the battle to see it was still not going well for the Gauls. Though those remaining on the battlefield were probably the best Gaul had left to offer, they were from different tribes, with various languages, petty rivalries, and different commanders.

As I looked back on it later, it was clear that though they probably hoped to defeat the Romans and kill Caesar, their ultimate goal was simply to die before they were brought under Roman rule. Death in battle assured them ascendency into their mythical idea of heaven. The alternative was too hard for them to bear.

Having dressed myself in full armor, even though much of it was still black with drying blood, I marched with Remmy in tow to the back of the lines where I hoped to find the nearly mythical Julius Caesar. You can imagine then, my surprise when a contingent broke from the rear ranks and headed our way.

"Identify yourself," a *centurio* demanded as he moved ahead of the others and approached me, hand on sword.

"I am *Optio* Marcus Aremus, of the 6th *centuria* of *Legio XI Claudia*. Our fifth and sixth *centuriae* were the ones who attacked the enemy from behind."

To my surprise, the *centurio*'s scowl almost turned into a look of admiration. "State your business with the *imperator*."

Standing as straight as possible, I answered, "I must speak with *Imperator* Caesar. I have information from a captive about a threat on his life."

The man huffed a laugh. "There are always threats against our *imperator*, but if the conspirators wish to kill him here they will be disappointed. He left early this morning for Rome with a *cohort*."

He what? screamed in my head, but I wisely kept the thought to myself.

"This threat is not from the Gauls," I explained as calmly as I could. "The captive did not know the name of the conspirators, but they are certain it was someone from Rome. I believe our *imperator* is being deceived, and is heading into a trap."

"The senate is honoring him with a triumph," the *centurio* said proudly.

I shook my head. "According to this captive, that is part of the deceit."

His scowl returning, the *centurio* shook his own head. "The decree came by messenger straight from the senate."

"With respect, Sir, where is the messenger now?"

"He returned with the *imperator*."

I looked toward the battlefield and watched the remaining Gallic fighters retreating into the wood.

What a waste of lives. Why would they... I turned back to face the *centurio*.

"These pathetic people were sacrificed to keep most of the legion here while Caesar continued on to Rome."

"To what end? He still has enough men to fight off any remaining Gallic forces."

I felt a tap on my shoulder and turned to see Remmy's excited face.

"The Stranger!"

"What?"

"He's a skinny, pale guy," she insisted, "and he's not from this time."

"So he has knowledge of the future?"

Her head shaking, the corners of her mouth turned down, she locked eyes with me. "Worse than that," she nearly whispered. "He killed the guy who kidnapped me first." She held up a hand, arranging the fingers to look like a pistol. "He shot him and then forced me into his cart."

The idea hammered my brain and it took a long moment for me to realize what she had said.

"But how is that possible?"

Her head shaking, she sighed. "I'll explain later, but it's possible."

"Crap!"

"*Optio*?" the *centurio* demanded. "What is your slave saying?"

It was only then that I realized we were speaking in English.

Turning to face him, I snapped to attention.

"I stand corrected, Sir," I said. "The *imperator* is not heading into a trap. He is already in it."

Chapter 85

"I can't do it," Miriam protested as she sat next to Marcus, but glared desperately at Jasmina.

Struggling to contain an exasperated sigh, Jasmina shook her head. "I just saw a police cruiser moving slowly through the neighborhood. We have to resolve this soon, or that doctor will find us."

Her eyes still on Jasmina, Miriam held that pose for a long moment before jerking a nod, putting her hands on Marcus', and closing her eyes.

Within seconds her eyes were open again, hands flat against her chest.

"What happened?" Jasmina insisted.

Miriam took in a deep breath and slowly let it out.

"It's OK. They're not fighting anymore, and Remmy is with him. They're marching somewhere, almost running along with other soldiers."

When Jasmina remained silent, she scowled at her. "OK. I'll admit it. This is overwhelming." She jerked her eyes to Marcus for a moment before lowering her hands to look at them. "It's not just the brutality." She hesitated, biting her lip as her head shook. "This kind of thing isn't supposed to be possible."

Moving close, Jasmina put a hand on hers. "I know this is difficult, but you need to focus on getting your son back."

Fear flashed across Miriam's face, and was just as quickly replaced with resolve that slowly faded.

"I don't...I don't know..."

"You have to trust me," Jasmina insisted. "There's no time for debate."

Her heart pounding, she fought down her fear and gave a quick nod before lowering her hands to her lap. She took a deep breath in a vain attempt at relaxation, and reached out to grasp Marcus' hands.

She immediately felt the shock of Gerry's mind, questions rapid-firing around it, his concentration completely on the problem at hand as he ran in full battle gear alongside the *centurio* and in front of a *centuria* of legionnaires.

What is going on, Son? she finally asked.

Mom? Is that you? Where have you been?

Her mind flashed back to the events of the last few days, and wondered how much she should tell him.

We've had a few problems here since Marcus and Enid arrived. What is happening with you?

His thoughts raced again, and though she could catch random threads, the story they told was so disjointed it made no sense.

Listen, he finally said. *I think I know how they are going to kill Caesar, but there's no way to get a message to him so we're running to catch up.*

How far ahead is he?

About half-a-day, but they will be traveling at a slower pace, so we should reach him by nightfall, and that's when I think the attempt will be made.

Jasmina has an idea about that as well, Miriam said.

She does? What is it?

She paused, and immediately knew that her son picked up on it.

Mom?

She thinks it will be Enid.

How can that be? Remmy is in Enid's body and she wouldn't hurt him.

I don't know, but then I have no idea how you got into this situation in the first place. They could trade places at any moment.

But how do I...

Miriam sucked in a breath when he stopped so abruptly, but her stomach cramped when she saw Gerry look over at Enid, his thoughts unclear, but anxious and conflicted.

You have to speak with Marcus alone, he finally said with a flat tone that gave his words a scary finality.

About what?

There was another long pause, and she bit her lip as she squeezed the hands she was anxiously gripping.

You need to tell him that if he finds himself back in his own body...

He looked away from Remmy, and the intense turmoil and fear Miriam felt made her want to pull her hands away, but she couldn't.

He has to kill Enid.

She more felt than heard his last words, the intensity of them exploding in her head, making her jerk back and pull her hands from Marcus'. Stunned beyond reason, she pressed her hands flat against her chest as her eyes flew open.

"Oh God, no!" she gasped, her vision blurred, lungs refusing to take in badly-needed air.

When her eyes finally focused, she saw the others gawking at her, and suddenly, desperately needed to get away. Pushing with her feet, she slid the length of the couch until her butt hit the arm rest then flew to her feet and hurried into the kitchen.

Slamming through the door, she ran straight for the sink, and leaned over it, gasping in air, fighting her cramping stomach, struggling to keep her wobbly legs under her.

An instant or an hour later, Jasmina was by her side, turning on the tap.

"Quick. Splash water on your face."

She couldn't release her grip on the edge of the sink, those words, repeating in her head: *Tell Marcus to kill Enid. Tell Marcus to kill Enid. Kill Enid. Kill Enid.*

The broiling, mad, horrifying, insanely loud turmoil in her head touched off a firestorm that blotted everything, even the overlapping shouts of someone else that seemed so close, yet so very far away.

Miriam!

Kill her!

Miriam!

Kill her!

Miriam! Kill her!

"Me? No!" she cried before falling into the sudden peace of unconsciousness.

Chapter 86

You need to tell him that if he finds himself back in his own body he has to kill Enid.

I felt myself suck in a sharp breath at the realization to what I'd just said, or maybe it was because of Mom's strong reaction to it. I looked quickly around, thankful that my gasp had been drowned out by the pounding feet and noisy armor of over eighty Roman legionnaires running behind me. It even covered the second gasp when Mom vanished so suddenly it felt like she had been sucked out of my head.

Crap!

I don't know how long we had been jogging, but soon after my mother disappeared, the *centurio* called for a halt. Despite my heavy breathing, I was pleased to realize my body wasn't all that tired.

Wish I could be in this good a' shape, I mused as Remmy moved toward me, hands on hips, sweat beading on her forehead.

"What's the plan?" she asked.

I hadn't had time to work out what I was going to do once we caught up to Caesar's *cohort*. I was still struggling with what just happened when another thought came to me.

What if Enid comes back before Marcus? Can I kill her?

"I'm still working on it," I finally answered, my eyes on her.

Still breathing hard, Remmy was looking at the path ahead as I watched her, and wondered if Enid should die just to save the future I knew. I couldn't help thinking this was a cop-out. Yes, I wanted a future to go back to, and I also wanted Remmy and my parents, and everyone else I know to live, but that life seemed so far away. Enid was alive here and now. She was a beautiful woman, and some day might be a wonderful mother. How could I deny her that chance?

"Have you heard from your mother?" she asked without looking at me.

The simple question made me pause before nodding. "Yeah, but only for a minute. They've got their own problems to deal with."

Now was one of those moments in which I wished Remmy wasn't so inquisitive.

"What problems?"

"I don't know exactly. She didn't have time to explain before she had to leave."

She finally looked at me. "Is this like last time when that Chinese doctor tried to kill you in the present while the guy you were linked to fought his counterpart in the past?"

I nodded. "It might be, except I'm totally in the past now, at least mentally, and I actually have to kill people."

"Yeah," Remmy said while rubbing her shoulder.

"How's your shoulder?"

She shrugged. "Not too bad. The Greek slave gave me a vial of something he called *the juice*. It really takes the pain away, but he told me not to take any more than I actually needed, or it would steal my soul."

"Geez, Remmy! It's probably opium," I protested. "Be careful with it."

She scowled at me. "I'm not an idiot. I only take it when the pain gets bad."

I suddenly had an idea that might solve my dilemma.

"Maybe you should stay behind and wait for us. That sore shoulder might get you killed."

Remmy bristled noticeably. "I have just as much at stake here as you do."

Though I wanted to continue the argument, a sudden thought made me look around, thankful that no one was close enough to hear us.

"We need to remember that you are my slave," I said as I turned to face her. "You could be whipped for talking back to me."

She scowled. "Enid is Marcus' slave. I'm not yours."

I nodded. "I realize that, but we have to pretend or…"

Still scowling, she interrupted, "I know. Shit! This isn't exactly easy."

"Yeah, but we have to do it."

When she looked past me, I followed her gaze to see the men gathering into formation again.

"You realize that when we get back to our time, you're going to pay dearly for this."

I turned around to see a smile on her lips and concern in her eyes.

I shook my head. "Let's not get ahead of ourselves. We still have to survive this first."

Chapter 87

"Miriam," Jasmina cried and then lurched forward to grab her as she started to tilt over.

Marcus burst in as Jasmina carefully lowered Miriam to the floor.

"I was afraid this might happen," she said as Enid joined them.

"What is that?" Enid asked.

Jasmina looked from Enid to Marcus. "Your way of life is far different from ours. This connection requires us to be a part of things we find repulsive." She looked down at Miriam. "Sometimes it is just too much to bear."

"You no have war in this time?" Marcus asked.

Jasmina shook her head sadly. "Yes, we still have war, but we don't take slaves or the possessions of the losers."

Enid and Marcus gave each other questioning looks.

"But it is the right of the victor," Marcus protested. "It was always so."

"And there are still people in our time who believe that, but in our country it is not permitted. We fight only to preserve peace."

"But what of the people you conquer?" Enid asked, her puzzlement obvious. "Will they not just rise up against you again?"

Shaking her head again, Jasmina looked down at Miriam. "When we can, we try to help them rebuild their country in the hopes they'll see that thriving economy is preferable to war."

"And does that work?"

"Not always, but it has produced a stable Europe, and much of the Far East. Over time, we hope to bring the rest of the world around to this way of thinking."

"What are these places?" Marcus asked.

"Europe is roughly the area incorporating what you used to call, Hispania, Gaul, Germania, Greece, and Italia. It's divided up more than that now, but they live together in peace."

"Under Roman rule?" Enid asked.

Jasmina shook her head. "The Roman Empire no longer exists."

"*Non potest*!" Marcus shouted angrily. "We are most powerful nation ever to exist. No one can defeat us."

"And no one did, Marcus. Rome crumbled from within."

"How do you mean?"

Jasmina hesitated a moment before shaking her head. "Listen, I don't think I should tell you anymore. If you learn too much it may affect your future, and possibly ours."

"But how can we help," Enid argued, "if we not know what is happening."

Jasmina looked at the unconscious Miriam and sighed. "You can help by giving me the information I need to help Gerry and Remmy save Caesar's life."

Marcus looked around the room but stopped when his eyes fell on Enid.

"Tell me," he said while returning his attention to Jasmina. "If we help, do we go home again?"

She nodded. "Saving Caesar is the key to getting you back home."

He kept his eyes on her for a long moment before turning to Enid. "And if you get the chance, you wish to kill my *imperator*."

It was Enid's turn to hesitate, but before she could respond, a gasp pulled their attention down to Miriam.

"Miriam?" Jasmina asked as she rushed to her. "Are you OK?"

Her eyes flooded with tears, Miriam sat up and opened her mouth to respond, but stopped when she noticed Marcus and Enid behind Jasmina.

"I'll never be OK again," she sighed, but when Jasmina did not respond, she shook her head and continued. "Caesar left camp with a small contingent just before the battle. He wants to get to Rome to celebrate his triumph, but Gerry's group should catch up by nightfall."

"And what is he going to do when they arrive?"

Miriam shook her head slowly, her attention moving from one person to another before she said, "I don't know."

Her attention also shifting to her companions, Jasmina hesitated for a moment before asking, "How long before they get there?"

"I got the sense that it would be a couple of hours."

"So that gives us some time to figure out..."

Pounding on the front door interrupted her. When Tim and Alvin raced in from the kitchen, Jasmina held up a hand to stop them.

"Why didn't I sense his presence before this?" she nearly whispered while moving to the door.

The rest of them followed her, and when she opened it, all but Jasmina gasped.

"Hello, Doctor McFaddan."

Chapter 88

By the time we caught up with Caesar's *cohort,* the *castra's* walls were already up, guards were manning the watch towers, and a small contingent of men led by a well-decorated *centurio* marched out to meet us.

Our *centurio* took care of the greetings as the rest of us stayed in formation, thankful for a moment's rest from the forced march.

"We come with an urgent message for the *imperator*," our *centurio* announced. "We must see him at once."

Being from the same legion, these two *centuriōnēs* knew each other, so there was no need for verification: checking driver's licenses, Social Security Numbers, and other things these guys had no concept of. I guessed they'd probably shared a bowl of wine the night before, so what did they need that stuff for?

My heart skipped a beat when our *centurio* pointed a stubby finger at me.

"This is Optio Marcus Aremus of the *Legio XI Claudia*." he announced. "While interrogating a captive, he learned of a plot to assassinate our *imperator*."

The look on the second *centurio's* face made it clear mine was an often-repeated story. After all, who in Gaul didn't want Caesar dead? His tight jaw and compressed lips meant that he didn't expect to have to ask the obvious question.

"The captive claimed that the plan is to separate our *imperator* from his men," I explained. "They would then use a larger force to overwhelm him, and cut him down."

I was suddenly struck with how similar that was to the way he would actually die in roughly eight years.

"He is never without his guards," the *centurio* stated dismissively. "How will they get past them?"

I shook my head. "I asked, but he did not know, unless it is one of his own."

The scowl deepened, and the eyes widened for only an instant.

"His men are handpicked, and loyal beyond question. None of them would side with these savages."

I wanted to shrug, but fear was melting my resolve, sweat pouring down my back as I fought against uncertainty and doubt.

"The captive did not say specifically, but I had the impression the threat was not Gallic. The captive said our *imperator* would receive notice of a triumph, but that it is a fake. Maybe the messenger is the assassin?"

"An assassin from Rome?" Though he was still glaring, his attention shifted to the men behind me for a moment before his eyes again met mine. This time, I saw disgust. "*Pompeius?*" Not waiting for me to respond to the rhetorical question, he spat. "He calls himself Pompey the Great, but that idiot couldn't lead a horny bull to a cow in heat."

Not sure what to say, I remained at attention as those angry eyes bore into me for another endless moment before he turned to the other *centurio*.

"Get your men fed and rested." To my surprise he pointed a finger at me. "You come with me. *Imperator* Caesar will want to speak with you."

When I started to follow, he added. "Not your slave."

I turned to see Remmy's muscles tensing, her mouth forming the expected protest.

"Go with the men," I commanded as firmly as I could while handing her my *pilum* and shield. "I will find you shortly."

Not only was she a woman in a totally man's world, but a slave to boot. One angry word from her would get her whipped or... That was one dark alley I didn't want to go down.

Knowing I had her attention, I shifted my eyes briefly to the men behind me. I could see her eyes follow mine, and it only took a few seconds for her face to show recognition of what I was indicating.

The one thing any slave-owning people feared most was a slave revolt. As successful conquerors, the Romans had a lot of slaves. To make sure they remained obedient, even though their numbers often exceeded those of their captors, punishment for disobeying a master was often severe. A rebellious slave wasn't just put to death or beaten, they were often brutalized. And when the civilian population couldn't deal with the problem, such as the rebellion of Spartacus and his fellow slaves, the army was called in to deal with it, and their brutality made that of the Roman citizens' abuse look like child's play.

Our history instructor had been a bit obsessed with this subject, so I knew Remmy was aware of what I was referring to, and was relieved to see her head bow.

"Yes, Master."

As the *centurio* and I marched away from the others, I struggled to keep from looking back, all the while wishing Remmy could come with me. I was again alone in a dangerous world, fettered by my 21st Century Christian upbringing. Marcus might be comfortable in this situation. I was ready to pee my pants.

I have to be ruthless, ran through my head. *Caesar is looking for someone who is obedient, but not cowed. To be convincing, I must meet his eyes and speak with conviction.*

And more than anything, I had to keep Remmy out of the conversation. If she got close to Caesar, and Enid suddenly returned to her own body...

"Stand and be recognized," a deep baritone voice demanded.

Lost in my reverie, I hadn't realized we were at the north gate to the *castra*. Stopping along with the *centurio*, I looked up to see two soldiers staring down at me from a watch tower next to the gate. My lungs deflated at the sight, but the *centurio* slammed a fist against his chest, and without so much as a "How are you doing?" he identified himself and his objective.

"The *imperator* is in his tent with the senatorial escort," the guard announced as the gate slowly opened.

Without further comment, the *centurio* marched to the gate, passing through when the doors were open wide enough for him. I quickly followed, trying my best to look as confident and determined as he did.

Inside, I found a blur of activity: some men setting up their tents, others finishing parts of the camps interior, erecting poles for flags, or raising the last of the perimeter wall. I heard hammers pounding, donkeys braying, men talking and marching. My legs were aching from the long march, but as much as I wanted to stop and sit, I knew it was important to keep pace with the *centurio*.

As we approached the largest tent in the compound, a challenge was shouted by someone inside. If it was Latin, I did not catch what the person said, but the *centurio* stopped in his tracks. Moments later, a huge soldier appeared, his broad shoulders being the first thing I saw, but as he appeared, and straightened, it became obvious this guy was easily a full head taller than anyone around. His armor was also different. Instead of being segmented iron, he wore a full breastplate with various gold-plated disks attached to it. Unlike the Gauls, this man's hair was short, face bare, except for a blue tattoo of an eagle on his right cheek. A moment later, a second man, as big as the first, and similarly dressed, came out and stood behind him.

Two of Caesar's personal guards? No wonder it is hard to kill him.

The *centurio* saluted and announced himself and his business. Both of these giants glared at us, their eyes jerking from one to the other until the first one took a step forward and motioned for us to approach. When we were close to them, the leader held up a thick, meaty hand, palm out. After we stopped, he pointed to a group of men raising the last of the posts that made up the perimeter wall.

"*Chatti*," the *centurio* muttered derisively as we marched in that direction. "The *imperator* captured those dirty Germans last season and they still don't speak a word of Latin."

It was all I could do to stop myself from gawking at the two towering guards who reminded me of those big bulky professional wrestlers back home. The most obvious difference was that these guys fought for real.

Hurrying to catch up with the *centurio*, I followed him to where the men were constructing the remaining part of the perimeter wall.

As we approached, I looked around for Caesar, assuming he would be in full uniform with his distinctive red cape, but there was no one around who fit that description. I finally found the cape draped over the side of a cart, and only then realized that everyone nearby was staring at the men pushing the final pole into place. One of the working men wore a finer tunic than the others, though he was nearly as dirty.

When the log slammed into place, the watching crowd cheered and the man in the fine tunic straightened, showing he was taller than the rest. As the others finished securing the post, he strode over to the wagon and put on his red cape. I was stunned to see that this thin, though not scrawny, pale-skinned person was none other than the famous general I'd read so much about.

"*Imperator*," the *centurio* announced as he approached Caesar. "This *optio* has heard of a conspiracy to murder you."

When he spoke, I was surprised by the high, almost feminine pitch of his voice. "Why do these Gauls vex me so?"

The *centurio* waved me forward, and as I approached, I had to resist the temptation to gawk at this curly-haired man whose brilliance on the battlefield was legend, even in his own time.

"Sir...*Imperator*...I..."

"Out with it, Soldier," he demanded with a wave of his hand. "By the time you get around to telling me who my assassin is, he'll have already killed me!"

Hearing the men around me laugh flushed all thoughts from my head for a moment...too long a moment.

"Which tribe are we talking about?" he asked. "I've defeated all of them by now."

"It is not a tribe, *Imperator*," I finally answered. "My captive told me the threat came from Rome itself."

My statement obviously took him aback, but he quickly covered it by brushing dust from his curly hair and barking a laugh.

"Who in Rome conspires to kill me this time?"

I shook my head. "He did not know, but since he also told me that there is no triumph planned for you, it might be wise to look more closely at the messenger who brought you that decree."

"And where is this captive?" he asked, his expression still one of amusement. "Perhaps I should question him myself."

I was preparing to say, "Sorry, *Imperator*," but the words stuck in my throat when I remembered my teacher saying that Caesar insisted that his soldiers never show the weakness of apologizing for their actions.

"He was badly wounded, and died soon after making his confession."

His expression turned cautious. "Why would a dying Gaul want to warn me of danger?"

Good question, I thought, but then remembered that Marcus would not have been gentle with a captive enemy.

"He died of his injuries, but to get his cooperation, I brought it on sooner than he expected."

To my utter shock, he smiled. "You continue to surprise me, Marcus Aremus."

I glanced at the *centurio*, but his scowl gave nothing away.

"Sir?"

Waving a hand dismissively, he said, "Don't think I haven't heard of your fight with the giant Gaul. Though I am sure he grows larger with each telling, he must have been as formidable as my Germans."

Another thing I knew about Caesar was that he hated false modesty in his men.

"As tall, if not more so, but he moved too slow for a skilled legionnaire."

"And yet not too slow to take out half-a-dozen of your men, I'm told."

"I suspect they were intimidated by his size," I responded as confidently as I could. "I was not."

"I also understand that your *centuria* has lost its *centurio*," he stated. "Is that so?"

"Yes, *Imperator*. I am acting as temporary *centurio* until a replacement arrives."

The other men went quiet when he did not respond, his eyes on me, feet squared, jaw set, hand on the hilt of his sword. I felt the sudden urge to crack a stupid joke to break the tension, but didn't need Marcus to tell me not to.

His eyes still on me, he pulled out his sword, and held it up while waving his free hand at one of his massive German guards.

"Ein ring."

The German pulled a sack from his waist and opened it. As Caesar lowered the tip of his sword toward the man, he lifted a golden ring and placed it over the end of the blade. Before I could react, Caesar walked up to me and held the tip inches from my chest.

"He is here now," he said, and though his eyes flashed merriment, the rest of his face was serious. "Your posting is now permanent, *Centurio* Marcus Aremus."

Are you shitting me? screamed in my head, but for reasons that totally escape me, I had the presence of mind to shout, "Sir! Yes, Sir, *Imperator*." Taking the ring, I struggled to think of what else to say. *Thanks boss. Gee this is great. Cool.*

"I will not let you down, *Imperator!*"

Expecting applause or cheering, I was surprised when he sheathed his sword and the merriment in his eyes vanished.

Did I say the wrong thing?

I glanced over at the still-scowling *centurio*, but before I could do more, Caesar spoke,

"Now let's address this issue of my triumph," he said while turning to one of his guards. "*Lädt die messinger aus Rom.*"

I made out 'messenger' and 'Rome', but struggled with the context as the German snapped a salute and marched off.

I was sweating bullets as Caesar turned away from me and faced the men standing in front of the now-completed wall.

"Finish the watch tower and hang the doors. I want the camp secured within the hour."

"Yes, *Imperator!*" the *optio* responded with a salute, and before he could turn to repeat the order, his men hurried to the tasks they had performed many times before.

His attention now on the *centurio* who had escorted me in, he said, "Double the watch tonight. We may soon learn if this threat is real."

"Sir!" the *centurio* barked before doing a quick spin around and marching away.

Caesar looked at the sky for a moment before dropping his gaze to the men around him. "Return to your duties. We have much to do before settling in for the night."

As the others moved away, I froze, still holding the ring that designated my promotion, but unsure how Caesar's order applied to me or the men I came with.

I didn't have to wait long before his attention was on me.

"Bring your men inside the *castra*. I assume they came lightly provisioned to make better time."

I almost said "Yes, Caesar," but remembered that the title was never used by him, only those who created and maintained Imperial Rome.

"Yes, *Imperator*."

He looked up at the clear sky again. "They will sleep under the stars tonight, and we will return to the legion in the morning where they can be reunited with their provisions. I will instruct an *immunes* to find blankets."

"Yes, Sir."

When I didn't move, he held up a hand to wave me away, but was stopped by the German calling to him.

"*Imperator! Ich konnte nicht finden den Boten.*"

Caesar's eyes went wide for a moment before he laughed. "Your conspiracy theory is no longer a theory."

"Sir?"

"The messenger from Rome is not to be found."

When I didn't respond, he apparently took that as a sign of strength, but this time he did not smile.

"Go get your men, *Centurio,*" he said solemnly. "We have conquered these people, but it is not yet safe to linger among them."

"Yes, *Imperator!*"

Gripping the gold ring tightly, I marched out of the *castra* and back toward the men I came with.

"What happened?" Remmy cried when I was within earshot.

When I saw her running to greet me, I slowed so that we could meet out of earshot of the others.

"This is getting weirder by the minute."

"How so?"

I held up the golden ring. "Julius Caesar just made me a *centurio*."

"Oh my God," Remmy exclaimed. "You're not serious."

I barked a laugh. "Yeah, I am. This should make Marcus happy."

I almost laughed again when Remmy gave me a puzzled look.

"He wants to die," I explained, "and the mortality rate of *centuriōnēs* is way higher than for foot soldiers, even *optiones*."

"But how does that help us?"

"It doesn't, but being a *centurio* gives me more flexibility, especially if the attempt on Caesar's life happens tonight."

Shaking her head, she looked back at the men gathering into ranks. "I don't follow."

"Once I take command of the sixth *centuria*, I'll be bogged down in the day-to-day running of it, but tonight I don't have anyone to command. That leaves me free to move about the compound watching for an assassin."

"But what if it doesn't happen..."

I stopped her with an upheld hand. "It just has to happen tonight. There's no other way for it to work."

"But that's not how things..." Her eyes went wide. "Wait a minute."

"What?"

She looked around for a moment before answering, "We're not alone. Someone else is on our side pulling strings and keeping the *Tsabbat* from overpowering us."

"How do you know that?"

"Because somehow they transported me in Enid's body to another time and place."

"What? How?"

She shook her head slowly. "I don't have a clue, but this guy who kidnapped me..." She shook her head. "Well, he wasn't the one who actually kidnapped me, but he killed the guy who did it."

"Remmy! Get to the point."

"This stranger ties me up, puts me into a wagon, and covers it with a tarp. For the longest time, we were plodding along on grass and then I fell asleep. I woke again when some kind of irritating buzzing surged through my body, like I'd been shocked or something."

Impatience was making me testy. "And?"

She threw up her hands. "And then it was suddenly hot and the cart's wheels were crunching on something gritty. When he finally stopped, we were in the middle of a desert."

"A desert? There's nothing like that around here."

She nodded emphatically. "Well that's where I was: sand, dunes, and hot sun burning my skin. Before I could do anything, they locked me inside this old mud-brick shack."

"How did you escape?"

Her shoulders shrugged. "That's when I met this merchant. He waited until nightfall, drugged my captives, opened the door, and brought me back to the transfer point."

I felt a smile form on my face. "The merchant must have been Beauregard. He knew you were in trouble and he... Wait a minute. What's a transfer point?"

She shrugged. "I guess there are places on the planet where you can move from one time period to another."

"To anywhere?"

She shrugged again. "I don't know, but that's not the point. It got me here."

"So what happened to Beauregard?" I looked behind her to see if the merchant was still at the edge of the wood.

"The merchant wasn't Beauregard."

My attention returned to her. "He wasn't? How did you know?"

"Because I got the feeling he was stuck in that time. Maybe he was some other guy's Beauregard." Her eyes widened. "In fact, I think it was the young Muslim boy guarding me when I escaped. The merchant said he had to survive to do something in the future."

"Any idea what it was, and will we be part of it?"

She shook her head. "He wouldn't say, but then I was only interested in getting out of there."

Puzzled beyond belief, I looked back at the *castra* and realized something was wrong about it.

"Oh shit!"

"What is it?" Remmy asked anxiously.

"I know how they're going to try to get in."

"They? Who are they?"

"Don't know, and this might be a shot in the dark, but I have a plan."

"Shot in the dark? Shit. I forgot one more thing."

"What is it now?"

"The stranger who had me kidnapped is from our time as well."

"How do you know that? Did he tell you?"

My stomach cramped when she shook her head, made a fist with only the first two fingers straight. Pointing the fingers at me, she pulled back on her thumb and made a cocking sound.

"Double shit!"

Chapter 89

Dr. McFaddan stood in the doorway looking less confident than when Jasmina had last seen him. The female psychic she had seen at the mall agitated on his right, standing slightly behind him, her dark eyes glaring, wide mouth scowling, hands fisted by her side, and even her mussed, black hair looked pissed.

When the doctor hesitated, Jasmina felt a disturbing sensation as the woman started to move past the doctor, but he waved her back.

"Not now, Jana!"

Her face showing strain, she stopped, her eyes locked on Jasmina, her body shaking as though she were about to explode.

"What can I do for you, Doctor?" Jasmina asked as Tim, Alvin, and Miriam moved up behind her.

She suddenly felt tired and weak. Tim's gasp and a groan from Alvin told her that they were all being mentally attacked.

"We should talk," McFaddan said as though he were unaware of his companion's actions.

She felt compelled to agree with him unconditionally, but knew that feeling was being projected into her mind.

"What is her name?"

Looking slightly amused, the doctor looked down at his companion. "Jana Hostetti. I assume you've heard of her?"

Jasmina did not look at Jana. "No talking as long as Ms. Hostetti continues to mentally harass us."

McFaddan smiled, seemingly impressed with how well Jasmina was resisting his attempts to control her.

"That will be enough, Jana," he said without emotion.

Jasmina had to fight to keep from gasping when her whole body jerked as though an oppressive hand had just been lifted from her head. Her eyes instinctively went to Jana's taught face: glaring eyes, compressed lips, flushed cheeks. She had the impression that if not for McFaddan, Jana would lurch forward and physically attack her.

"She's not looking very much in control," Jasmina said as calmly as she could. "If she can't behave, you'll have to leave her outside."

Jana started to lunge forward again, but McFaddan stopped her with a hand on her shoulder. They locked eyes for a long moment, McFaddan keeping his expression neutral, Jana glaring. Finally, Jana lowered her head and took a step back.

Acting as though nothing had happened, McFaddan turned to face Jasmina.

"May we come in?"

"I don't think so," Tim blurted angrily. "The last time we saw you, your goons tried to kidnap my wife."

His eyes still on Jasmina, McFaddan said, "It was a very dangerous situation. We had to act quickly for the benefit of everyone."

"It's still a dangerous situation and your being here isn't helping."

"I have to meet them," McFaddan said to Jasmina. "This could warp space and time as we know it. The effects could be catastrophic."

"It already has," Jasmina responded, her voice steady despite the mental turmoil making her stomach ache. "People are disappearing, their entire history wiped out, and the cascade effect will only get worse if this isn't resolved soon."

"It's you who's messing things up," Jana growled.

"You don't understand," McFaddan protested, his voice soft, but stressed. "If Caesar dies earlier everything will be better. The Romans won't spread their Nazi-like thinking across Europe and into the Roman Catholic religion. Europe will get the chance to evolve into a more peaceful place, ruled by a single entity who loves us like a devoted father. Instead of centuries of despotic rulers with their wars, plagues, and the slaughter of millions. Mankind will get the chance to flourish, to grow, to invent even greater things. Disease, poverty, famine will be a thing of the past. Instead of barely making it to the edges of our solar system, mankind will be travelling to distant stars, populating other worlds, establishing a peaceful, productive empire that will grow until it encompasses the entire galaxy."

"Are you serious?" Tim laughed. "The *Tsabbat* doesn't want…"

Jasmina stopped him with a hand on the arm. Everyone was silent for a long moment, their faces tense until Tim sucked in a breath and nodded. After nodding back, she turned to McFaddan.

"That all sounds rather grand, but we like our present just as it is."

Raising a finger level with his face, McFaddan opened his mouth to protest then stopped, his unfocused eyes looking up toward the ceiling, expression curious, finger still pointing upward, as though he was listening to something. After a moment, he jerked a nod and returned his attention to Jasmina.

"We could stand here all day arguing about this, but I don't think that is what is going to happen."

"So you're leaving?"

His head rotated slowly from side-to-side while he lowered his hand to wave it at Jana.

"You think she is the only one who has psychic powers, but you're wrong." He smiled broadly and redirected his wave to the three men behind him. "We all do."

Before any of them could respond, the room seemed to distort, the upper part twisting to the left while the lower went right, as though a whirlpool was forming in the entryway.

Jasmina pushed her companions back as the effect slowly moved toward them. Glass shattered, floor tiles exploded, sheetrock dust billowed out to envelope them. The doctor and his companions disappeared in the dust, but Jasmina could still feel their presence, was still hampered by their oppressive thoughts, with despair and the sense of failure blotting out everything else. Over the noise of the cataclysm, she more felt than heard the cries of her companions.

"Stay with me and concentrate," she bellowed over the racket. Lifting her hands to shoulder height, she screamed, "Hold hands and focus on me!"

As hands gripped hers, she closed her eyes and though the mental cyclone Jana and McFaddan created roared on, she felt immediate calm.

"It's all a trick," she howled. "Repeat after me as loud as you can! It's all a trick."

Tim's deep baritone was the first voice to join in, but as she chanted the mantra, she could hear the others. Soon after she felt their confusion, anxiety, fear as the effect of the mental storm increased in intensity. She could feel five minds in the storm, all working in unison to distort their reality. Walking slowly backwards to give her companions the sense that they were staying just ahead of the destruction, she kept pushing against McFaddan and his group with her mind, chanting as loud as she could, hanging onto the hands of her companions until they bumped into the wall at the back of the entryway.

As their backward motion stopped, it felt as though they were making contact with the mental cyclone. Though she knew it wasn't really happening, her senses were telling her that her head was being pulled in one direction while her feet were sliding in the other.

"Don't believe what you are feeling," she cried out. "Only believe what you know. This isn't real!"

She felt their strength. Sensed them pushing with her. She felt Alvin lose his balance, his hand yanking on hers, interrupting her concentration for an instant before he quickly regained his footing. She felt the storm trying to spin her like a propeller. Taking a quick step to one side, she felt the floor tilting away from her, but despite what her senses were telling her, she knew she was still upright.

Push! screamed in her head, but she knew they were outnumbered and outgunned. All five of Dr. McFaddan's group were trained in mind control. None of her companions had ever experienced it before.

As they pressed against the wall with nowhere else to go, Jasmina felt the floorboards being torn from under her feet and the ceiling above her disintegrating into dust.

They're winning, she moaned. *Someone help us. Please!*

Chapter 90

As I led the men into the *castra*, it became more obvious that this fort was designed for failure. Each *castra* has four entrances and on each side of the entrance for the north, west, and eastern gates were two towers with a guard on each. On the two corners attached to the north side, there was also another tower with a guard.

After dismissing the men, I motioned for Remmy to follow me to a position where I could see the entire south wall of the camp. The setting sun was peeking through a gap in the clouds just at the horizon, producing dramatic contrasts of light and dark, making the south wall's flaws even more obvious.

"I don't see the problem," Remmy complained. "That wall is as stout as the others."

I shook my head. "It's not the walls I'm concerned with. It's what's missing."

Huffing angrily, Remmy turned to look at the north wall, and it took her less than a minute to see what was wrong.

"Oh shit," she exclaimed as she returned her attention to the south wall. "There's only one guard post on that entire wall."

I nodded. "We have to tell Caesar."

Seeing Remmy nod as well, I started walking in the direction of his tent, but stopped when a figure appeared from a shadow, one arm up as though he were pointing at me. As he moved into the open, light reflected off his chrome-plated pistol, and I felt my heart stop.

"Oh crap!"

"Yikes!" Remmy added.

"Your interference stops now," the stranger growled confidently. "I'm tired of putting up with the two of you."

We all froze for a moment before he smiled and motioned for us to approach.

When we were ten-feet away, he said, "Stop right there and drop all your weapons."

I looked around, surprised to realize that in the busy, confined space filled with nearly eight hundred soldiers, not one of them was looking our way.

"You're controlling their minds," I stated, though I wasn't sure why it even occurred to me.

His only response was a shrug, which I initially took as a yes until Remmy shook her head.

"Jasmina told me that there are people who can do that," Remmy said, her voice almost squeaky from fear. "She never mentioned anyone controlling this many people."

"You hired Quintus to kill me, didn't you?"

The harsh light cast his eyes in dark shadow, making him look ghoulish.

"Just drop your weapons or I shoot you here. No one is going to care one way or the other."

"How strong is their control?" I whispered to Remmy as I slowly untied the belt holding my sword and knives at my waist.

"It's probably more a suggestion than anything," she answered. "Jasmina says you can't make anyone do something they really don't want to do."

"Stop talking and do as I say."

It was obvious by the strain in his voice that he was expecting something to happen and didn't want to be anywhere near here when it did. Time was on our side, if I could just find a way to stall him.

"You have to realize you're destroying your own future as well as ours."

He jerked a no, but his earlier look of confidence was gone.

"He promised to protect my people from the change. We will be the elite of the new world he will create."

"And who are your people?"

Scowling, he opened his mouth to respond when voices behind him stopped the words.

"Without turning around, he leveled the pistol at me. "I guess there isn't time for what I had in mind for you. A quick end then."

"Put those extra men with the sixth Cohort until we get back to the legion, and then…"

The stranger jerked around to see Caesar walk into the open with three guards and two *centuriōnē*s.

"No," he protested. "It's too soon."

Seeing he was distracted, I snatched up my fighting knife by the blade and heaved it at him. He howled when the blade embedded itself in his left shoulder, and everyone around Caesar yanked out their swords in a useless effort to protect him.

I wanted to yell, "He has a gun!" but none of them knew what a gun was.

Instead, I charged at the stranger, hoping I could get to him before he recovered his wits. Unfortunately, all my remaining weapons were on the ground, so I cried, "He's an assassin!" which created even more confusion, because as Remmy would later tell me, in my panic I actually said it in English rather than, *"Non percussor ille est!"*

Recovering enough to realize his time was limited, the stranger started to turn toward Caesar, but since his guards didn't yet know what was going on, they didn't close ranks around him, or try to move him out of sight, and that gave the stranger an open shot at their *imperator.*

"You missed one!" I shouted, and upon seeing the stranger turning back toward me, I wind-milled an arm as though I was going to throw another knife at him. Since I was a more immediate threat, he gasped against the pain in his shoulder, pointed the gun at my forward-moving hand and fired.

I am pretty sure I screamed when my wrist exploded with pain, but have no memory of it. Losing my footing, I started to go down, but kept my feet pumping long enough to crash into him. He howled like a banshee when we hit the ground, and immediately tried to squirm out from under me. My attempt at hanging on was a waste of effort because my now-useless right hand was spurting so much blood I couldn't get any kind of grip on him.

Groaning loudly, the stranger pushed me off and clumsily rose to his feet. Through his legs, I could see Caesar and his men still standing in the same place, trying to make sense of what was happening. I tried to rise, to crash into him, to cry out for them to move, but my throat wouldn't work and my legs gave out on me. I was flopping on the ground like a grounded fish when something dark and growling flew past me. The stranger cried out, his gun discharged, Remmy screamed, and I watched my over-excited heart pump life-giving blood from the mess that was once my wrist.

Everything seemed to go quiet all at once, and when I looked up again, Remmy was on her knees, her back to Caesar and his entourage as she grabbed the pistol and shoved it into her satchel. Before I could even think to speak, she snatched up one of my arrows and sprinted toward me.

"What in the…"

My question was interrupted when she snapped the arrow in two, slid to her knees next to me, and quickly started smearing my blood on its broken ends.

Before I could reason out what she was doing, the whole scene was swallowed by blackness.

Chapter 91

Seeing Gerry crash into the stranger, Remmy's instincts kicked in. Without even thinking, she charged forward, her only weapon a small knife.

I'm too far away, exploded in her head as she strained to run faster.

The two men were wrestling, but it was obvious that Gerry could not fight effectively with one useless hand. He grabbed the stranger's cloak with his good hand, but the man pushed him off and jumped to his feet.

As the distance closed, she saw Gerry hold up his injured hand, blood flowing freely from the hole in his wrist and she started to reach for the leather belt around her waist when she looked up and saw the stranger pointing his pistol at Caesar.

God, no!

Changing direction slightly, she lowered her shoulder and hammered the man from behind. He screamed on impact, the gun discharged, and they both hit the ground hard. As she rolled off him, she realized her knife was gone, as was Gerry's bow.

The stranger rose to hands and knees, his face down, his empty hands swiping the grass around him in a desperate search for the pistol. Not knowing what else to do, she launched herself at him, knocking him over. When he hit the ground, she landed on top of him and the impact knocked the wind from her.

As she gasped in short, useless breaths, she looked up to see his attention suddenly shifted from her to a spot on her right. Just as he started to lunge in that direction, her grasping right hand closed around a fist-sized rock. She had no idea as to what she was going to do, but as the stranger moved past her she brought the stone up to his forehead, hammering it with all her remaining strength.

The effort sent her onto her side at the stranger's feet. Her breathing now approaching normal, she unsteadily pushed herself up, to see the stranger's head bent at an impossible angle, and a large gash in his forehead. His open, unmoving eyes, and the stillness of his body made it clear he was no longer a threat.

The sight froze her in place for a moment until she heard voices behind her. As she was turning her attention to Gerry, a flash of light pulled her attention to the gun only inches from the stranger's lifeless hand. She immediately dropped to her knees and scooped it up. While she was slipping it into her satchel, she saw the bow on the opposite side of the stranger's body and an idea popped into her head. Making sure her back was still to Caesar and his guards, she grabbed an arrow and sprinted towards Gerry

Dropping to her knees, she could hear the armor of the men clacking dully as they ran toward her. Pulling the arrow close to her belly, she snapped the shaft in two and dipped the broken ends in Gerry's blood.

"What is going on here?" Caesar asked with a puzzled tone. "What was that noise?"

Pulling the soft leather belt from around her waist, she wrapped Gerry's wrist several times before tying it off and answering, "This assassin tried to kill you, *Imperator*." She pointed at the broken arrow. "My master saved your life." She wanted to add, "by risking his own" but knew that would not be well received.

Hesitating only a moment to scan the body next to them, Caesar waved for his men to come forward.

"Take him to my tent." Without waiting for a response, he pointed at a third man. "Have my Greek physician meet us there."

"Yes, *Imperator*," they all shouted at the same time.

Remmy wanted to stay close to Gerry, but knew her place was behind the small procession following Caesar.

When they reached the tent, a short, dark figure in an off-white flowing robe stood by the entrance. A broad-brimmed hat covered his head and over one shoulder he wore a light gray shawl with elaborate red and green embroidery along its edges.

"You call for me, *Imperator*? Are you wounded?"

Caesar pointed at Gerry. "This soldier saved my life. Treat him as you would me."

Though Remmy thought she saw a flash of disgust as the doctor looked at Gerry, it was quickly replaced with a generous smile.

"Where should I attend to your very brave soldier?"

Caesar waved a hand at the entrance to his tent. "You will use my cot until he is ready to stand."

"As you wish, *Imperator*," he said with a bow. "I will do as you ask."

Caesar turned and waved his men inside, but when Remmy tried to follow them, he held up hand to stop her.

"Wait here."

She looked into his face with the intent of protesting, but immediately saw there was no room for negotiation in his expression.

"Yes, *Imperator*," she said while quickly looking down again.

As she watched his feet, Caesar hesitated for a long moment before turning and peering into the tent.

"I have matters to attend to. Send someone to let me know when you are done."

As he walked away, Remmy started to sneak into the tent, but one of the German sentries blocked her path. When she looked up at him he spoke in his native German.

Flustered, Remmy shook her head. "I have no idea what you just said."

The guard pointed at a small bench. "*Einen Sitz haben.*"

Though she was anxious to learn about Gerry's status, the bulky man in front of her was too big an obstacle to pass.

"Yeah. Right," she muttered as she moved to the bench and sat.

Nervous energy only allowed her to sit still for a moment before the need to see Gerry almost overcame her fear of the guard. Fidgeting on the bench, it felt like she was going to explode.

What can that doctor know about sewing up nerves and tendons? She thought while looking at the guard again, and surprised to find him staring back at her.

"Not so much to worry, *Fraulein*," he said as he moved closer, but did not sit. "*Der* Greek is *ein guter Artz*...err...*doktor*. He many battles sees."

The guard's assurances did little to calm her, but when he continued to stare at her, she moved back into the bench and crossed her arms. Appearing to think that was the end of it, the guard watched her a moment more before returning to his post, his eyes forward, expression blank.

Once his attention was off her, Remmy looked around. "I've got to get in there," she muttered. "Who knows what a hack this Greek doctor is? No matter how many battle wounds he's dealt with, no one in this time had the skills to repair nerves or tendons. Hell, they may even try to cut off his hand."

She started to rise again, but felt a jolt of electricity shoot through her body. It wasn't enough to kill her, but it stopped her from moving, and the shock of being shocked in pre-imperial Roman times kept her from moving.

Then a sudden realization struck her.

"No! Wait! I can't go now."

She tried again to stand, but the electrical charge glued her to the bench. As she struggled, her body felt as though she were starting to float away. She tried to grab the bench, but her hands passed right through the wood and soon she was above Enid's body. When she was higher than the German guard, she looked down to see Enid leaning back on the bench as though she were sleeping.

No! Don't take me away now. I'm his only chance of...

She stopped when a figure appeared beside her and she quickly recognized the sleeping Gerry.

As they continued to rise, the scene below them slowly faded until they were in total darkness. She looked down to see her body glowing slightly, as did Gerry's, and before she could process this, two more glowing figures appeared far away in the blackness. Initially, she could not tell if they were moving or not, but over time she realized they were growing in size. After a long period she could not gage, she recognized Enid.

What is happening? Enid asked anxiously.

You are returning to your time, and we to ours.

How is this possible? We did not ask for this.

Nor did we, but you need to know that Marcus killed a giant Gaul, but later an assassin tried to kill Caesar and Marcus was wounded saving him.

Enid looked down at the sleeping figure next to her. *Your master is injured as well.*

He is not my master, Remmy protested. *We are friends. I am no slave!*

Enid stared at her for a long moment. *You are a free woman?*

Yes, Enid. Slavery is forbidden in our world.

But there are dangers there as well.

No less so than in your world.

Enid's laugh came as a shock, but before Remmy could respond, she continued.

I will do what I can to free my people from Roman rule.

Remmy shook her head. *Marcus will treat you well. I think he loves you, and you could do worse.*

I will not be the wife of a Roman pig.

Though the words shocked her, Remmy got the distinct feeling they lacked the conviction she felt when they first traded bodies.

I don't think you will be a slave for long. You should give him a chance.

Enid shook her head. *The place we were in. That was the future?*

Yes it was.

What will become of me now?

For the first time, Remmy detected a sadness in Enid's voice that made her heart ache. Everything had been taken from her: home, family, fiancé, and her future. She looked at the ghostly image of Gerry and felt her heart ache as well, but then her attention drifted to Marcus who was furtively watching Enid.

I think, my friend, you will be treated like a queen.

Chapter 92

Her mind twisting and churning against the powerful storm attacking it, Jasmina struggled to hold onto her own sanity and that of her three companions.

Someone help us!

Had she spoken it or was it just a powerful thought? It didn't matter now because she knew she couldn't hold out much longer, and when she crashed, the other five would come down with her.

Five? Where did the extra two come from?

An instant later, she felt movement on her left: two forms running. She pushed with all her remaining strength just before the storm shuddered, weakening only slightly. It shuddered again and she felt her self-control coming back.

Hit them again!

A sound, much like a ringing bell burst into her head, and as it faded, the sound morphed into a high-pitched scream.

Her eyes popped open to see a blur of movement: a fist striking McFaddan's face, a body impacting the screaming Jana. McFaddan went down like a sack of bones, crashing onto the floor as Marcus plowed into the men behind. Though big and muscular, they were no match for the man who moved so fast she could not focus on him.

Enid gave Jana a fist to the face that abruptly stopped the scream and sent her to the ground. Without stopping to watch her fall, she grabbed a small table near the door and raced into the fray, hammering it onto the head of the nearest of McFaddan's men.

By the time Jasmina's vision cleared completely, McFaddan and his four companions were on the ground. It was only then that Jasmina turned to her own two companions to find them hanging onto each other and gasping for air. She turned back to see Marcus and Enid standing over their defeated enemy.

"Don't let them back up," she commanded. "I'll get rope."

Both Marcus and Enid nodded, and when one of McFaddan's men groaned and started to push himself up, Marcus gave him a kick to the head that sent him back to the floor.

Though appalled by the violence, Jasmina said nothing as she raced through the kitchen to the garage. Once there, she searched shelves and cupboards until she found a bundle of twine, grabbed it and sprinted back into the house, pausing in the kitchen only long enough to grab a knife.

"Here," she said while passing the rope and knife to Enid. "Tie them up, hands behind their backs, feet together."

The pair worked quickly, and knowing their experience far exceeded her own, Jasmina turned her attention to her companions who still had not recovered from their ordeal.

"Wha…what just happened?" Miriam moaned, her arms around her husband who was holding onto Tim who still had his eyes closed, body pressing heavily against the wall as though the mental storm was still raging.

"Tim!" she called. "To break the spell, you must open your eyes."

"NO!" he shouted. "I'll be swallowed up in…that…thing."

Moving close, she grabbed his hands and felt the tension in his body. "Trust me, Husband. You're holding residual energy from the vortex. Opening your eyes will dissipate it."

He forced his eyes open with a gasp, jerking his body as he reacted to the sudden loss of the vortex's spin.

"What the hell was that?"

Jasmina shook her head. "I'll explain later." She pointed at the front door. "We have to secure these people and then reestablish a connection with Gerry and Remmy."

When he didn't react, she looked at the four men and one woman on the floor.

"It seems Marcus and Enid have them well tied up." She turned to her husband again. "Keep an eye on them until we're done. OK?"

Gulping in a breath, Tim nodded clumsily.

"Good," she said while taking Miriam's arm. "Let's check on our children."

"We should kill them," Marcus insisted as Jasmina moved in his direction.

"No, Marcus," she pleaded, her hands outstretched. "It is very important that we do them no harm."

"Why is this?" Enid demanded. "They try to kill us."

Jasmina shook her head. "They are needed to get you both back home, and I'm hoping we can do that very soon."

"*Quid hoc sibi vult?*" Marcus asked.

The question caught Jasmina off guard because she had no idea what he asked.

She turned to Miriam. "Do you know what he said?"

Miriam's eyes went wide as her head shook. "What does this mean?"

Her mind in turmoil, Jasmina stared at her for a long moment before gasping, "It's starting."

"What?"

"They're starting to return to their former lives. We're losing our connection to them, and their language. We need to get…"

"Ieeeee!" Marcus cried, his left hand clamped around his right wrist as blood oozed from between his fingers.

"Good Lord!" Miriam shouted, her hands flying to her mouth.

Without speaking, Jasmina rushed to Marcus' side, her mind reeling, eyes searching for what was going on. His face distorted in pain, he dropped to his knees as Jasmina nearly rammed into Enid.

"Let's see what happened," Jasmina commanded as she slipped past Enid and reached for his wrist. Her fingers were less than an inch from it when Marcus yanked it away.

"*Non intelligo.*"

Enid muscled Jasmina aside. "*I auxilium mihi in eum.*"

She pulled the cloth belt from around her waist and said, "*Ego conturbaverunt eam.*"

His face distorted by pain, Marcus hesitated for a moment before releasing the wound and holding it out to her. Blood spurted from the wound, splattering her face and chest, but Enid ignored it as she wrapped the belt several times around his wrist and cinched it tight.

Groaning loudly, Marcus' face went pale as his attention jerked from one woman to the other and back before his eyes rolled up in his head and he collapsed to the floor.

"Tim!" Jasmina cried. "Call an ambulance."

"What about them?" Tim asked, his attention on McFaddan and his people.

"Call the police as well, but get that ambulance here as soon as you can."

Tim was just starting to turn when a distant siren worked its way through the walls of the house.

"What the…"

His question was interrupted when an ambulance stopped in front of the house.

"Quickly," Jasmina demanded, her free hand waving for him to move to the door. "It's Robert."

"How do you…" Miriam started to ask as she watched Tim yank the door open. She stopped speaking at the sight of Robert jumping from his vehicle and hurrying toward the back.

As he extracted a bag from the ambulance, Alvin stared out the front window, surprise obvious on his face.

"How did he know to…" He turned to Jasmina. "This is your doing?"

She shook her head. "Not intentionally, but I'm glad he's here."

Moving quickly toward the front door, she stepped carefully around the prone McFaddan and his crew. When she opened it, Robert held up his bag and smiled.

"Thought you could use some help."

She waved him in. "Come quickly. Marcus is bleeding."

"Whoa!" Robert exclaimed when he saw the people on the floor. "What's this?"

Moving past McFaddan, Jasmina urgently waved Robert forward. "Don't worry about them right now. Time is precious!"

Still eying the people in his path, Robert made his way into the living room to find Marcus on the floor, Enid leaning over him as Miriam held a death grip over the belt wrapped around his bleeding wrist.

"He's going to bleed to death," Miriam moaned. "Please help him."

Putting his bag on the floor, Robert waved Enid back. "Please step back, Ma'am. I need room to work."

She hesitated briefly until Jasmina got her attention and motioned for her to step back. As she moved out of his way, Robert looked down to see Miriam give him a questioning look.

Smiling at her, he said, "You keep squeezing on the wound until I can get to it."

He turned to Enid. "Help me get him laid out." He pointed at Marcus' feet. "You take those…"

"Eh?" Enid asked, looking confused.

Jasmina moved in between them. "She doesn't speak English anymore."

"How'd that happen?"

Nodding toward Marcus, her voice cracked as she said, "Let's deal with him first."

"Oh yeah. Right. He take any shots to the head when he fell?"

"Not that we know of."

"How did his wrist get cut?"

"We aren't sure, but I'm suspecting it is something that happened in his past life."

"You mean what happens to a person in his past life affects him in this life too?"

Jasmina shrugged. "Not usually, but in this case, it does."

Nodding, Robert said, "Then let's move him more into the middle of the room so I can work on him. You take his feet. I'll get his shoulders, and we'll carefully slide him there." He looked at Miriam. "Keep a good grip on his wrist and follow as best you can."

Her face tense, eyes locked on her son, Miriam walked on her knees as they slid Marcus out of the pool of blood he was laying in and into the center of the living room.

Dropping to one knee next to Marcus, Robert asked, "What about those other guys? They from the past as well?"

Jasmina released Marcus' feet and shrugged. "I'm not sure, but they are part of what's going on. We just haven't figured out what."

"You call the cops yet?"

When Jasmina looked at her husband, he shook his head. "We were going to call when you showed up." He nodded at the five people on the floor. "Now I think we'll wait until you have this one stabilized. Those guys aren't going anywhere."

"Good," Robert sighed. "I called a cop friend of mine who's sympathetic to the psychic thing. He's on his way now, and should be here in a few minutes."

"What are we going to do?" Miriam moaned. "We can't go back to the hospital."

Robert smiled. "It's OK, Ma'am. Your son will be safe in the hospital." He nodded toward the front door. "The cops now know this guy isn't McFaddan, and they want to speak with him."

"They'll need to be careful," Jasmina warned. "He's telepathic. He and his cohorts almost took us down without even touching us."

After slipping an IV needle into Gerry's arm, Robert connected a saline bag to it and nodded, his expression somber. "I know all about those kinds of people, Missus Maxell. So does my cop friend. We won't let them get away."

When Robert turned his attention to the bleeding wrist, Jasmina looked over to see the person who claimed to be McFaddan stirring. Gasping in air, he shook his head, struggled with his bonds before looking up at Jasmina. She sucked in a breath when she realized his blank expression meant he did not recognize her.

Turning quickly, she saw Enid straighten, her mouth open, eyes wide, and knew that she was Remmy once again.

"Remmy!" she shouted as she rushed to her.

"Aunt Jasmina? We're back?"

After injecting something into Gerry's wrist, Robert looked up. "What does that mean?"

As the two women screamed and hugged each other, Miriam stared into her son's blue-gray eyes, ran her fingers through his blond hair and let out a sob. While Robert wrapped a pressure bandage around the wound, she crawled forward to hug her groaning son.

Chapter 93

Blackness filled my vision and my mind, but I could hear bits and pieces of faint, dull, distant sounds that grew sharper and louder until pain exploded in my wrist, forcing my eyes open. As I looked up at blurry figures, my ears were filled with familiar sounds: men running, voices, uncorrupted Latin. I smelled leather and sweat, and something sulfuric and burnt that I didn't recognize.

Blinking several times to clear my vision, I discovered that I was on the ground inside the *castra*, grass tickling my good arm, the bright sun warming me. I finally focused on the beautiful face above me, her expression tense.

"That's it, Marcus," she said anxiously. "You are awake now."

"That's what?" I asked, or thought I did. My tongue felt funny, lips numb.

She looked up. "He's awake."

It was only then I saw I was in the middle of a circle of people, all eyes on me. When I realized one of them was Caesar, I struggled to rise, but my muscles would not respond.

"What happened to me?" I croaked, my mouth dry, tongue swollen, and limbs so weak I could hardly move.

Though I continued to try to stand, Enid easily held me down as she shook her head.

"You were injured in the attack, but you are now safe. The surgeon has dressed your wound and given you opiate for pain. You have lost much blood and will not be walking for some time."

Feeling as though I'd had too much wine, I held up the wounded wrist, now cleaned up and bound tightly with a leather strap and stared dumbly at it. To my dismay, none of my fingers on that hand would move, no matter how hard I tried. I was at a loss for what to say or even think when the Greek physician leaned over me.

"Heroic warrior of ours is awake," he announced, but when I looked at him, his expression was stern. "Not to try moving fingers for a while."

It took a moment for the words to register. "A while?"

Scowling, the surgeon shook his head. "Do I no speak good λατινικά?" Smiling, he shook his head. "Gods preserve me, I mean to say *Latine*."

I felt my own head shaking, though my cramping gut kept me focused on him. "How long?"

He held up his hands, palms up while shrugging. "Two weeks, maybe more. We wait. We see."

I was preparing to ask another question when I noticed movement on my right and turned to see Caesar walking toward me.

"You saved me, *Centurio* Marcus Aremus," he said solemnly as he waved a hand at a man standing behind him. "And in return, my Greek surgeon saved you. However, I am afraid he said it is time for you to retire again."

I grimaced slightly from the pain and looked down at my bound injury so that my *imperator* would not see my expression. "Can nothing be done, Sir?"

Caesar's only response was to scowl, but when I turned my attention to the surgeon, the large brown eyes in his narrow, pinched face looked sad as he made only the slightest side-to-side move with his head. He might as well have shouted it, the impact being so profound I felt my head jerk back.

"Don't worry," Caesar blurted. "Your bravery will not go unrewarded. There is a very fine farm just outside of..."

He stopped abruptly when I held up my uninjured hand, palm out. "I do not wish to seem ungrateful, *Imperator*, but I have already tried farming, and..." I looked up at Enid briefly before dropping my gaze to him again. "If I may, Sir, I'd like to return to Rome."

"You have family there?"

I debated my answer. To me, *yes* meant there was someone there I cared about, but neither of my siblings, if they were even still alive, cared one whit about me, nor I them. But then I thought about Helena Antonius, my late wife's sister, and the only person in her family who considered us a good match.

"Yes, Sir," I responded. "I do."

"What will you do?"

His question caught me off guard. Except for my short and painful attempt at farming, I had never considered life outside the army. With my military career permanently and painfully at an end, I was at a loss for an answer until I remembered my mother saying that I had such a lovely way with words, I might someday run for public office.

As a politicus, she would say with a laugh, *you can steal the people's money and they will love you for it.*

Smiling, I nodded at Caesar. "Maybe I'll run for office. I could start as an *aediles plebis*. Who knows where that will lead?"

"You will need money to do that," he countered. "Rome will give you a decent retirement, but that will not be nearly enough to run for office."

"Then I will find a wealthy sponsor."

Caesar smiled. "With that, I can surely help." He laughed heartily. "Even if I can't yet go back to Rome, I can give you a few letters of introduction to get you started."

"Thank you, *Imperator*."

He nodded, and started to leave, but turned back one last time. "You may come to hate me for helping with this," he said with a smile. "Politics in Rome can be bloodier than any military campaign. I can attest to that."

When I laughed, he smiled and walked away, shouting commands to his *centuriōnē*s as he went. Despite the ache in my wrist, I could not help feeling good about having something to work toward. After a moment, I felt Enid's hands on my shoulders and looked up to see her worried expression.

"What is the matter?"

She looked at the departing soldiers for a moment before returning her attention to me.

"What is to become of me?"

I shrugged. "You will come with me, of course."

"As your slave?"

The involuntary laugh that erupted from me felt good, and I thought of my lovely Maria, and how she touched me so deeply I could never say no to her. To my utter surprise, I realized this "savage" woman had the same effect on me.

"I doubt you've ever been my slave," I chuckled.

Clifford M. Scovell

Chapter 94

Miriam jumped to her feet when the surgeon pushed through the doors leading to the surgery.

"Oh God," she cried softly. "Please let him be OK."

As the doctor approached, he gave her a pleasing smile and clasped his hands together at chest level.

"I have good news," he said when they were close enough to speak privately in the very public waiting area. "It was a clean through-and-through, so thanks to the wonders of robotic surgery, I was able to reconnect the tendons." His tired eyes shone with pride. "It will be a while before he can use that hand again, but if he's careful with it, and gets proper rehab therapy, he should regain full functionality."

Tears running down her cheeks, Miriam leaned against her husband and resisted the urge to hug the surgeon.

"Thank you, Doctor," she finally managed to say. "You've answered my prayers."

"He's asleep now, but the nurses will be taking him to his room soon. I'm guessing he won't be waking up for a few hours at least," he said, but then his expression turned puzzled. "Any idea where the bullet came from?"

When Miriam and Alvin looked at each other, Jasmina moved up beside them and said,

"It literally came out of nowhere. We didn't even hear the shot."

The doctor shook his head. "That is strange."

"*Strange* doesn't begin to cover it," Miriam mumbled more to herself than anyone else.

Finally giving an over-exaggerated shrug, the surgeon held up a finger. "Make sure he gets to therapy. It's vitally important that those tendons get the right amount of stretching or the scar tissue with bind up his wrist and we'll have to go back in."

"We will, for sure," Alvin assured him. "How long will it be before he's fully recovered?"

The doctor shrugged. "Four to six months, depending on how well he sticks to the regime. Overdoing it can be just as bad as doing nothing, you know."

Page 340

He turned. "I'll talk to him before he leaves the hospital and get him an appointment with the therapist as soon as can be arranged."

"Thank you, Doctor," Miriam said again. "I know he'll do whatever you tell him to do."

"Well, good luck to you," he said while already walking away.

When he was out of sight, Miriam straightened, her face a mask of determination as she turned toward Jasmina.

"You have to stop this past-life thing from happening. Gerry can't take any more."

Her lips pinched together, Jasmina shook her head. "I would if I could, but I don't have any say in it. The best I can do is help him get through it."

"In my opinion, you're not doing a very good job."

"I'm doing the best I can under the circumstances. No one's ever had to deal with this kind of thing before."

"There has to be something we can do," Miriam pleaded. "Find that Beauregard person and make him leave Gerry alone."

Jasmina shook her head again. "I'm not even sure he has any control over this. I think he's here to help as well."

"Well you both suck at this, if you ask me," she shouted. "Do your woo woo thing. You and this Beauregard person need to figure it out. Someone has to be responsible. There has to be a way to…"

"Hon," Alvin interrupted. "Let's go home and get some rest. We can come back later when Gerry is awake. We'll all think better if we've had some sleep."

"I'm not leaving until he does," she insisted. "Someone has to watch over him."

"The nurses can do that."

Miriam's head shook. "The nurses are not his mother."

"But you need rest."

Shouldering her bag, Miriam started walking toward the waiting area. "I'll find a seat and wait. You can go home."

His features strained with fatigue, frustration, and concern, Alvin tried to cover it with a smile. "I guess we're waiting."

Jasmina nodded. "I guess *we* are."

Chapter 95

The mists of its ethereal form roiled with angry energy as the *Tsabbat* glared at the small, blue planet floating in the darkness of space. It could not approach the blue and green orb because the gravitational well would suck it in like any passing space dust. The frustration welled up a raging anger that upset its concentration, and for the first time since before this meager planet even had occupants, the moaning of the millions of captured souls trapped in the folds of its essence made it difficult for the *Tsabbat* to concentrate.

A name -- unpronounceable in human language -- appeared in its mind, recapturing the lost concentration, and the tempest that was its body churned even more. Bolts of lightning flashed through it, the thunder absorbed by the vacuum of the void, but the *Tsabbat* felt it just the same, as did those millions who writhed in the agony of it.

"He has accomplished nothing!" it bellowed.

A part of the roiling mist began to condense into a form that looked roughly human. As the *Tsabbat* seethed and spit angry epithets at the blue planet, the shape grew more and more distinct.

"He will pay dearly for his defiance," it grumbled with a voice that flew through the mist like rolling thunder.

The shape's details came into clearer view, and gradually shifted in color from coal black to those of the human form the mist had assumed: pink for the skin, green for the eyes, red for the curly hair.

The grumbling was replaced by malicious laughter that stung the souls of the millions and made them scream from the pain of it.

"His agony will be worse than crucifixion, more horrific than burning in Hell's fires, more debilitating than a crushed spine. He will know mortification and pain like they were his own self, because they will be."

As Remmy's shape finally looked identical to the real person, a wispy finger of dust reached out and touched it. The eyes popped open, head began twisting, hands grabbing the throat as though she were suffocating.

"Yes," the *Tsabbat* laughed maliciously as the form continued to writhe. "A high price indeed!"

Chapter 96

Though his brain and motor skills were numbed with a flood of opiates, Gerry's consciousness raced like a scared rabbit with wolves on its tail.

Remmy!

He saw her floating in the nothingness of his consciousness, her body writhing, eyes bulging, mouth agape as though she were trying to suck in air, but could not. He wanted to reach out to her, but his arms and legs were stiff and unresponsive. A cry of alarm stuck in his throat, blocked by uncooperative vocal cords and lips that would not open.

No! screamed in his head as he struggled against invisible bonds, unable to do more than make his body vibrate.

As she floated closer to him, her body was silhouetted by an eerie green cloud of dust that seemed to fill the darkness behind her. A part of the dust started to coalesce into a frothy bulb that floated up beside her. The bulb hung there for a long moment before slowly condensing into a caricature of a face: the eyes and mouth merely depressions in its surface, simple blobs where there might be ears, and a bulbous nose more befitting a clown's face than anything else Gerry could imagine.

When the mouth moved, loud, scratchy noise, interspersed with squeaks and honks, raked his ears so brutally he feared his ear drums might burst.

What are you saying? he howled against the vocal assault that temporarily distracted him from Remmy's struggling form.

The static slowed and dropped in tenor for a moment before it evolved into more recognizable sounds as though a person without a tongue were trying to speak.

Rrrrrough. Gaaahhhouk. Marrrrrrrufff.

I don't understand.

The strange mouth kept moving, but the sounds began to shorten, the pitch increasing slightly.

Raa. Gaa. Maa. Pooo.

He was prepared to speak again when a sudden movement on his left brought his attention back to Remmy. To his utter horror, she looked as though she were immersed in water, hair inflated around her head; eyes and mouth open, but not moving; arms floating in front of her.

Oh God, no!

You are interfering! a deep baritone voice stated.

With great effort, he tore his eyes from the floating Remmy to see the dust-face scowling at him: vacant eyes squinting, lipless mouth curved down, and that bulbous nose seeming to grow longer and more pointed as it glared at him.

I don't under…

His thought was stopped by a bitter, mind-numbing cold that slammed into him. He flinched only because he could do nothing else.

I, the Tsabbat, will not be played with, little human, it growled with a malice that seemed to punch into his chest and clamp his heart. *You will pay for what you did.*

The head turned toward the image of Remmy and started to laugh: a deep, malevolent laugh that sent Gerry's body into a fit of spasms as he struggled against the invisible bonds.

NO! NO! NO!

Chapter 97

"Doctor," the recovery-room nurse cried. "His heart rate just jumped to one-twenty and he's starting to convulse."

His unbuttoned white coat flapping, the doctor hurried to her side.

"When did this start?"

"Just now," she protested. "He was normal a minute ago, and now this."

"What was the last thing given him?"

Her head shook. "Nothing since he came in from surgery."

"Allergies?"

In two quick steps, the nurse was at the foot of Gerry's bed, snatching up the metal clipboard holding his charts.

"None listed."

His eyes jerking from Gerry's face to the monitor and back, the doctor hesitated for a moment before turning to the nurse.

"Bring me..."

The sudden silence stopped him, and he twisted around to see the heart rate had already dropped to one-hundred then ninety. Seeing his patient was no longer convulsing, the doctor reached down and took his wrist as though he did not trust the lighted numbers on the machine next to Gerry's bed.

"He's ice cold," he whispered aloud, his puzzlement obvious.

Putting the clipboard back on its hook, the nurse moved to the other side of the bed and put a hand Gerry's right arm, just above the bandages covering his injury.

"That's not possible," she gasped, her eyes moving to the monitor as she gasped again. "His temperature is down to ninety-seven..." She hesitated a moment until the readout dropped a tenth. "And falling."

"Let's get some hot-packs in here, and call in the crash team."

"But what could be..."

He waved her away. "Don't worry about that until we get him stable."

Jerking a nod, she ran from the room, but when he did not hear the automatic door close, the doctor turned to see Jasmina standing in the doorway.

"Only authorized personnel allowed in here," he declared.

Moving further into the room, Jasmina shook her head. "I know what is happening," she said with a calmness not reflected in her eyes as she looked from the doctor's face to Gerry's.

"How could you?"

"It's complicated," she answered, "but if I don't get to him soon, he will die."

"I beg your pardon? Who are you?"

Waving his questions aside, she marched up to Gerry and took his ice-cold hands.

"Fight him, Gerry," she demanded angrily. "You can do it."

For a moment the doctor stared at her, his mouth open; hands at chest level, palms down; eyes following Jasmina's progress through the room.

After she spoke, he lowered his hands and demanded, "What on earth do you think you are doing?"

"Saving your patient, Doctor," she answered sharply.

His surprise turning to anger, the doctor moved quickly to her and reached up to grab her shoulder, but just as his hand was about to grip her, someone shouted,

"Stop!"

Though Jasmina did not look up, the doctor turned his head to see Miriam and Alvin standing in the open doorway.

"And who are you?" he demanded.

Glancing at her husband, Miriam answered, "We're his parents, and..." She looked at Alvin again before returning her attention to Jasmina. "God forgive me for saying this, but she is the only one who can help him now."

"What the hell are you talking about?" the doctor protested. "We don't even know what..."

A desperate gasp from Gerry stopped the doctor in mid-sentence, and when he looked around, Gerry's eyes were open, his uninjured hand gripping Jasmina's.

"Son of a..." he started to say, but stopped when his eyes met hers. "Where's Remmy? She's in danger!"

Before anyone could respond, he sat up and looked around the room, his expression growing desperate when he realized Remmy was nowhere to be seen.

"I don't see her!"

"It's OK, Gerry," Jasmina assured him, though when she looked at Miriam, her expression showed she was not so certain. "Remmy passed out when the transfer took place. She's been sleeping since then. I don't think she is in any danger."

"I'll go and check the room," Alvin offered as he made a quick about face and hurried out.

"No! You don't understand," Gerry protested as he tried to rise from the bed, seemingly oblivious to the pain in his wrist. "The *Tsabbat* has her and he's going to kill her if I don't stop interfering with him."

With the doctor's help, Jasmina forced him back down, but he continued to struggle against them.

"Your father is going to check on her," Jasmina said as she gripped his good wrist and refused to let go. "Let's wait to see what he finds out."

Gerry struggled a moment longer before collapsing back onto the pillow, but the tenseness in his face remained.

"He's got her," he whimpered.

"Who is this *Tsabbat* person?" the doctor demanded.

Jasmina kept her eyes on Gerry for a moment before she turned to him. "Someone who may have kidnapped his girlfriend."

"Kidnapped? When did this happen?"

Jasmina shook her head. "I'm not sure, but we should check to see if she's still in the hospital."

Looking confused, he looked at Miriam for a moment before returning his attention to Jasmina.

"You mean she hasn't been kidnapped?"

She opened her mouth to respond, but stopped when Alvin and Robert rushed into the room.

"Sorry to interrupt, Doctor, but we've got a problem," Robert announced between gulps of air.

"I met Robert in the hallway," Alvin announced needlessly. "He just came from Remmy's room."

"What's happened?"

Both men seemed to freeze, their mouths open, jaws flexing, but no sounds came out. After a moment, Robert jerked as though he had been slapped.

"It's Remmy, Missus Maxell," he blurted. "She's gone."

"Gone?"

Looking confused, Robert nodded. "It was totally freaky. I was sitting next to her bed reading my magazine and I heard…well, sort of this strangled noise, like she was choking." He closed his eyes for a moment before popping them open, his face awash with surprise. "When I looked over to see what was going on, she wasn't there."

"She fell out of bed?" the doctor asked.

Robert shook his head. "No Sir. I searched the whole room. She is like, totally gone."

"Oh God!" Gerry exclaimed. "He really has her."

Moving to the foot of her son's bed, Miriam cried, "What do we do?"

Jasmina glanced at her and then turned her attention to Gerry for a long moment before she nodded.

"We have to get back to my house," she said calmly. "That's where it all started, and that's where we'll find Beauregard."

"Beauregard?" Gerry asked, his confusion obvious. "How can he help? We haven't even seen him this time."

"Yes we have," she said while looking at Robert. "Haven't we?"

Robert's face expressed panic for a moment before he nodded. "Yeah. I guess so."

"You're Beauregard?" Gerry asked.

"Oh no, man," Robert exclaimed. "Whoa. Would that be a trip." He looked at the people around him. "I've just had these…visions, like I'm tripping on something really good and I'm all happy and comfortable and he's in my head, ya know?"

Gerry glanced at Jasmina and then at his parents before focusing on Robert. "And?"

Robert shrugged. "Well, he tells me what to do to help you guys."

"And how do you make this connection?"

"I don't, man. I mean, he just comes to me."

Gerry once again looked at the others. "We've got to connect with him. He might be able to help us find Remmy."

"Yes," Jasmina said as she slowly nodded, her eyes unfocused, lips tight. "He may be the only one who can."

Chapter 98

The cloud of dust and energy that was the *Tsabbat* flowed around the Voodoo-doll-like form in the shape of Remmy. At random intervals a tendril of dust coalesced and stabbed at the image making it squirm as if it were in pain.

She is mine now, it stated triumphantly as it stared at the blue-green planet moving around its yellow star. *I have only to wait for the humans to come for her.*

The *Tsabbat* turned its attention back to the figure as it continued to writhe and twist, its mouth wide as though it were screaming, but the sound was absorbed by the vacuum of space.

It does not matter that I cannot enter the planet's gravity well. Your pathetic human emotions will be your undoing. By the time you realize what is happening, it will be too late for both of you. When the Gerry human is destroyed, the planet will be mine to...

It stopped when the figure became still, as did the moaning souls caught up in his energy.

You can't have him, the figure seemed to moan. *Before you even get close to destroying him, I will do the one thing you cannot control.*

The statement puzzled the *Tsabbat*.

You lie, Human. What can you do to stop me from destroying him?

When she did not immediately respond, the dust began to swirl around the image, whipping the hair and arms around like a doll inside a tornado.

What is it you can do, pathetic one? it asked again.

The figure turned its head up as though it were looking at the *Tsabbat* and the creature could feel a determination that grew from something it did not and could not understand.

Die.

Chapter 99

Jasmina burst through her front door with Gerry and the others close behind.

"Remmy!" Gerry shouted, the fear obvious in his voice.

When there was no response, Jasmina motioned for him to head for the kitchen, "Tim? You and Alvin go upstairs, and Miriam will come with me."

"I can feel her in the house" she added, her own voice high with stress, "but there is too much energy in here so I can't say for sure where. However, if you find her, do not touch her."

"Why not?" Miriam asked, her eyes scanning the living room.

"There's no time to explain. Just stay back from her and yell out."

Turning, she led Miriam through the living room to the back hallway as they heard the two men pounding their way up the stairs.

"Why would this *Tsabbat* bring her here?"

"He didn't…well, not exactly."

"What does that mean?"

Without responding, Jasmina slammed through the door to her office and quickly scanned the room. When she did not find her niece, she stopped and faced Miriam.

"When we moved to Salem, I looked at many houses, and though I liked the layout of several of them, they just did not *feel* right to me. That is, until I entered this one and immediately knew it was a place imbued with the power of love." She moved out of the office and yanked open a closet door, her breath catching when she found it empty.

"I know it might sound corny, but there is no power stronger than love, and Remmy would know that."

"You mean, we can destroy this monster from here?"

Jasmina shook her head. "It will take a lot more than what we have here to destroy the *Tsabbat*, but if we can overpower its connection to Remmy, we can at least free her from its control."

Miriam's eyes were wide as she looked up and down the hallway. "How do we…"

Her question was interrupted by a shout from the basement. Without waiting for Miriam to finish, Jasmina ran to the stairwell and peered into the dim light.

"What did you say?"

"She's down *here*," Gerry shouted, his voice thick with tension.

Without hesitating, she rushed down the stairs with Miriam right behind. The sound of moaning drew her to the darkest corner of the basement where Gerry stood, his eyes on something on the floor behind a stack of boxes.

Her heart racing, she sprinted to the spot to see her niece writing on the floor, her face scrunched up in pain, her body jerking one direction then another as though something was stabbing her.

"Everybody please stay back," she commanded, her attention totally focused on Remmy until she seemed to realize something. "But don't go very far away. I may need your help."

Gerry remained where he was, apparently not hearing her. Pushing past him, she knelt next to her niece, her hands only inches above her body, moving up and down from head to waist and back several times before she asked,

"Remmy? Can you hear me?" When she got no response, she slowly took the girl's flopping hands and pressed them to her chest. Closing her eyes, she hesitated for only a moment before barking a yip of pain.

"Oh my God," Miriam cried as she started moving toward the twosome, but was stopped when her son moved in front of her, his hands out to stop her.

She was so confused, it took her brain a moment to process what was happening, and she did not stop until his hands were on her shoulders. To her surprise, an electric-like shock knocked her back a step.

"What in the name of…"

She stopped when she saw the look on Gerry's face: anger, confusion, frustration, and fear. Before she could speak, he turned and squatted next to Remmy.

"Jasmina."

Jasmina rocked back onto her heels, lifted her hands, and opened her eyes. "It's too dangerous," she said as though she already knew what he was thinking.

"Remmy and I have to face this together," he insisted. "There's no other way."

As Tim and Alvin entered the basement, Miriam moved close as well, but did not touch her son. "Face what?"

"I can't help you," Jasmina said, her eyes still on Gerry. "Apparently, only you can make the connection."

"Yes you can," he responded, his own hands only inches above Remmy's body. He waved one hand at the three people now standing behind him. "Everyone! Focus your thoughts on us. We're going to need all the help we can get."

"What's happening?" Alvin asked anxiously as he and Tim moved closer.

When Gerry turned his attention to Remmy and seemed not to have heard the question, Jasmina straightened and looked at Alvin.

"It appears the *Tsabbat* has Remmy's soul."

"Her soul?" Miriam asked. "As in the devil?"

Jasmina hesitated for a moment before nodding her head. "You might think of it in that way, but the *Tsabbat* is not without its weaknesses."

"What weaknesses?"

She shrugged. "It can't come to Earth directly. It must work through an intermediary." She looked down at Remmy for a moment before returning her attention to Miriam. "It usually uses the souls of a people from another dimension." She shook her head. "I can't even pronounce their name, but…"

"How does this help us?" Miriam demanded angrily. "Will this *Tsabbat* creature attack Gerry as well?"

"I don't know. Maybe."

Miriam glanced back at her husband before returning her angry glare to Jasmina.

"What do I need to do to destroy this monster?"

Jasmina held out both hands, palms out. "Let's take this one step at a time. We have to free Remmy first."

"Won't killing this thing accomplish that?"

Sighing, Jasmina shook her head. "Remmy's soul is intertwined with the *Tsabbat's*. If we destroy it, we might destroy her as well."

A collective gasp from the people in front of her made it clear to Jasmina that they understood what was at stake.

"What can we do?" Miriam asked.

Jasmina turned to look at Gerry, seeing him slowly move to take Remmy's hands in his. He shuddered when they made contact, but rather than jerking away, he kept a firm grip on her as Jasmina turned back to the others.

"We have to form a circle around them and give them the strength of our combined energy."

"Another one of those séances?" Miriam asked though her tone was not dismissive.

"Something like that," Jasmina answered as she motioned for them to take their places. "Gerry will try to find the intermediary, and if he does, we have to give him the strength to tear it away from the *Tsabbat's* grip. If we can do this, Remmy will be freed as well."

"And if we can't?" Alvin asked anxiously.

The question seemed to startle Jasmina and she stared at Alvin for a long moment before turning her attention back to Gerry.

"Then we might lose them both."

Chapter 100

Blackness. The feeling of tumbling, spinning, disorientation.

Remmy! Where are you?

I felt no sense of direction. No up or down, just the dizzy spinning.

Remmy? It's Gerry. I'm here to help you.

Help her? a malicious gravelly voice laughed. *You can't even help yourself.*

Who are you?

The laughter angered me, less because it was dismissive than the inhumanity of it.

What can you do for that silly girl?

She's my friend.

More than a friend, I think. I'm sensing love, and I know the Tsabbat would very much like to absorb that useless energy and put it to better use.

Something soft bumped into me, sending my body tumbling in a different direction, if I was even moving at all. The darkness was so complete I couldn't see a single dot of light, no matter where I looked.

Another soft bump and I was somersaulting backwards.

You're too much of a coward to show yourself!

The laughter was nearly hysterical.

And why would I want to? You are no more to me than a baby flea on a mouse. I can extinguish you at any moment.

I was suddenly struck with how familiar that voice sounded.

Quintus?

The silence that followed gave me a flash of hope.

You killed me, and now it's my turn to destroy your life.

It took me a moment to realize that though two-thousand years had passed, to Quintus it might appear as though he had died only moments ago, and he thought I was Marcus.

You still don't get it, do you? The Tsabbat wants me alive. You're just an intermediary. Once he's done with me, you're toast.

Toast?

He will banish you to the cold blackness of space, a place so dark, so torturous, so agonizingly painful that even the most hellish punishment you can imagine would be pleasant by comparison.

You don't fool me. He promised me wealth and power beyond anything I could ever imagine. I will be a king in my own domain.

The absurdity of his last statement made me want to laugh and cry at the same time because there is nothing so frustrating as seeing someone on the verge of crashing into a brick wall and know there is nothing you can do to stop them. But he held the key to getting Remmy back. At the very least, I had to try.

King of the damned is what you'll be if you don't help me.

Why would you say that?

Because the Tsabbat doesn't share. Once he has me in his grip, you'll not be far behind.

You don't know what you are...

Don't I? You're dead, Quintus. What good is millions in gold going to do you now?

Well I... He stopped, and I took solace in the long pause before he spoke again. *You don't know nothin'! He'll send me back.*

Did he promise that?

Another long pause. *No, but...*

You're a puppet, Quintus, I interrupted. *And when the marionette releases your strings, you'll fall into the same black abyss, suffer the same endless agony as everyone else who believed the Tsabbat's black lies.*

To my surprise, I felt a shudder in the void and soon after, an amorphous shape appeared on my left. Turning toward the new manifestation of Quintus, I began to wonder why the *Tsabbat* hadn't participated in our discussion. Where was he and why was he letting this idiot do the talking for him?

In the eternal darkness, a light came on in my head.

He can't!

What? Quintus asked, his tone now anxious.

The Tsabbat can't communicate with you when you're close to Earth.

I don't know what you're talking...

Yes you do! He didn't speak with you directly, did he?

He did! Uh...at least I think it was him.

How would you know?

I dunno. Never thought about it. Wasn't that who the stranger was?

The stranger is just another puppet like you.

Don't talk nonsense. He had a weapon that could kill with a tiny pebble. He could travel through time. Deus homo, ut se habitu.

The stranger wasn't a god in a man's body, but a man being fooled into thinking the Tsabbat was a god. You've both been lied to.

Quintus' indecision was palpable. Though he uttered no sounds, I felt the argument going on in his…disembodied mind.

ENOUGH! I screamed. *You either help me or we both fall from Charon's boat and into the River Styx where the greatest torments you can imagine await us.*

I could sense more than see his slow mind working: fear battling greed, the lust for power countered by the fear of failure. In the end, it wasn't his response that gave me what I wanted, but mingled within the turmoil that raged within him was the one thing I was looking for.

The image was faint at first, but as I focused on it, panic tightened my chest when I realized it was a writhing Remmy. It took a moment for the panic to clear enough for me to realize I now knew where she was, and it wasn't in the darkness of space.

I'm coming, Remmy! I shouted as loudly as a disembodied spirit can shout.

Chapter 101

I popped awake disoriented and cold, still leaning over Remmy, my hands no longer on hers.

"Gerry!" my mother screamed as I struggled to sit up.

"It's not the *Tsabbat*," I blurted as I felt my mother's hands on my shoulders.

"It isn't? Then who?"

I shook my head to clear it, and after a moment my vision cleared enough to see everyone around me.

"It's Doctor McFaddan, or at least the spirit that once occupied his body."

"But he's in jail."

Continuing to shake my head, I tried and failed to rise, and finally did so with my mother's help. Once on my feet, I fought to steady myself while turning toward the others.

"The spirit that was in McFaddan provided the link to the *Tsabbat* and that spirit controls his followers, not the *Tsabbat*."

"How does he do that?"

"The spirit makes McFaddan a telepath, and he used that to control people."

"But we have Remmy," my mother protested. "Why do we care about this doctor, whoever he is?"

I felt my head shaking, but my chest felt tight and my stomach burned.

"We have Remmy's body, but he has her mind tied up in some way." I turned to Jasmina. "Do you know what I'm talking about?"

She nodded slowly. "Robert," she announced. "You must tell Beauregard that we need his help. If we can't save Remmy, we're all doomed."

"How do you contact him?" my mother more demanded than asked.

His face showing his confusion, Robert shrugged his shoulders. "I don't. He's always been in charge."

"Then you have to concentrate," Jasmina said as she moved in to grab his arm. "The doctor has Remmy's consciousness and we have to break that link before he destroys her."

"But I don't..."

"Everyone, close your eyes," Jasmina interrupted. "And take my hands."

Doing as commanded, Robert stood in an informal circle formed by the rest of us. Jasmina's attention was on him.

"Clear your mind of everything but finding Remmy."

Robert tilted his head back, pinched his lips together and hummed.

"What's he doing?" my mother whispered to me.

"Whoa!" he barked. "There's all kinds of stuff whirling around me, like storm clouds stuck in a whirlwind. Damn that's cold!"

"Hang in there, Robert," Jasmina cried.

Another few moments passed, but to me they seemed like back-to-back eternities.

"I've got to do something," I finally announced.

Before anyone else could respond, I moved up behind Jasmina and put my hands on her shoulders. My mind was suddenly filled with the deep blackness I'd seen before, except that all around us were swirling clouds. An intense cold slammed my body, and it was all I could do to stop myself from breaking my connection to Jasmina.

"That's the McFaddan spirit!" I shouted, or at least thought I did.

"We have to resist him and fight for what is ours!"

A freezing wind hammered me, its intensity threatening to knock me down. I struggled to stay in place when I felt a hand on my right arm and my mother suddenly appeared beside me. Another hand on my left and there was my father.

"Oh Hell. Here we go again," he cried over the din of the storm now raging around us.

"You cannot defeat me!" shouted a voice I recognized as McFaddan's. "The *Tsabbat's* power is far greater than all you puny Humans combined."

"Then you'll have to destroy us," Jasmina shouted back. "We're not giving in."

The storm clouds above us spun faster, as though trying to pull us into a whirlwind.

"We defeated him before, we can do it again," Jasmina cried. "Just stay together."

"That will do you no good," McFaddan's disembodied voice laughed. "I have the power of a god."

The intensity of the storm increased again and soon our feet were sliding as we slowly turned in a circle around Robert. The clouds above us darkened.

"Don't let go!" I warned as we were plunged into total darkness, the bitter cold cutting into me as though it would tear the flesh from my bones.

My fingers slipped on Jasmina's shoulder. As I gripped tighter, Dad leaned into me, but Mom was losing her grip on me.

Beauregard? Where are you?

Moments later, a light appeared above us then a second and a third. One of my hands slipped off Jasmina's shoulder, and I think I elbowed my father in the nose, but my extremities were too numb to know for sure.

The lights started to spin in the opposite direction of the clouds and they flashed on and off as they moved behind and then between the clouds again and again. The storm began to weaken and the friction between the clouds and the lights began to warm the air still blowing past us. By the time the lights stopped flashing, and the clouds came to an abrupt stop, I was dripping wet with sweat.

A sudden explosion overhead sent us all falling to the floor into a tangle of arms and legs, but the storm resumed in the sky above us.

"What is happening?" I barely heard my mother cry though she was lying across my stomach.

Someone else responded, "We're going to die!"

I didn't recognize the voice, but what surprised me even more was that as I watched the clash of two powerful entities I felt no fear, and for reasons I couldn't even begin to articulate, I was OK with that.

If Remmy's dead, I might as well be.

I tried to rise, but the wind and the weight of my mother's body held me down.

No! This is wrong, exploded in my head. *Remmy can't die!*

Sweat was now dripping off my nose and being sucked into the storm as it seemed to devolve into a series of lightning-like flashes accompanied by deafening thunder. I held onto my mother, but something else caught my eye and I turned my head to see Remmy's body sliding across the floor.

"Oh my God!" I screamed before releasing Mom and crawling to her.

As soon as I was close enough, I reached out to grab her, but just as my fingers started to wrap around her arm, a violent gust of wind sent us rolling. I slammed into the wall and was pinned there by the force of the gale, barely able to breathe, let alone move. Fighting the unrelenting pressure, I slowly groped around until I found Remmy's hand, and gripped it as tightly as I could. We might die here, but at least we were going to die together.

And then the room filled with a slow-motion flash of blinding light, followed by a silence so intense I thought I'd gone deaf. My mind remained in a shocked-blank state until the hand I was holding twitched.

"Gerry?"

My heart nearly leapt out of my chest as I jerked my head up to look at her confused, battered face. Blood was trickling from one nostril, and there were half-a-dozen cuts on her face. Her hair looked like a frozen red explosion, and one eye was only half open, but it was, without question, the most beautiful face I had ever seen.

"What happened?"

I looked up at the room's ceiling and saw not a single cloud or spot of light. In fact, the only light I saw was rays of sunshine pouring from windows high up on the wall.

"Another nightmare prevented," was all I could think to say.

Chapter 102

Marcus led Enid out through the gates of the town, and she gasped when the expected open road was lined with large and small structures, crammed together much like the houses inside the town's walls. Merchants loudly hawked their goods from small booths on each side of the road, but beyond their dozen or so stalls, a completely different collection of edifices appeared.

"Marcus?" she asked as we moved beyond the merchants. "What is this?"

"What are you talking about?" he responded irritably.

She pointed at the double row of mismatched buildings lining the road. Some were large with doors, like houses, but no windows. Others were barely taller than she, some with pedestals or a statue on top, others with no more than an engraved stone plaque on the front.

"These don't look like houses. What are they?"

He shrugged. "They are houses, in a way. They house the dead."

"They are tombs?"

"Of the most distinguished people in this town. You can only build here if you get special permission from the town council, and they don't grant it lightly."

As though that should satisfy her curiosity, he continued on, seemingly paying little attention to her as she hurried to catch up.

"You bury your people along a highway?"

He stopped and pointed at an elaborate tomb with paintings of gods on its edifice, and several niches sheltering statues. "Read the inscription on that one."

After giving him a cautious look, as though this were some kind of sick joke, she moved closer and peered at an inscribed block on the tomb's façade for a moment before shaking her head.

"It is in your strange Roman abbreviated style," she protested. "I can't read it."

Moving up beside her, he squinted at the densely-packed script.

"The carvers charge by the letter, so some abbreviate to cut down on the cost." Shaking his head, he recited, "By council decree, freeman Antonius

Claudius Fastio, *aedile, duumvir*, *prefect*, and *quinquennial duumvir*, has been permitted to build this monument for himself and his family, and awarded three-thousand-five-hundred *sesterces* toward its construction." After stepping back, he added, "This person held some pretty high offices within the town."

"But why be buried here?"

He shrugged. "Where else can you be assured hundreds, if not thousands of people will see the monument you built for yourself? Would you have them hide it behind the town proper next to the trash dump? Who would remember them then?"

As he moved on, she hesitated, staring at the scene in front of her as a shiver of revulsion ran though her body.

He led her nearly three-quarters of a mile before turning down a path between two large tombs. For the first time since they had moved through the gates, she realized there were more rows behind the first ones. These additional monuments were much smaller. Some had statues or busts in front, while others were marked with crude paintings and badly weathered inscriptions painted on their walls.

She was so entranced with the macabre display, she almost ran into Marcus when he stopped abruptly in front of one of the structures. A cherubic statue stood on each side of the only door, with the carving of a goddess she did not recognize carved above it. On each side of the goddess were carved busts of some very serious-looking men.

She watched while Marcus hesitated in front of the door for a long moment before his hand slowly rose to reveal a key she had not noticed before.

"This is your tomb?"

He seemed to ponder the question before shaking his head and moving closer.

"My wife's family had this built."

The lock grated as he turned the key and the hinges squealed when he shoved the door open. Dust billowed out, settling on them and making her cough, but he did not hesitate, moving quickly into the dark cavern. Though still standing outside, she felt a sudden bout of claustrophobia. It took two deep breaths for her to muster the courage to venture inside to see him using a flint to light a firebrand before holding it up.

To her surprise, the inside of the tomb was brightly painted, and though the space was small, and cool, light from his flame illuminated paintings on the walls, and a small statue of Apollo stood in the center. Numerous niches lined the walls, and in each one a beautiful vase stood, though most were covered with a thick coat of dust.

"These have been here a long time," she observed.

She heard his breath catch as his attention focused on the small funeral shrine on the floor against the back wall. A ceramic alter held a block of stone with the finely carved busts of a woman and young boy on its front. Tears filled his eyes as he gently ran his fingers over the names inscribed below the images: Maria Fredrica Metellus, XXXI, Marcus Antonio Aremus, III.

Fingers trembling, he carefully gripped the stone as though it were something delicate. As the stone rose, Enid could see a cremation urn carved from a single block of alabaster. Reaching inside, his fingers gently wiped a thin layer of dust from the urn's polished brown and tan surface.

"Your wife?"

His nod was almost imperceptible.

"They were both…so young."

"And I am too old," he said so sadly she jerked around to look at his face, and instinctively knew that at that specific moment, she did not exist to him.

"You reenlisted to die," she whispered, more to herself than him.

When he did not respond, she looked again at the shrine, noticing for the first time a broken stump of rock on one side of the stone top, as though something had been knocked off.

"What was here?" she asked as her fingers gently touched the rough surface, and she saw what remained of the hem of a long dress with two feet protruding from under it.

"It was a statue of Fortune," he sighed.

"Your goddess of luck?"

She waited for his reply, but he remained silent, his eyes again on the urn.

"What happened to her?"

His head snapped back as though he had been slapped, and after he recovered, his hand rose to gently finger the broken stone.

"She abandoned me, so I banished her."

"*You* attacked her likeness?"

She was surprised when he chuckled. "I wished for her to bring bad luck upon me, in the hope I would quickly die in battle and rejoin my family."

"But you didn't die."

"Be cautious when making wishes," he sighed. "They might just come true."

"I do not understand."

"I offended the goddess of fortune so I would have bad luck, but little did I know that meant I would never get what I hoped for."

"To die?"

Sighing, he carefully lowered the cover back onto the mini-tomb. "Instead of dying, I have become nearly invincible."

"That is irony, no?"

His hollow, sad laugh made her heart ache.

"Yes."

He pressed a palm against the cold stone, drew in a deep breath and slowly let it out. She waited for him to breathe again, but he remained quiet and unmoving like the small statue of Apollo behind them. The moment stretched out in a deafening silence that made her stomach clench. No breath, no movement, not even the flicker of his eye lids for what seemed like nearly forever.

When he finally gasped in a breath, she jerked back, startled.

Without even looking at her, he turned and moved out of the mausoleum.

"What are you going to do?" she asked anxiously as she hurried along behind him.

He stopped suddenly, making her run into him, her arms wrapping around his body as she struggled to keep from falling. He grabbed her roughly under the arms, lifted her up and held her out at arm's length, as though he were holding a troublesome puppy. Frowning, he set her back onto the walkway.

"I will not kill myself," he said matter-of-factly. "Suicide is only permitted in our society under honorable conditions. Grieving over your lost family is not one of those conditions."

"So what then?"

Turning away, he sighed again. "The surgeon says my wrist will heal, and if it does, I might return to my unit and serve my country until death relieves me of that duty."

"And what about me?"

He glared at her. "I cannot take you with me."

"You must. It is only a matter of time before one of your so-called friends tries to rape me again and I will have to cut his throat."

Moving quickly to him, she grabbed the knife from his belt and jumped back. When he tried to grab the weapon she danced out of his reach, but did not point the blade at him.

They froze, each staring intensely at the other until she held the knife out, handle toward him.

"You must kill me now and save me the torture of your sadistic justice."

When he did not react, she moved her right hand to the hilt of the knife and pointed the tip at her left breast.

"Then I will do it for you."

Closing her eyes, she folded her left hand over the right and stiffened in preparation of the move that would end her life. Her last breath was deep, but as she stiffened her body for the fatal stroke, his hands gripped hers, stopping the knife's fatal move and forcing her to open her eyes.

The face of the desperate man staring at her was not that of a captor.

"Why are you stopping me?"

He forced the knife from her hand and sheathed it.

"Why would you do that?" he asked, his expression puzzled, eyes questioning, his left hand still gripping her right wrist.

She looked away for a long moment before facing him again, her eyes sparkling with determination.

"If I don't serve you, I am better off dead."

Her statement seemed to surprise him and it was a moment before he released her, but she could see a smile on his lips.

"Would you be happier if I went into politics?"

To his surprise, she rushed to him, threw her arms around his neck and gave him a passionate kiss.

"That settles it then," he laughed.

Epilogue

"I have to protect you," I protested angrily. "Who else…"

Charging at me, Remmy hammered the flat of her hand against my chest, surprising me with her strength and forcing me to stagger back. She kept pace with me, and though I was a good head taller, her angry eyes were locked on mine.

"I can take care of myself," she declared defiantly.

"But…"

Another fist to the chest. "I've nearly been raped twice, beaten to within an inch of my life, threatened with extinction, and tortured by a monster just for the fun of it." She hit me again. "I will *not* be treated like a weakling just because I'm a girl."

"No," I blurted. "I didn't mean…"

"The hell you didn't!"

"But I love you," I protested. "I only want to…"

"Treat me like a helpless woman?" she interrupted. "Well, screw that." She stabbed a finger at her chest. "I've also been a warrior, and I've learned a lot about taking care of myself. You might remember that it was me -- in Enid's body -- who saved your ugly butt."

I held up my hands in surrender and the sight of my right in a cast seemed to take the steam out of her anger.

"So how do you want to handle this?" I asked when she said no more.

She tried to glare at me, but her lack of enthusiasm made it almost comical.

"What do you think they will say?"

I looked at the doorway into Jasmina's living room, but could see no one, so I shrugged.

"Guess we won't know until we tell them."

She also looked at the doorway as though it were the gates of Hell.

Shaking my head, I put a hand on her shoulder, bringing her attention back to me.

"I'll concede that you can take the lead on this, but I'm going to be right there beside you."

Giving me a half-smile, she nodded and started for the door. When I followed, she held out a hand and I took it. As we walked into the living room, the six people turned to face us, their expressions curious.

"What was all that yelling?" my mother asked.

Nodding, Jasmina took a sip of wine. "Is everything OK?"

Looking at Remmy, I saw her jerk a nod, her hand squeezing mine.

"Look…uh…there's something we want to tell you."

Though our mothers and Jasmina kept their attention on us, Remmy's dad gave Alvin a questioning look, and getting no more than a shrug, turned his attention to Tim who shook his head.

After taking a deep breath and letting it slowly out, Remmy's shoulders drooped slightly.

"Mom, Dad…" she pulled her hand from mine and rubbed them together as another puff of air whooshed from her lungs. "I asked Gerry to marry me."

Six pairs of eyes went wide as they gawked at her for a moment before all of them jerked in unison toward me.

"And I said yes."

THE AUTHOR

Growing up on the Oregon coast, Cliff has enjoyed telling the stories rattling around in his head. His books are an opportunity to share his out-of-this-world adventures with a wider audience.

A fifth-generation Oregonian, Cliff has been a farmer, logger, and business owner. He now lives in the Jefferson, Oregon, working as a computer support consultant for small businesses up and down Oregon's beautiful Willamette Valley.

Photo by Andre Lindauer

Promise of Victory

www.ingramcontent.com/pod-product-compliance
Lightning Source LLC
Chambersburg PA
CBHW022245020726

47496CB00004B/1072